wally

Also by Greg Kramer

Novels:
The Pursemonger of Fugu: A Bathroom Mystery
Couchwarmer: A Laundromat Adventure

Short stories:
Hogtown Bonbons

wally

Greg Kramer

Riverbank Press
an imprint of Cormorant Books Inc.

Canada Council for the Arts   **Conseil des Arts du Canada**

ONTARIO ARTS COUNCIL
CONSEIL DES ARTS DE L'ONTARIO

The publisher gratefully acknowledges the support of the Canada Council for the
Arts and the Ontario Arts Council for its publishing program. We acknowledge
the financial support of the Government of Canada through the Book Publishing
Industry Development Program (BPIDIP) for our publishing activities.

Printed and bound in Canada

National Library of Canada Cataloguing in Publication Data

Kramer, Greg, 1961–
Wally / Greg Kramer.

ISBN 1-896332-19-6

I. Title.

PS8571.R356W35 2004   C813'.54   C2003-907264-9

Cover and text design: John Terauds

The Riverbank Press, an imprint of Cormorant Books Inc.
215 Spadina Ave., Studio 230, Toronto, Ontario, Canada M5T 2C7
www.cormorantbooks.com

"Light blue touchpaper and retire to a safe distance."
—Instructions on British fireworks circa 1950

THANK YOU TO

Ed Stockham, Bob Paquette, Alma Lee, Richard Cliff,
Michael Sinelnikoff, Jeffrey Aarles, James St. Bass and Ian Brown,
Marc Coté and Cormorant Books

TO
Attila Berki and John Terauds
with apologies for the kettle

Act I

1

Out of the west, a storm descends as ferocious as a blowtorch. It breaks with a thunderclap, just after sunset, and pummels the Lower Mainland into submission. For the next few hours, the rains pound and flatten the long grass down by the beach. They strip needles from trees in the park, splatter the ocean with pox, and blast the comics out of a newspaper caught against a chain link fence. The city is held hostage as if at gunpoint; pistol-whipped; clinging to the memories of summer with pointless desperation, like the memories of the year before, like a suicide kissing the bullet and then pulling the trigger.

Most folk hunker down in their homes, not daring to venture outside—outside, where sewer gratings clog with leaf and twig, where gutters burst, where fords of soupy mud seep across the roads. The good people of Vancouver are trapped in their living rooms; they float on their cushions, stuff their brains with Johnny Carson and reruns of M★A★S★H★.

Only an idiot would go out in this weather, careening out of the house and down the garden path, the front door slammed on the back end of a domestic squabble, with nothing more than a flimsy coat and a curse to ward off the rain. And only an idiot would carry on, a sodden mass, a fuming swamp, for a mile and a half down the hill, trudging along the edge of False Creek in the worst of the deluge, determined to stay out for the rest of the night.

Around two o'clock, power lines go down, plunging everything west of Cambie Street into darkness. Those still awake in Kitsilano, False Creek, and around Granville Island either switch to candles or call it a night. Some households search for batteries in kitchen drawers, or curse over lost flashlights, but not for long. The crises die down as the novelty of utter darkness wears off. Obstinate and monotonous, the storm continues, as storms do, out of human control.

Just before sunrise, things shift into a lower, less aggressive gear. A grand ennui settles over the city—a narcotic ache like the suffocating onset of the flu. Vision is restricted to less than twenty yards in a twilight that's going to last all day. It's still raining if you look hard enough but it's not so much falling from the sky as bleeding from the air.

Strike a match.

The flame is an affront. Blistering auras float before the eyes. Sulphur fumes mingle with the smells of paint, dust, glue, kerosene and moldy sackcloth. The workshop: quiet and solid.

Shivering from the damp and still half asleep, Wally nurtures the burning match caught between two of his spatulate fingers in the cup of his left hand. He allows the flame a few seconds to take hold, then carries it over to the storm lantern on the slatted shelf below the window. The wick catches with a blue *plop*, a smudge of black smoke curls toward the rafters. Within moments, heat touches Wally's cheeks and kisses the hollows of his eye sockets. He settles the flue into its brass rim and waits until the flame calms its crazed vaulting before he shrugs back to the beckoning warmth of his old armchair.

The power is still down. He can't remember falling asleep; he must have passed out around four or five in the morning, as the storm and his anger subsided. He has a vague recollection of talking himself down from his puffing indignation, damping the embers of his wrath in booze. Scotch, drunk straight, no ice, no glass, his head getting tighter and tighter until his eyelids squeaked shut and his whittling knife fell to the floor.

Now it's cold and damp. His corduroy pants are still soaked from last night's march down the hill, his sneakers are dipped in mud. Wood shavings scatter the floor, some cling to his trousers like giant flakes of dandruff. The small block of pine he's been working on lies by his foot; it feels like a withered apple; no discerning features yet, he's still roughing it out. He places it back on the counter and slips his knife back into his pocket.

It's gone nine o'clock. Today's the day Peggy's boy is due to turn up. There's about an hour and a half to go before the kid shows, assuming he doesn't get lost, or that he'll even bother making the journey with the power being out. The new apprentice. Peggy's boy: Ned. With a bit of luck, the lad will arrive shaking in his boots at the mere thought of having to work for crazy Wally Greene. The promise of a juicy game of How's Your Mother? sparks a glint of sadistic glee in Wally's heart: this could be fine sport.

Not that he can't use the help. The new season is gearing up: a Restoration comedy, an American two-hander, the Scottish Play, a small musical revue, a local farce, a couple of touring companies and a Greek tragedy. It's fewer productions than usual, admittedly, but last year's Expo fiasco took the wind out of the theatre's sails, and there just isn't the budget to do ten shows a year any more. Georgia's finally running out of money.

They don't do it over here like they do in England, thinks Wally. This season nonsense makes him laugh. Each show plays for four weeks, regardless of whether it's a hit or not. There's no flexibility to exploit a success or hide a flop. No wonder the theatres end up at the Council doors, knocking for subsidies. It's all upside-down.

A shudder runs along Wally's spine and he clenches his rheumy eyes shut for a few warm breaths. A recent thought troubles him, he can't tell what. His dentures stink. His beard aches. With the thumb and forefinger of his left hand, he pinches the bridge of his nose hard enough to equal the throb in his temples, a trick once shown to him by Georgia back in the days when she was all clever Buddhist ideas and deep breathing. The pain subsides.

Pain, superficially from too much alcohol. Or from sleeping in wet clothes coupled with the relentless drumming of rain on the tin roof hour after hour. Deeper pain, radiating from the argument that propelled him out of the house last night, the specifics of which are lost in a haze and which are, of course, irrelevant. Alex wanted more pocket money or some such—it could have been about anything, honestly, but all Wally knows is that he's not being taken seriously in his own house. It's been like this for years. Humiliation as if he were a six-year-old. Not understanding but fighting, regardless, putting on a show. When he slammed the front door, he so wanted them to come running after him, chase him down the hill shouting, "Come back! Come back!" knowing, of course, that was ridiculous.

Earrings. It had started with earrings, that was it. Alex wanted one put in his nose for twenty-five dollars, the new punk craze. Wally couldn't give two pins what bits of rusty metal his son wanted to shove through his flesh, but he was in an ornery mood and, if truth be known, he simply wanted an excuse to vent. Once the steam began to blow, Wally knew he would end up storming out of the house. He would come here, to the workshop, as some kind of twisted proof of his umbrage. They let him go; he pretended to be ousted.

Wally tugs the Afghan comforter around his square bulk as if he were some grotesquely large European grandmother. His pants chafe against his calves and the backs of his knees. For a while he sits, gnawing at his upper lip, playing with the suction of the dental plate in his mouth. One of these days, he thinks, he simply won't go back home. He'll move a cot into the workshop and he'll be lucky never to have to go through with that domestic rigamarole ever again.

But it's not going to happen. He's been gelded. How has he ever allowed himself to get so tamed? For as much as it pains him to admit,

Wally doesn't have the energy these days to stir things up as he would like. He knows that by the end of the day he'll slink back to the house, probably soak himself in a hot bath and pretend that nothing has happened. It is a slow suicide.

He sniffs. Morning. In a little while, he'll turn on the kerosene and warm things up. He wonders how long it'll be before the emergency crews restore power; he has a gas ring around somewhere to boil up a pan of water for some tea if he has to. Inevitably, he'll have to get moving, attack the day, but first, please, a few more minutes of stillness as blood runs through his veins.

Peggy's boy.

Why on earth had he agreed to take him on? To even have him in the same room? Breathe the same air? He daren't begin to think about it. He'd done it as a favour to Peggy, supposedly, and at his own suggestion, more incredibly. To rub her face in her eternal sickness, most likely; the woman has been on the verge of death for decades, it seems. Why can't she get it over and done with? Wally chuckles wickedly at this audacity in the face of Peggy's decline. He still hasn't said all the things he wants to say to her; she's been such a recluse these past years. Fine. Her boy can take her place; he'll torment him instead. It'll be like worrying a lamb to the edge of the cliff. Wally's determined to get some enjoyment out of it.

The boy is old enough to take it. Year of the Snake, 1965, three years older than Alex, Year of the Monkey. In his early twenties, then, but from all reports still battling his way through adolescence. The last time Wally saw Ned was almost a decade ago on a disastrous camping trip in Squamish. The kid had gotten the worst of it then and, according to Peggy, had never fully recovered. Most recently, there had been some kind of collision with the authorities; Wally hadn't paid attention to the details. He was more astounded at the sound of his own voice, blurting out the offer of something for the boy to do for a couple of days a week, how he could appreciate an extra pair of hands around the workshop, what with the new season starting up. He may have mentioned something about the Scottish Play, knowing that would put the wind up her for sure.

"It's the least I can do, Peggy, considering."

After hanging up, he'd stared at the phone, trying to undo the conversation, pick it apart like a faulty appliance, figure out where it had gone wrong. But Peggy remains impenetrable; it is a miracle she deigned to call him. For as much as their lives are intertwined across two continents and half a century, it is as if they live in neighbouring castles and he only catches glimpses of her brushing her hair in a distant turret.

South Wales, London, then Ontario, and now, British Columbia. He in Kitsilano and she over in West Van, across the water where the houses sprawl up the mountains and the roads twist and curl with money. She is as far off and yet as close as his scars, now smoothed by the passing years.

The McLeans and the Greenes. Two modern, expat families, romping in the Great Canadian Playground, making the fantasy of a colonial *National Geographic* ethos come true. Like hell. The two families are as comfortable together as a pocket of wasps.

Peggy, rather *Margaret*, McLean is, in Wally's judgment, a condescending coward, married to a Scottish moron, her four boys faceless acquisitions that mean no more to her than her fancy hairdos and posh shoes. She is as unsuited to motherhood and marriage as is Georgia—but if Wally compares the two women, and he often does, it is Peggy he thinks of as being the bigger fake. It has something to do with the way she play-acts through her life, whereas Georgia keeps her acting to the stage. Peggy's infirmity is her utter ignorance as to how the world really works. Sometimes Wally wonders if she really has cancer.

He mustn't think like that; it makes him bitter.

He checks the switch on the electric lamp beside him: there's still no power. Hoisting himself out of the chair, he shuffles over to the sink, where he finds an old pan to fill with water, then sets it on the gas ring he normally uses to heat glues. He sighs at the electric kettle, then whistles in its absence when the water boils in the pan, because he misses the noise; he needs it to complete the ritual of making tea. For Wally Greene's Welsh soul is so steeped in this ceremony that he must surely be rimed with tannin. So, whistling the missing boiling note, he runs through his time-worn preparations: heating the pot, doling the leaves, rinsing the cup, sniffing the milk, biscuits if he's lucky, tobacco pouch, and papers.

The oblique concentration required to prepare a proper tea tray is, Wally knows, according to Old Man Greene, womanish. But a shot of peat whisky sloshed into the milky brew shut up that old bag of bones. Like grandfather, like grandson.

"The acorns don't fall off the tree in this family," Old Man Greene would say. "Some shyster comes along in the middle of the night and picks them, sells them to a Chinaman for a packet of leaves."

The tea tastes off. Wally dreads to think what had once been in the old pan, but at least the water was boiled for a solid three minutes, so it's doubtful it'll kill him. The slightly metallic flavour suits the gloom of the day, suits his mood: a hint of something wrong beneath the familiar. He shovels two extra spoons of sugar into his cup, and pushes an entire digestive into his mouth as if it was a second dental plate. He leaves it in there for as long as he can while he sips, enjoying it slowly disintegrating into Pablum. Smiling, he rolls himself a cigarette.

Solitude. It isn't so bad if, like Wally, you can endure your own company. Not all the time, of course. There are periods when he is so sick of himself that every moment grates. There is the abysmal pain of compromise—no different, he supposes, than what everyone else endures—yet still he feels marked as an outsider. At worst, a failure hangs over his life, casting a shadow over what might have been, and which terrifies him at dark moments with its threat of calumny. But mostly, he finds amusement in his alienation, in how this particular apple-acorn of the Greene family has found itself going to seed in the far reaches of Canada, growing wrinkled and rotten among the fresh-scented evergreens and wide wet skies. It makes him laugh, the differences between the concentrated tea-and-biscuit world of Britain and here. Over there, they had an answer for every question. Somebody had done it all before him, laid the foundations, built the house, solved the problems, may as well have lived his life. Here in Canada, it's all new, all undiscovered. All wrong and back-to-front.

He gets up and lights his cigarette by holding it to the lip of the flue of the storm lantern until the paper flares and a stream of blue smoke twists off towards the window. Georgia has long since given up on getting him to quit. These days, her cry to change his habits is a muffled song, sometimes heard, even repeated on occasion, but never adopted. He doesn't have her gumption; he wouldn't want it if he had it.

The first nicotine hit of the day; it's worth the rush. The drug crawls through his bloodstream, buzzing to his fingertips as he stands at the window, staring at the filthy windowpane. Outside, the shadowy blur of the dark trees looms on the far side of the railway line. Inside, the orange flame of the lantern reflects in glass. Velvet cabaret drapes in the rafters. Smoke. Strange images like those in a hall of mirrors. Demons. A quick glimpse of the whites of his eyes, fearful.

And although he has promised himself not to think about her, Wally allows a fume of memory to seep in. There she is. The angle of her neck accompanied by the click of her heels as she staggers away from him, down the corridor and out into the streets of London. Or of her head flung back in surprise, her mouth like a little *o* as if an egg would pop right out of it. Smoke rings. The sound of blood rushing in his ears, the air trapped in his throat, the blooming chrysanthemum of ecstasy, then ultimate release—sweet God—

snapped shut, the golden moment extinguished, leaving him stuck like a badger in a snare.

The boy is coming. Peggy's boy is coming today. Ned. Wally feels as if he's kissing the bullet, the smack of metal on his lips.

2

The first time Wally laid eyes on Peggy was in Wales during the war. He was six years old and she was five. She was sitting cross-legged on the floor of the crowded assembly hall of the old flint schoolhouse in Fishguard. She wore a thick overcoat and a brown cardboard label with her name written on it: *Chingford, Margaret*. To one side of her sat *Chingford, Charles*, and on the other, *Chingford, Leonard*. The two boys, both clearly a little older than the girl, were dutiful brothers, casting suspicious looks at their surroundings.

Wally had never seen so many children gathered together in one place before. For morning prayers and assembly, the usual number was around fifty. The hall that evening must have had well over a hundred boys and girls in it. Strange-looking creatures with bags and boxes and suitcases, a tired but excited rabble. The chatter was deafening. Wally could hear it from outside the schoolhouse; it frightened him. He clung to his Ma's hand, tried to drag it behind her back, behind her camel hair coat, into the safety of familiar scent.

"That's them, Wally," Ma whispered, indicating with a tilt of her head. "The three of them together, with the pigtails in the middle."

It took a long time for Wally to figure out which three Ma was talking about. He'd scanned half the crowd before he found the right combination; even then, he wasn't certain. He furrowed his brow, let go of Ma's hand, then marched through the shallow sea of children, right up to his quarry. Scrutinized them, he did, from head to toe.

"Who're you looking at, then?" demanded one of the boys.

"Are you playing the Piggy in the Middle?" Wally asked the girl. "You have to come home, now."

Her mouth and eyes went as round as round, and her head wobbled a strange little dance. The other boy leaned over and poked Wally in the middle.

"Who're you, Tubby? You our new cook?"

Wally felt himself redden. "No!" The back of his neck prickled and he stamped his foot. "No!"

"Wally!"

Ma flew in to the fray, closely followed by Mr. Quarrendon in his tin auxiliary helmet, both eager to smooth things over. Introductions were made and welcomes extended, smiles and awkward handshakes, but the damage was done. A barricade of hostility between Wally and the new boys, Leonard and Charles, was firmly in place. And as the adults helped carry the bags out of the school to where Da was waiting in the van with the dogs, the new girl burst into tears. Wally wanted to smother her right there and then to make her shut her yelping.

His understanding of the evacuation process was shaky at best. A few months before, his Da had taken him along to a sheep auction, where they'd picked up a new flock. And, although he'd had it explained to him no fewer than half a dozen times, Wally was under the impression that this process was a similar one: they'd come to the old schoolhouse to pick out new brother and sister stock.

"Did we get a good bargain, Da?" he chirped. "Did we? Did we?"

On the drive back to the farm, once the girl had been quietened down, the two new boys kept up a salvo of questions. They were both intrigued by Ma's arm. Why was it in a sling? Had the Germans wounded her? "Polio, my lambs," Ma told them. "That's the polio, that is." They seemed satisfied with this and, as Wally sunk deeper into his seat, he became aware of how much they talked and behaved frighteningly like grownups. One of the farm dogs, Jessie, propped her head on Wally's lap, and for a while, he was comforted by her bony muzzle. When Da coasted the van down the hill with the engine off, Wally wanted to impress the boys with his knowledge, wanted to tell them how this silent ride was all part of "the war effort to save petrol," but one look at their pointy faces, at their sharp little London eyes, and he couldn't open his mouth.

It was dark when they reached the farm. The evening air was laced with wafts of dung and damp feed. Not wanting to spend another moment in the company of his new siblings, Wally scuttled around to the barnyard, rattled through the kitchen door and hid in the scullery, where Millie, a four-year-old Rambouillet sheep, was bedded down on blankets, recuperating from a recent illness.

"Budge over," growled Wally, claiming a portion of the blanket. "I'll sleep here, if you don't mind."

Millie didn't answer; she didn't have to. She rearranged herself to accommodate her new roommate, gave him a nudge of recognition in the ribs with her snout, and went back to sleep. Even though Wally tried to follow suit, resting his head against her springy curls, his heart was pounding too heavily for him to relax. He knew he was being rude to the newcomers and that he'd likely get punished for running away from them, but he couldn't see how he could stomach sleeping in the same room as those two boys. A bitter resentment he didn't understand crept into his head as he thought about how he, Da, and Ma had spent the entire afternoon preparing for the new arrivals: hauling mattresses, adding a chest of drawers, making up the beds with fresh linens and hospital corners. It had been exciting, then. Now it was unspeakable.

A renewed bout of weeping and wailing reached him through the walls of the farmhouse. The girl was in tears again somewhere upstairs. He could hear stampings and door slammings, Da's voice raised in annoyance, and he knew the search was on to find him. He closed his eyes and pretended to be asleep, pretended not to know a thing about the hubbub going on in the house.

Ma knew where he'd run off to. She called to him from the scullery doorway; she was no more than a shadow, he could just make out the tip of her nose and her sling where the edge of her arm jutted from her body.

"Wally, love, do you mind sleeping in the box room for now? Little Margaret wants to be with her brothers."

"Can't I sleep here?"

What with all the shufflings and changings that day, it seemed a reasonable possibility, but Ma wasn't having any of it. He was to go in the box room and if he got cold, he could have a hot-water bottle.

"Come and get washed up for your tea, there's a good boy."

He would have run to her side, such was the power of her command, but one of the London boys, exploring, burst past her into the scullery.

"A sheep!" he exclaimed, pointing. "Leonard! Come and look! They've got a bloody sheep in the house!"

So suddenly, as Millie lumbered to her feet, Wally found himself at the centre of attention. Little Margaret came too, astonished beyond belief to see the huge woolly animal inside a house. Wally tried as best he could to retain his dignity, explaining that it wasn't any old bloody sheep, that this was Millie, who was a better friend than any of them could ever be.

"Why's she called Millie if she has horns, then?"

"All sheep can grow horns," explained Ma, stepping forward and scratching Millie's head. "Male and female alike. But in this case, you're right, Leonard. Millie is a wether, which means she used to be a boy sheep, but isn't any more."

"What . . . h-how?"

Ma's eyes glinted with mischief. "With my sharp little knife, of course."

That shut them up. The two boys went as grey as porridge and looked nervously at each other, as if there was something nearby that could change them, too, from little boys into Millies. Taking advantage

of their docility, and chuckling at her own archness, Ma herded everyone into the kitchen, where she began to lay out a grand supper.
Mutton stew, with thick doorstops of bread for mopping the gravy.
Hot tea from the big Brown Betty, and for afters, they were promised a bowl of suet pudding with treacle and custard.

"Eat up, Margaret, love. You could do with some meat on your
bones."

"Her name's Peggy," interrupted the one called Leonard. "It's
short for Margaret, you know."

Peggy smiled weakly, as if she'd been caught telling lies, and she
stared at her food. Her eyes were still rimmed with tears, her cheeks
shiny. She pushed a lump of meat around her plate with a fork; suddenly addressed her hostess. "Mutton stew is a sheep, isn't it?"

"That's right, dear. And very lucky we are to have any at all, what
with there being a war on."

Peggy put down her fork and glanced quickly at the scullery
door, back to the table, then to Wally, who was sitting at her elbow.
Her body hiccuped, her lips crinkled.

"Please . . . I'm going to sick."

Which she did—all over the edge of the tablecloth, on Wally's
knees and slopping onto the stone floor. A jerky burping slew that
stunk of sweet, warm cheese, immediately triggering a sympathetic,
identical response from Wally. Two retching children at the tea table.
Horrors.

A howl of disgust went up from the boys as Ma and Da sprang
into action. Peggy was whisked off by Ma, while Da grabbed Wally
roughly by the elbow and dragged him over to the kitchen sink
where he was wiped down with a dishcloth.

"Bloody fine first impression you've made, *boi*," he muttered.
"Stop fidgeting, *Bobol bach*!"

"I'm not finished, Da. There's more."

So he was marched out to the privy where he sat on the cold
grey flagstones for a while with the old rusty bolt drawn on the door.

Just to get his breath back, really. Every so often he would lean over the pot and make retching noises to satisfy the audience he knew was listening. There was a horrid smell of carbolic and bog.

"You all right in there, child?"

Eventually, he pulled the chain and emerged, but not before he swore not to have anything to do with these awful children from London ever again. From now on, he would pretend they didn't exist.

With embarrasing ceremony, Ma cosseted him upstairs, into his pyjamas, then tucked him into a tight, unfamiliar bed with a hot-water bottle and a peck on the forehead. A yawn raced up his body.

"I don't care if they were a bargain, Ma," he managed to say before she left the room. "Can we send them back to London to-morrow, please?"

But, of course, the Chingfords were not sent back to London, where the worst bombing of the war was in full sway. Not the next day, nor the one after that. Wally was given a lecture on the virtues of being polite to his guests; little of it sank in. Ma suggested he could show Charles and Leonard his tin soldiers, but as luck would have it, the boys were far more interested in running around in the fields, climbing trees in the nearby wild garlic forest.

Whenever they returned to the farmhouse, they'd be flushed from exercise, ruddy, and smelling of fresh sea air, the kitchen door banging behind them. But as soon as they saw Wally, they'd assume an air of indignation.

"Where are the buses?" demanded Charles. "In London, we have double-decker buses."

"The King lives in London," boasted Leonard. "Who lives out here? Slugs and mushrooms, that's who!"

Wally would flush to the roots of his hair, a reaction he was beginning to detest. He would hang his head, not daring to look at either of them; he knew there was a fireball burning away inside him, that if he were to turn this dreadful weapon on them, they'd be fried to cinders as surely as if they'd been hit by a bouncing bomb.

He took refuge in the house, moving to another room whenever they appeared. Indeed, he wouldn't go outside at all, other than to go to the privy. The sun shone, the skies were clear, if blustery, but he couldn't bring himself to go beyond the barnyard. To run with those London boys into the open fields and beyond would have been treason. He couldn't even look at Peggy, short for Margaret. She filled him with such a dancing anger for making him sick on the kitchen table alongside her, as if he was as weak, as much of a blubbering sissy as she. So if he wasn't talking with Millie, he'd hang around the front porch where there was a built-in window seat and a stack of parish magazines that he'd flip through and look at pictures. He kept sneaking peeks through the window at the huge sky and the rolling hills. Then he'd poke his head around the front door, daring himself to cross the transom, telling himself that this was the most normal thing in the whole wide world, but all he could think of was being caught by Charles and Leonard and ridiculed for not being able to climb trees or run as fast as they could.

"Careful of that main road, Wally!" shouted Ma from the window.

He played with his soldiers up the back stairs that led to the usurped room. He imagined he was an army general, the Grand Old Duke of York, leading his men up the rising cliffs. Or he pretended the little tin men were Londoners, and he'd heap them all together in a big pile and drop lit matches on them. Part of him was terrified of getting caught; he'd had a thrashing from Da once in his life for playing with matches, and he didn't need to go through that again. But Da was out in the field and Wally felt brave to the point of not caring. He kept his wits about him, however, as he filled the stairway with the stink of sulphur, ready to run away at a moment's notice. The smell only added to the excitement of the pretend-Blitz.

"Would you like to play Mothers and Fathers?"

Peggy, in tight, new pigtails, had been watching him.

"Don't know how," shrugged Wally, his heart pounding at her closeness. "I've never played that before."

"That's all right, I'll teach you," she said, with a serious tilt of the chin.

Reluctantly, Wally allowed himself to be indoctrinated. She dragged him into the sacrosanct sitting room with its adult aroma of furniture polish and coal dust. Her bossy manner disarmed him as she led him deeper into Mothers and Fathers before he could object. Mothers and Fathers. It turned out to be a frustrating game with no rules, no goals to be scored, and no body count to be tallied up to decide winners and losers at the end—if indeed it ever had an end. The main gist of it was boring: she was the mother and he the father. They would pretend to wake up of a morning, and she would send him "off to work" into the hall, so that she could get on with her "chores"—secret make-believe rituals with dolls and hand-kerchieves in a corner of the sitting room. When Wally returned after a suitable period of tedium, he had to give Peggy a kiss on the cheek, call her "darling," and try to figure out what she'd been up to while he'd supposedly been out of the house all day, earning the daily bread.

"I give up."

"No-oo! Don't! I made your favourite supper!" Peggy managed to put on a most grown-up air, wagging her finger at him. "And you forgot to kiss all your children when you came home."

It was a loathsome game. The last thing Wally wanted was to be caught kissing dolls and rolled-up hankies in a pretend world he knew nothing nor cared anything about. Peggy constantly chastised him for ruining the fantasy.

"No, you can't sit there, silly. Fathers sit up that end of the table!"

When she tried to force him to slipper the doll children—six of the best for the naughty ones—he was convinced he was about to explode.

"Mutton sicker!" he yelled. "Stupid mutton sicker!" And he stormed out of the house just to get away from her, just to stop the rising wash of fury.

Freedom! He was out in the fields, galloping, with the sun in his hair before he knew it. And there was no sign of the boys. It was vast out there. Wide open and beautiful. A sweet, wet smell was on the breeze, not a building for miles; no double-decker buses, no Kings of England, just grass and trees and little stone walls and hedges into the distance. He ran to the edge of the field, climbed a wall, and launched himself into the air.

He stayed out all afternoon, hiding behind a wall, say, then running across a sharp, barley-stubbled field to the other side, wind rushing his ears. Then landing in a jump and a tumble, pebbles and chaff bruising his knees. He crawled on his belly, he crouched for an eternity as still as he could, he ran, he whooped, he scratched his legs raw.

After a while, he found where the sheep were grazing that day. They were in one of the standing stone fields, the one with the triangular arrangement on the little tor. He ran, shouting, through the flock, the slower ones skittering away from him in short, untidy gallops.

"*Twll dy din!*" he yelled as he reached the stones. "*Cer i grafu!*"

Then he leaned his back against the old smooth rock, his diaphragm aching from the exercise, and let himself slide down to the ground. Blood was oozing from where he'd skinned his knee; a dark, glistening patch that gave him no pain. He couldn't remember the actual moment when he'd wounded himself.

A passing cloud plunged him into sudden shadow, while a sunbeam hit the blue-grey hills way off in the distance. The sheep had forgotten about him, they'd closed ranks, surrounding him with mutton.

"You stay away from Soggy Peggy," he told a nearby ewe. "She can't even think of you without sicking all over the place."

And to prove how much he belonged to the tribe that killed and devoured without nausea, he daubed his finger in his wound, tasted the blood, the salt and grit, then spat a glorious arc of dark spittle through the air. Out from the druid's triangle it went, over the congregation of sheep, and landed somewhere in their midst, unseen, like a conspiracy, a secret wish. A seed, tossed down a well, to the roots of the earth.

3

"Alex! If you want a ride into the West End, I'm leaving in ten minutes!"

Alexander Greene, pale, plump, and naked except for a pair of powder-blue Jockey briefs and his Medicalert bracelet, has been lying on his bed, playing a flashlight over the posters that cover the sloping ceiling of his room. David Bowie, The Clash, The Eurythmics, and *The Rocky Horror Picture Show*. As the beam of light travelled from image to image, he would hum a couple of appropriate bars. He was totally absorbed, content, forgetting how much he hates still living at home. At the sound of his mother's voice, however, he stops humming and returns to a state of captivity, feels the prisoner's flame burn in his gut. It's been three months now since he announced to his parents that he would prefer to be called Xander, but has it sunk in?

"Alex . . . Xander?"

His mother pokes her head around his door. She squints momentarily as he hits her with his followspot. She starts to say something, but the words get caught in her jowls, and she merely huffs like a deflating bullfrog, little pockets of air escaping in silence. She ducks her head out of the beam.

"God, it's dark in here."

She picks her way across the floor to the window, yanks up the blind, letting in a miserable grey light through the dormer window.

By this, she consults her watch on the inside of her left wrist. She doesn't really look, it's just a gesture, she knows the time. It's time this universe evolved into something more to her pleasing.

"Do you want a ride or not?"

"Don't you ever knock?" Xander swings his legs off the bed, brings himself up into a sitting position. "I could have been in the middle of something."

He plays the flashlight over his underwear for a couple of seconds, where his morning erection of five minutes ago is subsiding. His mother returns to the door, ignoring him; they've had this banter before. How she'll say that she's not his type, or that young men of his age should be able to pick up where they left off at any time of the day.

"There's no hot water left. I'm sorry." She rubs her cheek against her shoulder. "But I'm sure Mr. Stradivarius won't object to your manly stink just this once."

She can't resist getting in a dig.

"Mr. Stadjykk, Mom. His name's Stadjykk, and I really don't think he's gay."

"He teaches piano, doesn't he? He looks gay."

Xander doesn't take the bait. Arguing with his mother on this topic when she's in this mood is pointless. She knows everything there is to know about homosexuality, except, of course, her own son's proclivities.

"Give me five minutes to get dressed. I'll meet you downstairs."

She bows deeply. "Your carriage awaits, my lord."

Which is supposed to be a joke—an old one, about her ideal job, where she plays the ancient servant who makes an appearance in the final act, utters this immortal line, then exits. That would be it: full Equity wage for ten seconds of stage time. It is a role she maintains she is looking forward to playing at the end of her career. But it will never happen. For Georgia Brandt owns fifty percent of her theatre and can pick and choose whether she plays Hedda Gabler or Saint Joan, which she does (never the servant, never the maid) and will continue to do until the day she expires. Moreover, after years of use, *Your carriage awaits, my lord* is now steeped in her chronic complaint that at home she is reduced to the role of domestic servant. Or, in this case, chauffeur.

Xander lobs a rolled-up sock at the closing door, hitting the dart board in its outer circle. He wants to shout "All right, I'll bloody well walk!" after her, but he bites his tongue, jumps off the bed and judders into his jeans. Two minutes in the bathroom, dousing his face and armpits with cold water, thirty seconds to shove a toothbrush around his maw, check the hair hanging over his brow, and he is downstairs in four and a half minutes. His mother, banging around in the study, isn't ready.

"Have you seen my book on eighteenth-century England?" she demands, when he goes to see what's taking so long. "Big, thick thing. Burgundy cover?"

"Give me the keys, Mom, I'll wait in the car."

In his mother's old Mercedes there's a radio that only functions on the AM dial, but it is better than sitting trapped for fifteen minutes in silence while the rain spritzes the windows. He listens to the CBC's smorgasbord of news, popular classics, and an eager phone-in about what the city intends to do with the newly abandoned Expo site. By the time his mother clambers into the driver's seat, he could have made it to the West End on foot. You just never knew with her; sometimes she was on track, sometimes she wasn't.

"Don't look at me like that," she says, reversing into the laneway. "I'm going as fast as I can."

Five minutes later they motor across the Burrard Street bridge, part of a steady string of traffic that moves along at a brisk trot. As they approach Pacific Avenue lights can be seen shining through the mist. The West End has power.

His mother is deathly silent. Xander can guess what's nagging at her: last night's stupid argument. Dad said some hurtful things to her. She keeps tucking her hair behind her ear and chewing the corner of her lips, while she focuses on maintaining her distance from the car in front. The windshield wipers pulse intermittently, marking time until someone says something.

"He's getting worse, isn't he?" she says, eventually. "Poor old Wally. Last night. I thought he was going to explode."

Xander stifles a laugh. The image of his father bursting into flames is too easy to picture: the red wiry hair and beard, the way his face blushes crimson when he's angry, the ever-present cigarette providing the whiff of smoke. The man is a walking Vesuvius.

"I don't know what gets into him, sometimes, I really don't," she continues, shaking her head.

Xander knows. Today is the day Ned McLean is supposed to start work as an apprentice, and if his mother can't grasp why that would screw things up, she deserves to wallow in her misery.

"He's right, though," he says carefully. "I should find my own place one of these days. Move out."

"Oh honey, no."

She says it with such simplicity, such assurance, that Xander sighs and curses himself for raising the topic. Now he's trapped again: on one hand she revels in his maturing into a young man, and on the other she protects him, smothers him, wants to hold onto his youth as if it were her own.

"Let me off here, Mom," he says suddenly, grabbing his backpack. "I'll walk up the hill and you can take Pacific Avenue round to the theatre."

He takes advantage of a red light, opens the door and gets out before his mother can object. Her mouth registers surprise, opening, then snapping shut again. A car in the lineup behind them honks as she leans over and rolls down the window to shout after him.

"Alex! Do you have your meds?"

Xander shouts over his shoulder that he does, indeed, have his meds, and he waves goodbye by saluting the air in angry dismissal.

He doesn't look back as he runs across the road and up into the one-way system where she can't follow. Freedom.

Up the hill, then, as fine needles of rain sting his face. He reaches Davie Street, picks up a take-out coffee from a muffin store, then shifts over to Thurlow Street and up to Nelson Park. The red brick of St Paul's hospital looms through the mist on his right, followed by the dark shadow of Mr. Stadjykk's New York-style brownstone apartment building, with its fire escapes that twist down the side like menacing sculpture.

Xander lets himself in. There are no buzzers, not even one for the superintendent, so visitors either have to wait until someone opens the door, or they shout up, throw pebbles at the windows, make idiots of themselves in the street. Enterprising tenants often prop the door open with a brick, but this is frowned upon by management. Mr. Stadjykk, customarily immersed in his music lessons, wisely issues his students with a front-door key.

It's dark in the lobby, a patchwork of faded crimsons and umbers, and the whole place reeks of cockroach spray from monthly treatments. This bug problem is an ongoing battle, up the north side of the building then down the south, chasing the pests from the seventh floor to the basement and back up again, never getting rid of them, but satisfying the municipal inspectors. It's an eternal topic of conversation for the tenants, as popular as grumbling about the weather, and just as pointless.

Xander passes the superintendent's office on his way to the elevator. The month's vacancies are posted on strips of wood slotted into a frame, like the day's hymns in a church. There are three bachelors available and a two-bedroom. He should put in a rental application; the rents are cheap, a bachelor goes for a couple of hundred a month and has its own kitchenette and Murphy bed. He would be among friends, or among those he would like to have as friends. The building is home to Bohemians: artists, musicians, photographers, poets and writers, some of whom Xander knows well, some that he's had sex with, some that he fantasizes over, and some who, like street dogs, terrify him. Living here would be so right, a step toward real freedom. Growth.

He would have to persuade his mother to help him out financially; right now he doesn't have a job and he can't touch the thousands in his bank account without his mother's signature. He knows he can get welfare in six months, but if he wants to make the move soon, some adroit handling of his mother is in order.

He shares the tiny, gaudily painted elevator with a pink-haired girl carrying a basket of laundry. She watches him from behind thick lines of kohl, friendly enough, but he knows she's summing him up, deciding that he's probably too young, too chubby or too gay for her. He says hi, more as recognition of being on the same planet than of wanting to know her better. The ride is slow and shaky. It is, in fact, much faster to take the stairs, but six flights is too much of a hike; easier to go down than up. The girl gets off at the fourth floor. Xander leans against the elevator wall for the remaining two, nestling into the corner, pretending to be a junkie renegade. He carves an X into the paintwork with his door key.

Muffled piano music can be heard the moment he steps onto the sixth floor. The nuances of a difficult passage of Schumann get louder as Xander approaches Stadjykk's apartment. Xander can imagine the lesson inside, the heated discussion over interpretation, arguments sometimes, often ending with Stadjykk shrugging, hands wiping invisible cobwebs out of his hair, walking away, "You choose, sweetheart, you're the one playing the little tune."

Xander walks past Stadjykk's door and continues down the hall to apartment 612, at the end on the right. He's at least half an hour early for his lesson, and as is his habit, he pays a visit to his friends to kill time.

"Xander-boy!"

"Juan de Fuca!"

"You're all wet."

Kisses and caresses, innuendo, smirks. Xander steps into another world, down a narrow vestibule crowded with leather jackets, and into the main room where the gang is draped around the couch, watching cartoons. Their eyes are glowing embers in ashen grates, the light from the television flickering over their faces.

"As you can see," says Juan, "No one's been to sleep, yet. It's been a bit of a binge." He extends a languid arm to stroke Xander's coat, his long fingernails scratching the military fabric as if he were petting a cat. "Take it off, baby, stay a while."

"Anyone got any grass?"

Roxie looks up from her princess spot on the orange shag. "Forget your pills at home, again?" she drawls.

Someone on the couch grunts "Heads up!" and a fat baggie of marijuana sails through the air. Xander helps himself, nips a baby sprig into a twist of silver foil from his gum wrapper before tossing the mother stash back. Someone catches it, wordlessly.

He then settles down cross-legged on the carpet to roll a joint. A packet of papers appears from his backpack along with his Swiss Army knife. He takes the task slowly, enjoying the ritual, the spread of accoutrements around him on the floor, the craftsmanship in creating the perfect doobie—not one of those string beans that Juan likes to slap together in twenty seconds.

At the next commercial break, Roxie rolls over, "Hey Xander, are you ready to get your nose pierced today or what?" She's eager to play doctor, having volunteered a month ago when the idea first surfaced. "Just say the word."

"My Dad won't let me," he mumbles.

"Do it anyway," jeers someone on the couch. "What's he going to do? Rip it out?"

Xander's hands start to shake.

"You OK?" Juan eyes him, doubtfully.

Xander nods yes, but he has to stop what he's doing. He pinches the bridge of his nose and breathes deeply, as his mother has taught him. It's not just a seizure he's trying to ward off, it's anger.

Juan grabs a big bud of cannabis from the floor, torches the tip of it with a lighter and waves it under Xander's nose like a bottle of poppers.

"Breathe in, baby, that's it. Breathe in."

Xander waves away the smoke, pushes away Juan's arm. It's all confusion, boiling inside him, confusion and heat. It propels him off the floor, away from the group, and into the bathroom. Suddenly, his legs give way, and he's staring at the hexagonal white tiles, kneeling at the john.

A spray of saliva explodes from his mouth. The desire to break something surges. Loathsome as always, the routine sensation of the seizure edges closer. He has just enough time to grab a towel, fold it into a makeshift pillow and climb into the claw-footed bathtub. It's an old trick; it keeps him contained and he's less likely to break anything.

He lies in the tub as the energy swells. The sound of the cartoons playing in the next room grows tinny, his lips buzz, an early electrical jolt, and he knows he's only got a few seconds left. Silence, while he concentrates on breathing. Here it comes, he thinks, the unseen hand, the unknown force. He should have stayed on the carpet with Juan. Juan, who knows how to deal with seizures the luxurious way: head on the lap and gentle stroking until well after the All Clear. Then again, he should have pocketed his Dilantin before leaving the house.

Something twists his body sharply into the familiar strain: the forty-nine degree entrance to unconsciousness. It's like being shoved off the top of a water slide. Down he goes, down, the taste of burning on his tongue, a tunnel opening up beneath him. Once again, slave to the masked master who keeps him chained to mystery on the dark side of his eyelids.

4

The power comes back on around noon. Wally is surprised at the number of appliances, lights, and switches that had been left on. With a gentle surge, electricity flows into the workshop, the overhead fluorescents stutter on, vent fans hum, and the old fridge by the sink chunks to life. Wally closes his book and turns down the storm lantern.

There's plenty of work to be getting on with while he waits for Peggy's boy; *She Stoops to Conquer* opens in three weeks, calling for a truckload of authentic-looking props and set-dressing. Two weeks ago, he rescued his copy of *England in the Eighteenth Century* from Georgia's clutches and it now has dozens of paper slips acting as bookmarks bristling down its three-inch thickness. It's a treasury of furniture design, architecture and costume, and it contains a generous number of reproductions of period etchings, drawings, and paintings; mainly Hogarths and Gainsboroughs, of course, a style of art that Wally always thinks of as being deliciously loose and lusty. For the past few hours, he's been flipping through the pages by the light of the storm lantern, which lent a satisfying element of verisimilitude to his studies.

Now with the power restored, he sets himself up at a worktable. He's still not certain which jobs he'll allocate to Peggy's boy if and when he turns up, most likely the fake candles, since there are so many of them to be checked, mended, and built. That should keep him busy and miserable for a couple of days. He hefts a cardboard box full of electrical bits and bobs—wires, Christmas lights, batteries and bulbs—and sets it at the head of the table. There you go lad, he thinks, sort through that lot.

For himself, he's part-way through constructing a sundial for the garden scene in Act Five. The armature is almost done, just a bit more shaping of the chicken wire, then he can start with the papier-mâché, a satisfying, messy process. His new apprentice can help him with that, too.

So it is that Wally is hard at work with wire-cutters and staple gun when there's a knock at the workshop door. It's gone two o'clock by this time, and Wally has forgotten all about the outside world, so immersed is he in the joys of what he's doing. He genuinely wonders who it could be.

The door to the outside sticks, needs an extra shove to get it open.

"Mr. G.?"

Wally blinks through the needle-fine rain at his visitor: a weather-beaten brute with a hull of tattered black leather, a six-foot press-gang of a chap in boots and chains. His hair is hacked short, bleached; his eyes are steady, dark; his mouth set in granite. A brindled bitch, Staffs terrier by the look of her, rears on her chain at Wally, eager to make a new acquaintance.

"Down, girl."

"Ned?" Wally steps instinctively forward, to offer his hand for the dog to smell. "Is that you?"

The last time he saw Ned McLean, the lad was a lanky version of Peggy, all open eyes and unintentional grace; now he's grown into something more approaching Wally's stance, solid and unyielding. Wally feels a tinge of fear, such as he might feel upon coming across a gang of hooligans in the street, then tells himself to stop being so silly; he's come across tougher yobbos on the streets of London, survived worse. It's simply that he was expecting Ned to be an innocent mouse like his mother.

"We got lost." Ned says, brusquely, quietening the dog. "Spent all morning wandering around Granville Island."

"Ahh." Wally glances anxiously at the animal; a bit hyperactive, but otherwise it doesn't seem dangerous. "The confusing wilds of False Creek. Didn't I give you directions?"

Ned's shrug speaks volumes.

The Phoenix Theatre rents this place from the city for a mere twenty-five dollars a month. Years ago, it was part of a thriving foundry, a collection of one-storey buildings scattered around a city block down by the edge of False Creek. The concrete and brick where the old furnace originally stood in the centre of the lot is still charred, a raised circular structure now cracked and overgrown with weeds. A few of the buildings have been torn down and the land is now used by a local housing co-operative for allotments—the usual cabbages, squash, and beans flourish in neat patches amongst the old foundations.

Hidden away, beyond the bulge of Vanier Park, Wally's prop shop is a swift hike of at least thirty minutes to the theatre if you go straight down the disused railway track to the edge of Granville Island, and then take the Granville Bridge over to the West End, and up to Davie. The distance from the theatre suits Wally fine. If he was closer, say squashed into the back end of the scene shop or the costume attic above the dressing rooms, people would bother him all the time with mend this or glue that. As it is, he's pretty much left alone; only the determined make it through. He has Georgia to thank for this arrangement.

"Do you have a dish or bowl or something?" asks Ned, about to loop the dog's chain around a pipe. "Then I can give her some fresh water and she won't be drinking out of puddles."

"Oh, you can bring her inside, as long as she's quiet. What's her name?"

"Schtupitt."

"Come on in with you, then."

So in they all come, the two men standing uncomfortably in the cramped area by the door, the dog sniffing around excitedly in corners. After an embarrassed pause, Wally forces a smile, squeezes out a "Well, then," and off he goes, fussing for a suitable water bowl.

"I was just about to get a pot of tea going," he lies, once the animal is sorted. "Can I get you a cup?"

"Got any coffee?" Ned looks Wally in the eye. "All that English crap reminds me of home."

Wally suppresses a shudder and mumbles something about there possibly being a small jar of instant coffee around. He gets to it, thankful for the activity—sorting out cups, rummaging around for the Maxwell House, filling the kettle—as the alternative is unnerving. Ned is civil enough; he hasn't said or done anything outside the usual bounds of politesse, but there's something dangerous about the man, a criminal element that wafts from his body like the steam from a grating in a back alleyway.

"How's your mother?" asks Wally, as innocuously as he dare when the drinks are almost ready. "How's she doing, these days?"

A fleeting vulnerability skitters across Ned's face, reminding Wally of the younger boy he once knew. "Still dying." Hardness returns to his jawline, the pointed edges of a tattoo on his neck peep over the collar of his T-shirt. "She was doing fine at home until a week ago. Now they've shipped her back to the hospice."

Wally doesn't know what to say. One thing is certain: he'll have to stop thinking of Ned as "Peggy's boy." He hands over the mug of instant coffee, granular lumps floating on the surface, manages a weak grimace, intended to be supportive, but which probably comes across as pathetic.

"Well, then."

They sip their drinks. The electric clock on the wall behind them whirrs as its second hand sweeps around the dial. Wally notes that it needs to be reset after the power cut. He'll have to get out the stepladder.

"Let me show you around."

"Sure." Ned leaves his coffee, untouched, and follows Wally. "Go lie down, Schtupitt."

They start with the storage area. The building, L-shaped and low-slung, is crammed on the longer side from floor to ceiling with theatrical stock. From musical instruments to incidental furniture, statuary to skeletons, body parts, flagpoles, halberds and other weaponry, coffers, barrels, books, flowers, lamps and mirrors, glassware, cutlery, and every kind of fake food you could imagine, shellacked onto plates or loose in boxes. Wally takes Ned up one aisle and down the other, all the time sneaking peeks at him out the corner of his eyes, trying to get a measure of the man: the way he stands, walks—more of an amble, really—his mettle. He points out items of interest and tries to explain his storage system.

"Here we have long sticks: dowels, rods, poles, staffs and the like. Shorter ones, like walking sticks or batons are here."

"Cool." Ned picks up a fake flintlock pistol. It's a bit dilapidated, needing its hammer mechanism to be glue-gunned back on. "You could fool a bank teller with one of these."

"I doubt it," says Wally, firmly. He waits, pointedly, until Ned returns the gun to the shelf.

Further down the aisle they pass Wally's carvings in the shadows. They take up a complete shelf: his whittled spheres, devil heads and fetishes, acorns and dice, sheep heads and strange beasts. He continues past without comment; avoids the possibility of either interest or ridicule.

In the elbow of the *L* is the washroom and wet area: paint spattered sinks, a fibreglass shower stall, and a rickety door to the yard where the big jobs are painted. Schtupitt joins them at this point of the tour, trotting at her master's heels.

"And this is where we do the work," announces Wally, leading Ned back into the other arm of the building where the workshop proper is housed. Paints, tools, glues, lumber, band saw, lathe, worktables and, of course, Wally's makeshift office, with his chair, his curtained throne, in the southwest corner. Schtupitt gets within sniffing distance of the armchair, bounds up onto the seat, paws herself around in a circle and plumps down on the cushion, claiming it for her own. She growls, not antagonistically, but with pleasure.

"And that's the lot." Wally claps his hands like a stage conjuror, hoping, perhaps, to roust the interloper from his favoured seat. "What do you think?"

Ned raises an eyebrow as if considering the question. Then, all jutting leather elbows, he goes through his pockets until he finds a wad of paper. Unfolded, it looks official, if a bit soggy. He hands it over.

"While I remember, Mr. G.," he says, "can you sign this for me?"

Court papers. Family Court and Youth Division. Wally's seen something much like it before. Fragments of his phone call with Peggy return to the forefront of his memory. There'd been some trouble with authority, and she said they'd arranged for the sentence to be commuted into community service. There it is in black and white: twenty hours a week for two months. Wally knows that means they're trying to correct some form of fairly harmless antisocial behaviour, like pot smoking or misdemeanour charges; and Peggy knows how familiar Wally is with those, she ought to, after all, it was she and that lug of a husband of hers who'd gotten Wally into trouble in the first place. He casts his eye down the sheet of paper. *Edward Leonard McLean, dob 21/02/63, Male, Caucasian, Mischief/Aggravated Assault.*

His belly jolts. A suffocating discomfort settles upon him; he's not sure where he stands, or how much he can keep himself under control. He realizes just how manipulative Peggy McLean has been. He hates her.

"This is for the whole week," he says, handing it back. "I'm supposed to sign this on Friday."

"I'm here now, aren't I?"

The papers go on the counter; neutral territory.

"You certainly are." Wally inspects his thumbnail for a moment, waiting for his heart to stop pounding. "For twenty hours a week, like it says. Now I don't mind if you do four hours a day for five days, three short days, two full days and a Saturday afternoon, or . . ."

"Excuse me?"

"Pick your own hours." Wally feels the grip of anger. "But do the hours you will, *boi*. Or I won't be putting my signature on that sheet, you can be fucking sure of that."

His outburst isn't prompted by any staunch views on Justice, nor is it because he won't stand for any nonsense from Ned, far from it. It's because of Peggy. Peggy picking at a scabbed wound. How her kid had fallen into trouble and how, in her sickness, she'd called upon him, Wally, to help sort things out; put the young man's house in order and perhaps—she hadn't said it, but the inference was there —perhaps there would be the murmur of a chance that a similar salvation might hit Wally by associative magic. She must be stupid. Does she think it's that easy? One phone call to twist the cooperation of an idiot beyond recognition. But the proof of all that old pain, the thousand ancient, obstinate emotions, is still there, standing before him in the workshop, sizing up Wally as if warming for a fight.

Son of the father, Wally wouldn't hold back a punch if it came to that. It would be worth it just to feel the blood of generations repeating an old dance through his veins.

"OK, Mr. G., have it your own way." Ned shrugs, backs down an inch. "I'll do a couple of days and make up the rest on the weekend. Are you going to clock my lunch breaks?"

"You bet, son. And every time you take a piss." He doesn't mean it, but he can tell he's being taken seriously.

"Look." Ned appears to be choosing his words carefully. "I don't give a shit what happened between my parents and you. I don't give a shit, honest. I just want to do my two months and get out of here."

Wally can't resist the temptation. "And what do you know about what happened?"

"Aw, drop it, man."

"No, no, no, no, tell me. Come on."

"Dad calls you a dirty fighter."

"Oh, yes?"

Ned grins, laughs. "Yeah. He calls you a certifiable psycho and says to watch out for your left hook."

Blood flushes up Wally's neck, pulses over his ears at the reminder. The veins at his temples stand out as if they've been embossed. Psycho? The memory of blood on his knuckles, the dull bruising along the fingers, and his opponent's saliva stitching the air. The battle of the moment won. The war, as everyone now seems to know, lost.

"He asked for it," he snaps. "I broke his nose because he asked me to, just as I'm doing this because your bloody mother asked me to. Call me an idiot, but here you are."

And with that, he strides over to the box of candle ends and electrical rubble, picks it up with both hands and drops it on the counter by Ned. It makes a satisfying noise as it lands; not broken bones, not an aggravated assault with a suspended sentence and social workers, none of that, but it does the job.

"Sort through that, will you, lad?"

In silence, he goes back to work on his eighteenth-century sundial, his cheeks burning, every tooth left in his head biting down, his jaw clenched to avert disaster. Year-of-the-fucking-Snake, indeed. Peggy McLean must think he's an idiot. He forces memories aside, concentrates on the hexagons of twisted wire. When he looks up again, Ned is deep in the process of sorting through the box, and the wad of court papers has vanished from the counter.

Act II

5

The small town of Fishguard—Abergwaun in Welsh—accommodated the influx of strange children as best she could. The old flint school was bloated to bursting; its seven classrooms proved inadequate. Classes were held in the assembly hall, even in corridors. Extra teachers, more baby-sitters than academics, were corralled from the community: Mrs. Glynn from the Women's Institute, Miss Fford-Davies from the Manse and, to Wally's torment, Mr. Maddox from the chapel.

Things were fine until September, when Wally moved up from Mrs. Blackmore's infant class to Mr. Maddox's introduction to genuine scholarship. Peggy stayed behind with Mrs. Blackmore when it was discovered how young she was; another year of nursery rhymes and clapping songs for her. Chaos ruled the school. Everyone muddled through, changing things and rearranging children, desks, and coat hooks as the need arose. Wally was glad to be rid of Peggy, but was soon wishing he too had stayed behind with Mrs. Blackmore when he started Class Three.

Mr. Maddox was a steaming, red-faced brute from Liverpool who never passed up the opportunity to flout his English superiority over the Welsh natives. He split Wally's class in two, further solidifying the breach between the evacuees and the locals. Wally was stuck at the back, in the corner, a mere chair-scrape away from the dunce place, where he was banished with regularity for no apparent reason other than being Wally Greene. Worse, Mr. Maddox was dangerous. A week wouldn't go by without him whacking Wally across the knuckles with the wooden blackboard duster as if he were a washerwoman whacking a mouse with her scrubbing brush. The crime: writing with the left hand. This hadn't been a problem the year before. Mrs. Blackmore had mentioned his left-handedness, certainly, but had done nothing about it, hadn't given him an inkling that anything was wrong, if anything, she made him feel special in his difference. Mr. Maddox, the self-appointed janitor of godless infants, however, was out for blood.

"Kack-handed idiot! Use the proper hand. The right hand, boy!"

It didn't take Wally long to discover that he only ever got punished if he got caught. He could fill the pages of his exercise book with line after line of left-handed scrawl, and as long as Mr. Maddox didn't see him wield the pencil, things were fine. It became a game, holding a second pencil in his right hand and hunching over his desk, pretending to do things properly, hating himself for having been put together backwards, kack-handed, ungainly, useless at football, and the guilty possessor of red, red hair that shone like a beacon through the copse whenever he tried to play hide-and-seek.

Most lessons were taught by rote and choral repetition, and every so often soloists were forced to the front of the class to regurgitate their knowledge for the benefit and amusement of the others. Wally could recite some of his times tables: his twos, threes, fours, fives, tens, sometimes his elevens and twelves, but had eternal trouble with his sixes, sevens, eights, and nines, which would cause him to blush uncontrollably, earn him a clip around the temples from Mr. Maddox, and invariably end with a visit to the dunce's corner.

Once a day, for a full twenty minutes, the entire school was made to sit and wear their gas masks for the war practice. Wherever they were—sitting at their desks, lined up along the corridors, or in the main hall—hundreds of rubber monkeys snuffled and snorted as the filters vibrated in their casings, a muffled cacophony. Vision distorted, imaginations dilated, they were as fearful of sneezing as they were of Hitler's mustard gas.

The division between Londoners and locals was most evident in the playground, where Wally, uncomfortable, hovered alone at the steps to the canteen. Soggy Peggy, who adored Mrs. Blackmore, was popular amongst the London girls. She was full of dancing games and Ring-a-Ring-a-Roses, and she could sometimes be seen trying to bridge the gap between her crowd and the locals. It was a futile endeavour. The division was as permanent and real as the one between the the Germans and the British.

Months of sleeping in the box room and talking to sheep had given Wally some immunity to Peggy's girlish enthusiasm. Now he could watch her eyes go as round as her mouth, watch a new idea descend upon her, watch her blow in the wind like a daffodil, watch her cry, puke, scream herself green in the face without getting the urge to kick her stupid. He was apart from her. She was a year younger than him, after all; there was his position to maintain.

Charles and Leonard Chingford, however, were as hostile as ever. With the other London lads, they formed a posse that was better avoided than confronted. They would scream around the playground, a gang of Gatling gun imitations, hot on the warpath for fresh casualties.

"Kack-kack-kack-kack-kack!"

On the couple of occasions Wally dared to stand up to their onslaught, they surrounded him, forced him down to the ground and sat on him, crowing their victory to the world while Wally's face was smeared into the mossy grass. Knightsbridge leather scuffed him in the bottom until his trousers were a mass of muddied footprints. He became adept at fading away whenever they appeared on the scene. Luckily, theirs was not the kind of contrariness that would search out and chase him down if he wasn't around; he had to be there for them to get the idea, which was worse, in a way. It made Wally feel as if his existence depended upon them.

Mid-December, one Tuesday morning after prayers, the head-master's wife made an announcement to the assembly. Due to the war, she told them, it had been the practice of the theatres in the land to close their doors out of respect. The conflict, however, had been going on for longer than anticipated, and some establishments were now turning their lights back on to help lift morale. Such was the case with the Grand Theatre in Swansea, which was announcing its Christmastime production of *Jack and the Beanstalk*, a panto for all ages. A tour bus was being organized, Saturday week. Any interested parties should speak to Mr. Quarrendon as soon as possible, and leave the appropriate deposit.

"Panto!" Peggy's face shone. "*Jack and the Beanstalk!*"

Always the last to be chosen for the football team, always the brunt of taunts, always to have prizes promised, then withdrawn as punishment, Wally wasn't about to count on going to the panto. If he was allowed, he would go; if not, he wasn't going to cry over the loss. It might be nice to have the house to himself for a change.

"*Jack and the Beanstalk*, is it, now?" said Ma, over supper, pursing her lips. "Saturday week? And how much is that scoundrel Mr. Quarrendon asking for this deposit?"

"Five shillings, Mrs. Greene," said Leonard. "It's only five shillings and that includes the petrol and sandwiches for the trip."

"But Swansea, Leonard love, that's a long way off." Ma shrugged her shoulders, cast a sharp glance in Da's direction. "And I suppose that's five shillings each."

"We have our own five shillingses, Mother Greene," burst out Peggy. "And we could treat Wally if you like."

"Well now," said Da, on one of his rare intrusions into the supper conversation, "I suppose I could drive the whole lot of you in the van, might be cheaper, come to that. We could kill two birds with one stone and pay a visit to Dinbych-y-pysgod while we're at it."

"Tin biccie piss god!" Leonard collapsed in chortles, which spread like wildfire to Charles. Both boys still derived amusement from the Welsh tongue, mispronouncing words whenever they got the chance, even when they were in danger of getting a clip round the ear.

But for once, Da didn't bristle at the boys' joking. Instead, he looked steadfastly at Ma, who shifted and shunted with her polio arm, trying to untangle something Wally couldn't see. Then she cleared away the dishes without a word, the plates talking for her, chattering against the cutlery as she stacked them on the draining board.

"Dinbych-y-pysgod?" asked Wally. "What's at Dinbych-y-pysgod?"

"Your Gran and Grampa," growled Da. "We're about due a visit."

Wally was dumbfounded. This was the first he'd heard of grandparents. He'd assumed that, much like in most areas of his life, he was different than other children who always talked of Nanny this and Grandpa that. He supposed his family didn't have grandparents; they had sheep instead. In fact, he'd told this to someone at school only recently, in all seriousness, and Mr. Maddox had put a stop to the argument by telling Wally how his grandparents were in all probability not of the ovine family, but likely deceased. Now, to suddenly acquire relations within the beat of a moment at the end of supper, was a shock.

"But my grandparents are dead!"

"Not on that side of the family, they're not," said Ma. And she left the room.

Saturday week arrived and early morning, bright and balmy, scrubbed behind the ears, fresh handkerchieves in pockets, and coats buttoned stiff, everyone piled into the van for the trip to Swansea by way of Dinbych-y-pysgod. Ma stayed behind. She said she'd been there before and besides, the animals had to be fed, there were enough chores to be getting on with.

"But the panto? pleaded Peggy, "Don't you want to see the panto?"

"Not really, love." She adjusted the ribbon in Peggy's hair. "But you be sure to tell me all about it tonight."

She gave them all sandwiches wrapped in wax paper, then she followed the van out of the gate and waved them all goodbye standing in the middle of the road and lifting her good arm in salute— no higher than her elbow, she wasn't putting herself out. Wally, looking through the little square window in the back of the van, watched one of the dogs chase them as far as the post office.

They arrived at Tenby—Dinbych-y-pysgod—in good time for lunch with the mysterious grandparents, which was the aim. It took a while to find the right street, but soon, Da parked the van and trooped everyone single-file along a curved, narrow street, where the slate-roofed houses were built right up to the road, with one strip of brick pavement. The sun blasted down their side of the street, the occasional crisp shadow plunging them into cold. They arrived at an old blue door and Da knocked hard and long on the wood as if waking the dead.

"What'll you be wanting down there?" A head with a halo of white hair stuck out of an upstairs window. "Be off with you!"

"It's David and the children!" Da hollered back. "Come for lunch!"

When old Grandma Greene finally appeared at the door in her dressing gown and slippers, Wally took an involuntary step backward as a waft of stale, fruity air reached him. Da was worried. It looked as if their visit was a surprise.

"Didn't you get my postcard, Ma?"

A long stare, followed by a sniff. When she smiled, she revealed a row of brown teeth like rusty eyehooks set in her gums.

"You'd better come in. Enough cluttering up the street with you." She led them through a narrow hallway, dark as an underground tunnel, and into a smoky parlour that was crowded with lace, glossy white pottery and polished black wood. She eyed the Chingfords as if she was sizing up meat in the butcher's window. "Heavens. Have been busy, haven't you?"

"These are the evacuees, Mam. They're from the City of

London." He presented them by pushing them forward: Leonard, then Charles, then Peggy. "And this is Wally, Mam. This is our Wally."

"Stupid name for a boy!" came a sudden, throaty voice. Wally looked around to see where the noise had come from, then realized the pile of old smoking clothes sitting on a chair in the corner of the room actually contained a human being. Its skin was as grey as the shirt around its neck, and as wrinkled. One clouded eye stared out, the other was covered by a sag of drooping brow. The head was nigh bald and covered in liver spots, a wizened apple left in the cellar too long and growing tufts of mould.

"Wally is short for Walter," offered Wally in the most polite voice he could muster. "But everyone calls me Wally."

"Gelding! Who are all these people, Doris?" demanded the old man. "What are they doing in our parlour?"

Da explained again how they'd come for lunch on their way to Swansea to see the Christmas Panto. Once more, the postcard was mentioned, and again, it was met with silence.

"Oh, there's nothing in the larder for so many hungry mouths," said the old woman, "but I could rustle up some tea and biscuits, I suppose. Sit yourselves down and try not to break anything."

"That's all right, Missus," Leonard explained, "we've got sand-wich lunches in the van."

For his pains, the mistress of the house pinned him with a sus-picious glare, her mouth pursed as if she were sucking lemons. "Oh, and I wonder who made those sandwiches for you, young man," she rasped. "A one-armed farmer's wife, I'll be bound. How she cuts the bread is beyond me."

At that, they laughed, the two of them, the old man and the old woman. They dredged a mocking cackle out of themselves, pleased at their joke, but it was devoid of any joy. It was the noise of souls scraping the bottom of the barrel. Wally, stunned, looked at Leonard. For once, they were on the same team.

While the kettle boiled, the children were taken upstairs to the

water closet to relieve themselves. Nobody really wanted to go, but
they had been cooped up in the van for an hour or so, and bladders
were undeniably full.

When Wally's turn came, and he stood before the ceramic toilet,
his eye spotted a dish on a shelf to his left. A box of matches, an old
postage stamp, and a little pocket knife, silver with fancy inlay. The
knife was in his hand before he realized it, smooth and cold, looking
like a sardine on his palm. Upon examination, it had a blade that
swivelled out from one end and a thin nail-file from the other. The
decoration made him wonder if it was real silver, valuable. In a flash,
he decided it was much too nice an object to belong to his grandparents, so he slipped it into his pocket, pulled the chain, and sauntered down the stairs with a thief's swagger.

Lunch, such as it was, was awful. Wally couldn't wait to get out
of that claustrophobic house. The tea was weak, the biscuits hard.
He watched his grandmother tip a slug of whisky into his grandfather's teacup, straight out of the bottle. The adults carried on a
painful conversation, all stutters and mumbles, mainly in Family
Welsh, punctuated by silences and short, loud English musings about
the terrible situation in Europe. The children were silent. Every so
often, they exchanged glances, wordless agreements: these grandparents were nasty, horrible people and if there was any way of
getting out of there faster, they'd do it. Wally thought back to when
he believed his grandparents were sheep, happily grazing on the
hillside, hooves in the mud, clover for supper, the wind whipping at
their haunches. And even though the evidence to the contrary was
right before his eyes, he managed to convince himself he had no
grandparents—not on this side of the family.

"Well, we must be off Mam. Nice to have seen you."

"*Pob hwyl i ti.*"

"*Diolch.*"

Outside, Da blinked in the sunshine, stood motionless beneath
the clouds for a while. They were an hour and a half ahead of

schedule, he told them, so he would treat them all to cream cakes, which they found in a shop on the Tenby seafront. Everyone sat on two neighbouring benches and shouted conversations at each other through the brisk wind while the gulls circled and cawed, hoping for scraps.

"Those were the worst biscuits in all of Europe!" Leonard declared. "Churchill could use them as ammunition against Heil Hitler."

"Agreed!"

"Agreed!"

Charles, sitting next to Wally, leaned over. "Now I know where the smell in your family comes from. Pee-hew." Louder, he shouted, "Mr. Greene, why do old people stink so much?"

"That's enough, boys," said Da. "They can't help being old. It might happen to you, one day."

"Not me!" shouted Peggy. "I'm never getting old."

She said it with such vehemence that Wally believed her. And just as she said it, with the sun in her hair, her ribbons coming loose, Wally took a picture of her, *in camera*, a mental archive signed and dated, preserved with every crumb of cake, smear of cream, powdered sugar dusted round her mouth. Click. Peggy Chingford, five years old. Forever.

Stay a little girl, he thought, that would suit him fine. In the meantime, he would grow up and leave her far behind. His fingers curled around the knife in his pocket, tracing the smooth metal edge where the blade lay hidden. It gave him strength; made him feel adult. Soon, he thought, he would be much, much older than Peggy could ever be. She could stay with Mrs Blackmore until the sheep came home.

6

Two months after the Grand Theatre's production of *Jack and the Beanstalk*, and Wally was still performing excerpts, still describing scenic details, and still taking curtain calls with a grand sweep of his arm. The entire show was in his head, preserved like an exotic marmalade, any image available at a moment's notice. He could do the Dame's clog dance, the King Rat's sneak and the Oh-yes-it-is, Oh-no-it-isn't chant until he ran out of breath. He was intoxicated, shot through the heart, and he was determined to take down everyone with him.

"For the love of God, Wally, put a sock in it."

"But they're magic beans, Da. The Genii said they were ma-a-agic beans."

"Oh, a Genii was he? Looked more like a fairy in disguise to me."

Two months, and it was clear this was more than a passing fancy, and no one was more surprised than Wally. When he'd taken his seat in the velvet-and-gilt auditorium of Swansea's Grand Theatre, he'd been grouchy. He worried the knife in his pocket. He was certain the panto was going to be horrible, an endurance on a par with prayers at assembly—or worse, since Peggy was so infatuated, beneath him. He didn't bother to pretend to read the programme like Mr. Quarrendon and the other bowed heads of Class Six. The whole affair was just a plusher version of being up in the chapel balcony, with its kneeling rail, psalters and sermons; he braced himself for the worst.

But in that gulf of time between the overture and the first scene, the chandeliers dimmed to a purblind buzz, the audience took notice, held its breath, and the anticipation became palpable. A fearful strip of sharp grey light appeared along the bottom fringe of the curtain, and Wally got his first glimpse of the stage. Something pulsed through his stomach, swallowed his tongue, and seared a glowing scar across the horizon of his imagination. Here was something new. And from the wave of fear that swept through the auditorium, he could tell it was something inexplicably naughty.

Then, as quiet as a sigh, the curtain rose. It flew straight up in the air with such speed that even though he was sitting in the Dress Circle, Wally swore he could feel a breeze against his cheeks; cool air rushing in from a distant planet. He was looking at a thatched cottage on the edge of a forest. He was outside! Or, rather, the audience was inside, looking out through an enormous window. The sudden freedom of being confronted with a vision so utterly complete and impossible made Wally spring out of his seat. He couldn't contain himself. Danced a furious, red-faced jig in the aisle, did Wally Greene.

Panto! He understood it immediately; he grasped the conceit, embraced the contradictions. Unlike Peggy, who later admitted she didn't know that the Principal Boy was a girl, that the Dame was a man in a frock, and that cows couldn't in reality do a tap-dance, Wally knew the moment he was exposed to them. He knew the Giant and the Giant's Wife were on stilts, knew that Jack's cottage wasn't really old, but painted to look old, knew the beanstalk grew out of a trapdoor with help from hidden conspirators dressed in black, timed to music, and lit with lights that made you think you were outside under the most indigo ink of moonlight ever. Leonard and Charles sneered at it all, sighed, and called everything "stage trickery," declared the illusions false. Wally was beyond them. To him, it was obvious the panto world wasn't real; it was simply the biggest, most whopping fib he'd ever seen.

Forget butcher, baker, teacher, sheep farmer. Wally now knew what he wanted to do when he grew up. Panto. Principal Boy, King Rat, or Mother Goose, he cared not which, as long as he was in there, counted amongst the feathers and the greasepaint.

"Yeah, the famous Wally Greene," taunted Charles. "Now appearing as the back end of the cow!"

At night, in bed, Wally would watch the crack under the door glow like the moment before the curtain went up. He could bring back that thumping in his chest, the blood rushing in his ears just by imagining himself in the theatre. He knew he'd stumbled across real magic when he felt his bed spin beneath him and the box room shift dimensions as the door raised, the crack expanded, and he was able to step directly into the land of his dreams.

He had a newfound confidence at school. Mr. Maddox could no longer make him cringe; the blackboard duster was just as vicious as before, but now, when hit, Wally would break into a theatrical wailing routine lifted directly from the Giant's Wife. He would squeeze invisible tears from his eyes with screwed up fists, stretch his mouth wide open, and ululate a lip-wobbling warble until his classmates would dissolve in hysteria. Sent to sit in the dunce's corner, he would play the King Rat, standing on his chair and posing with one sneaky knee in the air whenever Mr. Maddox turned his back.

In the playground, he was master of the comic chase, the slapstick pratfall, and most spectacularly, the five-minute death scene that on one occasion became so infectious that all the children joined in, moaning and writhing on the ground *en masse*. Mr. Quarrendon was almost fooled into calling for the emergency gas masks. For his punishment, Wally got a hundred lines: *I will not lead others down the path of deceit.*

He learned his lesson. From then on, he was leery of involving anyone else in his games. If he was going to take the path of deceit —which, in his view, led directly to the panto—he would do it alone.

And then there was the knife.

It was a secret so profound he carried it everywhere, brought it out only when he was completely sure no one was watching, told no one, showed no one except Millie. That it had arrived in his life on the same day as the panto was no coincidence as far as Wally was concerned. The two events were connected. One was his secret, the other his destiny. They were as intertwined as Jack's beanstalk ladder to the clouds.

Once, Peggy spotted him worrying away at the knife in his pocket and asked him what he had there.

"Pocket secret," said Wally, closing his fist around the knife. "Little girls don't have them."

That had been a close call. He resolved not to draw attention to himself in the future. He would hate to have to explain where he'd gotten a knife like that; it would mean big Trouble. So he got to know it by touch, by the way it knocked against his leg when he walked, by the speed at which it grew warm when he clenched it in his fist, by its shape through the threads of his pocket handkerchief when he wrapped it up like a boiled sweet.

He brought it out rarely. On the kitchen lintel, he had the opportunity to slice a nick out of the wood, marking his presence in a way that only he could see. In the barn, he stroked marks into a beam, tried to form a simple *W* but the knife wasn't a pencil and it wouldn't write for him in either hand. As spring arrived, he snicked buds from the trees, flowers from their stalks, poked at snail shells that the thrushes had left lying in the yard. He stripped bark from twigs, revealing the creamy white layer underneath. He scraped paint from an old cart in the yard, using the point of the blade to lift whole sections away from the wood. Eventually, these activities led him to the idea of carving.

His first attempt was with a branch he found in the forest up by Clwyd's Corner. It was about two inches thick and a couple of feet long. The end of this stick was deformed, a fist of knuckled wood where it had come away from the tree. He took it to the standing stones, a place where he felt safe, sat with his back against rock, took out the knife and started in.

Once the bark and loose fragments were cleaned away, a shape suggested itself to him from the natural curves. A tiny knot in the grain seemed to wink at him like a watchful eye offering encouragement, and so he continued. It wasn't like writing at all. It wasn't even like drawing or painting; it took both hands, one to wield the knife, the other to clean the wound. It was like a dance, or a song he made up as he went along.

Letting the knife do its work, Wally was pleased at how the more adventurous his whittling, the better the result. A flat callous formed on the side of his middle finger where the blade pushed against the skin. Soon, he had fashioned the backwards curl of a horn, the slope of a snout, nostrils, lips. It was a sheep's head, plain as Millie, sharp as an eye. It emerged right there beneath his fingers. And when he was finished, he thought he saw its lips chewing the cud.

He didn't dare bring it back home with him, so he pushed the uncarved end of the stick into the soft earth, right up against one of the druid stones, the head facing out over the field. He'd come back to it another day and finish off the rest of the shaft. He had an ambitious idea of covering it with curlicues and fancy Celtic knot fretwork, like those on the backs of the pews in the chapel. It would be his special stick, a weapon perhaps, a Jester's staff. He would carry it onstage with him when he played the Pantomime Dame; his very own wooden spoon with which to bonk the policeman on the head.

He came back to it two or three times, slowly working his way down, but the pattern ultimately proved too complex for him to carve. One day, after a rainstorm, he returned to the standing stones and the stick was gone. He pushed his finger down the muddy hole where it had been as if to make sure that it was no longer there. He wasn't particularly sorry to see the end of it, as he'd grown frustrated with the technical demands he'd set himself. He knew he could coax shapes out of wood with his knife if he put his mind to it. That was all that mattered, the knowledge and the memory.

That summer, Wally came home from school one afternoon to an unearthly noise sawing through the air. It sounded at first like an animal in pain, and then, perhaps, a high, insistent violin. He ran to the back of the house, following the sound to find Da sitting, shirtless, in the middle of the barnyard. It was a strange sight. His father's head was bowed, so the keening noise was coming from an unseen mouth that kept dipping down to the ground. His fists pounded the earth, bare shoulders rising and falling, a slab of pale, muscled flesh twisting and turning in the broad daylight.

Ma stood five yards away from him, watching, her hair caught damp against her cheek. Wally went to stand beside her. After a while, she put her hand on his head. "Your Grandma's passed on," she said, eventually. "In her sleep, peaceful, last Thursday night."

At the sound of her voice, Da stopped his carrying on, went stiff, still, as if he hadn't known anyone was standing there until that moment. In the distance, down the lane, the yelps of the Chingfords playing tag on their way back from school could be heard. Da stood up then, rescued his shirt from where it lay in the dirt, snapped the torn fabric like a flag, and stalked back towards the house.

Suddenly, he stopped and turned around. "You tell another living soul about this, Wally Greene," he said, "and I'll give you a hiding into the middle of next, so help me, I will."

Wally had never seen his Da's face like that before: ashen, drawn, his eyes like two faint coals in the grate, the creases of his skin like folds of rock. All this was harsh, but when Da opened his mouth, his teeth were dark, coated with soil where he had bitten into the ground. An image of the old woman with the rusty smile appeared to Wally then, a ghost. He saw in his Da the same deep grooves around the mouth and nose, the same nubby chin, the same teeth. By the time he had shaken her out of his head, both she and Da had gone.

He had seen death before, in sheep and dogs. It was when breath stopped and limbs stiffened. He didn't know it as a sadness that could overtake someone as strong as Da.

Over the next few days, Wally's parents took their tea in the sitting room instead of at the kitchen table. Wally was forever walking in on them in the middle of whispered conversations, which they'd stop, and wait until he left before resuming. Peggy, Len and Charles, sensing the disquiet, melded together and became ever more the Chingfords, a single entity instead of three. Wally resorted to long chats with Millie, the only creature in the house other than the dogs to take any notice of him.

The next thing he knew, Da came back from the funeral with Old Man Greene riding in the van beside him. Three battered suitcases had to be lugged into the sitting room, where the old man was installed in not the best chair, but the sturdiest, the one with a high winged back. His legs had to be bent into position and the shoes removed, replaced with slippers. It was like moving a giant doll. Silent, save for a dry clicking wheeze, the head swaying from side to side.

When the old man caught sight of Ma, who was sorting through blankets on the sofa, he gave a grunt, came alive. His spine lifted a few inches, his chin stuck out imperiously, and he spoke. "What have you done with my luggage, woman? Where's my baccy?"

He rolled his own cigarettes, five at a time, kept them in an old Navy Cut tin. In spite of himself, Wally was fascinated. The cigarettes manifested perfectly at Old Man Greene's fingertips, even though he shook like a fern. Hands crabbed with age, saliva bubbling at his lips, tobacco peppering the floor—a loose and messy process that should have resulted in anything other than the pristine, uniformly cylindrical cigarettes that ended up in the tin.

Wally wanted to ask if he could try his hand at rolling, but he didn't dare, as it would involve pretending to be friendly. He didn't like the old man; he'd made that decision months ago, and thus it would be treason to curry favour simply to see if he could learn to make cigarettes better than his grandfather. So instead, he hovered at the transom to the sitting room, watching the process with envy, hoping he was invisible, unable to explain himself when he was asked what he was doing.

"This is your Grandpa's room now," said Ma. "When Leonard, Charles and Peggy go back home to London, you can move back into your old room, and he'll go into the box room."

"I thought he lived in Tenby." Wally screwed up his nose as if he could still smell the mould in that place. "What's he doing here?"

"That was your Grandma's house, and now she's gone, we can't expect your Grandpa to be all by himself, now can we?"

She said this, not as if she believed it, but at least as if she understood it. It wasn't necessarily the real reason, but a reason she was willing to voice. Wally wanted to tell her how the two old people had made fun of her arm, something that not even the rudest children at school dared to do, not Mr. Maddox, no one. He stared at the intruder in the sitting room, remembered the awful laugh, the inedible biscuits.

"When are the boys and Peggy going home to London?"

"When the war's over."

Wally knew when that was: next week. The war had been on the verge of being over next week for as long as he could recall. It was like "jam yesterday, jam tomorrow, but never jam today." In other words, it never happened. He couldn't imagine there not being a war. It had become part of their lives, as immovable as mutton stew grown hard on the bottom of the pan. He might as well face it: his Grandpa was going to be in the sitting room forever.

Suppertimes were the worst. When they moved the old man into one of the Windsor chairs at the kitchen table, his mouth shook loose and he started to complain. A litany of grievances stumbled out of him, from chilblains to children, from Germans to Japs, bad cooking, bad weather, bad manners, bad English, bad everything. "Get me another cushion, woman, I'm wearing out my sit bones on this seat." He viewed the world as a rotten apple, he wouldn't shut up, kept it going for the entire meal, until he was helped back into his chair in the sitting room where he would fall asleep, a smear of supper growing crusty on his lips.

It was Peggy who remembered what to do. "Mother Greene? Don't you have a bottle of something you can put in his tea?"

Da sprang out of his chair at that. "Good thinking, Peg!" He rummaged in the dresser and came out with half a bottle of single malt. He wiped it, looked at the label, uncorked it, gave it a sniff and poured some into Old Man's tea.

The trick worked. A hit of whisky didn't shut him up completely, but enough. His sentences faded before they finished, resurfacing later for a word or two before diving back down to the depths of whatever ancient bog they'd come from. Now his outbursts were quaint instead of caustic. And so the bottle stood in pride of place on the sideboard like a soldier on duty, pressed into service twice a day or more. When the level got low, Da only had to pay a visit to the Red Lion for a fresh supply.

The smells of smoke and spirits entered the farmhouse with the arrival of Old Man Greene. The sitting room was now shrouded in smoke, whether there was a fire burning in the grate or not. The sweet, sharp odours of tobacco and alcohol followed the old man around like an aura. Ma complained that the place was starting to stink like a public saloon. Wally, on the other hand, was secretly excited by the adult flavour of it all.

Months passed. Wally forgot that Old Man Greene hadn't always been there, just as he forgot that the Chingfords hadn't either. If asked, he would include them all in his definition of his immediate family, along with Ma, Da, and Millie.

One morning, on his way to school, Wally put his hand into his pocket and the knife wasn't there. His heart felt as if it had folded into his stomach. Had the knife slipped out without him noticing? And how long had it been missing? Terrified, he retraced his steps, looked everywhere: in the garden, in among the mushroomed roots of the old apple tree, around the yard, under his bed, in the dirty clothes hamper, it was nowhere. He walked slowly out of the house, back to the lane, each step taking him closer to admitting that his knife had gone.

"Have you lost something?" Peggy appeared at his elbow, as if intrigued. "Can I help? What is it?"

Wally couldn't think straight. He couldn't tell her what he was looking for without telling her his secret, and he wasn't about to do that. He couldn't pretend that he hadn't been looking for anything at all, that he was just playing a game, for the moment for that ploy had passed. He couldn't lie; couldn't say he was looking for a marble or an old conker; his hesitation had already condemned him. So the more he stood there, cancelling his options, the more the horrible impossibility of the situation kept him frozen in his shoes.

His secret had left him.

"Is this what you're looking for?"

She had the knife. There it was in her grubby paw, so wrong, so misplaced, so impossible. The shock of what this meant so disoriented Wally that he missed his chance to grab it back.

Her questions continued, she was beginning to enjoy herself, knowing she had him trapped. He closed his eyes, dimmed the lights of his mental theatre, brought the curtain down on the scene, but the taunts continued, surrounding him, piercing his guilt with the broadside of her barbs. Merciless, she was; Wally was certain she wouldn't stop, that he would be stuck there for his allotted three-score years and three, forced to hear the mockery for which there was no possible response. Ever.

"What's wrong, Wally? Wally! What's wrong? Lost your pocket secret, have you, Wally-Wally?"

7

M r. Stadjykk moans and shoves his fingers deep into his hair, as if working up a lather. This action skews his spectacles, which he then has to correct.

"Boy, boy, boy. How can you expect to get any better if you don't practice?" He slumps into his chair, hikes a pant leg, crosses his legs, takes a deep breath. "Not that I give a shit, but the novelty of Shostakovich wears off when you can't play it."

"I can play it, I can play it."

"Not well enough for me. Not well enough for your precious judges in New York. You play like that, you'll be stuck in hotel lounges for the rest of your life."

"Or teaching."

Stadjykk takes the insult with a shrug. He looks out of the window, his lips moving to an unheard litany. "Your fingers are on drugs," he says, finally. "You're flopping your way through that passage like a dead fish."

Xander starts the piece again, plays it right through to the end without getting stopped, relishing the final chords perhaps a shade too much. When he swivels around to Stadjykk for comment, he gets nothing, it's like staring in the mirror.

"Well?"

"Well, nothing. I've told you what I think of your funny little tune. Your brain never made it past your wrists."

He's right, Xander has to admit. He hasn't practiced for over a week and it shows. The audition date for Juilliard is getting closer, just over five months away now, and it'll soon be time to either buckle down or blow the whole thing off. He might be able to fool some of the judges with his panache, much as he might be able to fool his mother into believing he's spending all his evenings practicing in the rehearsal rooms at the school, but a lot of good that'll do him if he fails the entrance exam that she has her heart set on him passing.

Hanging out with his friends, smoking pot and occasionally getting laid is far more attractive than sitting at a keyboard, training his muscles through dastardly fingering sequences. He hasn't been home to Kitsilano for three days, and he's played hooky from two sessions with Mr. Stadjykk in the past week. He has other things on his mind.

It's a full moon. Today's the day, tonight's the night, and Roxie is waiting for him at the end of the hall with her piercing needle. And later, there are at least three worn pathways to debauchery that he has every intention of following.

"Can I go now?"

"Let's hear your well-tempered prelude and fugue first."

The Bach regulates Xander's annoyance. From the opening bars, mathematical configurations surround him, take him on a journey as if through an architectural structure, colonnades and high vaulted ceilings, sacred geometry. He loses himself to the exquisite pleasure of an acquired and demanding art.

When done, he waits for Stadjykk's grunt of approval before grabbing his knapsack, mumbling his goodbyes and getting out of there. They'd gone twenty minutes overtime, which was Stadjykk's way of punishing him for skipping earlier sessions. Roxie won't mind. When he'd left her an hour and twenty minutes ago, she was still in her kimono, sitting on the couch, drinking strong coffee in the sunlight, trying to banish the shine of sleep from her face.

She hasn't moved, the music is the same; it's as if he never left. His time with Stadjykk feels like a diversion to another dimension, an eighty minute bubble kept afloat by rules, tradition, and the threat of the Juilliard Future. But Scriabin and Shostakovich are already sinking into oblivion, as if they had happened to somebody else.

"So . . . ?" asks Roxie, failing to suppress her grin. "Are you ready for this?"

"Ready as I'll ever be."

The sun pours in through the window, it's a glorious September day. Brian Eno, the modern-day Bach, is on repeat on the stereo, *Music for Airports*. Xander pulls off his T-shirt and sits self-consciously next to Roxie on the couch. He's acutely aware of his puppy fat. Trepidation makes his skin gooseflesh, his pulse pound in his neck.

"So have you decided yet?" Roxie unzips the smart leather case of her needle kit. A bottle of rubbing alcohol sits on the coffee table, along with a bag of cotton puffs. "Left or right?"

"I was thinking the left," says Xander, scrunching his chin to look down his chest, to compare his nipples. They look much the same from this angle. He can't imagine what it's going to feel like for one of them in a few minutes, having a shaft of metal forced through its nub. He wonders if he'll bleed, whether he'd bleed more from the left than the right, because it's closer to the heart.

Over the past few nights, ever since he knew this rendezvous with the sharp point of fashion was inevitable, he's been pinching himself as hard as he can, imagining what could be stronger, or deeper, until his vision would glow blood-orange at the periphery and he could smell burning.

Roxie dons her surgical gloves, swabs him down, takes a felt pen and spends a few pedantic minutes placing a mark at exactly the right entry point. A drop of perspiration runs down from Xander's left armpit in a plumb line towards his waist. He turns his head away, just wants her to get it done, wants it to be over, can't bring himself to watch.

"Last chance to turn back," she says, brandishing the needle. "Speak now or forever hold your peace."

"No son of mine is going to put a ring through his nose like some bloody pig!"

"Right, then. Breathe in."

She counts down from three, impersonating a NASA flunky. ". . . Ignition . . . Houston, we have lift-off."

There is no pain. He hears the scrunch of tissue, like someone biting into a thick slice of buttered toast. The sun is suddenly hot on his face, he smells his own sweat, warmth, salt. He laughs to release the pressure. Did the music skip a beat?

"Hold still, bubba. Almost done." Threading the sleeper ring through the new hole in his nipple triggers a high, smarting pain that makes his spine straighten. "There you go."

It's done. He feels lopsided. A distant burning.

Roxie leans forward, her latex-shrouded hands at shoulder height, still holding a bloodied cotton ball and her needle, and she kisses Xander on the mouth. The velvet down on her upper lip brushes his face—soft spice, heady.

"Congratulations."

He responds, if for no other reason than to allay the growing furnace of pain that starts as a tangled ball around his nipple, reaches up through his eyes and continues, flashing above his head and beyond, surely licking at the ceiling. His breath sings through his clenched teeth as his lips engage with hers.

"Mmm," she smiles. "Endorphins."

Her robe drops from her shoulders, as if in assent. The thought of Juan stumbling in from the bedroom and discovering them making love flits through Xander's mind, and is as quickly dismissed. He grips her at the elbows, holds her away from him, wants to embrace her, fights the desire to push himself into her, to bury his stinging breast into hers, rub the pain away, not caring what damage he might do.

"Don't."

She disentangles herself from his steam and goes to the window, adjusting her kimono. She becomes distant, as only Roxie can; she has an ability to retain every moment of history and deny it at the same time. Yes, they just kissed, almost had sex. No, nothing happened, it was all in his imagination.

She asks him if he's planning on going to the big bash in Gastown that evening: an underground event, art students and a Rockabilly punk band in a warehouse. Lots of drugs, loud music and dancing. It's not really a question, since everyone will be there, they've been talking about it for the past week, she asks merely to reassert her social position. She has to make sure that Xander understands she holds the keys to the clique. With a ring through his flesh, he can't help feeling like a branded steer. Ranch Roxie.

"It's a full moon tonight," he says. "I can't guarantee where I'll be."

"Well, if you want to come, we'll be going to the Scuzz Box first, around ten or eleven. Get a few games of pool in." And with that, she gives him a pert smile and vanishes into the bedroom.

He's dismissed. Not immediately, of course. He can hang around, sit on the couch, watch TV, make himself a cup of coffee, read a magazine. But the ritual is over.

What just happened? His wound is throbbing, proof that he just went through the ordeal he so wanted. His internal frustrations have transformed into something concrete, something he can point to and touch. Barely. It takes him an age to manoeuvre himself back into his shirt.

He calls home, gets the answering machine. His mother hasn't bothered to change the outgoing message for months, and is still wishing everyone a good summer. The tape has stretched, transforming her voice into a chipmunk's squeak. For once it doesn't bother him, he doesn't mention it. Instead, he reels off the lie that he'll be sleeping over at his friend Barry's again tonight. After a momentary twinge of pain, he adds that everything is fine, not to worry about him, and that he hopes rehearsals are going well. The story is easy to spin; he feels no compunction, just freedom. Good old Barry, he thinks, as dependable as ever, even though he hasn't seen him since graduation. Mother approves blindly of Barry, if for no other reason than his parents were draft dodgers from Seattle.

At the window, where Roxie was standing earlier, Xander looks out over the park. The grass is beginning to be covered with dead leaves; the deciduous trees are turning pale greenish-gold, some deep crimson. A woman plays with her dog along the rise; he can just hear the whistled commands and shouts. It's a typical Vancouver autumn day, reeking of sun-drenched beauty. Since he arrived in B.C. over a decade ago, when he was seven, Xander must have heard about the glory of the place a thousand times, a million times, read it on T-shirts, on licence plates, in newspapers. It's embossed onto the phrases of anyone who carries a provincial health card. *Beautiful British Columbia.* He would love to agree, if he could only be left alone to find the beauty for himself. It is surely the fear of rejection, this fascistic demand that its beauty be recognized. Yes, you're gorgeous! But after last year's Expo overkill, the city has fallen into a slump, like a prom queen the morning after, not daring to look at herself in the mirror for fear of weeping.

For all its vanity, he has to admit that the city has something. A lawlessness. A frontier land, fly-by-night quality. Superior drugs. The highest suicide rate in the country. A thriving nightlife. Youth. Sex.

It's full moon. Xander bows to the vampiric urge, the wolf call. All over the city, like minds are tuning to the same wave, the same promise of libertine abandon, the same pining for nightfall. Some will escape from the most surprising of prisons—bourgeois homesteads and straight-laced families. Tonight, all those who hear the summons will emerge from their holes and congregate in beer halls, dance clubs, warehouses, bushes, parks and parking lots. Xander knows where he'll end up. And with whom. His freshly pierced nipple guarantees it; he has to see if sex with the satyr-man is different, now.

It takes an age for the sun to go down.

At the Scuzz Box that evening, he plays three rounds of pool with Roxie and Juan. Every shot pulls on his piercing; he has to angle himself to avoid aggravation. First, it's the boys against Roxie, which she loses, no surprise. Then it's Xander and Roxie against Juan, which goes to Juan, because Roxie isn't really trying, no surprises there, either. Finally, it's Xander against the two of them, which goes on for ever, and starts to make him feel like an outsider. He gets angrier as the game progresses. There's not that much of an age difference between them, but Juan and Roxie manage to make five or six years feel like a decade. Sometimes he suspects that they merely tolerate his presence.

"Xander's feeling a bit of a titty tonight," taunts Roxie. "We'd better watch ourselves."

Xander's neck prickles. He wants to slam the eight-ball into the corner pocket and finish the game right there and then, but instead, he finishes the round on automatic pilot, winning easily, but without any sense of accomplishment. The mathematical configurations of balls, pockets, and progressions appear much like the melody line of a Bach fugue played at half speed. Done, he lays the cue on the table, grabs his knapsack and walks out of the club without saying goodbye. If they think he's going on to their shindig in Gastown, they're going to be disappointed.

Outside, the streets are charged. The full moon hovers high in the clear sky above the buildings, a silver disc so bright it's impossible to look at without squinting. It covers everything with a malicious light, harsh concrete and humans alike.

"Xander, wait up!" Roxie has followed him out, trots to catch up with him, makes a grab for his arm, which he angles out of her reach. "Are you jamming out on us?"

"I just need some fresh air. I'll catch up with you guys later."

He's already walking south, away from the club, away from Gastown. She must know where he's headed, so he knows his words ring false, but he doesn't care. Right now, he'll say anything to get away. "Come on back to the bar, Xandy!" she yells after him. "Juan's about to roll a joint!"

He doesn't even say no thanks, Roxie, another time, maybe. He doesn't look back, knows she's still watching him, can guess the expression on her face. At ten yards, he salutes the growing distance between them; snaps the invisible umbilical cord with a gesture. See you around.

Under the Burrard Street Bridge, the reverberation of cars on the ramp above echoes like the repetitive clanking of a giant machine. At first glance, the parking lot around the back of the Aquatic Centre looks deserted, but once Xander's eyes accustom themselves to the darkness, he can make out half a dozen figures standing in the shadows. Every so often one will shift, drawing attention to itself. One by a concrete strut. One by a tree. One by the jetty leading to the old burned out boat. The taste of the hunt is in the air. Predatory. Surreal. Male.

Across the water, lights shine. From boats, from buildings on Granville Island. He wonders if one of the fainter lights just visible through the trees on the far bank of False Creek is coming from his father's workshop, but the angle of the shore has to be wrong, the Old Forge is on the other side of the Planetarium, surely.

He shoves his hands deep into his pockets and saunters down to the jetty, his boots clopping on the wooden slats. A sign from the city warns people not to wander here. A yellow caution ribbon stretches across his way. He ducks under it, knowing that he won't be the first of the evening to do so, won't be the last. Behind him, he senses one of the shadows in the parking lot detach from the darkness and start to follow him. Only those who mean business come here, those who don't mind getting a bit of dirt under their fingernails.

His destination, the old boat, was once a floating discotheque moored permanently on the edge of False Creek, a popular night spot with the Top-Twenty suburban set until it burned down last New Year's Eve. Now it's a charred husk, abandoned, caught in probate limbo, falling apart, but strong enough and secretive enough to be taken over by the fairies. At the eastern end of the Fruit Loop, it's the extreme destination for those willing to risk the dangers for a momentary tryst.

Xander knows the way in. He jumps down into a stony gully filled with young trees, and climbs the other side, onto the lower deck of the boat. As he clambers over the railing, his coat brushes against the saplings, announcing his arrival to anyone inside who cares to hear. He pauses. To his right he can see the glow of a cigarette's end where someone stands near the stern. Someone else is to his left, moonlight catching on their elbow. Ahead, a metal railing with steps leading down into menacing blackness and to what used to be the dance floor. Xander goes down.

It's a disaster zone down there. The floor is littered with New Year's decorations; paper hats and noisemakers, broken glass, bottles. The stink of fire still hangs in the air, Xander can imagine the smell of panic as the partygoers realized the place was ablaze. Now, nine months later, there's also the reek of urine where people have marked off their territory.

Satyr-man is there, waiting for him. Over by the mirrored section at the far end of the dance floor, leaning against the wall, one leg bent. Light jeans, T-shirt, studded black leather jacket. Xander feels his excitement rising, his heart pumping, saliva flowing in his mouth.

Every month he comes here on the full moon. Every month he meets the same man, goes through the same heady dance of ritual advances. And every month, they'll consummate their desires with a different act, in a different way, which is what keeps Xander coming back, this variation. They know nothing about each other, except that they are both as daring, as cruel, and as nameless as the crevices they hide in. They know each other by touch, by partial sight, by imagination, by reliability.

Xander's legs begin to shake as he walks slowly across the wide expanse between them. He is being stared at by knowing eyes that can't be seen. Recognition in every step. Anticipation. He reaches the wall three feet away from satyr-man. The smashed mirrors reflect back crazy partial images; half a torso, the angle of a knee.

`   "Show me."

Xander doesn't know if the man actually says the words or whether he imagines them being whispered through the darkness, so low as to be no more than a thought. Regardless, he obeys, lifting up his T-shirt, baring his cold, steeled breast to that cold steeled gaze. The flick of a brass lighter an arm's length away illuminates the scene; a warm spotlight. Xander holds himself motionless, his gut rippling with fear. He thinks he can detect a gentle chuckle. The flame goes out. What happens next, he knows, is unstoppable. Even if a squad of police were to descend upon them, flashing lights and shouts, public humiliation and arrest, nothing could prevent the world from tipping over the edge.

A hand touches his ring and twists, slowly, clockwise. A yellow wash of pain explodes in Xander's brain like sheet lightning over the ocean. Another hand grabs him by the chin, squeezes, pushes a sour-tasting thumb over his lip and into his mouth. Xander moans, shudders, closes his eyes as his tear ducts overflow,

So safe, he can't believe it, but he feels so safe. Sanctuary fantastic. Here in the midst of forbidden danger, in amongst the party offal and the sordid shadows of the city, he has found a corner of his mind that is as raw as an exposed nerve and yet as delicious and as warm and as quiet as the womb.

If he should choose to remember.

8

If Wally takes Fourth Avenue in the morning, it means he wants to take the day as business. Even though the route is longer than going directly down the hill, the wide road, the traffic, the buses and the clatter of humanity somehow keep his mind on whatever projects he has on the go. It's a mental trick that stops him from falling into a slump when he gets to the workshop; perfect for days when deadlines start screaming or when he really needs to focus.

If, on the other hand, he takes Arbutus, Maple, or one of the other north-south streets down the hill, the quieter residential route and the looming mountains up ahead trigger a meditative state, so by the time he arrives at work, he is suitably relaxed, and the ensuing day will be a gentle putter.

Today, however, he stands like a melon at the corner of Arbutus and Fourth, unable to decide which route to take. He doesn't feel like bustling down Fourth. Things are going fine at work; if he went any faster, he'd have nothing to do but supervise Ned. But he doesn't want to wander down the hill either, because lately, whenever he allows himself the luxury, his mind will slip into an abyss with fulsome thoughts of mortality and his own personal failures.

He isn't helped in his indecision by the dead leaves, the bite in the September air, and the bruise of approaching rain. They contribute to an overall numbness of the brain, a reaction against the inescapable reality of his own approaching winter. And no matter which route he takes, all roads lead to Ned.

He starts to stride along Fourth Avenue and tries to engage with the mechanics of reality. Everything for *She Stoops to Conquer* is on track, the sundial is done, right down to the final touches: copper fittings and an ivy treatment. He's done the larger furniture: the benches, chairs and side tables; gave them all the same paint treatment. He's about to start constructing a frame for the three-fold decorative screen behind which Sir Charles and Marlowe will hide. Then it'll be the small stuff. The jewel caskets, the books, the tankards and the flowers, most of which can be pulled from stock.

But Ned. Ned, Ned, Ned. What is he going to do about Ned?

Predictably, the reprobate didn't show up for the two days following their initial meeting. When he finally put in an appearance, he brought along a brand new, hifalutin coffee press still in its box and some excuse about being on a bender for a couple of nights. He spent the rest of the week, and all of the following, fiddling around with the electric candles like a sullen child picking at his spinach. He's unraveled some wires, sorted some candle casings as to state of repair and size, tested a few bulbs and passed judgment: "Are these supposed to look real?" To which Wally replied, "You don't like them? Go ahead and see if you can make them better, then." Which Ned took as an invitation to sit at the counter, drink his stinking coffee, and ponder the mess laid out before him. For hours. Days. Weeks.

It might be more expedient to put him on sorting through the artificial blooms for the garden scene, except that Wally suspects he'd get much the same behaviour, possibly worse, given the innate girlie quality of flowers. Ned is just a big lump of testosterone-laden sludge. If there's a way to light a fire under him, Wally hasn't found it, and the thought of trying to find it fills him with instant lethargy.

He turns onto Cypress, hoping to find some peace, but finds himself thinking once more about Ned. How yesterday, he shared the last of his single malt, trying unsuccessfully to warm things up between them. Chatted about this and that, about theatre and

England, until Ned called him a colonial wanker and Wally realized
he'd been talking to himself for an hour. Just to stop the anger ex-
ploding down his left fist, he sent Ned off with thirty dollars to pick
up a fresh bottle of Scotch. Of course, he didn't come back. Wally
curses himself for being such an idiot, wishes he had more gumption.
Perhaps with a sharper attack on life, he could have made something
out of himself.

As he crosses Cornwall, he tries to remember which way the cars
come at him in Canada—the old British adage "look right, look left,
look right again" is so permanently embedded in his brain that he
can't rid himself of it. Is he really, after all, a colonial wanker, some
expatriate dilettante, floundering about in the outpost of British
Columbia, treating the place as his cultural playground? Ned may
be right. How awful.

There was a time when he would have laughed at such an accusation. Nowadays, however, the gods of mirth have abandoned him
and everything has turned serious, morose. Just more ugly noise in
a universe devoid of meaning.

If he were to spread out the tapestry of his life for examination,
it would keep threatening to hold together, but never would. The
repeating patterns never connect solidly as he suspects they do in
other people's lives. His weave is threadbare, worn out. Badly designed in the first place and mended with mismatched thread.

Look at him. He never fell in love, not really. He married a
woman who wanted him more as a novelty pet than as a husband,
and under her insistence he'd committed himself to an existence not
of his own devising. Years ago, his greatest ambition was to be an
actor, a character actor. What happened? He ended up a props builder.
He fantasized about siring a brood of bubbling children to care for
him in his dotage. What did he get? A neurologically damaged sissy-
boy, currently bent on the same self-destructive path he followed
when he was much the same age. He stifles a bitter laugh. Juilliard
isn't going to happen, never was. It's a dream of Georgia's, an

excessively high bar in the chart of her expectations, no matter how much money she throws at it. When Wally looks at Alexander, he sees a familiar tangle of petty lies, adolescent intrigues, and sexual experimentation that clouds youthful energy. It makes him wonder if the purpose of growing old is to watch your offspring make the same mistakes you did; to know that the fruit starts to rot the moment it leaves the tree; that there's no way to stop it, even if anyone knew how; that it's part of your punishment to watch.

Does Peggy, he wonders, see her own distorted reflection in Ned? With his tattoos and stubble, his convict ways, he couldn't be more unlike her. Or unlike her husband. But that is surface. After watching him from a distance, Wally can see that beneath the ink and bravado runs a stratum of Peggy's snobbery and obstinacy. In Ned's shrugs and sneers Wally recognizes his mother's disdain for anyone who didn't fit in with her way of thinking. Is that what gave her cancer? All that festering build-up of disappointments, one after the other, until her cells burst their boundaries?

There it is again: Death. The shadow in the mirror, the ever-present punch line for a joke between angels and demons. No, not a joke. If there are any gods left in this world, thinks Wally, they're heavy-handed with the irony and light on the humour.

Foul thoughts. Really foul, depressing thoughts. By the time he reaches the workshop, jangling the keys in the lock, he's already pining after a hit of something narcotic or alcoholic. He doesn't know if he can hack another day of Ned comparing fake candles against the real thing. Or staring at an empty space at the end of the counter where either Ned and a bottle of Scotch or thirty dollars ought to be sitting.

That's strange. The lights are on. Just as Wally starts wondering if he'd forgotten to close up properly the night before, the brindled pit bull appears at his ankles, no barking, just a silent sniff and a stare to establish identity and hierarchy. Wally checks his watch; it's working fine, he's not late. No, Ned must have gotten here early. An eager beaver! Wally is immediately suspicious. At work by a quarter to

nine in the morning to stare at a candle all day. But how did he get
in? And where is he now?

The answer to the first question is: through a window, easy
enough when they're never locked and can be prised open with a
dull twig. A couple of blue glass bottles have been knocked over on
the sill where he came in. Wally rights them as the dog returns to
the chair with a flop, its tawny haunches sticking out obscenely.

He is about to call out when he hears water running in the pipes,
and gets an answer to his second question: Ned's in the shower. It
strikes Wally as decidedly odd that Ned would be cleaning up first
thing. Perhaps he's been out on the town all night with the thirty
dollars, and smells of booze and women.

But no. On the floor behind the workshop counter, Wally almost
trips over a rubble of stuff that's clearly been used as bedding.
Cushions, velvet curtains, a plastic bag of foam industrial chips,
clothing, a candle stub on a saucer, a couple of army surplus kit bags.
Ned hasn't been out on the tiles; he slept here.

The audacity rankles. Wally has an urge to run to the kitchen
area, turn on the tap at the sink, and send scalding water into the
shower stall. He could pretend he'd forgotten how the plumbing
was all connected, that he just wanted to rinse out his teapot.

One of the kit bags is open. The detritus of a traveller peeks out:
dirty laundry, maps, the edge of a worn paperback, J.G. Ballard's
High Rise. Wally squats to have a closer look, aware that the dog's head
perks up at his move. But he knows Ballard's work, is particularly fond
of *Empire of the Sun*, and is curious about this one, what the jacket
blurb might say. At least, that's his excuse.

The moment he pulls the book fully out of the bag, however,
two things happen simultaneously. One, an orange-capped syringe
that had been used as a bookmark jumps out from the pages. Two,
the dog barks three loud, rhythmic warnings.

The shower stops.

Wally is caught in a time bubble. Memories of his own drug-filled years in London crowd him: trying to find a vein, blood streaming down the inside of his elbow, dripping on the carpet, Procol Harum playing on the record player. He shakes it off, hastily stuffs the needle back into what he hopes is more or less the same spot in the book, rebags it, stands up and makes for the kitchen area as fast as he can.

There, on the running board, standing like a soldier at attention —wonder upon wonders—a spanking new bottle of J&B. The cap has been cracked and there's about an inch gone, but the promise has been made good. Wally feels a right bastard.

Next to the bottle, and next to the half-full carafe of stinking coffee, is a dirty glass with a spoon in it. Instant recognition. Wally doesn't have to see the little speck of cotton floating on the water, doesn't have to examine the spoon like Sherlock Holmes to know what he'll find: the faint smear of soot, the rainbow discolouration of heat shimmering like an oil slick, the kink in the shaft of the spoon where it's been bent back into shape. He hears Georgia's whine from a continent and two decades away. *Just not with my best silver, Wally, ple-ease.*

Last night's scenario plays itself out in his mind. Ned broke in, got high, a bit drunk, slept it off. It's time for a little man-to-man chat.

Spoon in hand like some damned trophy, Wally knocks on the washroom door. He stands there like a dummy, wondering how he ever got to be so polite. Knocks again and opens up.

Ned is drying himself off with a blue-and-orange striped tea towel. He grins at Wally as he slicks water off his face, over his body, plumes of steam rising around him. A veil of tattoos covers his skin: flaming hearts, capering devils, angels, roses, thorns, crucifixes, lucky dice, a swastika, yin–yangs, the whole works. If Wally was looking for track marks, he'd need a dermatologist. All those conflicting religious icons. He can't help thinking that this is what Peggy's self-righteous attitude has wrought.

"He-ey, Mr. G. What's up?" The smile is genuine and hits Wally unprepared.

"Uhh . . . have you finished with the shower?" He hides the spoon casually in his pocket. It will stay his little secret, for now. "I'd like to run some water. Make a pot of tea."

"Uh-huh, sure. I'll be out in a minute."

"The pipes are connected," mutters Wally, getting himself out of the steamy little room, ashamed of himself. "I could have scalded you to death."

So he busies himself with the tea things, worrying. Ned emerges shortly, unabashed, naked and damp, pours himself the dregs of the coffee, wanders off. Wally carries his tea tray into the workshop, keeps Ned in his peripheral vision as he waits for his brew to steep.

"You've got a lot of ink," he mentions. "Must have cost you a small fortune."

"Yeah."

"And a Prince Albert, I see." Wally nods at the pendulous ring through the head of Ned's penis—it tips a wink as the jeans are pulled on. "I had a friend in London had one of those done on a bet."

"Oh yeah? How much did he get?"

Wally almost tells him. A pony—twenty-five pounds. Twenty-five hard-earned quid, paid in cash, which, in 1954, ate into Wally's meagre wages and taught him not to make bets with daredevils, no matter how well you think you know them. "Can't remember. We all helped him spend it on boozing, though."

Ned laughs, as if he'd have done the same thing. He starts tidying up the bedding, piling it all to one side with the clear indication that it could be used again.

"Thanks for the Scotch. I was beginning to think you'd run off, never to return."

Ned shrugs, then jerks a thumb at his stuff. "You don't mind if I crash here for a while, do you? My girlfriend threw me out of the place where I was staying."

Wally sighs. Short of putting locks on the windows, he probably couldn't keep him out. "Just stay away from my booze. Stick to your smack. I'll keep to my Welsh tea."

Ned doesn't respond, so Wally lets the moment slide into silence, pulls out the designer's plans for the three-fold screen and starts to figure out how much lumber he'll need to cut for the frame. He buries his unease in the pit of his stomach.

The strange thing is that if Ned had been Alex, Wally would have hit the roof. He would have turned as red as a boiled lobster, veins punching out along his temples, arms snapping the air, and he would have exploded. But Ned's directness defuses the bomb, leaves it to tick away in Wally's gut, poisons him from the inside. He isn't sure which is preferable: holding it in or letting it out.

Lunch break comes and Wally runs up to Fourth Avenue to pick up a couple of sandwiches. When he returns, Ned's electrical wire mess has spread all over the counter, and he has the soldering iron and pliers out, working on what looks like jewelry.

"Hey, Mr. G. Look at this."

Ned holds up a funny little gizmo fashioned out of some copper wire and a candle bulb. The bulb rests on a coiled spring of thin wire that wobbles at the slightest movement.

"So is this what you've come up with, is it?"

"Yeah. See, I reckon the biggest problem is that these things look like tacky restaurant lighting fixtures."

"Best we can do short of having open flame onstage."

"So I had this idea," Ned is excited, despite Wally's cynicism. "If the movement is in all directions . . ." He pushes the coil of wire over a candle tube, much like a sleeve. Once in place, the bulb shifts around, magically.

Wally's spine unbends like an old spoon being snuck back into the cutlery drawer. "What happens when you run power through the wire?"

"I don't know, yet. It might melt the top of the candle."

"With a nine-volt battery? Come on. Let's see."

In less than half an hour, a prototype is up and running. It doesn't feel like work. It doesn't feel like invention. It's simply a vast improvement over the old, now obsolete model. The light of the bulb dazzles the eye so that even at a reasonably close distance the supporting copper wire vanishes. The idea is smart and direct. It has all the eloquence of a good illusionist's method.

"You know they'll fall apart as soon as an actor so much as looks at them," warns Wally. "They're much too fragile."

"No, look," counters Ned, shaking the contraption around. "They're strong. Strong."

"You don't know thespians like I do." He sees the disappointment in Ned's face. "But I think you might be onto something, lad. You might well be."

"You know it."

"Fancy a shot of weed killer to celebrate?"

"I thought you said . . . Sure, why not?"

So Wally fetches the bottle, pours out two healthy inches each. They raise their glasses, toasting not only Ned's invention, but also an unknown and unknowable bond between them.

"*Twll dy dîn, bychan.*"

"What?"

"It's Welsh. Means up your asshole, buddy."

"Oh." Ned scrunches his nose. "So does that mean you won't sign my court papers?"

Wally shakes his head disappointedly, like a headmaster saddened by the persistent aberrations of his underlings. "Hand them over, lad."

He smoothes out the well-folded packet, pretends to look for where he has to sign. "So what kind of mischief and aggravated assault exactly did you do that landed you in all this trouble, then?"

"You don't want to know."

"Try me."

Ned shakes his head, says nothing, stares at the bottom of his glass.

"Drugs, am I right?"

"Nope."

"Stolen goods?"

"Nope."

Wally isn't having any more of this monosyllabic guessing game, it could go on all night. "Are you going to make me ask your mam? She'll tell me, you know."

Ned keeps his eyes averted, but he's clearly embarrassed to be forced into this confession. Finally, he takes a swig of Scotch and mutters, "Vandalism, kind of."

"Kind of? What do you mean, "kind of," boy?" Wally is beginning to enjoy his power. It's actually fun, now that he's found the buttons to push. "Did they catch you spray painting the beach down at English Bay or something?"

Ned snaps. He turns on Wally, furious. "Fucking flowers, all right?!"

"Flowers?"

"Yeah, flowers. I got caught picking flowers from outside those fucking office buildings downtown."

Wally can't stop himself. He bursts out laughing. Handsome, thundering peals of mirth. Flowers. Not drugs, not carrying a concealed weapon, not even shoplifting fancy coffee machines or receiving stolen goods. Aggravated assault on poor, defenseless tulips! A great big brute like him got nicked for pinching pansies! It's hilarious. The gods have a sense of humour, after all.

Laughter, Wally's defence against the ills of the world, has returned to him.

9

"What a laugh!"

"It was ghastly, Wally. I loathe auditions!"

From his hard leather change-purse, Wally shook a few coins into the lid, extracted a shilling and two three-penny-bits. One was a new coronation issue coin with the unfamiliar Queen on it. He knew the amount through habit: three sixpences make one-and-six. He was still slow with arithmetic, especially when it came to making calculations in base twelve, as was required for shillings, hours, and inches. The mathematics of ounces and gallons were far beyond him, a secret coterie of numbers best left to bakers and chemists.

"Sticky buns all round, yes?"

"Lovely. Don't mind if I do."

"Miss Brandt?"

"Of course."

"Oi, Parker!" Wally, adopting his standard barrow boy accent, waved at the lad working the counter. "Three sticky buns wiv teas over 'ere, mate!"

They sat at their usual table by the window, where they could, by using the long, dusty mirror that ran along the length of the wall, watch both the street and the inside of the café without craning their necks. The three of them: Wally Greene, Monty Gower, and Georgia Brandt, the American. Just another clique of students from the Bloomsbury Academy of Dramatic Arts. Tufnel's Bakehouse was their clubhouse, a fifty second run down the hill from the Academy that squatted at the top. It was more Camden Town than Bloomsbury really, but that didn't stop the Academy from having pretensions. From its Victorian eyrie, the school had a panoramic view of North London crumbling away into the second half of the twentieth century. The joke was that your accent had to descend as you ran down the hill for a cup of tea and a sticky bun.

"Oi, Parker, you forgot the slice of bleeding lemon, mate, for our American visitor."

Tufnel's Bakehouse was a welcome escape from the Academy. It was a bakery more than a cafeteria, but there were half a dozen wobbly tables in the front of the shop which were usually crammed with drama students, smoking and eating and chatting. Framed theatrical "cards" covered every inch of wall space: the celebrated and the not-so celebrated alumni from the school of cream-puff acting up the hill. Any unsuspecting customer who wandered in from off the street would quickly grasp that there was something not altogether proper about the place. Too much airbrushing on the black-and-white studio portraits, perhaps. Too many effete young men with loud diction. Too much dust on the mirror.

"How did your audition go, Wally?" asked Georgia, plopping sugar lumps into her teacup, followed by a lemon slice that floated like a layer of sanctimony on the surface.

"Well, I managed to keep my blushing at bay, thanks to your little trick with the breathing. Worked like a tinker's charm."

"Thank the Buddhists."

"But I don't think Old Compton is going to cast me," he continued. "I'm only first year, after all."

"Don't you be so tough on yourself, Taffy." Monty dug Wally in the ribs. "You may only be first year, but you look like you're middle-aged. He needs you for one of the old fogey parts, just you watch."

"I'm not so certain of that," Wally took out his pack of ten

Woodbines, offered them around. Monty took two, one for now, one for later. Georgia declined as usual, preferring one of her imported Chesterfields. "Old Compton hates the ground I walk on."

"That's perfect then," smiled Georgia. "You're in for sure."

They all laughed, but Wally felt uneasy.

Here he was, at drama school, his first steps along the road to panto fame and fortune, and he was already out of his depth. Everyone else was beautiful of limb and erudite of tongue; it was a miracle that he'd passed the entrance audition, an ordeal if ever there was one. He'd taken the train to London especially for the occasion, with Da chaperoning him; then, they'd swiftly got lost in the tangle of soot-stained buildings and roaring traffic. Once the Academy was found, Wally stuttered his way through the opening Chorus speech of *Henry V*, warbled "All Through The Night," and for his pains, elicited the stinging comment, "We thought all Welshmen could sing," from the panel of adjudicators, which, as far as Wally saw it, put the kibosh on his acting career right then and there. When the acceptance letter came in the post, seven weeks and three days later, it was as if an archangel had descended from the heavens to tell him of the existence of God. That it was more like Beelzebub or Baphomet clearing his way to Hell only became apparent months after he got to London, alone, suitcase in one hand, forty pounds in his pocket, and, in his other grubby paw, the Academy's typewritten prospectus, which included a list of approved lodgings for out-of-town students.

He took up digs in a narrow, four-storey row house a few doors down the hill from the Academy. HMS Pinafore, they called the place, on account of its constant creaking and the big brass knocker on the door. Two dozen students roomed there, eight to each of the upper floors, in cubicles the size of broom closets. Wally was downstairs in the hold, while Monty, because he was in second year, was in the mid-ship. There was no captain—a caretaker lived on a nearby street, nobody seemed to know exactly which house—and no real crew—there was a blackboard in the hallway which displayed a schedule for the sharing of chores, of which no one took the blind's notice. Yet the place managed to stay afloat.

The house had a common room on the main floor that boasted an assortment of sturdy church furniture and an upright piano. At any given time, day or night, there would be students rehearsing, limbering up, drinking, smoking or gossiping. Without being obvious about it, they cowed Wally, until he was forced into the porch, which had a little seat by the front door where he would drink his tea and whittle his fetish projects.

For five months he watched his dreams erode. He began to suspect he'd been accepted at the Academy merely as a political gesture. The Welsh were artistic geniuses, everyone knew that: Dylan Thomas and Emlyn Williams. As were the Irish, but there were no Irishmen in his year, though there was one in the year above him. In the third year there was a Scotsman. The rest of the student population was made up of either smart, sophisticated snobs from London and the Home Counties, at least a social class above him, or Americans getting their British theatrical training at exorbitant fees.

So Wally's presence was token, he was sure of it, a living, breathing example of what not to be for the other students. He was ungainly, overly plump, had flaming, wiry carrot hair, and worst of all, spoke with an accent that couldn't be eradicated. The elocution mistress was a ghastly spinster with piano teacher fingers that would stab Wally unexpectedly in the diaphragm or in the small of his back to correct his posture. She was of the opinion that anything other than her cherished Received Pronunciation was an abomination. Since she had to go easy on the Americans for financial reasons, her wrath-that-rhymed-with-froth was reserved especially for Wally.

He had no friends, none, until Monty and Georgia came along. Monty Gower was a stylish blond lad with a round, romantic lead's face and a vicious quip always a muscle's twitch away from his lips. Georgia Brandt was another second year, but she had the bearing of someone who had always been there, as if the Academy depended on her force of personality to exist.

They found him at HMS Pinafore one unseasonably warm Friday evening in late February. Wally had moved outside from his soliloquist's bench in the porch, and sat perched on a little wall, surrounded by daffodils. He was whittling a ball out of a child's building block, making a lovely mess of chips. Just as the dusk began to turn the edge of his blade invisible, a taxicab pulled up, not six inches away. From where he was sitting, he could see that the occupant was having trouble finding the door handle, what with a cardboard box of books she was carrying, so Wally reached out and opened the door, and went back to his carving. It was no more than that, really, he just happened to be sitting in the best spot.

"Who the hell are you?" she asked, emerging from the cab. She spotted the knife in his hand, his work, then smiled, wryly, as if having solved a mystery. "Mr. Left-handed, that's who you are!"

"I'm Wally. Wally Greene." He didn't look up, knew better than to engage with an American.

"Well then, Wally Greene," she produced a ten shilling note. "We won't be long, I just have to dump this crap. Dangle this in front of his face if he gives you any trouble."

"Do I look like your doorman?"

"Please?"

He knew who she was, of course. Everyone knew who Georgia Brandt was. Gracile, violet-eyed and raven-haired, she was said to be the only daughter of a railroad tycoon from Boston. The Boston Brandts. Rumour had it that she kept a fully staffed apartment overlooking Regent's Park, scattered money to the winds every time she sneezed, and indulged in every excess, the most notorious of which was her taste for women. Lavender Brandt. Worth waiting for.

She returned shortly with Monty in tow. Wally recognized the face, but had hitherto assumed, probably correctly, that because he was a second year, Monty wasn't someone with whom a first year could simply strike up a conversation.

"Fancy a trip up Shaftesbury Avenue tonight, all expenses paid, Wally Greene?" drawled Georgia Brandt.

"Well, I hadn't thought . . ."

"Excellent," she whispered. "The less thinking, the better. Go get your coat."

So he joined their folly. Why these two peacocks had befriended him was a mystery beyond Wally's ken. That entire evening, all the way up Shaftesbury Avenue, from the Lyric to the Palace, he expected the truth behind their sudden amicability to descend upon him in the form of some awful practical joke or other. But nothing of the sort happened. They poured a goodly wealth of alcohol down his gullet and laughed at his jokes when his timidity eventually wore down. And if they were acting out of pity, he never felt it. At the end of the evening, he was dropped off at HMS Pinafore while Monty stayed in the cab, smirking at the prospect of continuing his evening with Miss Brandt.

"Let's do the Haymarket tomorrow, Wally Greene," said Georgia, as if it had already been decided. "There's a sneaky little cocktail bar off Jermyn Street you simply have to go to."

After a week of continued partying, Wally loosened his dread and began to enjoy this newfound company. Georgia was, reliably, impossible. Loud, opinionated and full of rubbish, Wally thought she was the first real person he'd met at the Academy. Monty, however, was quite different: superior, sneaky and vicious. But they were both constant to their own scruples, and confessed that he, Wally, was the first they'd come across who could hold his drink as well as they. Which was true. Wally was an alcohol sponge. No matter how much he boozed, he rarely got more than tipsy, and he could always roll out of bed the next morning as clear-headed as ever. He put it down to the large quantity of tea he'd drunk in his lifetime that had lined his innards with a preventative coating.

They laughed, drank more, ran screeching at the moon through

Regent's Park or Golden Square or howled Shakespearean sonnets
for a taxicab outside the Ritz on Piccadilly, right under the nose of
the liveried footman. They burned the Brandt fortunes with no
compunction.

What a future they envisaged. Georgia was going to be the biggest, brightest leading lady in the West End, Monty the dashingest,
smartest leading man, while Wally would get all the character roles.
Theatre was going to be their oyster; their talents would be the
pearls of fame for generations to come. They promised to always
leave their dressing rooms open to each other; it was a pact.

With these aspirations, Wally learned something of the moneyed
class. Both Georgia and Monty could have whatever they wanted;
in truth, all they had to do was lay down enough cash. But to be
acknowledged for their talents, to succeed in their intent—that was
what mattered. Wally realized this was an equal-opportunity fantasy,
as much his as it was theirs. And so he was just as vocal in outlining
his future success as a character actor. Shylock, Gloucester, and Vanya
—the roles were as good as his. He kept apace.

Tufnel's Bakehouse was their starting point of an evening, their
common room where they planned the night ahead. They always pon-
tificated loudly, so the other students had to flap their envious ears.

"Enough about those bloody auditions," said Wally, puffing
away on a Woodbine. "I really don't care if I get a part or not. Where
are we going tonight? How about slumming it in Soho?"

"Ooh, I could try out my Henry Higgins in the Berwick Street
Market." Georgia rested her fingers at her throat, caressing an invisible necklace. "See if I can catch me an Eliza."

"That's not all you can catch down there," mumbled Monty
through a mouthful of bun. "All praise Sir Alexander Fleming and his
miraculous mold. Tuck in, chaps. There's probably enough penicillin
in these here sticky buns to see us through the night."

And off they'd go into the charms of the London evening. To
Wally, it was as if a curtain had descended around him while he

danced a wild, ecstatic dance, a curtain of heavy, worn brocade, of glowing lamps in public lounges, of gothic stone arches, spiked iron railings, sooted statuary, and the screeching brakes of taxicabs and buses, of faceless souls in shabby raincoats, fellow glad-baggers, of dark wooden beams in pubs and cocktail lounges, and always, always, the whiff of stale beer or whisky that hung from the rafters, rose from the carpets, mingled with smoke and yellowing teeth. Old Man Greene would have been right at home here. But Wales, Fishguard, and Millie the sheep were on the far side of this curtain. The Bloomsbury Academy was on the far side of this curtain, too. Wally, on this side, was dancing a mad, three-handed waltz, extempore, across a stage with no off, the only thing forbidden was abstinence.

"You got the Stage Manager?" Monty's voice hit the higher nasal cavities so beloved of Madame of the spider fingers. "That's the best part in the whole play! Bugger you, Wally Greene!"

"I didn't believe it myself," Wally shrugged, blushed. "I thought there was some mistake, but I checked the list twice, thought they'd meant any old stage manager, probably assistant, you know, not *the* Stage Manager. Look, see for yourself."

The notice board for the first year students had the list, alphabetical by surname on the left, role to be studied on the right. Against Wally's name was, undeniably, *The Stage Manager*. He knew it was madness to think it, but he felt like Adam, touched by God. When he put his finger to the list, he got a kind of electrical buzz that shook his hand.

"What are you so afraid of, Wally?" Georgia demanded. "I think it's wonderful. You're perfect for the role. And everyone else is going to eat their hats."

"You're just saying that because you landed Emily," sniffed Monty. "You wouldn't be so magnanimous if you were playing

Social Injustice Man."

"Like you are."

"As I am," Monty agreed, correcting her grammar and holding up his hand to his brow as if to shield himself from the irony. "Don't get me started. As Social Injustice Man, I get to sit in the audience the whole first act and watch you lot prance around in your New Hampshire dialects. I think I'm one of the dead in Act Three, if I haven't actually died of boredom by then. I must have done something awful in a past life to deserve this."

"It'll do you good, darling."

"Darling, I don't want to do me good," he smirked, letting everyone know he'd gotten over his umbrage. "Come on. Let's go celebrate Wally's success. And yours, of course, Georgia. Ever heard of the Apollonian Room? It's terribly grimy, just off Rupert Street, but filled with the most fascinating rough trade . . ."

Wally didn't care where they went. He was ecstatic. He couldn't keep it hidden: first year, lead role, unheard of. He was vindicated, it gave him clout. All of a sudden, his awkwardness became hep. His devil-may-fright thatch of hair was an indication of his inner genius, the way his shirttail never stayed tucked in was because the Muse energized him. When he smoked, it was as if sparks flew off the ends of his fingers to light his Woodbines and salamanders flicked their tongues when he opened his mouth, to splash the air with vivid purple spots.

He wrote home, proudly announcing his *coup de théâtre*, and invited everyone to the opening night. He couldn't resist a dig at Da's prediction that he'd be out on his ear before the year was over, back on the platform of Fishguard station with his suitcase. *I'm playing the lead role*, he wrote, *which is very rare for a first year student. This bodes well for my future career, don't it, Da?*

At the end of the letter, in a postscript, he asked that anyone who wanted to come should consider themselves invited: Mr. Quarrendon, even Mr. Maddox—oh, how he would drive the train himself the two hundred odd miles to get Mr. Maddox in the audience. Exclamation mark.

. . . and not forgetting Millie!

He didn't expect the letter from Peggy two weeks later, saying how Ma had written to her relaying the good news. She, Charles and Leonard would be thrilled to come and see him in Mr. Wilder's Pulitzer Prize-winning play that she had read but never seen. She was back in London, of course, in Hampstead. After she and her brothers had left Wales, everyone had kept in contact by way of Christmas cards mainly, and the occasional birthday greeting whenever anyone remembered. But since his big move to London, Wally had forgotten all about the Chingfords. He'd had a twinge of memory at his first view of a double-decker bus, but it was no more than a chuckle at Leonard's grand, childhood bragging games. It hadn't crossed his mind to look them up.

Thursday, June 25th at 8 p.m., he wrote back. *Three complimentary tickets at the Bloomsbury Academy Theatre reserved under the name of Chingford!*

"You didn't really invite your parents, did you?" asked Georgia, unbelievingly. "Oh Wally, how common. I thought you were smarter than that."

"Who do you take me for?" Wally retorted. "I'm the result of a good chapel upbringing. We'll be having a one-hundred-voice Welsh choir turning up for our Grover's Corners church, just you wait."

"Except that Grover's Corners is supposed to be in America," chimed in Monty. "Oh well, I suppose it'll be the same place as your accent, *boyo*."

"You shut up about my accent, *bach*."

First day of rehearsal, Wally was ready to impress. He'd read the play at least six times, knew his lines by gist if not by heart, and was bloated to the rims of his eyelids with pride. The entire cast of more than forty trooped into the Academy's theatre, where trestle tables had been set up on stage, with extra chairs around the perimeter.

"First years around the edges, please," barked Management.

"But I have a speaking role," Wally protested, underplaying his importance in the cast.

"First years," repeated Management, with a directional nod of the head away from the tables, "around the edges, please."

Wally shrugged, lounged in one of the chairs as instructed, patiently waiting for Management's mistake to be made clear. The room filled up quickly. When Old Compton bustled in, Wally tried to catch his eye, but there were too many flunkies around, too much flappings of scripts and glasses of water being poured.

"Introductions!" boomed Old Compton. "Clockwise round the table. Name and role."

He looked around his immediate company like the patriarch at Christmas handing the carving of the goose over to his beloved heirs. He nodded at a curly-haired youth. "Reggie, you start!"

The young man coughed into his fist and stood up, addressed the room. "Reginald Prudhomme. Playing the role of the Stage Manager."

Wally shuddered. His bum jumped off its chair.

"*Y diawl bach!*"

Everyone turned to stare. All those pairs of eyes, whites glistening like the points of knives. Someone had played a nasty trick on him!

"An interruption so early from the gallery," said Compton. "Yes, young man, what is it?"

"Excuse me," Wally managed to blurt, frantically grasping for his politeness, "but how is it that there are two of us playing the one role of the Stage Manager?"

A few snorts of laughter erupted from the second and third years at the table. Nudgings and eye-rollings. Georgia's face was granite blank as she stared at her glass of water—one look at her and Wally knew that something was up. Something had been seriously miscommunicated, and she knew exactly what it was. Had known all along.

"Oh, dear me. There's always one who doesn't read the lists properly." Old Compton was simultaneously a sad, kindly uncle and a triumphant torturer. "First year students are never, *never*, cast in lead roles in the year-end production," he explained. "They perform understudy duties only."

"*Under*study?"

"Precisely. Some of you may get a small role in the play, which I haven't decided upon yet. Varying townspeople, those three bloody baseball players, Men and Women among the Dead, and so on. I'll allot them as we go through. Please pay attention."

"Understudy?"

"You can sit back down, sonny."

But Wally couldn't sit back down. The world had changed in an instant. Why, oh why hadn't he looked more carefully at the cast list? Not "role to be studied" but "role to be *under*studied." He had seen what he had wanted to see. Brimstone cursed his veins, his skin nettled. He was being roasted for his vanity, his presumption, his inattentiveness, his left-handedness.

"I said sit back down, sonny." Compton scraped a laugh out of his gullet. "Tell you what, I'll give you Man amongst the Dead in Act Three. Can't say fairer than that, now can I?"

The room joined in the laughter, merciless. Wally rang down the curtain on them all, shut them out, pretended they didn't exist. People were talking, but he couldn't hear them, it was just a distant, sawing hum that pushed against his sinuses. The introductions were continuing around the table, but Wally's anger was too great to concentrate on anything other than his personal hell. A discolouration surged up his neck, to his ears, feeding a twitch to his left eye, which watered hotly.

In his pocket, his fingers found the wooden block he'd been working on. Over the past few weeks it had progressed from a sphere, then to a roughly dimpled ovoid, and finally a rudimentary head had emerged with no real features other than three worn sockets. Eyes and nose. In his imagination it was no more than a skull, what was left once the flesh had fallen from the bone, the core of a man's apple. His fingers gripped and squeezed, gripped and squeezed, worming into the holes, and the more he squeezed, the more his vision sharpened, the shimmering, scattered fragments melded together into a vibrant stew with Old Compton disseminating poison at the very centre of it all. The desire to explode was intolerable.

"You bastard!" he screamed, rushing, crimson-faced at Compton, the wooden fetish flying loose from his fingers, flying like a cannonball out of his hand, flying into the face of his surprised enemy. A dull crunch, a loose tendril of blood like a lazy plume of smoke, the sound of a roaring ocean in his ears. "You fucking bastard! You fuck . . ."

The words curdled on his tongue into a collection of meaningless sounds. It was just so much keening into the wind. He felt hands grabbing at him, clutching at his elbows, yanking him down to the floor, to his knees. His nostrils filled with the stench of sulphur, the forgotten smell of a sunny farmyard more than nine years ago, and he couldn't stop himself—couldn't—from banging his teeth into the dirt. Repeatedly. Man among the dead!

10

"Why didn't you tell me? You cow!"

Georgia ignored him, thrust a mug of steaming liquid into his hands. "Drink this."

Wally shivered into the luxurious pile of a voluminous white bathrobe. He was wrapped up like a sausage roll on Georgia's sofa. His hair, soaked, clung to his bruised skull like oxidized seaweed. Beneath the robe he was naked; his sodden clothing had been peeled off him by his hostess. To get the job done, she'd transformed herself into a brusque nurse, as disinterested in his cherry cluster of genitals as if he'd been an infant. He'd been incapable of helping, just let it happen to him. Now he was sitting on the sofa, disoriented and vexed, staring at the empty fireplace.

He sniffed at the mug. "What is it?" The liquid smelled of warm peat and licorice. "It stinks."

"Valerian root, motherwort and a shot of Pernod. It's the best I can do." She was being deliberately firm, standing over him, her arms folded. "Drink it up, it'll calm you."

Because Lord knew, Wally needed calming. Nothing had stopped his raving. Not a rugby scrum of Academy students, not a cheat's punch in the solar plexus from an unseen fist, not his lunatic keening at the floor, nor, eventually, a fire hose trained on him full blast, skidding him body and limb across the stage floor, upending tables and chairs, papers strewn in his wake, until he was cornered against the back wall. He'd lost all grip on who he was, where and why. He was a jiggling marionette, still bouncing with rage when he was unceremoniously shoved into a taxi by Georgia. She was in no keen mood either, she had to give a sharp word and an extra guinea to the driver over the wet on his seats.

Her residence was, indeed, a Regent's Park address, one of those grand white buildings on the Crescent. But the opulence of his surroundings hardly registered with Wally as he dragged his sorry carcass up the sweeping stairway, following Georgia to a second-floor apartment the size of the entire farm back in Fishguard.

"I'm finished," he complained into his calming brew. "It's a bloody disaster. They'll throw me out of the Academy!"

Georgia sniffed, nodding. "I wouldn't be at all surprised."

"You knew!" He was back on his rant. "Why didn't you tell me? Understudy!"

"There's always one," she replied, quietly, moving away. "It's almost a tradition."

Except that a tradition would merely burn the cheeks of the poor sod who'd made the mistake. It would cause a few hours' embarrassment, at the most a few days; teach them a lesson about jumping to conclusions. The fool of the year-end production wasn't supposed to physically assault the principal of the school. In that regard, Wally had indeed broken the mold of history and carved himself a niche in the list of famous students. It didn't, however, bode well for his future career.

"What am I going to do?"

"I haven't the foggiest notion, darling. Perhaps I should hand you over to one of your bobbies? I'm sure they could think of something."

"Oh, aye, I'm sure." Wally remembered someone shouting to call the police, the fire brigade, the coast guard, anyone who could respond. An ambulance arrived first and, in that shift of energies as the wounded principal was borne out on a stretcher, Georgia suddenly took charge of him. They escaped in her hired chariot before the boys in blue showed up. "Thanks for getting me out of there. You didn't have to."

"Of course I did. What are friends for?"

"I don't want to get you into trouble."

"Too late for that. Drink up."

Monty arrived at the door within the hour. He was excited and nervous, but a layer of gravity dampened his usual flippancy. He moved around the room in fits and starts, hands in pockets, hands out, absently lighting two cigarettes in succession, sitting, standing, pulling his forelock, grimacing, and stage whispering, "All I can say is you're bloody lucky. You're bloody lucky, Wally Greene. That's all."

Georgia kept Monty's glass topped up, which got the story out of him in reasonably cogent parcels. How Old Compton wasn't badly hurt—he'd returned to the Academy with a sticking plaster on his face and a coterie of clucking assistants. How the read-through of the play was off, thank God, otherwise Georgia's absence might have been noted. How Wally's absence, on the other hand, was the topic of much conjecture. No one had spotted him leaving with Georgia. Lucky. How a posse had descended on HMS Pinafore, searched behind the piano in the common room and ransacked his digs. When they couldn't find him, they came up with the idea that he'd done a bunk. Back to Wales was the blunt assumption. So the police were given his address in Fishguard, but they didn't seem eager to start the manhunt.

"Oh, no-oo," moaned Wally. "They can't tell Da."

"I don't see how you can stop them," said Georgia. "That is, if they get around to it. Pray for incompetent bureaucracy."

"What am I going to do?" Wally repeated.

"Well, you can't go back to the Academy or HMS Pinafore," said Monty, lightly. "You'll get lynched."

"You can stay here," offered Georgia. "No one need ever know."

Wally gently prodded the swelling around his nose and upper

lip. It was puffing tight, tugging at the corner of his mouth. How the world had turned! It was incomprehensible to him, this cruelty of events, this chain of chaos that had, in an event-crammed hour, bungled his world unrecognizable.

So nothing would ever be certain again.

"What about all my things? They're all back at my digs."

Monty offered to sneak out as much as he could fit into a taxi; he was chuffed at the idea, wanted to do it right away. Georgia, with a paltry flap of her hand, told Wally to leave everything at HMS Pinafore, to buy all anew.

"Oh, stop being so bloody American, Georgie!"

Wally tuned out the two of them. There was no fire in the fireplace was all he could think. There was the ashen remains of a log. Soot. Cigarette ends. The last blaze must have been at the end of winter. He was surprised that no one had cleaned out the grate, it struck him as slovenly.

"I have to go back." He was suddenly very clear on the matter. There was only way out of this mess, and if he didn't confront it, get it out of the way, it would always be there. If the police wanted to throw him in gaol, so be it. It wasn't their affair, really; Wally had discovered the gaping wound in his character all by himself and carried out his own form of punishment. Anything meted out to him now by the authorities would be therapy. "I have to go back and apologize to Old Compton."

Opening night of the Bloomsbury Academy's year-end production of Thornton Wilder's *Our Town* found Wally selling threepenny programmes in the balcony. His name was decidedly not in it, not as Man among the Dead, not as sundry townsperson, nor even as an assistant to the assistant stage manager. He was, as he'd been told, fortunate to be allowed back in the building, to set foot on hallowed ground. But apologies carry a certain amount of moral weight, and Old Compton was New Testament to a fault: Wally could finish what remained of the year and that would be it. No charges would be laid, the incident would be forgotten, the term would end, and Wally would never be admitted back to the Academy, not the next year, nor any year thereafter. No other school in the country would touch him, except perhaps that Bolshevik outfit in Pimlico, where he'd wait for Godot the rest of his life. His panto career was over.

Old Compton, of course, never really forgot the incident; he'd merely said so out of form, following the role he'd found himself cast in, the Quality of Mercy, etc. It was even debatable whether or not his offer to let Wally stay on for the rest of the term was serious, but Wally chipped in with a "Thank you, Sir," before it could be withdrawn. So, by the grace of a milquetoast forgiveness, Wally lived out the last two months of his theatrical training in a no man's land, where his presence was tolerated but never fully acknowledged. Whenever Compton passed Wally in the corridors, Compton's hand would involuntarily rise to the little scar on his cheekbone, as if to hide the proof of Wally's impact upon the Academy.

Up in the balcony, Wally wasn't alone. A second-year, Claire Bottomsly, was stationed at the railing to house right. She was playing, not surprisingly, The Woman In The Balcony. She was swathed in full turn-of-the-century costume, give or take a few decades, lace, mostly, none of which fitted well, so she was constantly shifting and pulling at her folds, trying to get comfortable. Although she wasn't supposed to talk to Wally, she was so full of nerves, she couldn't stanch her babble.

"Is the house open, yet? Do I have time to spend a penny?"

Wally ignored her, stared over the rail at the seats downstairs as if watching for something important. Audience dribbled in slowly, a few venturing up to the balcony, where they'd sit as far away from Claire as possible. Wally could see without asking that someone from downstairs had already sold them a programme, so he stayed where he was, watching the tops of heads below.

"Oh, not too close, Lenny, how about here?"

A couple was trying to decide where to sit. She was in powder blue with a brimmed straw hat, he was dark-suited, comb-slicked hair, pink ears. They settled into a pair of seats, one in from the aisle, six or seven rows from the front. The angle that Wally was watching them from meant that he could just see the tips of their knees. Lenny? Would that be Leonard Chingford? With Peggy?

It wasn't long before another man joined them, taking the empty aisle seat, sandwiching the young woman. This second man was a bit plumper, a bit ruddier, a bit darker. Charles? He appeared to be out of sorts, huffing and sighing, making a pother with the bills in his wallet, leaning across to distribute programmes to the others, or slumping into his seat, black browed and mulish.

It had been a decade since Wally last saw the Chingfords, and they had all been children then. If this was indeed them, Time had stretched their limbs and squeezed their flesh into shapes that were only hinted at before. Memory had smoothed their features so that now, looking at the sharp point of a nose, or the crisp angle of an ear, he couldn't tell whether these were the originals or not.

But the human intuition relies upon infinitesimal clues beyond the physical. As Wally's suspicions about this trio grew into certainty, his initial moment of dread gave way to fascination. From an angle of the neck, a nervous laugh, a comfortable lean against a neighbour's shoulder, an adult identity emerged, sylphid, from childhood. It was Peggy, Len and Charles, there was no doubt. What were they doing here? Hadn't they gotten his postcard? He'd sent them a note, he swore he had; he could see his hand at the pillar box, posting it along with the one he'd sent to Ma and Da, explaining that there'd been an accident, that he couldn't perform in the end-of-year production after all. Ma had written back, expressing curiosity and sympathy in equal measure, but nothing had come back from the Chingfords; he'd just assumed they'd crossed the date off their engagement list and carried on as normal. But here they were, like weeds in the garden.

From Charles' sulking fume, Wally suspected there had already been trouble at the box office, when he'd tried to pick up the non-existent complimentary tickets. Now they were poring over their programmes, conferring, and although he couldn't hear what they were saying, Wally knew they were puzzled at the absence cf his name in the cast list.

He was watching a drama that had slipped off the stage, seven rows into the house. The auditorium began to crawl with theatre-goers, but Wally was transfixed by the Chingfords' performance. That he was intimately involved in this scene was something that his body understood better than his brain. He hid behind the balcony rail, his eyes peeking over the top, his heart pounding with embarrassment.

Charles stood up, he'd had enough, started pulling on his coat. Peggy's arm pleaded and stroked for him to stay, while Leonard, caught by indecision, rose halfway out of his seat, braced against the backs of the chairs, looking like a sprinter at the blocks caught out by a foul starting pistol.

Wally felt a touch on his shoulder. It was the lace-shrouded Claire, satin glove extended.

"Can you keep an eye on my place?" she begged. "I really have to go spend a penny."

Wally nodded, furiously, and tried to shrink away from her. But it was too late. Her conspicuous dress, white and anachronous, had caught Charles' eye. He nudged Peggy to look, but only as a point of interest, as one does when spotting a robin at the birdbath. Peggy, polite and merely curious, followed his gesture to the balcony. She locked eyeballs with Wally.

"There you are!" Her first expression was one of delight, as if playing a game of Hide-and-Seek. Relief played across her face as part of the evening's mystery fell away.

From Wally's point of view, the proceedings were surreal. The trio stood facing him in tableau, their chins lifted, slight smiles spreading in expectation. Actors taking their call. Peggy waved and Wally was propelled into the scene whether he liked it or not. There were no lines for him to recite, no eloquence to save him from the impossibility. Besides, he'd been watching *them*; he was the audience, not the performer.

So he sprang to his feet, rudely, as if at the opera, colour rushing to his face, panic fuelling his hands, and he applauded, loud and long.

"Bravo! Bravo!" he cheered. "Encore! Bravo!"

The Golden Hart, being the closest pub to the Academy, was usually where everyone went after hours once Tufnel's was closed. It had a decent enough lounge, with enough space to pull up a few chairs around one of the circular tables and make a jolly party. Wally found himself in with a crowd: the Chingfords, Monty and Georgia, two of Monty's friends from Tufnel Green, and a couple of Americans, a large young man in an expensive blazer and a skinny dowager in chartreuse silks who clung to Georgia like a sycophantic barnacle. Wally wanted to hit her, to pry her loose with the flat blade of his knife and toss her in some dark alley.

"You were so marvellous," this hag declaimed, feathering her bejewelled hand the length of Georgia's arm. "I'm so glad I got the chance to see you in action. I'll have to tell your Mom and Pip when I get back!"

"Well done, Georgie," said the young man, quietly.

"Thanks, James."

Georgia smiled at the assembled company. She was basking in glory, as well she ought. She'd acquitted herself well in the show and given the entire audience gooseflesh on her final line when she'd accused all humans of being blind. Wally thought she'd overdone it a bit on her hysterical breakdown, but he was willing to hand it to her on managing to avoid the bathos in the script. Ever since he'd found out he wasn't in the production, he'd allowed himself to admit to how much he hated the text. It was, in his opinion, cloying in the worst American tradition, pandering to an artificial sentimentality he found abhorrent. Its underlying moral of living life to its fullest struck him as absurd; how could you not live life to its fullest?

"So, Wally Greene," said Leonard from the far side of a pint of bitter. "You haven't changed a bit, have you, then?"

By which he meant he wasn't surprised Wally wasn't in the play, that something had gone wrong, clearly, as it always did with anything that came into contact with Wally's immediate surroundings, that they should have expected no less than to be dragged out to the theatre on false pretenses, then to be greeted by a one-man standing ovation.

"If I haven't changed," muttered Wally, "then neither have you."

"But I'm an Assistant Managerial Clerk at Coutts," blustered Charles. "I'll be able to buy my own house in five years."

Wally shrugged; let them continue talking. It was a vile half hour of one-upmanship and gloat. In the missing decade, the Chingfords had become upper-class twits. Leonard and Charles were barrelling along predictable avenues of privilege, while Peggy, practically mute between them, sipped her bottled pineapple juice and kept her eyes downcast and her comments to monosyllabic nods. She wore no makeup, but there wasn't a pore on her skin that hadn't been attended to, not a strand of hair that hadn't been brushed the requisite hundred strokes every night, not an expression that hadn't been schooled into submission. Wally felt his hackles rising.

"Married yet then, Peggy?" he asked, pointedly. "When do you start playing Mothers and Fathers in earnest?"

She flushed slightly at the reference. Then she cleared her throat into her fist, as if catching it there was more polite than merely covering her mouth.

"Mothers and Fathers," she said, thoughtfully. "Yes, I remember that. I'm so sorry, Wally. You must have thought I was an absolute monster."

Wally was so surprised he found himself denying it before he realized fully what she'd said. "No, not at all! I mean, I was much younger then. I don't really remember." Yes, he thought she'd been a monster: an ogress, a giant's wife, the back end of the cow. She had apologized. Wally felt the moral weight crush him, control him, make him say things he didn't mean.

Then she laughed—a snatch of music from out of the past—and he was transported back to cream bun smeared around her face with seagulls circling up above. The sea air, Carmarthan Bay. *I'm never getting old!* He caught sight of the swell of her breast beneath her pale-blue cardigan, the pearl hanging from her earlobe, the finger on the left hand waiting for a ring, and the joke became his. He laughed along with her. His voice had broken since he'd last done that.

He insisted on buying the next round, even though he didn't have the money on him. He knew he'd have to ask Georgia to cover for him when the slates were tallied up at the end of the evening. He relished the idea; it was a form of showing-off, a one-downmanship.

"You know I got thrown out of the Academy," he confessed, loudly. "I brained the principal with a block of wood when I found out I wasn't playing the lead in their little play. He deserved it, though. He was such a *toff*!"

"How long have you been smoking?" asked Peggy.

"But what I don't understand," he leaned in, conspiratorially, his finger bent against his chin, "what I don't understand is why you don't know this. Didn't you get my postcard?"

"We moved."

"We bought a new house."

"We're in Saint John's Wood now."

"Oh, Saint John's Wood?" Wally mocked. "Really? How nice.

We're practically neighbours. We have a place in Regent's Park, don't we Georgie? On the Crescent."

Georgia, who was deep in a conversation elsewhere, heard her name. Turned and smiled. "What's that, Wally?"

"Do you have a spare ten shillings, darling?" he asked. "I seem to be a little fucking short again."

He escorted the Chingfords to the closest taxi rank where, teeth bared, they exchanged addresses and promised to keep in touch. He waved them goodbye, good riddance, good Lord, then ran back to the Golden Hart where he got in another three rounds with Georgia and Monty before they all decided to move on to fresher waters.

He didn't care any more what was going to become of him. Laughing at the Chingfords had made sure of that. He had no idea what he was going to do, where he was going, or what he was going to tell Ma about next year, should he even tell her. He wouldn't tell her. He wouldn't tell anybody, not even Millie the sheep! He would simply disappear into the folds of London, follow his own nose to wherever it took him. It was an intense freedom, this business of growing up. Nobody else really cared. Why, then, should he?

Act III

11

The bar of the Phoenix Theatre after the opening performance of *She Stoops to Conquer* is filled with Vancouver's
own peculiar set of culture badgers. A year after Expo '86
and old habits die hard. The nightly fireworks have stopped; the free
samples, the publicity stunts, the attention given to A World in a
City, the flags of all nations, gone. The cocktail sausages and devilled
eggs may have shrunk to a bowl of chips 'n dip, but the patrons are
still expecting to be courted with cake. They hover, uncomfortable,
in well-pressed clumps or sit at tables with too many chairs squished
in, so as to keep the party together.

Wally and Ned are at the bar, on stools, scarfing their way
through a second bowl of peanuts and accompanying beers. They
are the scruffiest people in the place, and they're both wearing fresh
clothes. Other than the student waitresses and the wag who keeps
the bar, no one dares come near them. They exude danger like a mist,
keeping the intelligentsia at bay, which is, Wally freely admits, a state
of affairs that neither side would wish to change.

"So, one more month to go," Wally says. "How're you liking it
so far, then?"

Ned shrugs dismissively, but Wally can tell the job, or rather the
role, sits well on him. Ned is a functionary, much as he is. Together,
they get things done so that the high-flying artistes can do their thing
unfettered. During the final week of production, when props were

breaking and being returned for repair constantly, and problems had
to be solved with a glue-gun and a staple, Ned kept up with Wally,
running beside him almost as an equal. Thinking on the fly; he has
a natural aptitude.

"I'm not sure if I'm glad this one's over," Wally says with a grimace. "I mean, the next one's no big deal. Just a short two-hander
for a couple of weeks; a chair and an ashtray, that's all it'll need. But
the one after that promises to be a real stinker."

"What? Macb—"

"Shh-shh!" Wally grabs Ned's arm. "Don't even mention the
name. This may be the bar, but we're still in the theatre, you know."

"What?"

"Can't mention the Scottish Play or quote from it in a theatre,
my lad. It's tradition. You'll bring down the curse."

Ned looks as if he'd quite like the idea of doing just that, but
he holds his tongue. Wally smiles, sheepishly, as if to say it was all so
much rubbish, but he can't quite pull off the nonchalance. Not in
front of Peggy's boy.

"How're they going to rehearse the play?" Ned rubs his nose,
like a junky thinking about his fix. "If they can't quote from it in a
theatre, I mean. Do they all stand around miming?"

Wally laughs at the simplicity. He can't begin to explain how
the Macbeth curse functions; it just does. You could do the play, of
course you could do the play, anyone could do the play. But it
comes with a warning. Everything about Mackers is shrouded in a
black fog. Disrespect it, and a smidgen of evil will seep inside you.

A spattering of applause stirs the air to signify someone important has arrived. Ned jerks his chin toward the door through which
cast members have been making their public entrances. "Here comes
your old lady," he says. "Do I have to say something nice?"

"Don't be daft." Wally concentrates on rolling a cigarette. "If
anyone can take the truth, it's her. Thick-skinned Brandt. I believe
she's related to the rhino. Anyway, she'll be a while, yet. She has her

fans to contend with."

"She wasn't that bad." Ned plays it soft with his praise. "But she should have been playing the other part. You know, the daughter instead of the mother."

Wally raises an eyebrow. Oh-hoh, he thinks. Georgia would love to hear that, wouldn't she? Play the soubrette!

"No she couldn't," he says aloud. "She's too old."

"Sure she could."

Wally feels like saying something about mutton dressed as lamb, but catches himself. He doesn't want to continue the argument, it would only depress him. Georgia has grown old in mind as well as body, something he never thought possible. But he's seen her standing at the bathroom mirror, tilting her chin this way and that, stroking the pockets of flesh, curiously, with that sad expression in her eyes that makes her look even older. He's even found himself doing a similar kind of search on his own body: inspecting the veins and spots on his hands, poking his dough bag of a stomach, wondering when his liver was going to drop out of his arsehole. No, he daren't raise the topic of age. Especially with a young buck who treats his body as a carnival ride.

He glances over to where Georgia is entangled in her usual coterie of gaunt, rich American women. It doesn't matter which city she plays in, she attracts them, these doyennes of Chanel, who pop up like secret service agents keeping tabs on their target. They know Georgia's résumé better than she does herself, they can recite, word for word, speeches from roles she performed decades ago, and they are guaranteed to get Wally's back up in less than thirty seconds. Georgia claims to despise these creatures too, but she never snaps at them, never shoos them away, never commands them to crawl back into their wormholes never to emerge again.

In Wally's view, she encourages them by wearing her best couture on openings, tonight being no exception. If she dressed down after the show, he thinks, she'd be treated with respect and left alone.

Not so in that sleek forest green number with the ambergris jewel-
lery accents. The American mavens recognize it as the high-ranking
uniform of one of their own. The Boston Brandt connection, and
General Georgia deserves all she gets.

It's another ten or fifteen minutes before she joins them. She rolls
her eyes madly to let Wally know what a maelstrom she's just been
through. Then she positions herself at the end of the bar, where she
can keep an eye on the room.

Wally hands her the glass of bourbon that arrived not thirty
seconds ago. Left hand to left hand, it passes wordlessly. She removes
the straw and knocks back her drink. Medication taken, she holds
herself still, head down, no breath, waiting for the alcohol to hit. Then
a deep lungful of air—in and out—like a vocal exercise. Energy
returns. She glances at the ashtray.

"You've been smoking a lot, I see."

"No more than usual." Wally thinks about lying, decides against
it. "We've been out here since intermission. Missed the end, sorry."

"I thought you were going to quit."

"I am."

"No you're not, pal, don't give me that crap."

Tension whips up out of nowhere. Wally glares at her, daring
her to continue. Smoking is such a dumb issue to get all riled up
about, but he'll do it if she pushes him.

She backs down. "You left at intermission?" She strains her
features. "Was it really that awful?"

"You were good," Ned responds, jumping in. "Better than the
girl playing your daughter."

Georgia studies her compliment through slit eyes. Wally can
almost hear her thoughts—*Better than the immature, talentless bitch
playing the lead, you mean*—he's heard it all for the past month, nightly,
over and over. The unbridled venom she saves for when they're
alone together. Over the years, it's gotten worse, at the expense it
seems of her creativity. Each show, one more complaint, one less

original idea. The slow, poisonous creep of bitterness.

"Ned, right?" she says aloud. "You're our candle whiz, aren't you? Peggy's boy."

"Oh, come on, Georgie. Back off. He's hardly a boy any more."

"I can see that." She decrees her approval. "I hope you're going to stick around, Peggy's boy. We could use a talent like yours. Barkeep! Refill!"

She talks about the events of the evening for a while. How Tony Lumpkin needed a paper bag at the five-minute call to dispel a nasty attack of stage fright. How the fat little cow playing her daughter had ripped her dress in a quick change. How the godawful accent of Young Marlow travelled all over the British Isles before finally dipping to Australia where it stayed, leaking vowels all over the front row. She isn't obvious about monopolizing the conversation. Like all skilled performers, she gives the impression that it's a two-way street, but when all is said and done, Georgia's done and said it all with nothing but sympathetic nods and murmurs of agreement from her audience.

"Well, enough about me." She drains her second glass and turns her attention to Ned. "I haven't seen you since, oh, that camping trip up Howe Sound, wasn't it? Nineteen seventy-something, it must have been—ouch—ten years ago."

"Squamish, right. Eight years ago."

"Lots of family. Lots of tents." She flutters her fingers in a careless, erratic flight, and Wally can see her conjure up the clearing, the cluster of orange-and-khaki tents, the stone-rimmed firepit provided at the camping site, the lone-standing faucet outside the wood-slat latrine, the ambulance stuck in the mud with half a dozen kids trying to push it out, Wally's left hook, the taste of cedar chips and blood. The fireworks. All this comes back with the gesture of Georgia's hand, the whole mad mess reduced to a manicured fugue in the air.

"No, you're wrong," Georgia is saying. "It must have been ten years ago at least."

Ned looks as if he's about to correct her. After all, he has reason to know it was only eight years ago, not ten. However, he keeps it to himself, lets her stay with her inaccuracy, and with it, her passing years, her generation gap, her deterioration of memory. He doesn't want any part of it.

"I can't remember," he mumbles dismissively, rubbing his arm. "I've got to go."

He slips off his barstool, ready to leave, but Georgia stops him with a hand on his arm. She apologizes for being so thick, of course it was eight years ago, what was she thinking?

"Stay awhile." She releases him. "Or perhaps you have something better to do."

If I were you, thinks Wally, I'd run. She's playing him, can't he see that? Besides, Wally knows that Ned does, indeed, have something much, much better to do than hang out in the Phoenix bar: getting lost between the pages of Mr. Ballard's book. Wally's seen the hankering in Ned's eye all evening.

But Ned stays. He readjusts himself back on the barstool and waits for Georgia to make it worth his while. She searches for a topic of conversation.

"How's your Mum?"

"Still in the hospice."

"Oh, well. I'm sorry to hear that." She falters, trying to find the right thing to say and fails. "You will let us know when she finally dies, won't you?"

That's Georgia for you, thinks Wally. Sometimes she's a conversational ringmaster, keeping acrobats and clowns going in opposite directions while the trapeze artist swings above the whole crazy mess. Other times she has the verbal prowess of the blunt end of an elephant.

Ned blinks. He swallows her remark like an unexpected flavour. *You will let us know when she finally dies, won't you?* Then he bursts out laughing. Georgia acts confused, shifting her view from Wally's reddening scowl to Ned's guffaw and back again.

"What did I say? I was just being honest. I'm sorry."

Ned chuckles off to the washroom. Wally fiddles with the peanuts in his hand, disturbed.

"It's not as if anybody likes her, is it?" mutters Georgia.

"Even so."

She snorts. "Don't be such a fucking prude, Wally. Oh, right, excuse me, I forgot. You've slept with her."

"Don't be silly."

"Yes you have. I know you have." She purses her lips in the way Wally's seen so many times before—when she has something deliciously evil trapped inside her mouth, and can't keep it in. "I know, Wally Greene. I heard you. I was there."

This is news to Wally.

"But that's . . ." He stops himself from being careless. "You've never voiced this madness before."

"I know. Full of surprises, aren't I."

Wally's heart beats hard as he tries to reconcile the impossibility of what she's saying. Eating peanuts becomes an all-engrossing activity. She couldn't possibly have heard. She couldn't possibly have been there!

"You're bluffing."

"I am?"

"You would have said something, you would. I know you."

"Maybe I saved it for the right time."

"What, like tonight? What's so special about tonight?"

"Nothing," she admits. "But while we're on the subject of waiting for that sour, righteous cow to kick the bucket, I thought we might as well get it all out in the open." She angles her view to the crowd. "Oh, look, there's Dickie. Got to go." And she leaves to socialize.

As she passes him, she leans gently on Wally, her confidence smothering him. "It's no big deal, Wally. I mean, it was a sympathy fuck, right?"

"Right."

"You forget, Wally Greene: I had the room next to you at the Red Lion, remember? Those walls are terribly thin."

Alone at the bar, Wally orders a scotch. He understands, now. He understands how Georgia could be so terribly mistaken, and how it would be best—no, *imperative*—to leave her that way, secure in her ignorance. He's always wondered how he managed to keep the incident with Peggy a secret from her. The answer is simple: she thought she already knew!

The peanuts suddenly taste stale. He can't tell whether everything's unravelling or whether it's safe. Nobody's actually said anything; certainly not Peggy, not even to him. The thought of asking her about it rises, not for the first time, to the forefront. No, he should just let her leave this world in peace. No use making a scene. Georgia was right: they are just waiting for Peggy to kick the bucket. Here he is, sitting in a bar, eating peanuts, waiting to be told that she's gone, waiting for some relief from the prison he's been trapped in for twenty-five years and for the tumblers in the lock of his deadbolt to turn and set him free.

But there, back from the washroom, immovable as a granite slab and standing in his way, is the truth of the matter: Ned.

"You're drunk!"

"So are you! Drunk, drunk, drunky, drunky-skunk!"

"Where the fuck are my keys?"

Georgia plumps down on the top step of the house and scavenges through her bag. On her way through, she pulls out items that annoy and slams them into a pile beside her: a chequebook, a bag of mints, a tampon. Then she upends the whole kit at her feet.

"Aha! There you are!"

Wally, taking a piss behind a nearby conifer shrub, watches her through fronded branches. He wonders what it is that keeps her going, what motor drives the woman, now that ambition has taken a back seat to maintenance. He marvels at her ability to keep it all hidden, because surely it must be there: the fear of her sandcastle crumbling into the ocean. But to watch her, they could be back in Piccadilly Circus chasing taxis up and down the Strand.

She has trouble getting the key in the lock, laughs at the corniness of it all, shrugs Wally off when he comes to help, and gets the door open by sheer determination.

"Shush!" she whispers. "We don't want to wake the baby."

"He's nineteen years old and he's not home," says Wally, flicking on the hall lights. "Hasn't been home for weeks."

"Rubbish!" She slams into the small washroom under the stairs, kicks off her shoes, yanks down her panties, gathers her green gown around her waist and sits on the can, leaving the door open. "He's just spending a couple of nights over at his friend Michael's."

"Barry's."

"The McAuleys, right."

Wally wanders through to the kitchen to avoid an argument, even though he can tell that Georgia's itching for a fight. It's a new behaviour that he's noticed in himself, recently, this backing down from confrontation, this walking away. Usually, he pushes his luck any chance he gets. But not lately. He tries to remember when this change in him started; he isn't sure whether he likes it or not. It feels womanish.

He raids the fridge for some milk, drinks it straight out of the carton, then wipes his beard with the back of his hand. Staying the night over at the McAuleys? When was the last time a nineteen-year-old spent the night with a parentally approved family?

Georgia storms in, dumps her bag on the kitchen table, pretends to be efficient. She busies herself at the sink, filling the kettle with water to boil for one of her herbal teas. She's purposefully provoking Wally with her every move. He tries to weather it out, but each click of the tea-making ritual is like a war cry. She can't find the words to express her anger. He imagines that she's trying to find the demeaning phrase simple enough to destroy him. Wally is compelled to preempt her attack.

"I'm just saying, he's not at the McAuleys."

"Hmph."

"And don't give me that line about being close to UBC. He hasn't touched a piano in over a month."

"He likes to be up near the practice rooms." Georgia's voice is low and quiet. She doesn't even turn round from the stove. "He's got Juilliard coming up soon."

"Oh, Jooll-i-ard," announces Wally, pulling out his tobacco pouch and tossing it on the table. "Who are you kidding? He'll never get in."

She turns to him, sad-eyed. She's too drunk to hold back the argument, but too wise to pretend she hasn't said it all before. "He's your son as well," she points out. "And if he takes after you, then yes, you're probably right, he won't get in. If history is anything to go by."

"That's just your posh family talking."

"What's that supposed to mean?"

The argument stalls. Wally would so dearly love to throw whatever he could grab at her, physically or verbally. Her rich American family, her assumed privilege, it doesn't really matter what ammunition he uses. They've fought this battle so many times before, they both know the rules: there are no rules. It is all about saying the first most hurtful thing that comes to mind under the guise of unburdening yourself. But for now, the argument has stalled. Wally rolls a cigarette. The argument chokes back to life.

"So when are you going to quit smoking?"

"Never."

"Because you can't."

"Sure I can."

"Two thousand dollars says you can't."

"Fine." He offers his hand. She rises to the challenge; they shake on the bet. "But this isn't about my smoking."

"Starting now."

"All right."

He takes his tobacco pouch, along with the cigarette he's just rolled, and tosses them, casually and neatly, into the bin beside the sink. He doesn't even get up out of his chair. He realizes how perverse his enjoyment of all this is, but he can't stop himself.

"There. But I'm telling you. This is about Alex being a Monty, isn't it?"

"Oh, come on!"

"Come on yourself, Georgia. Face it: he's a big fat poofter in training, trawling the queer bars every night in the West End, giving those old nellies the time of their lives."

She stares him down, unable to comment for a few beats. She recognizes her own suspicions. "You're just saying that because, because . . ."

"I'm saying it because it's true." He stands. He feels calm. "Go on. Call up the McAuleys and ask them if he's there." He grabs the receiver from the wall-phone by the fridge and offers it to her. The McAuley's number is on the white board in blue felt pen: 687-3374.

"It's two o'clock in the morning, Wally."

"So manufacture a crisis. You're a professional, aren't you?"

The kettle whistles, calling the end of the round.

She turns away from him, opens cupboards, fusses with mugs and tea bags, gets a lemon slice from a plate in the fridge. He contemplates dialling the McAuley's number himself, manufacturing his own crisis, finding out the truth if only for the satisfaction of being right. He replaces the receiver with a flourish, as if the call has been made, that he's made his point. Georgia ignores him.

She breathes in silence. She doesn't speak until after she's poured her cup, until after she's stirred her spoonful of honey and added her lemon, until after she's carefully waited the requisite three minutes for her concoction to brew.

"That thing about Peggy really got to you tonight, didn't it?"

"Hunh?"

"Peggy. So what is it really with you and her, Wally?" She squeezes out her tea bag with her bare fingertips, shifting her grip from hand to hand to avoid getting scalded. "My God. You screw the stuck-up bitch; you'd think that would do her a favour, but no. It's like you killed her mother, the way she behaves towards you."

Finally. Wally relishes the excitement. It's like the plunger of the syringe being pulled back on a perfect flag of blood, the first step of that crazy journey to the brain. Georgia's voice gains a tinny harmonic, as if the station is slipping on the radio.

". . . and now she's almost dead, for real maybe this time—God knows she's been knocking on death's door for so long she must have bleeding knuckles—now you're almost rid of her, after almost a decade of sickness, but somehow that makes it even worse. Christ, Wally, do you want to go through the rest of your life with the ghost of Peggy on your back? And what you're doing with Ned around all the time, it's like he's some kind of twisted reminder . . ."

She stops. She squints at him. Wally can see her lips move as she does the math.

"There's something not quite right, here," she says, dangerously. "Something you're not telling me."

Wally senses the room pressing in. It's unravelling. The whole mess is coming apart!

The edge of the table is suddenly too close. He shoves it away, palms out, elbows locked. He hears Georgia's yelp. Good. He hopes she's got first-degree burns from the steaming liquid now drenching her expensive dress.

"Once!" he roars. "I only ever fucking screwed Peggy Chingford once!"

"Oh really? Is that so?"

He's standing, she's standing, he's yelling, she's yelling, herbal tea is dripping off the table onto the floor, he's pushing, she's pushing back. Welsh phrases colour the air, joined by some choice Shakes-pearean epithets. The dance is in full swing.

A shadow shuffles at the doorway. Wally is only vaguely aware of maroon-striped pyjama trousers. White flesh. Jet black hair, sleep-cracked eyes. Nipple ring.

"Hey, please . . . Dad? Mom? . . . Do you guys mind keeping it down? I'm trying to get some sleep here."

12

Peggy appeared at the door to Tufnel's Bakery like a wraith. The moment she took off her rain hat, Wally noticed her. He broke off his talk with Georgia mid-sentence.

"What's she doing here?"

It was raining out—one of those lowering, godless days that are supposed to build character—an endless, cold-edged drizzle, so typical of London. Tufnel's, damp and noisy, had kept shelter all day. Abuzz with students, smoky haze, electric lights and dust, it was more like some Parisian café than Camden Town.

Peggy caught Wally's eye directly. Something in her deportment made him jump up and go to her.

"Peggy!"

"Wally, thank God!" She hunched forward with relief. Words came rushing out of her as he led the way back to their wobbly table by the window. "It's Fishguard . . . I didn't know how to find you . . . Nobody did . . . Then I remembered . . . you were friendly with Miss Brandt, and, well . . . I couldn't find her in the telephone directory . . . so I called up the Academy, hoping, but they said they weren't a message service for the students . . . But I pressed and they told me she usually came down here for a cup of tea in the afternoons . . . Miss Brandt, that is, and . . ."

Wally felt his world crumbling around him. This was what he'd feared. Peggy had kept up correspondence with Fishguard. She'd told them about Wally getting thrown out of the Academy, and now he was being called to the mat to explain himself. Which was difficult to do, since Wally had no explanation that would be understood by sheep farmers in Wales. It was all a haze, especially the past few months.

Since term had ended, and all through the long summer holidays, Wally had been on a few binges—not all of them with Georgia and Monty.

He hated the idea of mooching off his friends, so he'd gotten himself a job. A casual summer position, tending the grounds in Regent's Park—raking leaves and picking up litter, mostly. Sometimes the deck chair boys would ask him to keep an eye on their punters while they went off for lunch, which would net him a few extra shillings and some rowdy drinking companions later on in the evening. The deck chair lads would take him to establishments that Georgia would never dare set foot in. Places like the Anchor in Paddington, or a stream of hidden taverns around the back of Blackfriars, or down by the docks on the South Bank. Three or four nights a week, he slept on Georgia's couch. Otherwise, he dossed down wherever he found himself. He became London flotsam.

Somewhere in there, he lost his virginity. He wasn't sober enough to remember it, but when he found himself in a Tufnel Park bedroom with a woman gasping beneath him, her sex pulsing around his, he realized he'd done this all before. He just couldn't remember when.

Autumn came, school started up again for Georgia, and Wally didn't dare write home to tell them what had become of him; of course the longer he left it, the worse it got, until his responsibility hung invisibly in the air three paces behind him. Always there, never acknowledged. He kept telling himself that he'd find some way of explaining to Ma and Da what had happened. But he could hardly explain it to himself. Now it was too late. Peggy had blabbed.

". . . and, well, we knew you were no longer at the Academy, so it was a bit of a long shot . . ."

"Would you like a cup of tea?" Wally interrupted. They had

reached their table, and he pulled out a chair for her. "It's the specialty of the house."

"Don't forget the sticky buns," chirped Monty. "Care for one? They're very . . . well, very sticky."

"No, thank you." She smoothed the palms of her hands on her coat. "Well, all right, I think I will. Thank you."

So she sat, like a porcelain teapot, at the edge of her seat, knees together, ankles turned just so, elbow to elbow with the rest of them. She folded her rain hat and smirked at the company, but mainly at Georgia.

"Hello," she said, beaming with charity. "I'm Margaret. Peggy. Chingford. I met you after *Our Town*. You were very good."

"Yes, I remember," drawled Georgia, referring to herself.

"Oi, Parker!" yelled Wally. "One more tea wiv a sticky bun over 'ere mate! Chop-chop!"

Peggy looked askance, a little worried. "Do you always shout at him like that?" she whispered.

"Who? Parker?" Wally looked at Peggy as if she were a little simple. "I suppose so, yes."

"Doesn't he mind?"

"Mind? I shouldn't expect so. It's his job."

"But he's not a servant."

"Yes, he is."

Monty broke the awkward silence by dangling his hand above the table at Peggy and introducing himself. "I'm Monty, the Social Injustice Man from Act One. I'm going to be on television." They shook, after a fashion. Everyone laughed because it was so ridiculous. Monty rattled on about the televised coronation, among other things.

When Parker brought Peggy's tea and bun on a tray, she thanked him with extreme politeness. Her eyes followed the dark-haired lad as he slunk back behind his counter. Wally felt uncomfortable.

"So," he said. "I didn't expect to see you here. Ma sent you out looking for me, yes?"

"Yes, Wally, well no, I . . ." She put a hand on his knee. Wally felt a warmth, like velvet, wrap his leg. "That's just it. It's your Ma. Mrs Greene. She . . . They didn't know how to get a hold of you."

Dead. Ma was dead. Wally guessed the truth before he was told. And all he could think of was that he had no idea how he was supposed to react; it felt like a drama improvisation exercise. Georgia and Monty were watching, taking notes. He was in a very public place. Admittedly, he wasn't a student at the Academy any more, but the rest of the population of Tufnel's certainly was—and they all knew who he was, all those ponced-up theatrical vultures in training. He didn't dare throw a scene, no matter how genuine. They'd critique him into the ground. *Remember Wally Greene, the Welsh idiot who got chucked out at the end of last term?*

"It's your Ma. She passed on."

"I'm sorry?"

"Two weeks ago, Monday night. They were frantic. Your Dad's in hospital, near death's door himself, and nobody knew how to get a hold of you."

"Well, it's a stroke of luck I was here today," Wally said, not really taking in the information. "You could have made the trip for nothing."

"I did." She smiled at Georgia and Monty. "Yesterday afternoon. Nobody was here."

"Wednesday, half-closing," sang the whole table, in chorus.

Her hand was on his knee again, patting him. "I'm awfully sorry, Wally. It's horrible, I know, but I think it was quick. There's a mercy."

"What was?"

She showed him the letter from Mr. Quarrendon. Full of complicated apologies for bothering her, it took a few paragraphs of explanation before it got to the matter. The Greene farmhouse had burned down. Fast asleep in their beds, they were, and the blaze had started downstairs in the living room, where Old Mr. Greene used to sleep. He'd been taken too, in the tragedy; they thought perhaps an ember from the fireplace had caught his bedclothes.

"I bet it was his smoking," muttered Wally. "Set himself on fire, he did. I know it. Selfish old bastard."

Mr. Quarrendon, apparently, had been riding his bicycle along the St David's Road and seen the blaze. He'd organized the rescue team, and was, by his own account, mainly responsible for dragging Wally's father, face down, by the ankles, out of the inferno and into the yard. Wally found himself thinking of Da's teeth scraping through the dirt. He kept reading the same portion of Mr. Quarrendon's letter over and over. The even copperplate hand made no sense. The under-lined words, scattered throughout the letter like clues for a treasure hunt, competed for his attention: *urgent*, *next Friday*, *11th inst at St Giles' Cemetery*, *consideration*, *trouble*, and *claimed they'd never heard of him!!*

"The funeral's tomorrow?" said Wally, bewildered. "What am I going to do?"

The question was rhetorical; he hadn't meant for anyone to answer it. Indeed, he'd forgotten Georgia and Monty were there, the drama was all his. Peggy, he could feel, a tending presence on his right, emanating a concern that utterly failed to touch him.

"There's a train from Paddington tomorrow morning that gets in at a quarter of two," she said.

"I don't have any money." Wally was simply stating the truth. "Not enough to take the train."

It came to him then: he didn't want to go. He didn't want to see his mother in a box, burnt to a nine-day-old lamb stew in the bottom of the pot. Didn't want to see his Da, dirtied teeth, gasping to fill his lungs on a hospital bed. Didn't want to say thank you to Mr. Quarrendon. Fishguard grasped at him like a rotten stink.

"I know!" Georgia clapped her hands, dispelling Wally's fug immediately. "Let's all go! Let's all go to Wales tomorrow! My treat!"

She was mad. He loved her.

That night, between laughter and horror, Wally fell into Georgia's bed, onto her breasts and down, down, down into the grip of her thighs. Semi-clothed, she took him purposefully, as a challenge, manoeuvring his limbs like a stuffed animal's at a doll's tea party— he was out of scale, wouldn't fit, but she was determined to get him a place at her table. That it was their first time together was all Wally could think of. Surely there'd been an accident, she must have made a mistake. Or worse: it was a sympathy screw. Hardly surprising that he didn't perform well. He banged his elbow on the bedside table, jammed her knee against his testicles, and finally, had to stop when her silky, boned brassiere reminded him of Ma. The curious construction of women's undergarments, white elastic, sharp hooks, smooth gussets between the stays, and that satiny fabric, triggered a memory of the bandage material in Ma's sling. What happens to elastic when it catches fire? he thought. Does it melt?

"I can't go." He looked for his trousers, started dressing. "I can't go tomorrow. I can't."

"Sure you can." She rolled over on the bed to light a cigarette. "I'll be there to hold your hand."

"That's what I mean, Georgia. I can't go and you can't come with me."

"Half an hour ago, you thought the idea was hilarious."

"It's a funeral, for God's sake."

"It's not yours."

"No. It's my mother's."

It coursed through him, then, in a massive shudder: grief. One foot halfway into a sock, his string vest half-tucked into his underpants, the bed catching him from hitting the floor. Life was happening to him the wrong way around. Everyone else was facing the opposite direction while he blundered through the back alleys, tripping over gin whores and barrow boys, oblivious. He tried to think of where he'd been two weeks ago, Monday night, and couldn't remember.

Fishguard was sunny, breezy, the sky punched with cumulus clouds. A preponderance of slate and rock, wild grass and hedgerows, and a familiar distant smokiness overpowered Wally. Out in the fields, he could see a plume rising from where they were burning the stubble, getting ready for winter. This was where he was born. The flagstones on the platform at the station knew who he was: his name, his weight, his sins of abandonment. When he breathed the air he tasted blame.

Georgia and Monty stepped off the train like explorers in the Amazon. Peggy slipped into the shadows behind them, a distinct figure, watchful and discreet. No one had brought much luggage; it could all be carried by hand. They all wore black; Wally's suit had been bought that morning. He was under Georgia's command; only ten minutes earlier she'd given him two little white pills to calm his nerves.

The taxi knew where they were going without being told. Mr. Davies, the driver, lived over by the waterworks and had a daughter who would be sixteen that summer. He drove them without a word to the cemetery and refused payment, leaving them at the lych-gate —*Adwedd*—the resting place, where, centuries before, they turned away the corpses from the Black Plague and sent them off to the unmarked grave pits in Clwyd's Corner. It wasn't lost on Wally that the Welsh for death also meant coming home.

Mr. Quarrendon strode towards them, his ears shining red in the sun. His air of seriousness was the same as he wore for all church events: a grown-up, responsible tweed that had sadness and pain woven into its core. Behind him, a dozen people in the requisite dark cloth looked at first unfamiliar, but Wally knew that if he gave them longer than a glance, he would recognize each and every one of them. His head bowed, it felt heavy.

"It's the tranquilizer," whispered Georgia in his ear. "Just enjoy it."

Wally knew it wasn't the pills.

And then Peggy was out in front, grasping Mr. Quarrendon by the forearm and murmuring something, the important somethings, no doubt, that Wally was unable to articulate. Gratitude for Peggy flushed through him, for keeping Fishguard at bay, for smoothing the sharp edges of his presence. But his respite from Quarrendon was, inevitably, short-lived. The man bore down on him, his ears glowing like a demon's.

"Walter. Wally. It's good to see you here."

No it's not, thought Wally. It's a nightmare. Nothing good about it at all. It reeks of punishment. Stick me in the dunce's corner. Go find Mr. Maddox to whack me over the knuckles with the blackboard duster.

"Mr. Quarrend . . . Qua . . . Quarrendon."

"Easy there, boy." Wally felt a worker's grip on his shoulder as Quarrendon steadied him. "Do your Ma proud, now."

"I'm fine." His nostrils were warm; the air flowing up the back of his throat tasted rank. He feared for his balance, but fought it off, if for no other reason than to prove Quarrendon's warning unnecessary—to "do his Ma proud" indeed! The suggestion that he couldn't was preposterous. So he swallowed his ire and introduced Georgia and Monty, who were received coldly, politely, suspiciously.

"American, then?" asked Quarrendon of Georgia, pulling his nose away from her. "Are you having any family in England?"

"I hadn't planned on it."

"Best you all follow me."

Over by the yew trees, on the side of the graveyard where the Chapel congregation was buried, a dozen mourners stood around a new gravesite. A uniformed nurse stood beside a wicker contraption on wheels. As Wally got closer, this contraption proved to be a high-backed Bathchair. Inside, was a man, sitting half in shadow, his neck catching the light, looking like a turtle's head emerging from its shell. Wally recognized the man only by inference—from his clothing. He was dressed, awkwardly, in his Sunday best jacket, with a yellowing shirt buttoned over bandages that swaddled his neck and head like a nun's wimple. Black, gnarled skin spread across his face, and turned grey around the eye sockets. The eyes were closed.

But above all, this man was thin. He was so gaunt, so bony, hollowed and spotted, that for a few seconds Wally thought he was looking at Old Man Greene.

"Is that Da?" Wally asked, surprised at his own voice. "He's so thin!"

"It's hard to believe, isn't it?" agreed Mr. Quarrendon, nodding. "But the fire melted his fat clean away. Like butter in the pan."

Did it dribble out the soles of his feet, wondered Wally, unable to imagine the heat necessary to do such a thing. Da must have been seared like a sausage. It was incredible that he was still alive, still breathing. Wally watched his father's chest rise and fall, a small, intimate movement, barely perceptible, more fragile than the seeded dandelions underfoot.

Quarrendon was talking, a medium-pitch ramble that made little sense to Wally. The occasional clutch of words made it through; he was spinning a tale of heroics, of a dark night full of mud and smoke, shouts and effort. Quarrendon was painting himself in Boy's Own Adventure Story terms: the plucky albeit overgrown lad who saved the burning farmhouse. As the tale progressed, it began to dawn on Wally that something was being expected from him, a thank you, perhaps, an expression of gratitude or admiration. Except that there was nothing to be thankful for. Certainly nothing left to admire. To Wally, watching the face of the man in the Bathchair, Quarrendon sounded more and more like a middle-aged meddler in need of a toy train set.

"Can he hear me?" he asked the nurse. "Da, it's me, Wally."

The eyes remained closed. A finger may have twitched in the sun. Wally wanted so much to touch, skin to skin, to feel the reality of substance, but he couldn't. Whatever their relationship may have been once, it was no longer. It was done between them.

The rest of the interment floated by at a strange angle, at a remove, as if viewed through the shadows of the fingers. It was the dark greens of the yew tree that stayed with Wally, and the scent of freshly turned earth. And the sun, which prevented the whole proceedings from sinking into mud. When Ma's coffin was lowered into the ground, it was merely a box, about two feet square, with mahogany curlicues. It felt like a farce to be burying something that had already been cremated, but burial had been her wish, so into the ground she went. The joke caught in Wally's gut, hardening like a cannonball.

Flowers were thrown in. The nurse swung a wreath down for Da. Wally, at a loss, balled up his handkerchief and dropped that. He kept waiting to hear the splash.

That night, he fell out of bed. Right in the middle of impenetrable dreams, which shrivelled at the touch of waking logic, he found himself nose to the old oak floorboards, pain radiating from the new bonk on his forehead. Upstairs at the Red Lion Bed and Breakfast. The next train back to London was in the morning.

They'd all been drinking downstairs in the saloon bar. Georgia had fed him two more pills and the whisky had done its rounds in a predictably forced ritual of eulogies which, thankfully, turned into singing before the bottle got to Wally. Peggy stuck like a limpet to him all night, he was sick of her.

On the hard floor beside the bed, he now felt the physical costs of the evening. A violent headache gripped his left eyeball. He felt ill and shaky, so he stretched out on his back and let the cold boards chill his fever. Nausea flushed along his spine. To his right, a faint light came through a crack in the door, but he was too scared to look at it in case it transformed into a curtain that would rise on some mortifying fear. To avoid throwing up, he held fast to the reality of the pain running from his temple and into his eye. He was determined to stay there on the floor, if necessary, until dawn.

Moaning gave voice to his predicament, an indulgence that may not have helped him physically, but gave him something to do. The sound attracted Peggy, who was in the next room and came a-knocking on his door.

"Wally? Wally, can I come in?"

He heard her let herself in to his room, felt her kneel beside him and tend to him, floorside, like a Florence Nightingale. Unaware of the narcotics he'd taken, she mistakenly assumed he was suffering from a manifestation of grief, and phrased herself around this delusion.

"She's at peace now, Wally. It's all for the best."

He groaned louder, hoping she'd leave. He tried to bat her away like an annoying moth, but she was as tenacious as she was mistaken. She stroked his hair, then when he shook her loose, she clasped his right hand in both of hers.

For ages they were stuck there. His moaning. Her cooing. It could have been the sounds of passion, a heated coupling in the sweetness of night.

"No-o-o, Peggy, leave me alo-o-one."

"Did you drink too much?"

"Please." Swearing seemed the only way to get rid of her, to shock her away. "Fuck off, Peggy. Ple-ease."

"Sh-sh-sh."

At which point, it all became unbearable. A wave of nausea returned, stronger than he could control.

"Oh my God, fuck, oh my God, oh my God!"

He rolled over onto his elbows, dragged himself up from his

knees and staggered to the door, pushing through the tangle of concern from Peggy. Only dimly aware of her following, he made it
downstairs and out into the alley before he finally doubled over and
retched, mercilessly, into the gutter. The world span. He braced himself with both hands against the brick, but he had no more idea of
which way was up than if he were a twig spiralling down a storm
drain. He could have been doing a handstand, could have been
leaning against a wall, or—and this was the illusion that stuck with
him—he was somehow suspended in mid-air, reaching up, up,
above his head, reaching for the cobbled stars that were stained with
his own vomit.

13

Wally knew nothing of his moans being overheard through the walls of the Red Lion Bed and Breakfast. On the train journey back to town, Peggy sat next to him, but not by his choice. He leaned his head against the comforting vibrations of the window and tried to absent himself as reflection met reality in the glass. Fields and posts, sky and rain. A couple of times when he looked up, he noticed Georgia looking at him with a crimped smile on her face. He thought he'd let the side down by succumbing to the effects of drugs and alcohol.

"Did you enjoy yourself last night?" Georgia asked him when they arrived at Paddington Station.

"Not really," he admitted. "What was that stuff you gave me anyway?"

"Some morphine derivative, I think."

Peggy wouldn't leave them alone until she got their phone number, so that she could keep Wally abreast of how Da was doing. It riled him, but he gave it, emphasizing Georgia's ostentatious address.

"God, I hope she doesn't come over," he said.

"Me neither," agreed Georgia, archly.

For the following month, he waited for the phone call. Da didn't have long, Wally knew that from the moment he saw him in the Bathchair. He now understood what was meant by the phrase, "waiting for the other shoe to fall." Meanwhile, guilt crept like a parasite into his brain. Although he knew it to be unfounded, he felt responsible for Ma's death. It was ridiculous—the fire was an accident. Old Man Greene, Ma and Da wouldn't necessarily have fared any better had he been there. But he couldn't shake the thought that he'd abandoned them. He'd gone off, gallivanting, to the big city; he'd chased after a selfish and unattainable dream, leaving the farmhouse to burn to the ground. Disgusted with himself, he felt, at eighteen, unable and unfit.

When the phone call from Peggy finally came, he'd already heard it so many times in his head, it was old news. It was like an echo in a swimming pool, jangling and muffled. Peggy's voice down the wire annoyed him.

"The funeral's next Tuesday. Would you like to catch the train with me? I'm taking the 11:40."

He had to stop himself from screaming. It was impossible to go back to Wales, the thought repulsed him. The logic of making the trip with Peggy, his pseudo-sister, failed him. It seemed perverse. He understood, but couldn't explain, how Fishguard was best left as a memory, that there was nothing to be gained by going back, just more guilt and shame.

"You go, Peggy. Tell them I'm sorry, but I can't . . ."

"But Wally, it's your *father*, you *have* to."

"I can't."

"You mean you won't."

"Both, actually." And he hung up.

Tuesday came and Wally was at work raking leaves in Regent's Park. After 11:40, he had the sensation of playing truant, even though he put his back into his labours more than usual. He kept imagining the graveyard in Wales, the same sunshine as before, the same smells of turned earth, the same sniff of disapproval from Mr. Quarrendon, the same nauseating blanket of narcotics that offered relief, at a price. A twinge of self-pity made him stop and lean on his rake when he realized he was now officially an orphan. At eighteen, he was alone in the world, answerable to none, with respect for none, apparently, not even his father. He was committing a despicable crime by his absence from the funeral that was taking place hundreds of miles to the west. The very leaves at his feet whispered of his treachery.

He'd failed the Academy. And in so doing, he'd failed Ma and proved Da right. There was only one thing to do. He had to find his way back into the theatre, just as he'd sworn to do after the panto. It was why he'd left Fishguard: to find that freedom he felt when the curtain went up and everyday life disappeared. Georgia and Monty understood. Peggy didn't. To her, life was a web of connections from family to teacher, to vicar, to innkeeper, to bus-conductor. You were supposed to keep your place in this rigid latticework, where history and other people told you who and what you were. Wally had tasted, however, the joy of the Big Fib, the place where you could be anywhere or anyone just by announcing it to an audience. To be royalty, you just had to stick on a crown. To be a judge, you merely had to don the wig and robes. Real life was no less of a sham— everything was just an amusement on the way to the grave. You were born naked; everything thereafter was some form of a costume. The false world of the theatre suddenly struck him as being incredibly honest.

He put down his rake then and there and walked off the job, ignoring the catcalls of his workmates at the groundskeeper's hut. He took a bus down to the West End and presented himself at the stage door of the first theatre he found.

"I have to work here," he announced to the doorman. "You have to give me a job."

Something in his tone of voice stopped the doorman from laughing outright in his face, although the guffaw lurked in the corners of the man's bemused eyes.

"Can't help you, mate. I'm not the boss around here. You'll be wanting a talk with Mr. Postlethwaite. The Professor. Good luck."

Mr. Postlethwaite, a shiny, pugnacious little man, inhabited a dark office crowded with memorabilia and ephemera. Everything about him was a-shine and a-gloss: his bald head, his eyes, his lips, his patent shoes, his watch chain. He was dressed formally enough to greet the prime minister and spoke with such strange emphasis and floridity that Wally had trouble understanding him.

"Perchance, my titian youth, you have some gnosis of the trade?"

"I, er, I beg your pardon?"

"Do you have any experience in the *théâtre*, Master Greene?"

"Oh." Wally thought for a moment. "Well, I did a year at the Bloomsbury Academy, but I—"

"I do not engage thespians," announced Mr. Postlethwaite, flatly. "You'll have to go through proper channels like the common, sundry herd for that. Good morning."

Wally felt himself redden. "No, I mean, I don't think I'm suited for the stage, not acting," he admitted. "I think I belong behind the scenes."

"Indeed?" Mr. Postlethwaite looked suspicious. "And what do you know of the gaffer's world, eh? What makes you so certain?"

Blankness filled Wally's mouth, a gaping hole where an answer should be. He couldn't find a single syllable to call upon in his defence. All he could think was that at that very moment, he was supposed to be in Fishguard, tossing a flower on his father's grave.

"I just know," he said eventually. "I don't fit anywhere else."

Surprisingly, this answer mellowed Mr. Postlethwaite. He cleared a few ledgers and some papers from his desk, then waggled a finger at the area of burgundy leather desktop thus revealed.

"Empty out your pockets, Squire Greene," he said, donning a pair of spectacles. "Let's see what you're made of. I have the nose for such things."

Wally hesitated, shrugged, but did as he was told. First, he emptied his left trouser pocket: a coat button, his penknife, a whittling ball wrapped up in his handkerchief, a spare shoelace and a safety pin. Then his right: a lucky farthing and a bus ticket. These items were scrutinized for at least thirty seconds, accompanied by varying tongue clicks and muttering. It was the strangest interview imaginable.

"Larboard, are you?"

"I beg your—"

"Are you left-handed? That is to say, sinistral?"

"Er . . . Yes."

"Ahh." Mr. Postlethwaite's eyes were hugely spherical behind his lenses. He walked around Wally as if appraising a piece of Chippendale. "Yes, a *Gaffer*. An *Urning*. Assuredly, I do believe I spot the mark, old man. I do believe I do. You have the *métier*."

"I have the . . . ?"

"You are a Creature of the Theatre," pronounced Mr. Postlethwaite, heavy on the assonance. "A man of the Gaff. You were born to pull the ropes and prompt the dry. You live to drop, fly, and trap." He gathered Wally's belongings in his hands and returned them, like a pickpocket in reverse, to their rightful places. "Your left is house right, you live your life from front to back, you belong in the whispering wings behind the veil. You are best when you're invisible. I can start you off on Tuesday next at seven guineas per. What do you say?"

"Well, I . . . er . . . Thank you, sir."

"Excellent." They shook hands. "Shall we say at eight-thirty then, on the thirteenth instant? Pantaloons and espadrilles!"

What a buoyancy to his step! Such vigour in his chest! Confidence shone from Wally as he caught the bus back to the apartment on the Crescent. To be sure, a few months earlier, he'd experienced a glow not unlike this when he'd believed he was playing the lead role in *Our Town*. But that had been competitive, and ultimately, deluded. This had come as a direct appraisal of his very being, one on one, man to man, scried through the contents of his pockets laid out like chicken giblets on the altar. He was born to be in the theatre. A man of the Gaff. Pantaloons and espadrilles!

Georgia wasn't home yet, so he sat on the couch with his feet on the coffee table and smoked three lazy Woodbines in a row, watching the smoke curl blue in the air. He helped himself to a celebratory bourbon, and eventually dozed off as he imagined clambering up ladders and swinging from backstage ropes. He awoke when Monty and Georgia returned from school, exhausted from the rigours of a stage-combat class. They dropped like wet sandbags into the chairs around the fireplace. Wally nonchalantly slid a five pound note across the table.

"I bet you a fiver I can make you insanely jealous," he announced.

"Not now, Wally Greene," sighed Georgia. "It's been a tough slog, the past couple of hours."

But Wally wasn't to be deterred. "Oh, well, I suppose you don't want to hear my news, then. Pity." He started to put his money away.

"Make it a pony and you're on," snapped Georgia. "You're already making me angry. Jealousy would be a relief."

"All right, then." He held out his arms like the William Blake *Glad Day*, making a spectacle of himself. "You are looking at a true man of the theatre. As of next Tuesday, the thirteenth instant, I believe, Wally Greene, Esquire, will be officially employed in the service of the New Whitehall Theatre in the West End." He paused for effect, which was unnecessary, as all attention was riveted upon him. "And not," he added, "not as an understudy."

"You got a part? You're in *Reluctant Heroes*?" Monty was blinking six beats to the second, not believing a word of it. "You're working with Brian Rix?"

"No," conceded Wally. "I'm to be a stagehand. A Gaffer. Seven guineas a week. Gentleman's pounds!"

It was real and they knew it. Admiration flooded across Georgia's face too quickly for her to hide it. "You win," she declared, slipping off her shoes and propping her feet on the footstool. "I'm insanely jealous. Now give my ankles a lovely massage, will you?

They feel as if they're about to snap off."

"Stagehand?" sneered Monty. "Cleaning the bogs, more like, I bet."

"Then bog boy I'll be," chirped Wally. "Bog boy at the New Whitehall Theatre, Trafalgar Square. I like the sound of that."

Monty cackled raucously, the momentum raising him out of his chair and over to Wally. Without warning, he cradled Wally's face in his hands and kissed him smack on the forehead. "The further adventures of Wally Wetlegs, bog boy!" he crowed. "You're a champ, you know. An absolute champ, and I'm spitting jealous, too." He went to the drinks cabinet and poured himself a drink, raised it in salute. "Here's to Wally Greene, the first of us to get himself onto the payroll of a West End theatre!"

They settled down after a round or two of congratulations and minor ribbing. Wally massaged Georgia's ankles as he relayed his story of meeting Mr. Postlethwaite and being judged by the contents of his pockets. A golden camaraderie enveloped the three of them, lightened by the booze and tempered by the softness of the furniture. These are my good friends, thought Wally. They care for me, they want me to do well.

"He told me to bring my pantaloons and espadrilles for Tuesday," he mused, bringing his story to a close. "I wonder what he meant by that?"

A snore alerted him to the state of his audience, his dear attentive friends. Fast asleep, the two of them, Monty with a cigarette still lit between his fingers, Georgia with her head lolled against her shoulder. The poor dears were fagged out.

Thursday night, Peggy called. Georgia answered the phone and, after Wally had made frantic hand signals to the effect that he didn't want to talk, told her that he was out, she didn't know where, nor when he would return.

"She said it wasn't important. But she said you should call her back tomorrow."

He didn't—and not because he forgot.

On Saturday, the telephone rang intermittently all day. Wally, alone in the apartment, knew it had to be Peggy, so he wouldn't—and couldn't—answer it. The last thing he wanted was to be chastised for not going to the funeral. In the end, he went out. For hours, he could hear a distant ringing.

Tuesday of the thirteenth instant and Wally was at the stage door of the New Whitehall Theatre bright and early with his kit bag in hand.

"Morning, Master Greene." He was greeted with a nod from the doorman, as if he had always worked there. "If you wait in the Green Room, Bernie will be along in ten minutes or so to show you around. Tea's in the pot."

"Thanks, er . . ."

"Jacko."

"Thank you, Jacko."

Wally took a deep breath, and in he went. The backstage world was an underground warren of corridors and rooms, ashlar walls the colour of butter, and black linoleum floors that shone like obsidian glass. The Green Room was easy to find, all roads seemed to lead there. It was peacock blue with a set of posh leather couches and chairs at one end, and a kitchenette with a simple table and mismatched stools at the other. The pot of tea was, indeed, fresh and made with leaves, not bags. Wally helped himself to one of the plain green cups stacked on the counter and was just about to choose a biscuit from the tin when a middle-aged man in a middle-aged brown work coat appeared before him.

"Biscuits is a shilling a week off your wages, if you like," he said, without a hint of malice.

His name was Bernie Bunting and the Green Room was his pitch. Everyone, he said, came through the Green Room: actors, gaffers, dressers, musicians, stage-door Johnnies, the odd punter and the occasional royalty, foreign and domestic.

"So if ever you get lost in the building," he joked, "just carry on walking, you'll end up here."

They went on a tour, which was giddying and impossible to remember. Dressing rooms, workshops, stairwells, corridors, rehearsal rooms, wardrobe, props, pit, booth, ladders, flies, prompt box, and finally, onto the darkened stage itself. The set was an army barracks room, shabby and worn. In the dim light, Wally could make out the back trusses of some of the flats, the stage weights and ropes, holding everything into place. He stood on stage facing the wave of seats rising up and into the velvet blackness, and his heart missed a beat.

"That's the house," explained Bernie, with a serious tick of the head. "Never let them see you. They don't know we exist. Got that?"

"Ye-es," nodded Wally, lost in awe.

Back in the Green Room, Bernie introduced five young lads sitting round the table having tea. Apprentice gaffers all, they were Messrs Glenhorne, Bilgeman, Titmarsh, Miller and Johns. Better known as Roger One, Roger Two, Nigel, Hamish and Dick. Wally's head swam with names and faces.

"Watcha, cock," smirked a skinny boy with protruding ears— Roger Two. "Welcome to the land of drop-yer-trousers."

"Taffy, are you?" asked one, responding to Wally's lilting helloes. "Better count yer teaspoons, Bernie!"

"There's nothing worth nicking here, mate," said another. "Leastways, anything that is, is bogus."

"What you got there?" asked Roger Two, gesturing at Wally's bag. "Did you bring your sleeping bag or what?"

"It's my pantaloons and espadrilles," said Wally, proudly. "Mr. Postlethwaite told me to bring them."

He showed off his brand-new pair of wide-legged, black Italian trousers and matching soft-soled slippers. After much debate with Georgia and Monty, they'd all agreed that pantaloons and espadrilles must mean something comfortable and practical to work in. And if he was going to be backstage, black was the obvious colour. The fine Italian quality was Georgia, paying off the bet.

His costume provoked a gale of laughter so loud Wally feared his blushing cheeks would explode. Had he made another "understudy" mistake? It certainly felt like it.

"Oh, that's rich, that is," sighed Bernie, as the tumult died down. "That's bloody rich."

"You poor sod," went Roger Two. "Imagine lugging all that in here on your first day, and all. No mate, pantaloons and espadrilles is trousers and shoes. That's what you're working on. Over there, in the wardrobe room: ironin' and polishin', that's what you'll be doing all day. You got bamboozled by the Professor's fancy talk, didn't you? A word of warning: he can throw a five-syllable word in your face and it'll take you a week to recover. Walking bloody dictionary, he is. He calls it a 'munificent intermezzo' when you take an extra five minutes in the bog."

It wasn't just shoes and trousers that Wally was put in charge of, it was also shirts, ties, jackets, socks, hats, and everything else in the costume bins. The wardrobe mistress came in twice a week to deal with anything important, but the day-to-day laundry, ironing, starching and mending was Wally's responsibility. It must have been the safety pin and shoelace in his pocket that had convinced the Professor as to where he belonged, he thought. Then he found out that the previous pantaloon and espadrilles gaffer had handed in his notice two weeks previously. According to Bernie, who had been there for years, it always happened like that. Someone would leave, and a replacement would mysteriously appear on the doorstep almost immediately. No doubt about it: it was a calling.

And Wally loved it. After his first few days of confusion and awkwardness, he fit right in with the misfits in the Gaff House, as they called it. He kept mainly to the other lads, but there were others who drifted in as the day wore on toward showtime. There were Stan and Dennis the fly boys, distant, muscular and fearsome. Mister Caufield, the head caller and front-of-house liaison, who moved in calculated angles. There were dressers, electricians, carpenters, Mr. Postlethwaite himself, and lastly, bang on five minutes to seven, the actors would arrive.

"Thespians!" the Professor would roar from the transom of his office, watch in hand. And the madness would begin.

Wally had been warned to keep out of their way, at least until he found his footing. "Stay on the other side of your ironing board," suggested Bernie. "If you're needed, a dresser will come to you." Wise counsel, for never before had it been so clear to Wally how different a breed the actors were from the rest of humanity. The world revolved around each and every one of them; multiple eddies in a bubbling stream that ran into the mouth of the Great Sea on stage. Get in the way of one and you could get pulled under as if caught in a whirlpool.

"Luvvy, drudge, *Auntie Nell!*" screamed a half made-up actor, his hair held back by a white elastic, a towel draped around his shoulders, a pair of shoes pinched in his outstretched hand as he marched up to Wally. "What did I tell you about my bats?"

"What's that?"

"Varda these stampers! Fake them up to the chinkers and leave the top mule flapping. How many times do I have to tell you, you naff cod?"

"I'm sorry, I—"

"Don't talk back!" The actor slung the offending shoes at Wally. "I'm late enough as it is. I haven't even started on the muck or zhooshing my riah. Bugger you, Nellie!"

Wally watched the retreating actor with bemusement. He examined the shoes, but couldn't see anything wrong with them.

"I see the Duchess of Bedford's already put the moves on you," muttered Roger Two into Wally's ear. "You want to watch that one, you do, she bites."

"I couldn't understand a word she said." It seemed quite natural to refer to the male actor as a "she." "What am I supposed to do to her shoes?"

"Oh, that's Polari. The Professor calls it the *lingua franca*. You'll get used to it. You might even get to understand it, one day." Roger Two put a brotherly arm round Wally's shoulders. "Do them up to the fifth lace-holes and no further. Then pull out the tongue so's that Cinderella can slip her tootsies in without having to use her delicate fingers as a shoe horn. Got that?"

"Thanks."

It was like looking after fussy houseplants. The actors required an inordinate amount of coddling or their leaves would wilt. Thankfully, they were only around for a small part of the day; when they weren't there, they became the topic of much ridicule, which lessened the pain of when they were.

Wally began to recognize thespianic traits in Georgia and Monty: a certain inability to function in the real world. They needed people like him.

He would come home in the evening, full of stories of his day's work, but only a fraction of them could be told. Georgia and Monty were still determined to be the toast of the West End when they left the Academy.

"So who's the toast of the town, now then?" challenged Wally.

"Um . . . Gielgud."

"Ellen Terry."

"Ah." Wally held his tongue. Gielgud wasn't playing in anything at the time. And Ellen Terry had been dead for more than twenty years. Clearly, toast was merely the scorched bread of one's own imagination.

14

Xander hears the telephone ringing from the bottom of the garden path. Through the intermittent rain comes the lonesome trill, repeating helplessly in the house like a trapped animal. Someone has forgotten to put on the answering machine again, most likely his mother, who is notoriously inept when it comes to dealing with technology. He lets himself in through the kitchen door, dumps his bag of laundry on a chair, then grabs the phone.

"Hello?"

"Alex!"

"Mom. Hi. What's up?"

"What are you doing home?"

"Forgot my toothbrush."

"You wouldn't be homesick so soon, would you?" she says. "You haven't been gone more than two weeks."

There follows a slight variation of the now-standard negotiated conversation about keeping up his side of the bargain and the importance of practice and discipline. Xander gives her what she wants to hear. She did, after all, shell out the damage deposit and three months' rent on his bachelor apartment in Cockroach Court. He did, after all, agree to really, really try for the big J and not to skip any more sessions with Mr. Stadjykk. He does, after all, have his freedom. Officially.

"So." His mother shifts from one topic to the next. "Is your father there?"

"Hold on, I'll check. I just got in." He leaves the phone to look through the house. In the living room, he picks up the extension.

"Yup, he's right here, watching some nature show on TV. Shall I put him on?"

"You might as well." Her voice carries a martyr's sufferance. "Oh, and Alex?"

"What?"

"Is he smoking?"

"Yup."

He holds the receiver out for his father, who snatches it from him, giving him a piercing squint. "What the hell have you done to your hair?" Not waiting for an answer, he barks into the phone, "Yes, what is it?"

On the television, a flock of flamingoes swarms across the screen, flying off, off and away. Xander follows suit, turning to flee the marsh-lands with a flick of his head, brazenly exposing the four-inch strip of freshly shaved scalp over his right ear. Merely walking creates a breeze that cools the smooth skin—a delicious sensation. Even more delicious now it seems his father hates it.

Back in the kitchen, he is about to return the receiver to its cradle, when the squeaking conversation in his hand tempts him. He seals his palm over the mouthpiece to listen in.

". . . how the fuck should I know," his father is saying. "I'm not his bloody keeper."

"Wally, I've got two of his brothers right here at the theatre, and they seem to think you should—"

"Well, I don't. Last I saw of him was a week ago. He's probably on a bender, somewhere. Have you tried that place in Gastown where he was staying?"

They're talking about Ned McLean. Renegade Ned, from the camping trip in Squamish, a good five years older than Xander, and the object of a pubescent crush that had been if not reciprocated, then at least encouraged. The two of them had shared a tent—and a sleeping bag when the thunder came. They'd jerked off together, if that counted for anything.

"You're lying. I can always tell when you're lying."

"Obviously not."

"He's at the workshop, isn't he?"

"What do they want him for?" His Dad is on the defensive, answering a question with a question. "Has Peggy . . . ?"

"No, not yet, but it doesn't look as if it'll be long, now. They're gathering the family."

The way she says it is full of ridicule. As if their ritual is pathetic, something that only idiots do. Xander feels a pang of loneliness. He's never known family beyond these two bickering fools. His father's side was all finished and done with back in the Old Country, and he only has vague memories of the infamous Boston Brandts, from when he was a baby. He has an image of a large house, hard furniture, and a towering plant reaching up to the ceiling, but it could well have been a dream. The reality was no siblings, no grandparents, no aunts, uncles, cousins, or relations beyond names and pictures in an album. Uncle James. He remembers him.

"Why don't you go look for yourself, if you're so keen," snaps his father.

"What, in this weather?"

"But you want me to go down there, I suppose? Well, bugger you, I'm staying in tonight. TV doesn't watch itself, you know."

Xander lets the receiver fall away from his ear, almost hangs up, as the thrill of eavesdropping loses its attraction. If it wasn't such a commonplace occurrence, he'd be embarrassed by his arguing parents. Instead, he merely feels sad.

Silence. The phone in his hand is ominously silent.

He puts it back to his ear, just in time to catch the sound of a strange, short, high-pitched exclamation, followed by his mother's controlled tones.

"Wally?"

"What?"

"*Is he yours?*"

There's another silence, this one more dreadful than the first.

"What? Mine?" His father's voice seems to be coming from neither the living room nor the earpiece of the phone. "No! Of course not. I told you, I only screwed her once!"

"I believe you."

"There you go, then."

"It's just that that one time wasn't the one time I thought it was, was it?"

"What are you talking about? Have you listened to yourself, lately?"

She launches into her Madwoman laugh as Xander replaces the receiver. Cut off, he can still hear her cackle, bunching up the wires, clogging the duplex coil. *Is he yours?* Downstairs, in the basement, measuring out the soap for his laundry, he can't get the phrase out of his head. He doesn't know how much truth lies behind it, doesn't really care, for even to entertain the idea for a moment is to open a door on something that would much better have remained hidden. *Is he yours?*

He loses his way more than once. The pathway is hard to follow in the dark. Wet branches whip his face, the mud is slippery underfoot. The nearest streetlight is twenty yards behind him, back through the web of trees and rain; he's stumbling forward into the pitch of his own shadow. He wishes the moon were full, although that wouldn't be much help in weather like this. Eventually, though, after he's caught his breath and steadied his internal compass, he breaks through into the clearing where the Old Forge once stood.

A dog is barking continually, reminding him of the telephone ringing back at the house. A faint, orange light comes from a window

on the west side of the *L* of the workshop, spilling onto the courtyard where old paint cans fill up with rainwater and a couple of
sawhorses are propped up against the wall. The dog, a blobby shadow
of a creature, is up against the window on the inside, knocking over
bottles on the ledge and scrabbling at the glass with its front paws.
The barking grows in intensity when the animal senses Xander's
presence. The tinny noise of crazy-assed music blares in the back-
ground—Red Hot Chili Peppers, it sounds like.

He can't see much of what's inside, the pane is so filthy, only the
glowing centre of a flickering light, which looks like a candle. Not
much else. The dog calms to a snuffle along the wood where the
window meets the sill. Xander tries the door first. Locked. The
window, however, opens inward after a firm push.

Inside, he knocks over pots and bottles. An old tin falls, clat-
tering, to the floor. The dog, now recognizable as a stocky pit-bull
bitch, bounds over to scent out Xander's ankles.

"Hey, there." Xander glances around as he squats to let the dog
lick his hand. "Who are you?"

The glow of candlelight reveals the workshop. Xander's only
been in here a few times before. It's his father's sanctuary; not a
welcoming place. It smells damp, chemical-doused, close, and there's
junk everywhere: things hanging from the ceiling, things stacked all
over, things under construction on the worktables. The music is
coming from a portable cassette player.

Finished with introductions, the dog scampers off with a sharp
bark to between two tables. Xander follows.

There on the floor, curled on his side in a fetal ball, is a man. A
large man. Silent and dark, he seems to be imploding, shaking.
A torn, grey muscle shirt curves across the shoulder blades of a
heavily tattooed, quivering back. Arms clamped to the head, pro-
tecting and hiding the skull. There is a faint, laboured breath.

"Ned?" Xander kneels beside the man. "Ned, is that you? Are
you OK?"

He lays a hand gently on the shoulder, and the whole body un-folds—blooms—at the touch, a slow, inevitable reflex, until it lies there, a *pietà* draped in Xander's arms. A soft moan rises from the rigid, weather-beaten face. Grey spittle foams on the lips; the eyes roll back, bloodshot and clouded. A syringe falls from a hand.

"Oh, Jesus."

Call an ambulance? Resuscitation? First Aid?

Xander finds half of his mind wondering what to do, while the other half watches, observes, more interested than anything else. Though this is unfamiliar territory, he does know it from a different angle. He's certainly been in something akin to Ned's position be-fore: when the *grand mals* take him, when he's lain in the safety of Juan's lap, separated from reality by his hissing neural curtain. If Ned were he and he were Juan, and this was something like an epileptic seizure, then all that needed to be done was to wait it out.

Thus, hoping he's doing the right thing, he stays the course. The music stops with a clunk when the tape gets to its end. Still, Xander waits.

Eventually, Ned's muscles calm and his breathing eases: colour and flexibility return to his face. He shifts his limbs as if trying to get comfortable. Now, he merely looks asleep. The dog has curled up on the sleeping bag, not three feet away. All danger seems to have passed.

Is this his brother in his arms, thinks Xander? The fruit of his father's one-time screw with Peggy McLean? His half-brother: half-dead, half-asleep, half-finished, raw, covered in scars and dipped in ink, spread out on his lap like a picture book bound in tattered linens. Envy surges along Xander's spine. He wishes, with a fervour that surprises him, that he were Ned. He could be, so easily; it's as if Xander is staring up through the waters at his own Narcissus, reaching up to the Other on the riverbank. Animus. Falling.

A sudden cough from Ned jerks Xander back to reality. Ned's face screws shut, then opens, eyes clear, focussed on Xander.

"Who the fuck are you?"

"Xander . . . Alex . . . Alex Greene, remember?"

"Xanderalex? Alexander? Ha!" He laughs into a rolling cough, slides off Xander's lap and tumbles onto the floor. "Whoo-ee! This shit's a bit strong! Man! Mmmmm!"

"What are you on?"

But Ned abstracts himself again. A dumb smile crosses his mug, he gurgles and coos like a baby. Then it's lights out and his jaw goes slack. Xander watches as Ned curls back into a ball, shudder after shudder, and the arms go back over the head. This would be where he came in. But now he knows that Ned is actually enjoying himself, twisted up into a tight little ball, shaking the sweat down his spine. It all feels a little selfish.

Xander could just kick himself. Coming to the workshop has been a misguided venture. What had possessed him? Perhaps his mother had merely been goading his father when she'd blurted *Is he yours?* It wasn't unknown for her to indulge like that, to say the first thing that came into her mind, for its dramatic value rather than sense. And yet.

He picks up the syringe from the floor, puts it by the spoon on the bench. Out of curiosity, he runs his finger round the rimed edge of the bowl, holds a grain or two to his tongue. The taste reminds him of marzipan. He sniffs. It isn't any drug with which he is familiar.

"What is this stuff?" he wonders aloud.

"Ecstasy," comes the reply, clear and cogent. Perhaps a little raspy. "Did you get the water?"

"What?" Xander glances down at the reniform bulk of Ned.

"I asked for water, did you get it? I need some fucking water."

Xander goes to the sink, fills a mug from the tap, knowing full well he hadn't been asked before. He plonks the water on the floor beside Ned. He shakes the spill from his fingers.

"I think your dog needs to go outside."

"Yeah. Probably."

The dog scampers for the door the moment Xander gets within

a step of it. He pulls the bolt and lets it out into the rain. He follows. The hard edge of the night is refreshing.

He perches on one of the sawhorses like a yokel on a fence. The paint-spattered courtyard glistens in the rain. Like a distant peasant in a medieval painting, the dog waddles to the edge of the wooded area to urinate, then sniffs around awhile, putting off the journey back.

Squamish. He was eleven, Ned was sixteen, the tent they shared was older than both of them—an ancient green canvas that when you crawled inside, turned the sunshine cold, put a milkish sheen to their skin, and cloistered them in mildew stink when it rained. There were no tattoos then. No nipple ring, either. Tuning their portable radio to a local student frequency and hanging it on the tent pole, Ned had filled Xander's head with the traitor's siren call of a modern world. The *National Geographic* sensibilities of their parents were in for a shock; the hippy movement was about to give way to the punks, the new wave, the anarchy. There they were, in the middle of all that nature, preaching the gospel of the Big City. It was all so important then. It still is, but it's older now. More painful. More real.

So much, however, is the same. Ned is in the workshop just as he was back in the tent, curled up on his sleeping bag, demanding water, reeling from this ecstasy coursing through his body. Back then, it had been beer. The gaping mouth frothing saliva is the same mouth that gaped at the tent's roof in the throes of ejaculation during their boyish masturbation competitions. The rounded shoulders with arms over the head is the same pose that Xander, then Alex, would find him in when he tried to get Ned to come to the camp breakfast. The same clear voice that spoke to him without looking. "Fuck off, it's too early." Ned was someone Xander once looked up to, admired. Even after the fireworks incident.

Everyone called it an accident, but the truth was shakier. That Ned had gotten the worst of it was an accident, but that was the extent of Fate's culpability. The fault lay with the four boys: the three

McLeans who were there (the eldest, Bill, was away) and the one young Greene. And if the adults hadn't been caught in their soap-opera, who's to say what might not have happened? It was impossible to share the responsibility, so it was called an accident.

All the kids had gotten into the game. It was Nigel and Ian, the twins, who produced the actual fireworks, a whole box of them—brown cardboard box with a blue-and-red printed label—which they kept in their tent, hidden under a plastic garbage bag and a blanket. They should have known better, being the eldest. The idea was that they'd wait until the grownups went to the local tavern one evening, and then they'd have themselves a special fireworks display. The whole thing stank of gunpowder and excitement.

But the adults were immersed in an unpredictable game of their own where they would leave one minute, friends, then return, minutes later, enemies. Ned's mom ended up poorly in her tent most often. So the secret fireworks night kept getting put off, put off.

No one can remember whose idea it was to take the arsenal apart, and try to figure out which of the little gummed-up balls of grey powder would burn blue, which ones red. Everyone was convinced they could figure it out if they looked carefully enough. A few were set alight on rocks around the firepit when the adults were momentarily absent. It became the grand experiment, the daredevil ride of the summer. Among them, they took turns at detonating the golden shower powder that blew out of the tail of the rocket, or the twisting silver-blue spiders that flew about the grass and had to be stamped out amid whoops of terrified laughter. It was just Ned's bad luck that he got the ferocious white sparks that blew through the screech valve.

Before he had a chance to put the Zippo lighter away, the screech tube flew up his arm and onto his chest, where it seemed to stick like a magnet. The noise was unbearable, coupled as it was with Ned's screams. Xander remembers staring at the brilliance suddenly in the darkness of the evening. White light. Ned was at the centre of a shooting star. The sparks held onto him as if he were an old friend; they grabbed his arm, his leg, his right side, all the way up to his neck and squeezed him tight. And everywhere it touched, his T-shirt dropped away and the skin beneath shrank a little tauter, like a plastic bag on the radiator. And his face, gasping, breathless from the attention.

War wounds. It isn't surprising that he's covered them with tattoos. Obviously, the ink took to the scar tissue. It's like his own signature, approving changes on a document. Commendable, but no longer quite so enviable, is Ned.

He appears at the door of the workshop, silhouetted against the dim candlelight. He struts out into the rain, swinging his arms in giant windmills. The dog runs to his heels, bounces up his legs, first one side then the other.

"Hey, girl!" laughs Ned. "Schtupitt!"

Volatile knowledge holds Xander stymied. He wants to blurt out two things, neither of which he can voice. One, that Ned's mother is deeper in her deathbed, that the family is gathering for the inevitable. Two, that Ned and he could be closer than they ever thought. Unable to say either, he watches Ned pick up a stick and hurl it into the darkness. The animal chases after and Ned turns around.

"Sorry about that, in there," he says. "I was kinda out of it."

"You don't have to . . ."

"Yeah, I do."

There is a pause. Xander stares at his boots. "What was that stuff again? I've never heard of it before."

"Wanna try some?"

"Maybe later."

"MDMA. It's new, out of Montreal. One of those designer drugs, eh?" The dog returns with her trophy, which gets flung back into the void. "I'm all right now. It doesn't last long."

"Oh." Xander takes a breath and decides to broach one of the subjects. "Your mom . . . your mom's taken a turn for the worse. And I think Nigel and Ian are looking for you."

"Yeah, I know." He shivers. "I was there earlier today. I don't have to go back." He looks puzzled for a bit, as if deciding whether or not he's done the right thing. Then he nods in affirmation and strolls back to the door.

"Let's get in out of the rain."

He gestures with his head—the smallest jerk—at the workshop. Xander slips off his perch on the sawhorse. In they go, the dog racing between them, into the dry, into the candlelight, into the sanctuary.

For now, Xander knows he can't speak of the other topic. Not yet. Maybe he will never be able to. Maybe he can convince himself that he never knew, never overheard it in the first place. The knowledge is like a firework, waiting to go off at the appropriate moment, for when the adults aren't watching, for when they're alone in the tent, when the candle has been blown out, when the fart jokes have subsided and the groans of the oncoming storm are upon them.

Strike a match.

15

Whenever Wally travelled by taxi with Georgia and Monty, they usually took the back seat, and he took one of the flip-down seats facing. He loved the view out of the back window; it was the cinema's perspective of the inside of a cab. Who cared if he couldn't see where he was going? Not he!

One afternoon in February, 1954, Georgia and Wally went to pick up Monty. The taxi door opened, and a young girl was shoved in first.

"Go on, Boo, get in. They won't bite."

She was a slight, blond creature with porcelain skin that looked as if it would shatter at a breath. Monty followed behind her, and the two of them took the flip-up seats.

"Boo, this is Wally and Georgia," introduced Monty. "Everyone, this is Elizabeth Marswick, a.k.a. Boo, a.k.a. the future Mrs. Gower."

To which there was no response, just wide-eyed disbelief. Georgia was the first to recover. She extended her hand, drooped at the wrist, in welcome, as calculatingly languid as any Sheridan heroine. Charmed, she was. Delighted.

"Monty, you sly old queen," she drawled. "Have you been keeping something from us all this time?"

"Well, I never," said Wally, finding his voice. "Engaged to be married?" He could have kicked himself for saying something so stupid.

"The Marswicks are old friends of the family," explained Monty, as if this information made things any clearer. "Isn't it fun, luvvies?"

The eponymous Boo clearly loved fun, especially of the vaguely risqué kind. She was all giggles and smirks, betraying her age to be not much more than sixteen. The two of them sat grinning, speeding backwards into the oncoming traffic.

Wally was fast becoming disillusioned with the ways and wiles of thespians. He thought the whole thing smacked of subterfuge. Monty was up to something.

"Of course it's a total lark, loves," Monty admitted later, in confidence to Wally when they all went for a drink at a pub just off Shaftesbury Avenue. "But a serious one, really, I suppose. You see, my old man was threatening to disinherit me if I carried on the way I was. You know, all those Dilly boys and cottage trawling." He lowered his voice to a whisper. "Boo knows all about that, natch, but she doesn't care one way or the other, so it all works out neatly. Besides, I want to go into television, and a wifey will be very useful there, won't it?"

Wally nodded, mutely. Not able to think of anything suitable to add, he raised his pint mug and drank to Monty and Boo's future happiness. It was a good, dark bitter, strong and dependable, with a thick head—the only real thing around their table at the time.

At the rancid gentlemen's urinals downstairs, Wally and Monty stood side by side at a long, slimy piss wall, their streams playing a duet. When they'd emptied their fill, Wally zipped up, but Monty, tipsy, left his cock hanging out of his trouser fly. The fleshy tube twitched. The head pushed, pinkly, through folds of dripping skin. And there was the ring through the piss-slit—the winking Prince Albert piercing that had cost Wally a pony.

"Last chance," grinned Monty, wagging his hips, his half-erection flapping. "All aboard who's going aboard."

Wally felt himself redden. He knew that Monty was only fooling around, but all the same, he felt dangerously close to a challenge that had nothing to do with pleasure.

"Not tonight, Monty," he quipped. "I've got a headache."

"Give it a kiss goodbye at least." Monty staggered closer so that his boozy face was pushing into Wally's; the head of his cock nudged foreign trouser cloth. "You may never get another chance, luvvy. After all, you bought the ring."

"Bugger off!" Wally took out his Woodbines and lit one up. He tossed the spent match into the bubbling river of urine in the gutter, then gestured at Monty's hard-on. "You want to be saving that for someone who cares."

"Don't you?"

"Not really, no."

There was a pause as the scene was wiped from the chalkboard of experience. Erased, but not entirely forgotten; some shadow remained. Monty fumbled his cock away. "Not much fun, are you any more, Wally?" he muttered, trying to do up his zipper. "Bloody Welsh peasant." Then he staggered out.

It made Wally angry. The toffee-nosed rules of class hadn't been in his head. Now, with one drunken lurch, there they were: back again. He stomped upstairs and stewed over his peasant's beer.

Georgia was going on about how put out she was that Monty hadn't asked her to marry him. The way she saw it was that she should have been the obvious choice, considering what close friends they were. Monty, climbing even higher on his purebred horse, assured her that it was nothing against her personally, but that marrying an American, according to his family, was just as bad as being a bachelor with questionable proclivities.

"Besides," whined Boo, "it's all been arranged."

If Boo had been more corporeal, Georgia might well have gotten into a fight with her. Instead, the anaemic aura of the future Mrs Monty provoked a challenge.

"I'll get her," Georgia whispered to Wally, gripping his elbow. "I'll bet you a pony I'll have her legs in the air, gasping at the ceiling before the ink's dry on their marriage certificate."

Wally shook hands on the contract, but felt himself detach. He watched Boo's ungainly smiles, her adolescence desperately trying to add a few years to her green, and he knew she had no idea she was being wagered over. The knowledge disturbed him. Had Georgia placed a bet on him when they'd first met? He wouldn't put it past her. He wasn't happy being tight with them, any more.

Monty and Georgia, he began to see, were coming down with what Roger Two called "thespianitis." It wasn't their fault. They were creatures of artifice, who suffered from the necessary delusion of their own importance. *Les feux d'artifice*, the Professor called them. "Artificial combustion." Day after day, working as a man of the Gaff, backstage at the Whitehall, Wally was getting an appreciation for seeing fantasy for what it really was, or rather, what had to be done for the grand illusion to take place.

"The first rule of show business," propounded the Professor, "is *Never Believe Your Own Publicity*."

Thespians, he warned, fell into two distinct groups: those who knew it was all cockamamie folderol rubbish, and those who didn't. Monty and Georgia were slipping into the self-deluded camp. Wally now saw that their topsy-turvy, backstage-upside revelry, for all its attraction, was manufactured.

So he moved into his own bedsit in Islington: a cozy box on the middle landing of a Peabody building. To get to his front door, he had to run a gauntlet of cats, piss, yobbos, and dustbins. It was all very grey. But it was free of pretension. It cost him the very real sum of thirty shillings a week. Every Thursday, three crisp ten bob notes vanished out of his pay packet and into the hands of his gnomish landlady, who lay in wait at the top of the stairs, barring his way until he paid the toll. Georgia and Monty visited him there a couple of times at the beginning, but soon left him alone.

"It's a nice place once you get inside," said Georgia. "It's just getting inside that's the problem. Let's meet at Tufnel's."

He began to buy second-hand books from a dingy shop around

the corner from the Angel tube station. He tried a few detective stories before discovering speculative fiction from the likes of C.S. Lewis and H.G. Wells. Huxley, Peake, and Orwell. Also, uncharacteristically, a book of poems by Robert Service, a slim volume that grabbed Wally by the stomach and made him shudder when it fell open at the page, *There's a race of men that don't fit in.*

He had an idea of squirreling himself away for the rest of the winter, reading and waiting for spring. He would economize by cooking on a little gas ring and by wrapping himself in sweaters and blankets to cut down on the cost of feeding the insatiable gas meter.

At the beginning of March, the show at the Whitehall closed, and a new farce was prepared to take its place. The set transformed from army barracks to a country hotel. There were a couple more women in the cast, and Roger One left for greener pastures. So the Professor expanded Wally's job to include "accoutrements and portables"—property duties. He was required at the final rehearsals to keep track and to let the Professor know what was being used, what got broken, and so on. He got a raise of five shillings a week.

On opening night Wally listened from backstage. He knew every line, knew when the actors strayed from the text. The addition of the audience's laughter to the familiar words was a pleasant surprise. It comforted him; told him that all was right with the world. Laughter. The theatre absorbed the vibrations, drinking it in as if it had been starved while the show had been in rehearsal. The whole building shuddered with delight. Suddenly, it was no longer a chore to iron pleats into trousers and count buttons, paint fake banknotes and glue fallen book spines onto flats. People were cheerful, glowing. Even the Duchess of Bedford appeared to beam through her cold cream and Polari tirades.

A couple of nights a week, Wally would go out with the lads from work. Roger Two, who'd taken a shine to him, became his guide and showed him round the working-men's pubs of South London. Draught and darts. There was a pleasing grit to these evenings that made Wally feel at ease. Mostly, though, he'd catch the bus back to his little box, wrap himself up in a blanket, and read.

On Tuesdays, and on Tuesdays only, he'd go to Tufnel's. His excuse would be that he had to work the Wednesday matinee, so the evening would have to be curtailed. A cup of tea and a sticky bun, followed by a round or two at the Golden Hart. He was quite capable of enjoying Monty and Georgia in these weekly doses. He still thought Georgia a genuine marvel, but Monty's charm was wearing thinner than chiffon. More often than not, Monty would turn up late, with his pale Boo-bride clinging to him like a wet flag. There was something unhealthy about her, a neurosis that put Wally on edge. Boo would look at him sorrowfully, as if not understanding who he was or why he was there. And then she'd leer, showing just how short in the tooth she was.

It was all horrendously strained and polite. Monty would tell his awful jokes, or gossip about some terrible scandal in the aristocracy. Georgia would quietly smoke a cigarette and stare at Boo, waiting for her chance to pounce. Wally would lower his head and count his change for the bus.

"Boo wants you to be our best man," Monty told him, one Tuesday in March. "Don't you, Boo?"

"Oh, Monty, don't!" She bit her lip.

"What do you say, luvvy?"

Wally shrugged. "You can't be serious." It was going to be a big church wedding with a large society presence. Wally would be out of his depth. "Can't someone else do it?"

"Absolutely not. You're our man." Monty was adamant. "Our best man. Pater will absolutely flip his noodle, having to stand next to a sodding Welshman. Definitely."

"Oh well, in that case." Wally sighed. "Seeing as I've already cursed the ring . . ."

"Oh my God," breathed Georgia, suddenly grasping Wally's arm. "Look who it isn't!"

Wally turned to where she was gesturing with her eyebrows: over in the corner of Tufnel's, near the cash register, where the staff table was. There, sitting in a periwinkle blue coat, deep in conversation with the boy who worked behind the counter, was Peggy.

"How long have they been there, I wonder?" asked Wally. "Has she seen me?"

"Of course she has," snapped Georgia. "That's why she's here, isn't it? To see you?"

"I don't know," mused Monty, "they look pretty chummy together, her and that Parker lad, if you ask me."

Wally felt awful. He hadn't heard from Peggy for months. He'd simply relegated her to his past: she was someone he'd known once. Seeing her again brought back all those feelings of guilt. He ought to have stayed in touch, picked up the phone, written a letter, thanked her for going to Da's funeral.

"Peg-gy! yelled Georgia across Tufnel's, her arm sweeping wildly in the air. "A-hoy there, Peg-gy Ching-ford!"

Peggy and Parker looked up as one. An expression of consternation flashed across Peggy's face before she smiled flatly, and fingerwaved back. That was the extent of her effort: half an inch of smile and three notes on an invisible piano. This acknowledgment over, she returned to her *tête-à-tête*. Wally surged with indignation at the dismissal. Without warning, he was on his feet and storming across to their table.

"So. How're you doing, Peggy?" he asked, rudely. "Haven't seen you for months."

"Hello, Wally."

"And Parker, my goodness, what a small world." Wally wasn't used to handling sarcasm; it fizzled on the edge of his tongue and made his breath catch short. "Shouldn't you be tending the sticky buns?"

"Parker and I are engaged," said Peggy, simply.

"What, to be married is that, then?"

"That is the idea, yes."

"Oh bloody hell, everybody's doing it, these days." Wally's cheeks twitched, he felt a burr of anger rise in his chest. "Hey, Georgia," he turned to fling his voice back across the room. "Georgie? Looks like we're falling out of fashion! Fancy getting married?"

The words soared in a perfect arc through the air, travelling through a slick momentary lull in the ambient chatter. Everyone heard.

"Married?" Georgia shouted back. "Who to?"

"Me, you big ninny!"

She laughed. "Do you call that a proposal, Wally Greene?"

And so, with at least two dozen witnesses, Wally played out the ludicrous scene. Chairs scraped and turned for a better view as he walked over to the old, familiar table and knelt at Georgia's side. Likening her skin to Etruscan pottery and her eyes to moonlight glinting off a pond of stagnant water, he professed his unmatchable, ineffable love for her, and begged her hand in marriage.

"You do know I'm an American?"

"You do know I'm Welsh?"

Possible impediments aside, she accepted, as if the notion was just slightly fascinating. The whole place erupted in applause.

What a laugh! Out of the corner of his eye, Wally saw Parker fold up his apron, place it on the counter, grab Peggy by the hand, and drag her out of the door. What a laugh!

Later, at the Golden Hart, Georgia gripped his knee and whispered in his ear. "Don't think you can wriggle out of this one, Wally Greene." Her breath was tinged with bourbon, but there was an edge to it that surpassed clarity. "I'm going to marry you if it's the last thing I do."

He hadn't meant it. It had been a joke, surely. It was born out of the moment, out of his anger at Peggy's pert little wave, out of his love for the theatrical. But the joke threatened to turn on its salamander's tail and engulf him. Married! To Georgia Brandt!

"I'm serious," she drawled. "I think we make a wonderful couple."

"You must be soused out of your senses," Wally protested. "We're completely unsuited. You're out of my league. Just think!"

"I try not to," she quipped. "It's bad for the liver."

"Oh stop being so bloody smart!" Wally was fed up. "I won't be your little Boo-bride and that's final."

She was taken aback at that, which pleased him. She didn't think he had the intelligence to see the parallels between her and Monty. Well, she had another think coming.

"Wally, I would never . . ." She sighed, frustrated and terse. Then her expression grew angry and something reached boiling point. She took him by the wrist and hauled him outside into the cold street. Methodically, she put her purse down on the pavement and rolled up the sleeves of her cardigan. Then she brandished her fists at him, played them at chin level like a prize bantam weight. "Fight me," she said. "Either fight with me or tell me what it is you're frightened of."

"Nothing. I'm not frightened of anything. Especially you."

"Bullshit."

She pushed him on the shoulder with the heel of her hand, an ugly jostle that caught him off-balance. He glared back at her.

"Georgia, I can't . . . you're a woman."

"And you're a man. Fight."

He started to walk away, disgusted. Her taunts followed him down the street. "Wally Wetlegs! Willy-Wally! Boo-Boo!"

He stopped. He stared at his feet. He was surrounded by stone: bricks, mortar, pavement, asphalt, pebble-dash and concrete. And within him there was stone, too: in his heart, in his head and in his intestines. Everything, inside and out, felt like a cruel and impervious rock. So easily, he could hit her. So easily, he could walk back and punch her in the face. It would feel good, the crunch of flesh against knuckle. He knew it, and he felt himself ache for it.

"All right," he said, returning. "Let's do it."

They set to. His first punch she caught easily—her fingers wrapping around his fist as if she was picking an apple off the tree. She laughed, knowing that he'd tempered his swing so as not to really hurt. Right then, thought Wally, I'm not holding back. But she blocked his next left, parried with her right, and clipped him on the ear. He felt a dry pain, more embarrassing than physical; the blood rushed to his temple, generating heat. Bitterness ruled him, and in a flash, he lost control, flailing fists in the air, not one of them connecting. Somewhere in that crazed windmill, she got him full square on the mouth. A sudden jab that came out of nowhere and split his lip; the salty, warm taste of blood filled his senses. He pulled back, breathing hard, fighting the urge to fall to his knees and slam his head into the ground.

"What's the matter, Wally? Had enough?"

At that, he knew what he was afraid of. And it wasn't Georgia.

Spitting blood, he approached her. Without warning, he grabbed her head with both hands and kissed her, fully, mixing blood and saliva, fear and desire, thanks and revulsion. He felt her struggle, her confusion, her anger, her resignation. He drank her in like laughter.

For a glorious moment there, he fell. A velvet starlight with neither beginning nor end enveloped his senses, crushed his heartache; he felt suspended in mid-air. He fancied he could hear voices whispering to him, watching and giving encouragement, cheering him on. He knew if he didn't stop, the prickling on the roof of his mouth would spread to his groin and he'd take her right there, in the middle of the street, with a violence that horrified him. He hated himself then, loathed the mechanics of being human.

He shoved her away, and their eyes locked. She looked as if she was about to burst into tears.

"That's cheating," she gasped, her hand flying to her mouth to wipe away the mess. "You . . ."

"I know."

Silence on the empty street. It reminded him of a stage set, with the street lights just-so, glancing off the brick. Shadows angled across the road and turned up a wall.

"I know," he repeated.

"Wally? What . . . ?"

"You win."

"Win what?"

"Me."

No more to be said, he turned on his heel and walked away.

He tried to call Peggy from a phone box to apologize. She wasn't in, and it sounded as if he'd woken up one of her brothers, he couldn't tell which. He blurted something, he had no idea what, about wishing her well for her future life as Mrs Parker and as mother of a string of perfect, happy children, trailing like ducklings behind her.

"Who shall I say called?"

He daren't speak his name, so vile were the syllables on his tongue, so he hung up. For at least thirty seconds, he kept hitting button *B* in a futile attempt to get his money back. Eventually, he went home and sat in his chair with an unopened book on his lap, staring at the wallpaper peeling away from the plaster until exhaustion overcame him.

When he awoke, he went to work.

16

Monty made it into television. *Half an Hour with Monty Gower* first illuminated living-rooms across the nation with its grey ennui in 1961. Sunday afternoons at half past four was its slot and Wally did his best to avoid it. Georgia, when she wasn't on tour, was an avid watcher, pretending to follow the boring political interview that Monty would, inevitably, be conducting, and it was *de rigeur* that anyone within her immediate vicinity had to watch it too. *Half an Hour*, after the first ten minutes, felt like an eternity, during which Monty would scowl and pout in as seriously intellectual manner as possible, while showing off his blond mop and rugged jawline to the cameras. All traces of nellie-dom had been scrubbed from him; he never addressed any of his subjects as "luvvy," and he never, ever smiled. He was butching it up, with the result that Wally wanted to reach into the television set, pull him out by the scruff of his neck, and give him a good shake.

"Do we have to watch this rubbish?" Wally would complain. "Isn't there anything better on the other side?"

"*Songs of Praise*," Georgia would mutter. "Besides, we have to watch Monty."

"Can't think why. We haven't seen him for years."

"We're seeing him now, aren't we?"

"Not the Monty I know."

It was the closest they got to him. Ever since getting married to

Boo, Monty had simply slipped off the map. The wedding itself had been predictably stuffy. Georgia gave Wally a handful of morphine pills that he chomped down on throughout the service. A good thing too, since he would have bitten the head off more than one stuck-up inbred wedding guest if he'd been straight. When Monty got back from his honeymoon, it was as if he'd made a promise to his new wife not to associate with his old friends anymore. A couple of painful dinners in silver-service restaurants and that was it. Georgia lost the bet over Boo, so Wally was twenty-five pounds the richer.

His own marriage, at Marylebone Registry Office was a minimal affair. Roger Two was the best man, and some friend of Georgia, Patricia, was the maid of honour. A scattering of intellectuals from the South Kensington coffee houses, Mr. Postlethwaite and Bernie from the theatre. The Duchess of Bedford and the inevitable American matron rounded out the guests. Throughout the ceremony, Wally was transfixed by the cut-glass dish that held the ring—it looked more like a naff ashtray than anything else. He wished he could have brought something more suitable from the theatre's prop shop: a silver salver, for example, or a velvet cushion. When he kissed his bride, he missed the taste of blood.

A marriage born of whim and bravado. Surprisingly, it fared well. Their expectations were nil; their respect and admiration for each other was as mutual as their suspicion; their lives were so far off the canonical that there was no model for them to follow, so they had to make it up. Wally moved back into the flat overlooking the park, but he kept his bedsit in Islington as an escape valve. Oftentimes he went there to read and sit, especially when Georgia was away on tour or working at one of the provincial theatres. Occasionally they frolicked in their marital bed, always clumsy, usually stoned, sometimes successful.

Georgia kept saying she was going to introduce him to her family, but she kept putting it off until it became obvious that she had no intention of doing so. Wally suspected she hadn't even told her family of their marriage, a state of affairs that both appealed and appalled. They did, however, make vague plans to go to the States when Georgia got a break in her schedule. They'd visit the Boston Brandts then, and what a laugh it would be to break the news to Mom and Pip! But Georgia's career progressed solidly from one decent part to the next, so the chance of getting away turned into a worn-out illusion.

At the theatre, Wally plodded on, eventually becoming Head of Properties, leaving pantaloons and espadrilles far behind. Shows came and went—all successful farces, all feeding the bricks and mortar with dose after dose of laughter, night after night. The quotidian routine settled like a skin over Wally's life; he looked much older than he was.

Eight years slid by like overlapping chimes.

"Do we have to watch this rubbish?"

Georgia sprang off the sofa to the television console and turned it off. Without a word, she strode out of the room, leaving Wally sitting, staring at the contracting grey spot at the centre of the screen. Management had rung down the curtain, it appeared. They didn't have to watch the rest of Monty.

Out in the park, it was a brisk, spring Sunday afternoon, complete with Gainsborough clouds chuffing across an Oxford blue sky. Given the weather, the walks were well populated: couples, families, children, solitary strollers, all sorts. Wally sat on a bench up from the zoo entrance, at a high point of land, in the shadow of an oak. Wrapped in his scarf, coat, and Greek fisherman's cap, he looked out over the grassy slopes at the scattered deck chairs. It was all so quintessentially English, all it was missing was some Elgar and a child with a kite. It was all a load of bollocks. England, he thought, was coming down with a case of thespianitis, swallowing its own Jolly Old myth. And here he was with an American wife in a world that beamed pictures across the sky, across an ocean, and into a little box in front of the sofa. It puzzled him.

He watched a family wandering towards him up the broad pink path. Husband, wife, toddler and pram. There were two canopies to the pram, one at either end; twins, most likely. The woman had a gay mauve pillbox hat and a matching poplin coat, while the man was suited and tied, dark and sharp, with good brogues. She was laughing, a high, trilling sound, much as Peggy used to make.

Wally's stomach lurched. It *was* Peggy. Older, more drawn, perhaps, but unquestionably her, out for a Sunday walk in the park. It was like being back at the Academy's opening night of *Our Town* again: the same curious distortion of time, the same elaboration of gesture and feature that no one could have predicted, yet seemed inevitable.

Luckily, she hadn't spotted him. He yanked the peak of his cap down over his eyes and willed himself to merge with the weather-beaten wood of the bench, to become one with the shadow of the oak. Once they'd passed safely, he let out a sigh.

Children. Three of them already. That was fairly good going, considering she'd married so far beneath her. Parker couldn't be bringing in much. She must be leaning on the riches of her family to be able to afford one of her own. They all looked well-heeled and as bright as rain. The pram was new. She still had jewels in her ears.

Wally remained stuck on that bench for almost an hour, lost in discomfort. It was an elusive malaise, like a lost dream, a sense of imbalance. Much time had passed since he last saw Peggy that day in Tufnel's. But obviously, some guilt remained towards her, otherwise he would have jumped up from the bench, shouted a welcome and laughed at the coincidence. He compared his marriage with theirs, a ridiculous exercise, since he knew nothing of them, save three minutes' observation.

He didn't mention his chance sighting to Georgia when he returned. She wouldn't have cared anyway, since she was poised on her mat, midway through her yoga. He tried to imagine her pushing a pram through the park on a Sunday afternoon and realized the notion was impossible.

A year later, Peggy turned up like a lost doll. It was after the Wednesday matinée on the thirteenth of June, 1962. Wally was just sitting down to a cup of tea with the lads in the Green Room before resetting everything for the evening show. Wednesday afternoons were, as a rule, tedious.

"You have a visitor, Master Greene," said Bernie, raising an eyebrow. "He's in here, miss."

Her hair was stiff and coiffed, back-combed into a brassy helmet. She looked uncomfortable in a green cashmere cardigan and a shot silk skirt. Beneath her Jackie Kennedy makeup, her face was flushed and confused as she stood there, her head tilted to one side, clutching a programme, and listening to the muffled Polari of the thespians in their dressing rooms.

"Peggy Chingford!" blurted Wally. "Sorry, I mean, it's Peggy Parker now, isn't it? Hello!"

Without thinking, he bounded up and offered his stool. He was going to play the social game, it appeared. She scowled at his attentiveness, however. Then she let out a laugh, and he knew she was going to keep up the pretense for both their sakes.

"Hello, Wally," she said, perching on the proffered stool, her voice sounding as if she'd never stopped talking to him, that she was merely picking up where she'd left off. "We just saw the show. It was very good."

"You should have warned me you were coming," said Wally, brazenly. "I would have gotten you a free ticket."

She stared at him sadly, twenty years floating, invisibly, in the air between them. "Free ticket? Really?"

"Absolutely!"

"Wally Greene, you're the worst liar in the world. Look at you, pillar-box red!" She beamed, completely in control, then introduced herself to everyone around the table, making jokes as she went. "Roger Two? And there's no Roger One. Oh, I don't know why that's so funny, but it is, isn't it?" She caught her breath. "I do believe I've been laughing all afternoon."

The lads agreed that her amusement was a good thing, seeing as the show was a comedy. Boded well for the future run of the play, they said.

"By the way, Wally," she said with a warning tone. "Parker's his Christian name. Our surname is McLean."

"Peggy McLean." Wally corrected himself as if at school. "Mrs Peggy McLean."

"He's waiting for me by the stage door, actually. Silly thing wouldn't come in." She grimaced, apologizing for the bad manners of her husband. "And I use Margaret, now. Peggy makes me sound such a little girl, don't you think?"

Wally felt nauseous, unsettled. He recognized the feeling from the park—and his mates were watching. He smiled through it, though, forced himself to keep the conversation going, all the time wondering why Peggy-Margaret Parker-McLean had turned up, why she wanted to see him.

"And how are the boys? Len and Charles? How're they doing?"

She assured him they were fine. Len was in the City, and Charles had moved to the Continent. Brussels, she believed, or was it Berlin? She didn't see much of either of them any more.

"But I have three lovely children to keep me company. Boys. All boys." She laughed again, as if she'd swapped her brothers for her children and somehow managed to gain one extra in the process.

Wally nearly blurted that he knew about her brood, that he'd seen them out in the park, but he kept his mouth shut. The other lads at the table were losing interest. Roger Two knocked back the dregs of his tea and started making excuses. Wally decided the time had come to be direct.

"So what brings you here today, Pe . . . Margaret?" he asked.

"Don't tell me you just came to see the show and happened to spot my name in the programme."

"Well no, Wally," she admitted. "I knew you were working here. The thing is . . . well, I just came to say goodbye, really." She paused, realizing she wasn't making much sense. She hadn't bothered to say goodbye all those years ago. Why start now? "So anyway, we thought we'd come and see the show, see what you're up to, at any rate, and . . . You see, we're moving . . . *emigrating* actually . . . we're emigrating to Canada, to Toronto. Parker's family's out there, and . . . well . . . it's jolly well time I met them."

She snorted over another laugh and then continued, a steady stream of unnecessary explanations as to why she was going and how big a decision it had been and how she was now doing the rounds saying goodbye and Wally thought: You haven't come to say goodbye, you've come to gloat. You've come to rub my nose in your happy marriage and your three little pigs and your expensive aeroplane ticket and your success. If there hadn't been half a dozen Men of the Gaff standing around as witnesses, he would have punched her in the vile pink lipstick. His left hand started fiddling. He had his knife in his pocket; he wanted so to play with it, to feel its smooth comfort in his fingers.

"Canada?" He was just catching bits from her conversation. "How far away is that exactly, do you know?"

She caught herself short. She stared at him. For a moment, it seemed she could see through his façade.

"Why, it's on the other side of the world."

It wasn't far enough. Worms were crawling under his skin, the corners of his mouth were wrenching downward, his finger was tracing the same edge of the tabletop over and over. Couldn't she see what she was doing to him?

"Oh, well," he said.

"Goodbye, then," he said.

"Send us a postcard, will you?" he said.

If she didn't go within the next few seconds, he would explode.
"Oh, *Wally*, don't be like that."

"When do you leave?"

"Tomorrow. But, Wally . . ."

He blinked away, broke his gaze from the table and it just happened to land on the dressing rooms. Through the open door, he could see the Duchess of Bedford, slapping on the cold cream. In a flash, Wally knew what he was going to do. A chill ran through him.

"Tomorrow?" he said, standing up and parading into the centre of the Green Room. "Tomorrow, did you say?"

It was too late to turn back, now. He struck a pose. He took a deep breath. He felt himself careening around the edge of a precipice. Before him, the void, quivering. Somewhere, a curtain went up. He launched himself into the forbidden speech.

"Tomorrow, and to-morrow, and to-morrow,
Creeps in this petty pace from day to day,
To the last syllable of recorded time;
And all our yesterdays have lighted fools
The way to dusty death. Out, out, brief candle!
Life's but a walking shadow; a poor player,
That struts and frets his hour upon the stage,
And then is heard no more: it is a tale
Told by an idiot, full of sound and fury,
Signifying nothing."

The very walls of the theatre gasped. The floor underfoot rocked, as on a ship. Two actors, passing through the Green Room, froze *en tableau*. The Duchess of Bedford at her dressing table, a gargoyle.

Surprisingly, the mirror didn't shatter. Roger Two and the lads slowly turned their heads in disbelief. Never before had such an atrocity been committed on this ground.

Silence.

Eventually, the Professor's approaching footsteps could be heard on the linoleum down the corridor. He appeared, prim and correct. He stood at the transom of the room for a few moments, hands behind his back, jaw tilted, eyes evaluating the scene.

"What is it? What's the matter?" Peggy was confused.

"He quoted . . ." Roger Two didn't dare finish.

"What? Quoted what? Wasn't that *Hamlet*? Tomorrow, and to-morrow, and to-morrow, creeps in this petty pace . . . *Macbeth*? Oh." Her hand flew, too late, to her mouth. "That's supposed to be bad luck, isn't it? I'm sorry."

A moan emanated from the dressing room. Distant at first, like an army coming over the hill, then louder, louder, and more pained. The Duchess of Bedford made her looming entrance as one of the Furies in full combat. The cold cream was a mask of horror: eyes lined and popping, mouth stretched and wailing. She raised an arm, her bony finger stretched from the sleeve of a silk embroidered dressing gown and she pointed accusingly at Wally.

"Varda the black cod fogola, clinging to your screech!"

Peggy gave a nervous giggle.

"And you, you charvering donna with the naff barnet, you can wipe that smile off your eek. You're just as guilty!"

Wally smiled, but it wasn't from good humour.

The Professor held up his hand for order, stepped into the room and cleared his throat.

"The quoting of text from, or the mentioning of the title of the Scottish Play is tabu within the confines of a theatrical establishment." He spoke carefully, choosing his words for the greatest clarity to a layman. "Whether deliberately," he glared at Wally, "or by accident," he turned to Peggy, "the transgression is the same. The remedy,

commensurate with the vapours exuded. Into the mazarine oubliette with the two of them!"

And anyone who knew which side of their loaf was buttered,
obeyed. The mazarine oubliette was the term for the claustrophobic
cubbyhole below the stage, where the trapdoor entrance was. Unlike a real oubliette, which only has one entrance, the mazarine oubliette had another small door that led to the mazarine level below
the stage. If the trap was in use for the show, it would be reasonably
clean and functional, allowing thespians to get in and out without
bruising their shins. If not, as was the current situation, all sorts of
junk would be tossed in there, from cleaning supplies—a few old
mops and brooms—to broken furniture and out-of-commission
props and set pieces.

Peggy and Wally were pushed, brusquely, by a dozen hands toward the stairs. When that didn't seem to be fast enough, the two
were bodily picked up and carried down the final steps. Peggy started
kicking when she realized everyone was serious.

"Put me down! Put me down!"

Wally travelled alongside her, as if in a sedan chair, enjoying himself. He watched Barry and one of the fly boys move their grip up
Peggy's thighs. His sturdy arm was wrapped around her, squeezed
her, kept her bucking to a minimum. Her skirt rode up and Wally
had a view of her underwear and the pale gully of her groin where
she was hinged together. He could smell her struggle.

Down in the mazarine, where heads had to be bowed because
of the low ceiling, one of the lads tripped the latch on the oubliette,
and Wally and Peggy were thrust inside. Wally noticed that his
calves, curiously, were shaking, but it felt as if it was happening to
somebody else. He was calm. At the very last moment, he caught
the Professor's eye, which winked slyly, he was sure of it. A spark ran
between them, a secret communication identical to the look that
Millie the sheep would give him. Bony and true. The game was
afoot and Wally knew he had permission.

The door slammed shut. Blackness. The latch fastened.

Dust filled Wally's nostrils. An old aroma of sweat and neglect. It was pitch dark. He could just make out the crack of light at the door, but he could feel Peggy, scared and flowery, close beside him.

"Election of the Areopagites!" announced the Professor, his words muffled, from the other side of the prison door. "A quorum of three!"

They were playing the game through to its bitter end. Wally knew the trick well, having played it himself a few times in eight years. They were choosing three judges from their number outside, who would decide just when and under what conditions the prisoners could be set free. It was the gaffers' version of Mother, May I?

"We could be in here all night," he whispered to Peggy. "I hope you've got a good stack of swear words."

"What?" Her voice in the gloom was dislodged, adrift in confusion.

"They're going to make us swear our way out of here," explained Wally, trying to keep the triumph out of his voice, "It's a boring Wednesday afternoon. You'd better not have plans."

"What?" She was right by his shoulder. "Wally, is there a light in here?"

They were pushed up tight against each other, a bucket and a roll of carpet preventing them from moving around too much. There was a string to pull on the light, Wally knew exactly where it was.

"No, there's no light." He pinched her waist. A spark crackled. He ran flitting fingers, like flames, up her spine. "Look out for the spiders."

"Ow! Shush. Stop it, Wally!"

But he didn't. He couldn't and wouldn't stop. Not now that he'd started. She tried to wriggle away from his tickling; something crashed to the floor; he moved the spider to her leg. Red blotches appeared before his eyes. Then, before she started to scream, he clamped a large, knowing hand over her mouth and pushed her up against the wall.

Out came the knife. His pocket secret.

"We have chosen our council!" came the distant voice of the Professor. "Let the swearing commence!"

Wally snarled. The moment was sweet beyond expectation. He felt possessed by a power that reached back to the very bottom of a deep well, to a time before he knew, to the kernel of the flame, to the standing stone pit. He released his hand from her mouth to shift the knife to her neck.

"Bloody hell!" she gasped. "Wally, wha—?"

The crowd outside the door booed with derision. "Bloody hell" wasn't good enough for them. Wally knew what would work.

"Fuck you!" he shouted, loosening the belt of his drop-your-trousers and pushing forward, through the snapping haze of his delirium. "Fuck you, you piss-elegant, lah-di-dah minge, you bitch!"

A cheer went up. Some applause that degenerated into rhythmic handclapping.

He knew exactly where every part of her was as if he could see her. His fingers navigated her underwear and found her already moist with fear. He teased her flesh—tickle, tickle—in and around her opening until he could stand it no longer. Suddenly, the overture was over, the curtain went up, his cock thrust inside her and they both gasped. He lowered the blade from her neck, there was no need to silence her any more. He had her on his other knife.

"You bastard!" she moaned. "You fucking low-life, scum bastard, Wally Greene!"

"That's it," he muttered. "Let it all out, now."

And so the cursing breached like surf, like the sucking chatter of pebbles drawn back before the next wave crashed.

Tomorrow!! He could feel her breath, full, warm, on his face. Oh, how he was smiling, spinning, swearing in the heat. Cheers and sparking vision surrounded him as his rhythm took hold. He fancied he could hear encouragement. Jeering voices. Persistently, he drove into her.

...and tomorrow!! His cheek hit a broom handle. An elbow collided with a papier-mâché sculpture. They bumped into something soft, something solid, they spilled on the floor. A smell of turpentine.

...and tomorrow!! Through a gaping hole in his psyche, Wally pushed himself inside-out and back-to-front: a pitiable figure, inconsequential and unattractive made strong, all powerful, all lost, for a moment. This was the moment. He would take it and treasure it always.

Numb to any sense of outrage, his anger simply flowed out of him and manifested into a pulsing woman beneath him, sordid and treacherous. A devil perched on his central cortex, anaesthetizing anything with which it came into contact, daring him to stop, which he couldn't, for that would be to admit what he was doing.

...out, out, brief candle ...

Then in the midst of the storm, came a silver moment of indescribable beauty, where time slowed, stopped. A beryl lotus bloomed a thousand petals. A distant lilt of a flute. Seed fell. One moment of bliss. Then gone.

...damned spot ...

It was all over. Wally rapped on the door and asked, begged, pleaded to be let out.

"Granted!"

The door was opened and light flooded into the oubliette, blinding and real. They were lined up outside, knowing eyes in every face. Wally staggered out, drenched in perspiration, grinning, buckling his trousers back up.

Then Peggy emerged. She straightened her neck like a giraffe and walked almost elegantly past him without a glance, her heels clicking like a metronome as she walked away, walked away, walked away down the corridor. Gone. All Wally was left with was a faint prickling on the roof of his mouth and the disquieting scent of a vaginal broth on his hands.

Act IV

17

"Fu-uck-ing No-or-a!"

The beeping of the bedside alarm clock is insistent, intrusive, violent. Wally fumbles for the snooze button but his hand is asleep; there's no feeling in it whatsoever; it's just a useless flapping appendage, bristling with pins and needles. Finally, by clutching the contraption with two hands and using his chin, he is able to put an end to the squawking timepiece. He flops back onto bed, groans as his world shudders, realigns himself with this new form of consciousness and the late nineteen-eighties. Vancouver. Grey light forces its way through the fissures of his eyes.

Everything hurts in this mewling world. Remnants of his dreams skitter into the shadows of memory, peeking round corners and jeering at him. Nothing specific, just a vague sense of malaise. His temple throbs, his ribcage aches. He lies there, acclimatizing, until his morning erection slackens.

Georgia rolls over beside him, the scent of her hair couples with the rancid dew of sleep. He pushes her away.

In the bathroom, he runs warm water over his hand to try to bring some feeling back into it. He looks in the mirror and is confronted with the image of a blood red handprint across his chest. There it is, right in the middle of the broad, white expanse of flesh, symmetrically placed between his nipples. It's where he slept on his arm, cutting off the circulation, quite explicable, but it has the appearance of something more sinister.

He showers. The handprint has faded by the time he's finished, just a ghostly pink smudge remains. He lathers up to trim the edges of his beard.

Georgia appears, leaning against the bathroom door. "You're up early," she says, from the depths of her terry cloth bathrobe. "Don't tell me you have something to do."

"I thought I might pop down to the workshop. Have a little think about the play before the production meeting this morning."

"Have a little smoke, too?"

"No." He pauses mid-shave to show her the most honest eyes he can muster via the mirror, even though she'd read his intent accurately. "No."

"Just asking," she says lightly, giving him a playful slap on his towel-draped butt as she crosses behind him to the toilet. She hikes up her robe and squats. "I never know with you."

"Please, I'm shaving."

Georgia holds a finger to her lips for silence as she pees noisily. Wally finishes up in three strokes.

After a strong cup of tea, he takes the Fourth Avenue route to the workshop. It's a bright, late autumnal morning and his mood is chipper. He lets himself in, quietly, so as not to wake Ned.

But there is no Ned to wake. Neither is there any dog. All his belongings have gone, too. No signs left, save for a dirty spoon in the sink and a few stray dog hairs on Wally's chair.

He sits, tries to read his copy of the script, but can't focus. Has Peggy died finally? And has Ned, consequently, moved back home? Or has he just moved on to some other digs? There's one way to find out, thinks Wally, putting his coat back on: go visit Peggy. Dare he? He needs to see her anyway, he reasons, he's been putting it off too long. Deep down, Wally is in turmoil. Not smoking doesn't help.

He takes a bus downtown, hops on the SeaBus to the North Shore. It's quiet. Sparsely populated—businessmen and secretaries are going in the opposite direction. He scans a paper someone left on a seat nearby, but his eyes can't take in the meaning of the words.

A world without nicotine is noisy. There's a rhythmic rumble in his ears, of blood coursing through, but not with ease. And the red spots in his peripheral vision have got to stop soon. It's been two weeks, now, not counting the odd one or two he's had on the sly. Surely, if these are withdrawal symptoms, they would have gone by now? Instead, they appear to be getting stronger.

Once across the Burrard Inlet, he hikes up the hill in the sun to the hospice. He's piqued that Georgia called his bluff. There would be no satisfaction now in sneaking a quick smoke. Bugger it. She's robbed him of any guilty pleasure he might have had—she always seems to be one step ahead of him. If behavioural structures are, as he has read somewhere, like houses of the brain, then for Wally, smoking, along with taking other drugs, must be a decrepit Addam's Family mansion, rife with secret passageways and booby traps. And Georgia has the only floor plan. Odds are high that she knows about the pack of emergency cigarettes in his pocket.

St Theresa's Hospice is to his right. He walks along the semi-circular driveway and up the steps to the colonnaded main entrance. Once inside, he is surrounded by tepid hopelessness. An odour of decay runs beneath a layer of industrial disinfectant, barely masked. The ceilings are low, the beige walls are stained and the linoleum underfoot is spongy. A large colour photograph of Bernini's *Ecstasy of Santa Theresa* has pride of place on the greeting wall, above a drinking fountain. The Pope and the Queen share another wall, near a cluster of chocolate vinyl visitor's chairs. Nuns gently waddle through, on their ways to tend or minister to the dying. Despite the brightness of the day outside, the place is so dark that it must be lit by recessed yellowing light along the ceiling. Wally feels suffocated by brown.

"I'm looking for Peggy Ch . . . Margaret McLean," he says to the receptionist. "Mrs Margaret McLean."

"Are you family?"

Wally refuses to answer. He merely looks grim and firms his jaw, which could be misinterpreted as a nod. The name is checked on a rotary file. Then a typewritten list on a clipboard is consulted.

"Room 244D on the second floor."

He is pointed towards a flight of dark stairs that take him to an equally dark corridor that smells of death. On his way, he passes a large fibreglass basket on wheels, filled to the brim with soiled linens: winding sheets, yellowed and choked with sickness, stained and rank.

Room 244 is behind a brown door with a wire-reinforced porthole. White letters on blue plastic stick-on tiles: *A*, *B*, *C* and *D*.

He sees her feet first, around the edge of a grey curtain. Peggy's neat little toes rest atop a cardboard-stiff blanket. The bed is made up, pristine; her feet merely rest upon it, occupying as little space as they can. He is surprised to see her without shoes. He never thought of Peggy as someone who would ever go unshod.

He stops. At the edge of the curtain, unable to continue. He can see a strip of an Oxford-blue Wynciette nightie with lace edging, and he doesn't want to see any more. He no longer wants to see her, talk to her, or ask her why she'd lied to him—*if* she'd lied to him. His presence here suddenly feels dangerous. She's waiting for him, he's sure of it.

The legs are pale, inert, with blue veins bulking in varicose clusters. One foot tilts at a slight angle, as if abandoned. There are fresh, white edges to the nails where they've been recently clipped; one is torn at the edge. Wally imagines some grey penguin nun sitting there, cheerfully wielding the pedicure tools, growing frustrated with the one nail's refusal to acquiesce to the clippers, until she rips the troublesome nail halfway to the quick.

The arrangement of feet looks like something from the prop shop: fake. Wally wonders what he would make these leg-ends from if they were required in a show. Foam rubber around a wooden armature probably. Wax. Plaster. If he felt ambitious, he might carve them out of wood.

They move. A gentle shift, as in sleep, the feet move. A cough from an unseen throat. A cough that signifies consciousness. No longer anonymous, an aura of Pegginess emanates from behind the curtain, and, try as he might, Wally can't stop himself from shaking. Did he wake her up? Just by staring at her feet? He is caught in the act of trespass. He has no business being here. He wants to rush around the curtain, grab a pillow, and, before either of them realize, smother her. Push down on her cancerous face, squash her skull with all his strength until all movement, all wobbling pedicures, all troublesome scratching has ceased. He can see it all happening; he watches himself go through with it, right up to the police bursting in and clapping cold handcuffs around his wrists as they wrest the pillow from his grasp. His saliva tastes warm. He didn't realize it before, but now he knows: every cell in his body yearns for the End of Peggy. And he so wants to be the cause.

The pressure on his ribcage returns. The mark left by his hand in the centre of his chest burns, as if he were back in his bed again, asleep. A constriction of the heart, accompanied by a sickening self-loathing and fear of what he might do, his potential. He sucks on his dental plate. Willing himself to stop, his knee shakes with the effort.

"Hello?" Peggy's voice wafts, weak but identifiable from the other side of the screen. "Who's there?" Then she coughs again, a spongy singing cough.

Holding his breath, Wally leaves the room, backwards, sideways, along the wall, down the shadows of the corridor. He's suddenly damp with sweat. It's not until he's outside again that his pulse begins to descend and he sucks in great lungfuls of air.

The sky is enormous, and there's a crimson-grey glow to a mass of bulbous, deformed clouds. A seagull circles overhead, and for a moment, he too feels high up, vertiginous. To stop the shaking, he finds a bench in a thin garden overlooking the Burrard Inlet, sits and holds his chin with his hand, a steadying gesture that could be misinterpreted as musing. He stares out to sea at a few boats that flag the bay. Further out, beyond the mist-shrugged waters, he can just make out the teal-blue shadows of the coastline. He smells something burning.

He could have killed her. He wanted it. Not so much to put an end to her existence, but rather, in some peculiar way, to provoke his own. And now he's furious with himself that he did neither.

The sepia tones of the hospice are now replaced with the spectrum of nature. It's all too vivid to endure: the Canadian red of a mailbox to his left twinning with a clump of deciduous boughs amid the dark evergreen to his right. A school bus rolls by. Autumn leaves run underfoot. Orange-browns, deep crimsons, and brilliant yellows, like a kaleidoscopic jigsaw puzzle, all shoved together, overlapping, tessellating. He smears some mud from his shoe onto a leaf, fearful of the presence of madness, embarrassed at his escape from the hospice, like a vole scuttling along the wainscotting. He doesn't understand how he got here. Things used to be so simple, back in the days when he was just the bad guy. Damn Peggy and her cough.

Slowly, his world calms. A cloud dilutes the intensity of the morning sun and the colours around him dim. It grows cold.

Just before he gets up to leave, he stubs out his cigarette with his heel against the concrete surround of the bench. He stares at the butt, confused. The gold band identifier, the stripe of carbon ash, the yellow-brown blemish like a tiger's eye where he must have sucked it through the filter, the squashed oval tube that he must have held between his fingers. Vague, like a dream escaping. He is unable to remember even having lit the bloody thing.

The sound of Peggy's cough sticks in Wally's ears like so much wax. At the production meeting, a few hours later, he sits with a dozen others in the otherwise empty Phoenix bar, discussing deadlines and budgets. All he can think of is that ripped toenail, the sleepy clearing of her throat, and his sudden, murderous urge. Is he that volatile? That dangerous? It is as if he harbours chaos in his spleen; one mistaken move could unleash the entire vent. Throughout the meeting, Georgia keeps eyeing him with suspicion—and the empty chair beside him.

"Let's look at the maquette, shall we?" suggests Dickie Flemming, the director. "As you can see, Sasha and I have gone for the postmodern look, almost sterile, with lots of clean lines."

Sasha, the designer, and Dickie produce a scale model of the set. It looks like a reproduction of the classic Elizabethan Globe Theatre, but made out of shiny black plastic, which they hope will be built out of black obsidian glass when it comes to the real version. They pore over their model, spouting such phrases as "Jacobean anachronism" and "esoteric diaspora of culture" which would normally grab Wally's funny bone and make him guffaw out loud, but today leave him cold. Even when panels slide back, flats revolve, and Birnam Wood descends from the flies on an eccentric cantilever, he remains unmoved.

"Here, let's look at the opening scene." Dickie is beside himself with cleverness. "The three witches, right?"

He pulls out a pack of cigarettes, lights one, and puffs into a little pink rubber tube sticking out the back of the maquette. Wisps of smoke rise through cracks in the stage floor. Wally can taste the nicotine from where he's sitting. His lungs almost rush out of his mouth to grab the cigarette out of the director's hand.

On the model, a miniature trap door falls away and three yellow plastic cowboy figurines rise jerkily through the blue mist. One of them wobbles and falls over.

"You have to imagine bony hag fingers emerging from the fog," garbles Sasha, righting the figurine. "But you get the general idea."

"Brilliant," mutters Georgia, hypocritically.

"Very *Star Wars*," agrees the Costume Designer. "Complex."

Wally grunts, unimpressed. Sasha and Dickie often come up with such over-ambitious designs that invariably end up being compromised when the real building starts. But until their dream gets burst, they have their automated maquette which, in Wally's view, looks like a flashy shoebox harbouring a mechanical chrysanthemum and a dozen dancing miniature elephants brandishing kitchen knives. If Birnam Wood descending from the flies doesn't damage the actors, then the smoking ha-ha will surely finish them off. Murderous. Suddenly, he can no longer contain himself.

"Fucking smoke it if you're going to!" he yells, his voice charging out of nowhere. "Don't waste it, you big ninny!"

Hiccup.

"Wally's just quit smoking again," explains Georgia, after the pause. "I think your Players Light fog machine set him off."

Dickie swiftly stubs out the offending cigarette in an ashtray. They resume the meeting, collectively, as if nothing had happened . . . perhaps at a slightly faster pace.

And so the Production Manager grumbles about costing, the Costume Designer grumbles about deadlines, and Wally mouths his usual grumble about sourcing materials, but his heart isn't in it. Dickie wants all the weapons to be authentic—whether he means authentic period or authentic practical is unclear. And there's a morgue's load of body parts needed, including a replica of an actor's head that will require a live casting. Take an impression of Peggy's face from the inside of a hospital pillow . . .

"The budget's too small."

"We don't have enough time."

"We'll have to hire some extra jobbers."

Georgia, presiding as both Co-Artistic Director of the theatre and lead actor in this production, fields the complaints with her own brand of soothing ointment.

"It's a high bar, Dickie," she says, as if actually imparting real knowledge. "But if we all work hard and knuckle down, we should be able to clear it."

"But obsidian glass, Georgia?" whines the Production Manager. "Where are we going to find enough black obsidian glass to cover this set for under two thousand dollars?"

"We'll fake it. Use MacTac on chipboard." She smiles, grimly. "This is theatre, Don. It's not supposed to be real."

"Exactly," pipes in Dickie, aware that his directing of the project, as always, falls under a dastardly form of grandmotherly stewardship by Georgia. The Phoenix is their shared responsibility, their shared torture.

The meeting continues slowly. Wally wonders where Ned has got to. This show isn't small and he's going to need help, regardless of family crises, regardless of paternity issues, regardless of drug-smashed benders, regardless of him wanting to murder his mother on her deathbed. Where the hell has the lad got to?

"Well, that's about it, people," says Dickie eventually, reasserting his authority for the final few moments of the meeting. "Same time, same place, next week."

The production crew disbands, forming into smaller clumps for serious chats over blueprints or social clusters trying to decide where to go for a quick lunch. Georgia remains seated, idly flipping through her copy of the script, an old Signet edition. She has a curious, sad look upon her face as her eyeballs jerk across the page. As Wally wanders over, she puts down the text and sighs.

"They're using the same design they used for *Coriolanus* in Saskatchewan two years ago," she says. "It didn't work then. It's not going to work now."

"A bit Egyptian," agrees Wally. "But it has its good points. I liked the yellow cowboys."

"The costumes are all Edwardian," she says with a sneer, "except for the dream sequence, which is a Chinese Lion Dance. Most of the time I'll either look like Chung Ling Soo after the accident, or Lady Bracknell."

"A bit experimental for Shakespeare, then?"

"Hmm."

"Why don't you put your foot down? Tell them it won't do?

"She laughs in a loose, unguarded way that tells him his suggestion is impossible no matter how much she'd like to follow it. Dickie Flemming is a necessary evil; she's stuck with him. She can't direct herself.

"And you'll never guess who we've had to cast as my stupid husband," she sighs, shaking her head. "Tony-bloody-Lumpkin, the hyperventilating moron."

Wally glares at her, saunters off towards the door, past the maquette, which still has a sniff of cigarette smoke about it. A red spark zips in his peripheral vision.

"So where's that Ned of yours?" shouts Georgia when he reaches the threshold. "What am I paying him for? Has he lost interest in us already? Or have you lost control of him, too?"

"Actually," Wally replies, "I believe he's now on a municipal grant program. You're not losing a penny."

She scowls at him, her eyes probing into his, trying to discern the truth of the matter. But Wally's gambit accusing her of being cheap acts as a shield. His trip to Saint Theresa's stays a secret.

"If you want me, I'll be at the workshop," he says, breezily. "Welding a bunch of authentic swords and daggers."

18

"Did I ever tell you that you play like a woman?"

Xander stares at the ceiling, absents himself, waits for the tirade to be over. It's getting dark outside, his session will soon be over. Yes, Stadjykk has told him before that he plays like a woman. It has something to do with his bony fingers—meticulous hammers instead of splashing chisels. Feminine instead of masculine, as if there really was such a distinction.

"Needlework!" Stadjykk moans. "You're typing again!"

Xander says nothing. With his right hand, he worries his nipple ring through his shirt. Ned almost chewed him raw last night. It's still very sensitive, like an electric stiletto teasing his breast, warm and sharp. It reminds him of Ned's piercing. The first time he clapped eyes on *that*, the bottom fell out of his world, an ocean roared through his brain, and he quite literally fell to his knees, mouth open, blatant.

"I know little old women who play the zither like you play piano. They end up cold and lonely, dying in attics." Stadjykk huffs out of his chair, then slouches, hands in his pockets and traces a pattern in the carpet with his foot. "Try the passage again with no *rubato*, and perform the dynamics strictly on the mark."

Xander spins back to the keyboard and works through the Rachmaninoff passage again, as requested, but his mind is elsewhere. He smiles, running his tongue around the inside of his teeth, tickling the ivory memories of Ned.

"See? Isn't that better?" Stadjykk shrugs, hands raised. "So much better when you're cruel. There's nothing wrong with playing like a woman, just so long as you're ready to crush my heart." He runs his hand through his hair, shakily. "Otherwise I want to . . ."

He stops, mid-sentence, a bead of sweat glistens on his upper lip. And, without finishing his thought, he strides from the room. The bathroom door slams.

This is not new behaviour for Stadjykk, but neither is it common, this sudden evacuation. It happens once or twice a month. Xander will suddenly be alone, while Stadjykk recollects himself in the washroom. Nothing is ever said when he returns, but the unspoken assumption is that it's a medical condition. Today, for the first time, Xander wonders if it isn't more psychological. Or sexual.

But then, Xander's been getting a lot of action, lately, so he may be projecting his own hyper-excited state onto his surroundings. It didn't take him long to surmount his fear of triggering a seizure before trying out Ned's new-fangled drug from Montreal. He figured that any drug that had the nickname "ecstasy" had to have something going for it. It did. Within seconds, he was plunged into a singing marzipan landscape. It's a full-body aphrodisiac, kissing cousin to LSD, but with a more solid, less crazy vibration. "Clean" is the word that everybody is using. "Really, really clean," said Roxie on her first hit. "Juicy," said Juan. "Oh my God," said Xander as the syringe came out, and he fell, buzzing wet, into Ned's arms, where he has been ever since.

Sex with Ned. It isn't so much a shared experience as it is a competitive one. It certainly isn't gentle. Over the past moon or so, Xander has amassed bruises, bite marks, grazes and carpet burns all over his body, which he sports like trophies. Each one tingles with a secret story. His time spent in the sack with Ned is like a wrestling match with an orgasm occasionally thrown in to mark the end of a bout. If Xander's honest, he knows that his ardour, or at least his enthusiasm, is not reciprocated. Ned would gainsay any emotional involvement and blame it on the drugs. Under their influence, he is able to induce a euphoria that allows him to horse around with his roughhouse version of homosex. There's no doubt in Xander's mind that without the Ecstasy there would be nothing.

"Isn't there another way to do this, other than making a hole in my arm?"

"You can snort it, but it's not as much fun."

"Can you play doctor for me? I'm not very good at this."

"Hang on."

Which got him close enough to lean against, to smell his sweat and subsequently to dive into. That first time, in his father's workshop, the sex happened more through momentum than desire; it was difficult to tell, what with the drug laughing through their systems. When it progressed to rolling around on the floor, mouthlocked, they had to shut the dog in the washroom, to stop it from attacking Xander.

"It's OK," drawled Ned, staggering back from the door, jeans popped and open, yawning, boots singing along the concrete. "She's just defending her territory. Where were we?"

Incest. The word hisses through Xander's mind, delicious, forbidden. It carries anger with it. A cold anger, that keeps his mouth shut and his suspicion of fraternity a secret. Ned knows nothing more than what's always been there for everyone to see: family friends, shared history.

Now shared needles. Blood brothers.

Stadjykk is still in the washroom, so Xander starts playing his Bach prelude and fugue from *The Well-Tempered Clavier*, the piece with which he ends his sessions. He wants to get back to the party going on down the hallway in 612. Unattended, he indulges the sustain pedal, smirking joyfully at his transgression. Towards the last few measures, he eases back on his right foot as he feels Stadjykk return and hover behind him. A hand pushes down on his shoulder to correct his posture.

"Stop. Please."

Xander's never heard this tone from Stadjykk before. He pulls away from the keyboard. The hand stays on his shoulder, but it's no longer correcting posture. It feels forgotten.

"You must go now. I'm sorry."

Xander nods, absorbing this new strangeness into a mundane gesture. He collects his music and stuffs it into his bag. On the side table, he notices a collection of Debussy. Stadjykk hates Debussy; he calls it thin and sugary.

"Is anything wrong? Did I . . . ?"

"No. Yes." He coughs uncertainly. "A family tragedy. I'm sorry. It's nothing, we weren't very close, but still . . ."

"I'm sorry."

Stadjykk grunts, not even wasting breath by calling him a liar, dismissing him as one dismisses a servant. He turns his back on Xander and casually picks up the Debussy as if it was a magazine in a waiting room, then tosses it back down with disgust. He has a forceful rectitude that might be culture, might be seniority, or might be nothing more than arrogance. Whichever, the room is now impossible to share. There always were just too many gilt-framed prints on the walls, gathering dust. Too many dead composers pressed between the pages of manuscript collections.

Xander leaves, his smirk coagulating on his face.

Down the hall to 612, where Ned is holding court over a line of spoons on the coffee table. Roxie plays nursing assistant with a fresh bag of 100cc syringes, tearing off strips of masking tape and labelling each rig for each participant. The ritual is well-attended with three neophytes sitting wide-eyed and expectant on the couch —Xander recognizes them from the scene. Two Goths and a weekend punk.

"I guess you'll be wanting a hit too, eh?" asks Ned. "Or shall we save ours for later?"

"Later," agrees Xander, cool. He perches on the arm of the couch and gives Roxie a peck on her neck. "Hi, bubba."

"Maybe just a little one now, though?" Ned cajoles. "Just to keep these losers company?"

"Sure. Whatever." Xander glances around. "Where's Juan?"

"At work," mutters Roxie. "Graveyard shift."

Ned looks up from doling out the crystals and gives Roxie a meaningful wink. His lip curls *à la* Billy Idol. The inference is clear: with Juan out of the way, he intends to play the field. Roxie is going to experience the Prince Albert. Xander wishes he could feel jealousy, but he can't. Part of Ned's attraction is his rogue persona; so to be possessive would be not only pointless, but also hypocritical.

"Anyone fancy some tea?" Xander asks, skipping to the kitchenette. "I'll put the kettle on."

"Got any beer?" bleats one of the Goths, hopefully.

Xander scowls. "It's not," he says emphatically, like a teacher, warning of a possible transgression. "It's . . . Not . . . My . . . House."

When he turns on the gas burner, a couple of cockroaches pop in the flame. Others scurry erratically to safety. It isn't the first time that Xander wonders what it would be like living under constant threat of death from one's hosts. Always running for one's life when the lights come on. Was there ever any satisfaction in it? Or was it as unfathomable an existence as his own?

His own. On the surface, he has everything he has ever wanted. His own place. Fashionable, smart friends. Sex with the most desirable outlaw in town. Designer drugs. A delicious, incestuous secret. Freedom. His own.

But it all seems so much pointless running around. None of it is real, in that it could all evaporate in the wink of an eye across a coffee table. Someone could turn on the gas, and he would pop.

"Xander! Come and get it!" yells Roxie.

Is it his imagination, or can he taste the drug in the back of his throat merely through anticipation? A studious silence emanates from the other room as the darts players line up their shots. Then comes Ned's tuneless whistle as he blows on his vein. A laugh of recognition. Otis Redding blares from the stereo.

Xander waits until the kettle boils and he has a bag of herbal tea brewing in his cup before he saunters back in. Around the table, it's a parental horrorshow. One of the Goths, using a skull headscarf for a tourniquet, is having trouble hitting the vein. Blood trickles from at least three bloated sites as he prods and pokes around the inside of his elbow. Nobody else is in a position to help. Roxie and Ned are fucking in slow motion on the carpet, and the other two members of the party are just sitting, looking gormless, teeth snapping, eyeballs stuttering in their sockets in time to the beat of the music.

A full syringe marked with an *X* lies on the table. Xander, nursing his cup of tea, saunters right past it, picks up his knapsack and walks out. He leaves the apartment door open behind him, in some vague hope that the noise will somehow reach Juan, putting in his graveyard shift on the other side of town.

Try a little tenderness . . .

He takes the old wooden staircase down to his bachelor oasis on the third floor. He cradles his cup of tea in his palms, as if he were an avatar of Molech or Asherah, carrying his bowl of goat's blood from one chamber to the next. The surface of the tea swirls, a scent of chamomile rises. He gains strength from his independence; he doesn't see a role for himself in the orgy taking place on the sixth floor. His days with Ned are numbered, if not already done.

Just over a month. That was fast.

The superintendent is standing at his door, waiting for him

when he arrives. A grizzled, drawn man, whose posture suggests that he's hanging from a meat hook.

"You got a dog in there?"

"It's not mine."

"No pets. It's in the lease. No pets. Dogs is pets."

He hands Xander the remnants of his mail. A letter from Welfare with one corner of the envelope chewed off, still wet.

"I was just doin' the deliverin'," explains the super, spittle glistening on his chin. "Almost bit my bloody hand off."

"I'll take care of it," says Xander, slipping his key into the lock and nodding politely. "It's gone. Dog pound. OK?"

"You do that, buddy." He wipes his mouth, then shuffles away down the corridor. "No pets or aquariums. I could give you your thirty days right now if I wanted."

Xander sighs. The letter from Welfare isn't too damaged, thank God. He can still read the date and time for his appointment: next Wednesday at 14:00 hours. That bloody dog must have gotten territorial when the super had shoved the mail under the door. What a world! He takes a sip of calming tea before letting himself in.

He is greeted by chaos. The dog has not only been defending the door, but has also, it appears, been on a psycho bender throughout the apartment. Feathers float in the air, mixing with the warm stink of dog piss. Chewed bits of paper are strewn all over the floor. A telephone directory has tooth scars all down one side; one corner is obliterated mush. A small hardcover book of poems by Whitman has lost its spine, the orange linen exhausted from the battle. With mounting anger, Xander surveys the damage. The bowl of dry dog-food is upturned in the washroom, growing soggy in a puddle of water. The meds and cough syrups he'd kept on the toilet tank are scattered all over the tiles.

"All right, where the fuck are you?"

He can hear faint shuffles, but it's hard to tell where they're coming from. Xander divests himself of his knapsack, his cup, and his coat to start the search. He begins with the Murphy bed that takes up most of the room, now a crazy ruin of chewed bedding and laundry. The dog isn't on it, or in it, or under it. Neither is it in the little kitchen area, nor anywhere in the bathroom. Eventually, he finds the bitch, cowering, on his boots and shoes in the closet, back legs scrabbling with guilt over the Doc Martens.

"Right. Out."

Xander hauls the dog by the collar and yanks it out of the closet. Its hindquarters lock the moment it realizes eviction is in order. Out into the corridor.

"You, my friend," says Xander, snout to snout, "You. Are. History."

They stumble up three flights of stairs, Schtupitt dragged by the collar. Xander takes it at a speedy clip to fool the animal into thinking this is exercise. There are a couple of shies at the sharp turns of the corkscrew, but Xander isn't having any nonsense. Down the hall to the open door of 612 and Otis is onto a new song.

I can't get no satisfaction . . .

"Hey, Ned!" Xander bowls the dog into the room, where it picks up the scent of its master locked in apparent mortal combat on the floor, and bounds over to join the battle. "Keep the fucking bitch out of my stuff, OK?"

And he storms out, slamming the door behind him.

Nobody of worth is at the old boat, tonight. It's not full moon. It's much too early, it's only just turned dusk. Worse, it's a weeknight, drizzling, and the few cruising guys furtively shifting through the shadows of the burned-out husk have a sad, quotidian aura to them, as if the boredom of their other lives has seeped into this one. Satyr-man is not there, nor anyone else with a speck of vitality. Xander is relieved. He really only needs the air.

The possibility, however, of a quick, sordid dalliance appears in the parking lot beneath the bridge. A white Camaro pulls in with a towheaded jock behind the wheel. A red-sleeved elbow juts from the open window; a cigarette calls attention to the wait. Xander stares for a while, his hands nonchalantly thumbed into his pockets, until he is certain that his stare and intent is returned. Then he saunters slowly over.

"Been waiting long?"

"Could be. You a punker?"

"What do you think?"

"Cool. Hop in, dude."

The guy has a lazy eye, and a shiny, soft face like he's been in a fight recently. There is a cheap aroma of plastic seats, of cologne, and of pot. A wedding garter hangs on the rear-view mirror. Xander grins. Oh, it is all so deliciously sordid.

He scoots around to the passenger side, patting the Camaro's muscle-striped hood as he goes. This should take his mind off Ned and Roxie: a trip with a Duke of Hazzard, an episode of *Starsky & Hutch*, or Macmillan *sans* Wife, the British Columbian version, that is, which is at least twice removed from the original, but twice as desperate to make an impression. He just hopes he won't have to walk home from Burnaby.

"Alex! Alexander-fucking-Greene!"

The voice is coming from the Aquatic Centre, up the slope by the street. It's Ned.

"Yes, you, you shit! Hey!" He's panting, his breath coming in bursts of steam from running. Ten paces behind him is Roxie, carrying the dog in her arms. "Hey, you! What the fuck?"

"Ned . . . what?"

Xander turns as Ned bears down on him. He's screaming. His face is white and blue in the streetlight. Rigid.

"What's wrong with my fucking dog, man! What have you done to my dog!"

In a few strides, he's within range. Without warning, Ned swings his head back, then violently snaps it forward. There is a sharp crack of skull against skull. At much the same time, Xander feels a force in the solar plexus, his feet slip, jolt away from beneath him and the car's silver hubcap seems to defy gravity and swivel up like an eccentric frisbee to whack him in the face. Something smells warm in the back of his throat. Salty. A familiar taste.

"Ned, *don't!*" comes Roxie's distant voice. "You said . . ."

With a frightened squeal, the Camaro takes off in a stink of exhaust and rubber, so close to Xander that he's certain he's been run over. He hears the sound of the car door flapping like a porch screen in a thunderstorm. Goodnight, John-boy.

Xander tries to stand up, but is too woozy to be successful. He wonders what it is about the dog. It's hanging in Roxie's arms, limp, paws hanging. What was wrong with the dog?

"Is it . . . is it dead?"

"What?"

"Is your dog dead?"

Ned explodes again. "Dead? Fuck no! She's poisoned!" He shoves an open bottle of pills at Xander. Dilantin. A couple of orange-and-white capsules scatter. "She's stoned on your fucking seizure meds, man! What the fuck were you thinking?"

"I . . . I don't . . . I'm sorry."

Where had he left them? On the back of the toilet. He thought they'd been safe there.

"Sorry isn't fucking good enough!"

And then it hits. The energy swells as the seizure takes its victim. Xander's knees buckle and he's back pushing his cheek into the concrete. Jolts run down his spine, but it's like never before. For the first time, he can't tell if it's epilepsy working its way out, or Ned, working his way in.

His head shudders, harbouring tightness and incomprehension. It runs all the way along his body: straining, straining, waiting for something to snap.

Then, suddenly, a boot catches him in his stomach and he lets go, releases the tension. The taste of bile and day-old N-methyl-3, 4-methylenedioxyphenylisopropylamine floods into his mouth. The tarmac pulls him close, welcomes him to the soft and deep end of the pool, down, down. Happy. Wet. Buzzing. He understands, now.

He's found the part of himself that cares.

19

The price for one moment's bliss beneath the stage of the Whitehall Theatre was exacted insidiously. It cost Wally his perspective and he paid for it in ever-larger installments. No longer could he swim at the edges of the cesspool, occasionally pulling himself out of the waters whenever he had a convenient excuse or when he felt the moral current was just a bit too dodgy for him. Now he was fully-fledged pond scum, up to his neck in it, no longer an innocent.

"You really showed her, Wally, matey!"

"Those posh birds are always the biggest sluts, aren't they?"

"Bloody delicious," agreed Wally, sighing. "A slice of heaven."

The Professor gave a cold nod and walked away down the hall, with a deliberate, measured stride. There was implicit approval in every step. Wally had, somehow, passed a test and was now part of the fold. Nothing had changed on the surface, but on the inside, Wally felt a masonic connection with a new brotherhood. And it wasn't just red-blooded men who were members of this club, nor was it merely about sex. It was a way of looking at the world as a series of pleasures that must be taken by force if necessary. Georgia was a member. As was Monty. Boo wasn't. And neither was Peggy. Travelling on a bus, or on a train, Wally could look at a person's face —male, female, child or crone—and he could tell immediately who belonged and who didn't. One glance at the way their lips tightened with disillusionment, or the way their noses turned in expectation, and he recognized the difference between those who knew and those who were blissfully unaware.

Peggys and Wallys. The world was now divided. Charitably, Wally was glad Peggy had managed to get away to Canada. Perhaps things were different over there.

For London, as Wally knew, had never been a place to settle down, much less to raise a family. It was always too much of a whirlpool for most people to hold onto anything solid enough or for long enough to build a homestead. Attempts, sometimes successful, had been made over the centuries with the help of bricks, stones, walls and fences, much money and social clout. Pockets of such resistance still peppered the city but, by and large, the population was feckless. London was a magnet for those who'd shucked their families and wished to strike out on their own: selfish, opportunistic, adventurous and peripatetic souls. Roger Two was the only person Wally knew who regularly saw his parents and was thus considered strange.

"They're just landlords, really," was the disclaimer. "Landlords I happen to be related to. That's all."

Everyone else was a single agent, responsible to none. And even though they were married, Wally and Georgia were hardly a couple in the traditional, innocent sense. They were companions in expediency, each looking after their own needs first. The night after the shenanigans with Peggy in the oubliette, Wally came home and demanded his conjugal rights from Georgia. He took her by the neck and dragged her down, impaled her rudely. She, surprised, acquiesced, laughing, spitting. When it was done, Wally felt filthy strong.

The times changed. They moved out of the apartment on the Crescent, Christmas 1963, and into a little mews house off the Fulham Road. They were smaller, but more exclusive digs, with a large roof garden and a double garage. The move happened as if by abandonment; Georgia was spending seven months of the year on tour and Wally was retreating more and more to his little hole in

Islington. The old apartment started to get packed away into crates almost before he noticed, certainly before he was told.

"Remember my damned brother?" explained Georgia. "He's suddenly decided he wants to go to the London School of Economics. Mom and Pip said he could have this place."

"I didn't know you had a brother."

"Oh, didn't you meet him once? I thought you had." She made a face. "He's a Democrat, so he's a bit of an embarrassment to the family. He's also a jock."

From her tone, being a jock was obviously far worse than being a Democrat. Neither term meant anything to Wally, so he couldn't tell if he was looking forward to meeting this damned brother or not. He considered it progress to finally make contact with anyone from the Brandt family, since Georgia had always kept them distant, never talked about them, deftly skipped around the topic whenever it was raised in conversation. It was only with the approaching reality of the brother's arrival that Wally realized how subtly he'd been manipulated into not being more than merely curious about the infamous Boston Brandts for all this time.

He knew of Mom and Pop, Pip, Pup, whatever the term of endearment for the father was. They were the ever-present shadow across the cheque book, the unseen benefactors who (less and less, now that Georgia was a rising force of her own) had paid for everything through Georgia's trust fund. Wally had constructed a mythic version of these American parents, all sepia-print mansions and cattle-ranch Stetson hats. Mom, he decided, was a fading antebellum beauty who played exquisite piano nocturnes in an overstuffed parlour, whilst Pip was a bellicose industrialist with great bulging bags of silver dollars in his fists. Sometimes, when he indulged in this fantasy in front of Georgia, she'd laugh at his assumptions, but she'd never correct him. No photographs existed to prove him wrong.

And for a while, it looked as if Wally would never even meet the brother. There were three or four phone calls, always taken by

Georgia. There were two luncheon engagements that were cancelled due to scheduling problems. Finally, as if by accident, James Brandt, Wally's damned brother-in-law, arrived at the Crescent apartment on the very last day, mere hours before the moving van. He wore a cashmere coat, fur hat, and Italian shoes. He shared Georgia's intense good looks and poise, but one look at his broad, open face, and Wally knew that London was going to eat him alive.

Georgia embraced her brother with the briefest of emotion. There was an obligatory American hug, during which she adroitly spun him round and shoved him off to the next in the receiving line.

"Hi, you must be Wally. I'm James. Jimmy. Actually, we met after the opening night of *Our Town*, but I doubt you remember." He extended a hand like an oar, which grasped Wally's own in a hearty shake. "Congratulations, old man."

"How do you do?" muttered Wally, vaguely remembering the American lad from the Golden Hart. "Georgia didn't tell me she had a brother."

"Oh-hoh, didn't she!" laughed James, his square jaw barely moving. "I'm not surprised, no sir. She's a crafty one, is old sis. Just think, she never said a pip about you!"

"I'm sure."

"Planning any kids?" James then asked, following a predictable social script. "The matriarchs would love that, wouldn't they, Georgie?"

"If ever I have child, abortive be it," sang Georgia, sitting atop a packing crate, her legs bashing out a tattoo on the pine wood.

"That's not exactly what that quote means," mumbled Wally, intrigued at the way Georgia had donned the persona of a six-year-old. Then, louder, he picked up on the tantalizing reference. "Matriarchs? Which matriarchs would that be, then, James? They're in Boston, right? Would these be maiden aunts or grandmother matriarchs?"

James looked awkward as Georgia stilled her beating legs. The room became close. Wally wondered if Boston was the correct city;

he was certain that it was. Or, perhaps they were just known as the "Boston Brandts" because they'd made their fortune in Boston. Or perhaps "Boston" was an adjective meaning very, very rich. One thing he was sure of: he'd fallen headlong into another assumption pothole.

"Georgie didn't tell you . . . ?" James started, flushing.

"No, I didn't." Georgia jumped into the ring, businesslike. "And neither will you, dearest brother, if you know what's good for you. Come on, Wally, give me a hand with this crate. The movers will be here any minute."

But Wally, his antennae raised, wasn't going to be diverted that easily. He rooted his hands into a knot across his chest. "What wasn't I told, then?" he demanded. "Oh, wife of mine?"

She stared at him with a certain pride at his audacity, at his testosterone outranking her evasiveness. She shrugged, as if it was all some unnecessary fuss, something she was going to come round to eventually.

"The Boston Brandts," she said, lightly, "are not from Boston. We're from Long Island, New York, where we have property inherited from our grandparents who came from a long line of Dutch tinkers and gallipots. Mom and Pip—Phillipa—they're the matriarchs. Theirs is a . . . well, they call it a Boston marriage. They're both women. *Capisce?*"

"Georgie and I are adopted," added James.

"Oh." Wally shifted his mental image of the family. Two antebellum beauties, playing exquisite piano duets together, with a couple of mewling bundles left on the doorstep. "Well, that explains a lot."

"James and I are truly brother and sister," she continued, "but Our Father was no more than a prayer at the orphanage. Now you know. Thrilling, isn't it?" Wally looked around the large rooms, at the fancy moldings along the ceiling, the parquet floors, the marble fireplace, the French windows. "All this, too?" He scratched his nose. "They must have been pretty successful tinkers. Pots and pots."

"Yes, pots and pots," laughed Georgia, giving him an utterly fake kiss on the cheek. "And we haven't even come close to burning the bottoms of them. Brandt Pharmaceuticals, darling. When America gets a headache, we scoop the rewards."

"Actually, Georgie," added James, holding up a nervous finger, "you may not want to hear this, but—"

"You're right, I don't." Georgia grabbed Wally by the elbow and fairly dragged him out into the hallway. She slammed the door behind them, then leaned, exhausted against it, her hair straggling across her face. "God, I hate them all. Crazies. Thank God I'm in England."

Wally nodded. He was beginning to understand how, like a barnstorming biplane, the world turned upside-down over the Atlantic. How it twisted in upon itself and made virtues of its vices, repulsion out of its desires, and new lives out of the old. America was where the Europeans ran away to, and Europe was where Americans fled. Loop-the-loop. With each nod of his head, as he stood there, he finally understood things about his wife and her hatred of the other side of the door. It was like finding out about himself.

The mews house was a liberation for them both. They seemed to have more friends there. Georgia maintained it was because the place was cozier, the ceilings were lower, but Wally thought it more to do with location. Fulham Road was more alive than Regent's Park. Carnaby Street, the official mecca of cool, was a few miles away, but its influence was rampant throughout the West End with coffee bars, groovy pubs, and discotheques. Down through Knightsbridge the scene gathered money and prestige, so by the time it hit South Kensington and the select tributaries running down to the river, the hype and the momentum were rich indeed. There were flared trousers, velvet jackets, denim jeans and go-go boots trotting up and down the King's Road. Patchouli oil and long hair on the guys, short bobs and men's shirts on the girls. In the mews house, there were two guest rooms along with a comfortable couch and beanbags. They were rarely unoccupied.

In the bathroom, Wally built a toothbrush tree out of bamboo. It was a fantastic structure with a hundred branches, each end capable of receiving the handle of a toothbrush. Whenever anyone new stayed over, Wally would decorate a branch especially for them—a symbol or a glyph or sometimes an animal. His was an acorn. Georgia's was, at her own suggestion, a snake. She was playing Cleopatra at the time and got immense amusement from telling her friends that every night she stayed in town, she stuck her toothbrush up her asp.

The parties got rowdy and more demanding. Drugs had always been around, but now they got serious. Wally tried LSD a couple of times, but got frightened off when he caught sight of his monkey head in a mirror. Most of the time they smoked reefers of hashish with a smattering of coke. Inevitably, Lady Heroin slunk in. First, she was sampled as a novelty, out in the open lounge, around the coffee table, snorted from silver spoons more used to cocaine than smack. Then, she was smoked on tinfoil, chasing the dragon around the kitchen table. Finally, she was courted in syringes, privately, in the second guest room that was swathed in purple velvet and closest to the bathroom. She added a streak of morbidity to the festivities, an element of decay perfectly suited to offset the naïveté of Mary Quant minidresses and Op-Art.

Wally indulged sporadically. He knew the "one hit and you're hooked" myth was mere popular scare-mongering, but he was also wary of dependence, so he kept his treats to the weekends when he wasn't popping pills. Besides, it was too expensive a habit to develop, enjoyable as it was, and the last thing he wanted was to go crying to Georgia for party favours. He loved the way it caressed his entire body, how it ruffled up his spine to the very tips of his hair, how it squirrelled away through his every crevice, busy, busy, busy, while he lay, inert as a corpse. He loathed the way it sluiced his guts, how it kept him retching over the toilet bowl as sick as a Spanish dog.

The rot set in. To prevent addiction, he'd go on binges: three or four days at a stretch. His hair grew to his shoulders in a wiry mane, loose and abandoned. He sported rimless spectacles and developed a hunched, sagging posture. At work, when he deigned to turn up, they called him Hippy Dippy Wally. The Professor had a chat with him about his absenteeism. Then another about his attitude. Wally couldn't give a flying tinker's galipot. Finally, Wally was directed to Mr. Postlethwaite's office first thing in the morning, which could only mean one thing: he was about to get the chop. He was surprised that it hadn't happened sooner.

"Enter!"

The chair in the office had been moved off the carpet, so Wally had to stand as the Professor lectured on the topic of idiosyncrasy. It was a long, confusing lecture, but the theme was obvious.

"Peccadilloes, my dear Mister Greene," said the Professor, "are, theoretically, minuscule diversions of character that ought to allow one to continue in one's *métier*. When these motes have reached, as they have in your condition, Polyphemus proportions that threaten to usurp your ability to function, either with one eye or with both, open or polluted, then something must be done. Do I make myself understood?"

"Yes."

"Good." The Professor handed Wally a business card. "Go see Mr. Spratt of the Aldwych. I believe he needs some help in constructing the Forest of Arden. All the best, Greene."

He held out both his hands, one slightly forward of the other, in a gesture of finality. Wally knew that if he took those hands in his, he could never return.

"I'm sorry," he blurted, trying to put off the inevitable, perhaps apologize his way back into favour. "I'm sorry, I . . ."

"Don't milk the bull, chum." The Professor was waiting for his handshake. "Consider yourself fortunate and get out of here. Spratt'll look after you. Give my regards to your goodwife."

So they shook, civilly, hands crossed above the desk, right hand to right hand, left hand to left. Their seal was final. Wally left the building, angry, knowing that a door had just been shut, bolted, and barred behind him.

He had thought himself immune. He had thought himself a member of a club, a *permanent* member, with tenure. Then he realized that the name of the club was the International Machiavellian Cut-throat Bastards, and he kicked himself for being such an idiot.

Back home, he locked himself in the garage to sulk. He sat in the driver's seat of Georgia's BMC Mini, daring himself to turn on the ignition and let the carbon monoxide take him. But it was much too melodramatic a gesture for him to seriously contemplate for long. In the end, he merely smashed the rear-view mirror with his fist.

"You're back early," said Wally, looking up from his book. "I thought you were in Nottingham for another two weeks."

"I'm going to have to pop down to the Brighton tea shoppe again," sighed Georgia, dropping her tour bags in the kitchen to free up a hand for the cigarette that dangled from her lips. "That's the second time this season. I won't be able to afford it at this rate."

"Have you tried the hot bath and the bottle of gin?"

"Too late for that, I'm afraid." She took a haul on her smoke with such strength that Wally feared she would turn herself inside-out. "No, it's back to Old Mrs Pickle and her wire brush for me."

"Charming." Wally chuckled to himself. "And I suppose your understudy's a bright young whip, itching to jump into your shoes?"

"Hmmph." She rolled her eyes. "You got that right. And worse. The management's a disapproving Presbyterian, for Chrissakes. What business does he have managing a theatre when he's Presbyterian, I ask you!"

"Nasty," agreed Wally, getting back to his book. "Oh, whose was it, may I ask? Just in case I have to ward off an angry would-be-father while you're down at the seaside."

She blinked at him, dumbfounded. "Yours, you bastard."

He laughed so hard that he fell off the couch.

Mr. Spratt of The Aldwych was crazy as a snake pit. His clothes had that ill-fitting look, as if they were being worn back-to-front, but in reality, it was the body inside that was more in need of correction. His hips jutted, his shoulders sloped, his ankles shied at the ground. He stunk of ether.

"Oh my, my," he whimpered. "Mr. Postlethwaite has remembered me in his old age. How sweet."

"He told me you needed help with the Forest of Arden."

Spratt sized up Wally in a flash, his eyes cruel. "Oh, did he now. What sort of help would that be?"

"I would imagine it would be something to do with building props," Wally persisted. "I was with the Whitehall for ten years. Head of properties."

"And the Professor put you out to pasture, eh?" Spratt perched like a goblin on the edge of a worktable and poked Wally with a finger. "What did you do, parse a bad sentence?"

It was a test in the guise of a joke. Would Wally laugh? He did—a little, forced chuckle just to show his willingness, but Spratt's sharp finger hurt his ribs, so the laugh was transformed into a cough. Spratt moved his wandering fingers up, to run them through Wally's hair, as if he was arranging a vase of dried flowers.

"There, there," he said, almost crying. "You mustn't think of it as punishment. We'll look after you. Come."

He led Wally by the hand to a long, low-ceilinged workshop around the back of the theatre and across the yard. It was filled with rows of tables at which sat half a dozen grey old men at work with strips of raffia and brown paper, florist's wire, and glue. Along the walls was the usual set-building madness. The room smelled of the same ether as Spratt.

"They call me the Admiral," he said with a mock naval salute. "And this is my Sargasso Sea. Pick a raft and set to, Midshipman Greene."

"What, exactly, would you like me to set to, sir?" asked Wally, suspiciously.

"Well, let's see," mused Spratt. "Postlethwaite told you Forest of Arden, did he? Very well. I suggest you start with moss. Moss is easy to be getting on with. I'm sure one of our lads will show you all the necessaries. Luncheon is at noon. Pip-pip." Another salute, and Spratt vanished in the twist, closing the door behind him.

Abandoned, Wally sank to a place at a table, aware that he was a good fifty years younger than anyone else in the room. He knew what had happened to him: he was being retired, put out to pasture, as Spratt had called it. This was where gaffers came to die: the elephant's graveyard. Bitterness crept up Wally's gullet. He craved a drug of some kind, any kind, if it would have made any difference. He guessed that he could have rolled up his sleeve right there, slap-ped a vein to attention, and cranked a bucket of wallpaper paste into his system and no one would have batted an eye. Looking around, he noted that many of his fellow elephants were either pink-drunk or stoned. He stayed for an hour or more, playing tiddlywinks with one of the old gaffers, then went for a drink at the Lamb and Cross. He came back for lunch, which was a cup of hearty soup and a but-tered roll, then he left early.

At the end of the week, after two days off and three very late starts, he got a pay packet. It was exactly one guinea less than what he'd been getting at the Whitehall. If he wasn't such a man of the world, he would have wept at the cruelty of it all.

Four years passed in the Forest of Arden. Moss grew.

James Brandt got his Bachelor's degree from the LSE at much the same time as a class-action lawsuit scuppered the Long Island family coffers. It was a distant tentacle of the thalidomide scandal, but it still did enough damage that James was recalled home and the Brandt London properties were put on the market. Georgia was in the middle of a successful run of *Saint Joan* at the Old Vic and refused to be affected. She went into overdrive with lawyers to separate her finances from her trust fund. But in September 1967, she admitted defeat.

"I need you to do something for me, Wally," she said one afternoon on the roof garden. "I have to put some money into your account. Can I trust you?"

"No," said Wally, without looking up from his whittling project.

"Good." She sat with him at the wrought-iron table and poked her fingers through the grilles. "It'll be the house. I have to sell it. And some Treasury bills and maybe the car, but not if I can help it."

"What, this house?"

"No, the house across the street, you moron; of course this house. We have to liquidate."

She was, inexplicably, close to liquidating herself. Her eyes brimmed with tears and the corners of her mouth tugged down. Wally didn't care. He put down his ball of wood and wondered whether he ought to look at her more closely. Most often, these days, he didn't waste much time on her. He had entered into an assumption of her presence; she had become an artist's sketch, a loose description, a few simple lines, broad strokes, and he filled in the rest with his imagination.

"What's going on?" he asked, his eyes focussing on her suspiciously. She was getting older, rounder. "Where are we going to live?"

Like a shuddering crime, she wept. It lasted all of three minutes and then it was over.

"Fuck this crap," she said, wiping her tears. "I hate this, but I'm backed into a corner. We have to go back to Long Island and see the matriarchs."

"Mom and Pip?"

"And James."

"Well, we should look up Old Peggy while we're at it," he said, brightly. "Isn't she over there?"

"Peggy?"

"Peggy Chingford, remember? At my Ma's funeral?"

"Oh, *her.*" Georgia soured her mouth. "Didn't she end up in Canada? I thought you said she'd gone to Canada, not the U.S."

"What's the difference?"

"Oh, Wally!" She laughed, warmly, for the first time in what seemed like years. "Sometimes you're so sweet! It's disgusting."

He marvelled at himself, at his capacity for always misunderstanding the world. In some ways he was still innocent but—and it was an important distinction—only about things he hadn't been exposed to. Not in terms of things he wouldn't see.

He returned to his whittling. The penknife chipped away at his ball of wood, its blade sweeping over and over the same site, sometimes removing nothing, sometimes a whisper, like an attentionsuicide's wound, sometimes deeper. Layers ripped away, the puppet head began to emerge. Another little demon.

She sat beside him, watching the sun approach the rooftop horizon. It was a fading, cloudless sunset, orange and blue. Sparrows hopped on the chimneystacks.

"Oh, and one other thing," she said eventually, laughing gently. "I'm pregnant. That should help soften up the matriarchs."

"You're what?"

"You heard."

Pregnant? Now there was a word Wally didn't expect to hear out of Georgia's mouth with any seriousness. Usually it was a trip to Brighton and it was dealt with. He was surprised, after all the scrubbings that it had received over the years, that her womb was hospitable enough to entertain a visitor. He had assumed that her fecundity, like his virility, had undergone a form of atrophy in sympathy with their souls. For the last four or five years, it had felt as if they were living in a bubble of inexpressible ennui.

"How far gone are you?"

"Four months."

"Oh." It must have been conceived around May or June, he calculated. "Who's the father, then?"

She became coy, poking the table again.

When he started to ask her again, this time more harshly, she put her finger to his lips and shushed him, at which he knew the answer. It was him. This time, he couldn't laugh. He could barely bring himself to smile.

20

The Brandt House was at the eastern extreme of Long Island, on the South Fork, near Montauk, where the terrain turns barren, windswept, salty. The region was haunted by the ghosts of smugglers and whale hunters, along with the souls of quarantined soldiers from both World Wars. Set back from the cliff, the house—huge and stolid—faced south, towards the ocean.

Wally and Georgia arrived on a winter's mid-morning, driven by James in his station wagon. Georgia had three massive cases to Wally's smaller one. A further trunk of her stuff had been sent ahead by sea, but not expected for a couple of weeks. They were met on the verandah by the matriarchs, who stood like a pair of sea captains on the deck. They both wore doubleknit—which kept its form in the stiff wind—slacks and cardigans in purples, greens, and lemon yellows.

"Mom! Pip!" Georgia ran up the stairs to perform the introductions, *comme il faut*. "This is Wally. Wally this is Alexandria and Phillipa. Pip."

"And James," cheered the one on Wally's right, Pip. "Look, there's James! Hi, Wally, pleased to meet you. Hi, Jimmy! Georgia, sweetheart, are you ever pregnant!"

Wally had never encountered women like these before. They were both smothered in makeup, but drawled like sailors. The woman called Pip wore a tight-curled brunette wig—bits of tinfoil stuck out around the edges of the cap as if she was partway through a perm.

The other matriarch had her own hair, but it was wisping bald in patches over her scalp. They both wore men's slippers: simple, patinaed leather, no heels. Wally was inclined to think them nutty, but there was a sharpness in their eyes that warned him otherwise.

"Hello, there," he said, cagily. "Alexandria. Phillipa."

"Call me Pip. Come on inside, will you, where it's warm."

Not merely warm, it was tropical. Wally broke a sweat immediately, losing his coat and clambering out of his sweater as a matter of survival. The foyer was a claustrophobic mahogany-and-antler tangle, despite its size. The carpet was threadbare, but the lamps were Tiffany. A huge india rubber tree, *ficus elastica*, soared two storeys high where the stairs swept up to the second floor. A lobster net hung from the balustrade.

"Let's have a look at you, then," said tinfoil Pip, donning a pair of thick plastic spectacles and giving Wally the once over. "Well, you look harmless enough. How many languages can you speak?"

"Have you now or will you ever," demanded Alexandria-Mom, "or have you in the past ever been a member of the Communist Party?"

I can't take this, thought Wally. Ten hours' travel by air and land to be confronted with an incongruous mélange of old women demanding explanations. If it hadn't have been so important to Georgia—and by extension, him—he would have turned on his impulse, run out of the house, over to the pitching ocean and swum back home.

"How many whats?"

"Communist Party."

"Languages."

"Welsh and English. Why do you have tinfoil on your head?"

"Well, there's no need to be snippy, young man." Pip gave him a slap on the belly. "Sheesh, you're fat. You sure it's not you who's expectin'?"

The house was big enough to raise a football team in. Wally and

Georgia were installed in a northeastern bedroom, which had a bathroom and dressing room *en suite*. The view was dismal through grimy
windows: a luminous, grey horizon with radio antennae and power
lines. Wally lost his bearings even in relation to the sea, so surrounded were they by sameness.

"They're bonkers. Your parents . . . matriarchs, whatever they
are. They're a pair of nitwits."

"I believe the expression over here is 'nutty as a fruitcake,'" said
Georgia as she laid claim to the left side of the bureau. "And don't
you be fooled. Acting runs deep in our family. They've got their
beady hawk eyes on you, trust me."

"How long do we have to stay in this hothouse?" Wally sat on
the high bed and tried to slump with no success. "I'm sick of it
already."

She shoved him over for no real reason but to make space to re-
fold her sweaters on the bed. "We come out of this with an heir,
Wally Greene, and we'll be free to do as we wish."

"Oh yes. I remember, now."

"Sarcasm fails you, you should remember that."

So he kept his mouth shut and watched her flit about in her
native environment. It was strange. She twisted herself around, un-
packing, negotiating the swell of her belly, from suitcase to drawer
and back to suitcase. Her gestures were all familiar, her lazy confidence, her easy arrogance; but where in England these qualities had
seemed daring, here they appeared predatory. Something of the
meanness of the place invaded her being, or perhaps she'd stolen a
bit of it, whichever, but it slithered in her veins like owl's blood.

When she was done, she took a shower. He unpacked his own
case in thirty seconds, simply scooping its contents into a couple of
drawers, chucking his wash kit towards the bathroom, and scattering
a few books on the bed.

"Don't leave anything lying about," Georgia warned, when she
emerged a while later in a billow of steam. "James is a bit of a jackdaw.

Bathroom's free. There's tons of hot water. Go crazy."

Wally stood beneath a sluice of scalding water until his finger-pads pruned, until he felt the grit of England loosen from his skin and swirl down the drain. America, now. He didn't feel excited; he felt relieved. He took a nap, imagining himself pinpointed on a globe, with a red ribbon streaming behind him all the way back to London. The move was monumental, turning his earlier journey from Wales to London into triviality.

Dinner was around a long table swathed in a white plastic table-cloth. One of those turntable affairs, a Lazy Susan, heavily loaded with sauce bottles—catsups and dressings—served as a centrepiece. Alexandria sat at the head, with Pip to her right. Wally was to her left.

"They do experiments here," she whispered to him, as she peppered her soup. "At the military base. Secret experiments. They got Pip. But they won't get me. Or my orgone."

"That's why I wear the tinfoil," explained Pip. "Since you asked."

What else could Wally offer, other than burbles of concern through the clam chowder? He glared at Georgia or James to come to his rescue, but they were both, in their own way, treating his discomfort as amusement. It was a difficult meal. The food—soup, roast chicken with peas and mashed turnip, then Jell-o dessert—was bulky and flavourless, but it was served off Spode with good silver flatware. The condiments were necessary to make it palatable. Lazy Susan got a workout, as the matriarchs constantly reached for bottles of flavour. The cloth was soon dotted with stains.

"If you become a citizen," Pip asked, streaking a ribbon of cat-sup off her plate, "would you be prepared to serve in Vietnam? Are you a fighter or a boozer, Wally?"

"Lover, Pip," corrected Alexandria. "It's a fighter or a lover."

"We know he's a lover," snapped Pip. "He knocked up Georgia, didn't he? Married her, even."

"I'm a pacifist," admitted Wally.

"Aha. He's a hippy, Pip, a big, fat hippo-hippy. Free love an' all that."

"He's been gettin' lots of free love out of us, Lex, that's for sure. Over two million, huh? Pretty good going for baby gravy."

"I'm sorry?" Wally sensed that he ought to be offended. "What's that?"

Pip made clucking noises with her tongue, as if she was a doctor discovering a nasty infection. "Every orgasm changes the world," she announced. "It's a little-known fact."

"Every orgasm changes the world," echoed Alexandria. "For good or for ill. You should think about that!"

The coffee was excellent. Turkish.

When it was done, the matriarchs dashed from the dining room to the parlour, where they watched a news broadcast on a brand-new colour TV. Pip watched from the far end of the room through a pair of old toilet-paper rolls that she'd fastened together with paper clips to resemble binoculars. With the two gone, James cleared the table while Wally stretched his legs and stood around, amazed, although he did his best to disguise his unease. Georgia lit up a cigarette.

"Should you be doing that?" asked James. "I mean . . ."

"You're right." She handed the cigarette over to Wally. "Here you are. I only lit it for you."

"Oh Wal-ly!" sang Pip from the next room. "I smell tobacco smoke!"

He stubbed it out on a saucer, making a big, chunky black smear of ash. The house, he decided, was stifling. He strode outside and into the cold. Then, not having a hope of knowing where to go, he sat in the car, feeling stupid. It was a ridiculous gesture, he knew, but once he was out of the house, he simply couldn't go back in. Curtains twitched. He closed his eyes, but he still felt watched. Eventually, Georgia came out to collect him.

"You're being an ass, Wally. Come back in. Nobody gives a shit if you smoke or not."

That night, he took a long time to fall asleep. At his side, Georgia —his surreal wife, soon to give birth to his surreal sprog in this surreal country—snored. The thought kept circling in his mind: *Every orgasm changes the world.* For good or for ill. There was a truth to it that frightened him. What changes had he wrought on Georgia? What shifts were taking place in her womb as a direct result of a fuck he couldn't even recall? For it was true: even with the help of mathematics, calendars and newspapers, he couldn't remember when the child had been conceived.

And suddenly, that other name came to him in the dark. That name from the far side of a thousand spoons of heroin, nameless screws, and half-stuck yawns of ejaculation. That name he'd never quite forgotten: Peggy. Now he was on the same side of the Atlantic. Closer. Was she tucked up in bed, too, on this same night, somewhere on this same landmass? Was she sleeping as soundly as Georgia? Wally groaned. For the first time, the possibility that he might have irretrievably changed Peggy's world winked at him from the darkness, from the corners of the room, from a world across an ocean.

The Montauk house may have been physically isolated from the rest of Long Island, but the Brandts were well-connected socially. Not a week went by without at least two out-of-the-house social engagements that required drives to the Gold Coast or west along the South Fork. Wally was introduced as yet another nut in a family already lionized for eccentricity. There was safety in this, not least being the freedom of honesty, for which Wally was grateful. He watched some of the social twistings and compromises that went on around him with horror. Women forced to simper and fawn at the elbows of their men; chatterboxes with nothing to say who had the run of the conversation and could interrupt anyone; toadlike men who had everything brought to them on plates. There was no class system as Wally had known in England, but there was a definite pecking order that appeared to be based on a combination of money and clout. The Brandts, luckily, had both. They were automatically on the lists, and enjoyed the highest of privileges, namely that they were under no pressure to invite anyone back.

The import of Georgia's swollen belly was understood by everyone, discreetly admired, but discussed by none. Wally and Georgia would wander along the buffet tables, loading up their plates, eating for three amid smiling faces nodding with approval, while James straggled behind them, stuffing his pockets with teaspoons and forks whenever he thought no one was looking.

Small dinner parties were held at the Montauk house with a select few: thinkers and arguers, mavens, and protocol keepers. There would be the occasional appearance of a fantastically wealthy octoge-narian who turned up with a full, Chinese-liveried retinue, slurped the matriarchs' tasteless soup, and then went home. Pip and Alexandria treated all these intrusions as nothing special; they neither resented nor enjoyed these obligations. James would cook, and when the guests were ready to leave, Pip would return the silverware he'd pilfered the week before, wrapped up in butcher's paper.

Wally began to be fearful. He didn't understand a single moment of this world, even though he was grandly implicated. He was about to be the father of a baby sprog that had spent its last trimester feeding on vol-au-vent and caviar. He'd watch Pip, standing in the kitchen, replacing the tinfoil on her head and he'd find himself wondering if an insulating sheet of aluminum around the skull wouldn't be a good idea for him, too.

If sprog was a girl, she was going to be called Alexandria. If a boy, David, after Wally's Da. That was the deal that Wally thought had been agreed upon, so he wasn't prepared for a boy called Alexander.

"He'll have lots of choice when he's older," cooed Georgia into her armful of swaddled baby. "Alex, Lex, Sandy, Al."

"Alexander? What happened to David?"

"You weren't here, Wally."

The comment stung. He hadn't been present at the birth for a very good reason: he couldn't trust himself. His attitude towards fatherhood grew more and more volatile as the big day drew closer. He wanted it all to stop, or at least to happen somewhere else, quickly, with the door closed. But Georgia, he discovered, was cursed with an outrageous sense of occasion. She was determined to live the experience to the full, to play the role of birthing mother to the hilt. No dulling drugs for her. Brandt Pharmaceuticals was, after all, nearly bankrupt from the thalidomide scandal. The child was a symbol of the future not only for Georgia, but also for the family. Wally, on impulse, wanted to strangle it. He was terrified that he might carry out his fantasies, and so, on the day Georgia appeared in the doorway announcing, "Here we go, folks, Overture and Beginners," he bicycled east to Fire Island and hid in a homosexual Bed and Breakfast for three days until he was certain the show would be all over.

On the third day, he rode to the Southampton Hospital, where he found Georgia ensconced in a flower-bedecked private room complete with bassinet and baby. Alexander. Year of the Monkey.

"You weren't here, so I filled in the registration form myself." Georgia gently smoothed her baby's cheeks with the back of her knuckles. "Now that you've decided to turn up, Wally Greene, you can open an account at the First American. We shouldn't leave it much longer than tomorrow. This little lad's a rich bundle. Look at all his gifts. Look out the window."

"What?"

"See that maroon Mercedes? Pip got him that. Isn't it hilarious?"

"He's a bit young to drive, isn't he?"

"Would you like to hold him?"

"No."

But she insisted. Wally was terrified. He was sure that his mere presence in the same room as the baby was illegal. He would break it if he so much as looked at it. Didn't babies have soft skulls? He would drop it, squeeze it, choke it, for sure. He knew nothing, nor cared a jot about the mewling, wriggling creature, his son. He looked down at the infant's clenched features and did his best to engender a paternal concern but it was hopeless. He felt hoodwinked. Not just by Georgia, but by a faceless corporation that was using him and his seed to cream off funds that would otherwise go to the care and compensation of children born without ears or with phocomelia of the fingers.

"He's not brain-damaged, then?"

"Wally!"

He tried to apologize for having missed the performance, but she was too tired and too wrapped up in maternal concern to pay him any kindness. His fingers caught against the baby's blanket, the weight inside felt inconsequential, barely human. He faked a chuckle at his part in the drama but the pretense didn't bring him any real comfort, just frustration at not understanding this Miracle of Life he held in his big, ungainly hands. The baby Alexander opened his mouth to cry. The breath he drew was Wally's. It was as if the oxygen had been diverted from Wally's lungs straight to the baby's.

Once he'd handed his precious load back to Georgia, he couldn't wait to get out of that fragrant, suffocating room, and run down the street to the nearest bar where he doused himself with whisky, and rubbed his shoes in the sawdust.

His world, he was convinced, was now out of his control. The sprog, Alexander, Alex, Al, would grow up to be a defiant, insolent, disobedient clone of himself, who would point its accusing sprog finger at him as soon as it was old enough to lift an arm. Made from Wally's image, this creature would possess all the genes and hereditary traits necessary to be Wally's undoing. He'd known it, instinctively, from the moment Georgia first told him she was pregnant. It was confirmed when he held the baby in his arms and had his very breath stolen out from under him. Something intangible and un-stoppable had happened. The child—he knew it in a terrifying moment without either reason or logic—that child would some-how, however obliquely, be the death of him.

Georgia dropped the mother act the moment she was offered a better role Off Broadway. Busy, busy, busy, she got herself a *pied-à-terre* in Manhattan, took the Mercedes, and left Wally and James to ward the baby. Most often, of course, the duty was left to James, who loved it. The matriarchs pitched in where they could, but they were as unsuited to the task as was Wally. This incompetence created a bond among the three of them.

"Thanks, Jimmy," they'd shout in unison when the baby's cries interrupted dinner and James would dash from the table. "Thanks again!"

The matriarchs and Wally developed a relationship that pre-tended to be argumentative. Alexandria—or "Mom" as Wally began to call her—was so full of her conspiracy talk about the Air Force Base further along the coast, she was only really good for this one topic, as all-embracing and fascinating as it was. Time travel, mind control, alien contact, orgone reception, and radio waves were res-ponsible for everything that was wrong with the whole ball of wax, according to Mom. Wally recalled his love of science fiction. Their conversations were like flipping through a stack of Asimov.

Pip, on the other hand, was unpredictable. Some days she was so sharp and on the ball that Wally felt she could see right into his brain and read his thoughts. At other times, she regressed to a child-hood simplicity, adopting a hokiness that Wally gradually came to recognize, through television sitcoms, as being uniquely American.

"Aw, Wally, honey," she'd gurgle on such occasions, "are you ever just the cutest teddy bear!"

"I think you have me confused with my offspring."

"Na-ah." Pip wrinkled her nose. "You're cuter, you big lump."

So while James rushed around, feeding, burping, cooking, changing diapers and cleaning, Wally watched the news with Mom and Pip, demolishing whatever booze was in the house and raiding their medicine box, which had a neverending supply of powerful Brandt narcotics. He liked to lie on his back on the floor in the foyer, stoned, and stare up at the circular skylight. Up the giant rubber tree he'd climb in his imagination, using those tactile leaves as a ladder to reach a revolving castle in the clouds—Kublai Khan meets *Jack and the Beanstalk*.

"Wally Greene, you're nutty as a fruitcake," declared Pip, when she found him and asked him what he was doing. "Have you been raiding our meds again?"

"Yup. Is that okay?"

"Yeah." She plunked herself down beside him on the old carpet. "Just don't overdo it, you big moose. I don't want to be calling in the paramedics, we have dinner guests coming in half an hour." She handed him her toilet-roll binoculars. "Here. Have a look through these."

"Baby's crying, again," said Wally.

"Jim-meeee," wailed Pip from the floor, kicking her legs in a fake tantrum. "Little Alex needs a change. Jim-meee!"

Alexander was nearly three years old when he was packed into the Mercedes. They were moving again—this time to Canada, to avoid Vietnam. Wally was going to be travelling alone, taking the train north across the border to Toronto, while Georgia and James would take the baby by road. After some fancy footwork, they'd managed to squeeze an extra passport in Wally's name from the British Embassy. James would become Wally—a subterfuge neither of them had any conscientious objection to if it meant freedom from the recent Supreme Court ruling and the draft.

Much to the matriarchs' chagrin, Georgia picked up left-wing politics as a hobby. Initially, she saw it as a publicity tool, a way to get her name in the paper. But then, when she got into the details of Vietnam, she was converted to the cause. Everywhere she went, she carried a postcard-size photo of the Buddhist monk setting himself ablaze. She'd point to it, as if it were absolute proof, and bark, "See? See?"

The image made Wally want to throw up.

The journey to Canada was panicked and inelegant. Wally was, almost literally, torn into two people. Seeing James' luggage accumulate in the foyer next to Georgia's reminded him of London. "Are you sure I won't get in the way in Canada," asked Wally. "James makes such a good parent."

"Don't be an ass, Wally Greene." Georgia was snappy. "You're the father, face it. Sheesh! James is my brother."

"Weren't you both adopted?" retorted Wally. "I don't know, Georgia. It all seems a bit fishy to me."

"I've got bigger things to worry about."

By which, she meant her career, which was true. She hadn't dared tell them yet at the theatre that she was leaving, but she had already secured herself a part in a Shakespeare festival, somewhere in Ontario and she'd said yes. Their return offer of employment was on paper: an official letter in her purse that was guaranteed to give her entry into Canada. She was rightly scared about breaking her Off Broadway contract, knowing that she was already getting a reputation as a troublemaker, and thus smaller parts; she might never be able to return to the American stage. Her politics-hobby had been getting more and more public. She'd appeared in demonstrations and spoken at marches, denounced the war and once appeared on television in a debate.

"Stay away from the box," advised Wally when he saw her next.

"The camera doesn't really like you."

"He's right, honey," agreed Pip. "You looked like one of those transvestites. Over dramatic, I'd say. Stick to the stage."

Mom was convinced that the CIA now had a file on them all, thanks to the alien technology of television, and they'd all get arrested at the border and taken in for experimentation. The only way to solve it, she said, would be to go back down the time tunnel. She knew where it was, in Warning Area 105 in Camp Hero down the road, but she'd need help in getting past the electro-fence and the security guards.

"That sounds like an awful lot of bother just to change last Thursday night on the telly," said Wally. "What about the repeats?" and they all laughed.

"The fucking theatre'll figure me out in five minutes," said Georgia. "They'll get me blacklisted for life. Damn!"

"So tell them yourself," urged Wally. "Preempt them. Don't give them the satisfaction, am I right?"

She knew he was. It made her eyes brim with tears to admit it. Wally saw right into her, then. He saw her weakness for him; the hint of an answer to his long-standing question, "Why me?" She loved him! It was all Wally could do to hide his surprise; for he knew a good thing when he saw it. He'd use it against her, if it ever came to the crunch.

So off she went for her meeting with the theatre. True to form, she'd left it right up until the last minute and was hoping to drive into town and back—120 miles in each direction—before lunch. When she left, she was composed and efficient, magnanimously admitting that perhaps she'd miscalculated and that they could put off the big trip until the next day.

"I'll call you once I've told them."

The telephone didn't ring clear through to sundown, when Georgia appeared, careening off the Old Montauk Highway, all screeching tires and honking horn. She was a harpy.

"Get in!" she yelled. "We're leaving. Now!"

Wally quickly erected a mental shield to protect himself. He helped load the car and, along with Mom and Pip, made a big deal of ushering James and the sleeping Alex into the front seat. Georgia was pacing, furious, on the verandah, smoking.

"Once I get to Canada," she said, shaking her finger at Wally, but clearly still continuing her talk from theatre management, "Once I get to Canada, you wire me the rest of the trust fund, buddy, and I'll start up my own fucking theatre, my own fucking Great White Way, my Great White North Way, just you watch me! The phoenix will rise from the fucking ashes!"

"I'll be there, too, Georgia," he reminded her. "I won't have to wire you anything. It'll all be there."

"Right, then." She nodded sharply. Her theatre was as good as built. "All aboard!"

She gave Wally a rudimentary hug, then one for Mom and one for Pip. She tried to make it a business-like departure, but she was too flustered to carry it off.

"Bye-bye, honey."

"Bye."

"Bye-bye, James! Bye-bye Baby!"

Georgia chunked the car door behind her, settled herself in the driver's seat, started the ignition, and switched on the overhead light to adjust her lipstick in the mirror. Once she was presentable to the world, she then reached up, switched off the light. With a robust haul on the steering wheel, the Mercedes lurched onto the road.

21

The escape to Canada burnt in Wally's sinuses through a stinking cold that grew gradually worse as his train travelled north. By the time he staggered out of Union Station in Toronto, all his energies were concentrated on survival, of just making the next step, taking the next breath, counting his luggage —navigations of the simplest kind. A singing wheeze had settled in his lungs, and his head, dense with phlegm, felt twice its normal size. Thus, he was ill-equipped to start his new life in a new country; he feared that Fate, with a gust of wind would pick him up and dash him to death.

Anger stuck in him, frustrated by his sickness. He negotiated the insolences of securing a room at the Royal York Hotel with undisguised acrimony. The desk clerk, the bell boy, the chamber-maid, all caught the tail of his ill humour. Once in his room, he wrapped himself up in blankets and cocooned himself in a chair by the window, staring at the reflection of snow on his eyelids. Every so often, he would smoke a cigarette and make himself cough pitilessly. Whisky compounded the misery. He read a bit of Emerson—just enough to stave off the suicidal urge.

On a whim, he flipped through the telephone directory, looking for Peggy Chingford, but he couldn't remember her new name other than it was Scottish—Mc or Mac something. The book was full of 'em.

"How was your trip?" Georgia asked on the phone, three days later. "Sorry we took so long, but we stopped off in Niagara Falls and it took us a while to get sorted. We've found a house."

"Fine. When are you coming to pick me up?"

"Oh." The line was quiet for a full three seconds. "Can't you get here under your own steam?"

"I'm sick."

She sighed as if it was all so predictable, that Wally was totally incapable of doing anything without her, that his failures would always be her chores. It was, Wally realized, part of her charm. She agreed to come and get him as soon as was possible, but she couldn't promise anything, since she had to start rehearsals in a couple of days. In the end, of course, she sent James, who maintained that it was his idea to come in her stead.

They drove for hours along a flat, snowbound highway, the car smelling of vomit recently cleaned from its upholstery. The journey was mainly conducted in silence.

"It's all a bit strange," blustered James at one point. "It's not that I've got anything against Vietnam. I'd be off like a shot if I didn't think it would throw Georgie for a loop."

"It'd loop her," agreed Wally.

"But Canada!" continued James. "It's hardly a step up the career ladder for her, is it?"

"Well, I don't know."

"If you ask me, it's a bit like playing poker with matchsticks," said James. "You're not really part of the game when you're in Canada."

The conversation died, and the two men fell into a silent communion. They shared an inability, an utter failure, to understand what they were doing together in another foreign country. Eventually, their avoidance of each other became comforting, so much so that when they finally pulled into the driveway of a Victorian clapboard house, it felt as if they had shared a temporary peace.

Georgia was reading in the front room.

"You're not sick," she decided, after giving Wally the once-over. "It's just a sniffle. Come say hi to Alex, he's watching television upstairs."

She took Wally on a tour of the house. In comparison to Long Island, it was small, but of its kind, it was handsome. It only had three bedrooms, possibly four, if someone didn't mind sleeping in a seven-foot box. There were three storeys including the dormer attic, two sets of stairs (front and back) and a basement. The previous owners had left furniture and fittings everywhere, so that an absent personality began to emerge from the detritus. They'd had two children, as evidenced by the bunk-beds still in place upstairs, and girls, judging from the wallpaper and ghastly frilled curtains. In the master bedroom, there was a king-sized waterbed taking up half the room. It looked as if an effort had been made to remove it—drag marks across the carpet and scars from a screwdriver attack at one corner—but the beast had proved too massive to move.

"It's going. I hate it," said Georgia. "It makes me nauseous."

"It's soothing," said Wally, stretching out on the undulating mattress. "It's like being on morphine."

"Precisely."

Little Alexander was upstairs in the converted attic. He was hardly "watching television"; he'd been plonked on the carpet in front of a black-and-white television set that happened to be on, and was chewing his way through the corner of a plastic brick. When Wally entered the room, there was a momentary hiccup of recognition before the child returned to the task at hand.

"You left him up here all alone?" asked Wally. "What if something happened?"

"Like what?" Georgia picked up her son and carried him on her hip. "Look, Alex, here's Daddy. Wave hello to your father."

The child was much more interested in the plastic brick. Wally forced a smile and a wave, felt foolish. It was the real version of the vile Mothers and Fathers game that Peggy once tried to make him play—and just as repulsive. Just as false.

As it turned out, it was Peggy who found him. Or, rather, it was Peggy who found Georgia. She'd gone to see *Two Gentlemen of Verona* at the Festival and—wouldn't you know it?—Georgia just happened to be in it.

"Guess who turned up in the green room after the show last night?" Georgia asked.

"Peggy Chingford?"

"How did you know?"

"I didn't. I guessed."

It wasn't that difficult a leap, given Peggy's proclivities for culture, Georgia's profession, and that they were both in the same province. It was really only a matter of time before they bumped up again. What Wally did think mysterious, however, was Peggy's decision to pop by and say hello after the performance. Surely, she'd learned her lesson about backstage visits after the last time.

"She looked awful," said Georgia. "I think she's been dropping kids nonstop since we last saw her. She wouldn't shut up about how nice it was to get a night out away from them."

"How many does she have now, then?" Wally asked, as he played with Alex on the living room carpet, tiny fists gripping his big fingers. "Last time I saw her, she had three. Twins in there too, I believe."

"Oh, I'm sure she has more now. Bound to be a dozen, at least."

Wally thought he managed to hide his quickening pulse, but some of his nervous energy must have transferred to his son, because Alex started punching him to the same beat as his heart.

"Whoa, boy, easy!"

"She asked after you," Georgia continued. "Said to say hi."

"Oh? Did she leave a number?"

"She might have."

Wally glared at her to stop that nonsense. She backed down, but not before savouring the moment.

"Don't be a fool," she said. "Of course she didn't."

"Thanks."

"By the way. I've got you into the prop shop. They sounded quite thrilled to get you."

"Thanks. Really."

Alex started up again, hitting Wally with a cushion. It was easy enough to dodge, so it turned into a game for a while, then shrieks of laughter, ending in tickle-torture with Alex wriggling on the floor in a fit, gasping for breath like a salmon. Concern swept across Georgia's face, but Wally knew exactly when to stop. The room was still for a while, just the sound of Alex's breath returning to normal. Sunlight warmed the carpet through the windows, despite the cold outside.

"You know what I think?" said Georgia, lost on some distant plane. "I think, for all her smiles and chatter, I think that Mrs Margaret McLean of North York, Toronto, was terrified out of her wits."

"Don't be silly."

"No, I'm serious."

McLean, thought Wally. Not MacDonald, Macnamara, McCarthy or Mackenzie. McLean. North York, Toronto. McLean.

"Peggy!"

"Wally!"

Eyes, wide at the door, wide enough to obliterate the February afternoon. Windows to the soul, shutters flapping, unattended for that split second, allowing Wally to see straight through to the fear. Georgia had been right: Mrs Margaret McLean was terrified.

"Look at you!" he chided, gesturing at her apron and yellow rubber gloves. "Did I catch you doing the washing-up?"

"How did . . . When . . . ?"

"Sniffed you out, didn't I?" Wally wiped his feet on her doormat and slid inside the door before she could shut him out. "How are you, Peggy? You haven't changed a bit."

She was caught off guard. It was hardly fair of him, bursting in on her like this, but he didn't dare give her any advantage if he could help it. So he'd waited, first, until Parker had left the house, and then until the kids had gone to school. After that, he'd given it another half an hour before making his move. Up the garden path he sauntered, and round the side to the kitchen door. He wanted it to be casual.

The kitchen was clean, but not the kind of clean it really wanted to be. It tried too hard to impress and ended up stinking of cleaning products. It had a dull sheen instead of a sparkle, as if entropy was only ever a half-hour away. Wally felt giddy from all her housework.

"What do you . . . ?" she began.

"Georgie's in town doing a play, you know. We thought you might like to come and see it. When it opens."

"Well, I don't know, Wally, I . . ."

She hemmed and ha'd, fidgeting terribly, gained control over her fear, then wrestled with the problem of how to get Wally out of her house without it turning ugly. He could see her measuring the distance to the telephone, to the kitchen knives. It was rich.

"Oh well, never mind," he shrugged. "It doesn't matter. I just wanted to see you, really."

"Well, here I am," she laughed, flapping her arms.

"So I see."

Wally sat, uninvited, at her kitchen table and asked if it was too much bother for a cup of tea. She went along with him, rising to the challenge, playing the game, but drawing the line at his smoking. He got his tea, though, and a plate of plain cookies-not-biscuits into the bargain. Until the kettle boiled, they passed the time by listing all the differences between English and North American vocabularies they could think of. Faucets, autumns, crisps, chips, petrol, motor-ways and car bonnets, nappies and rubbish.

"Oh, speaking of nappies," Wally smirked. "We have a toddler of our own, Georgia and I. Alex. He's going to be three in a couple of weeks."

She lurched when the kettle whistled. "We have four." She poured the water into the pot without any sign of tremor. "You know about Bill and the twins, of course, and then there's Ned."

"Ned?" Wally was careful to hide his interest. "Is that short for Edward? How old is he?"

She showed no hesitation, no evasiveness, no sign of spotting his reason for asking. "Oh, Ned was born a couple of years after we got here."

Wally tried not to exhale with relief. *A couple of years after they got to Canada.* That was what he wanted to know. That was why he'd waited outside, what he'd burst into her kitchen to find out.

He kept the conversation charming and bright, however, commenting on how she'd gotten all boys in her brood, how tough it must be for her.

"Georgia's family's all girls," he lied. "I feel like I'm covered in frills."

"Alex is a girl?"

Wally nodded, his heart skipping a beat. He'd forgotten he'd given a name to the sprog.

"Short for Alexandria." He held her gaze. "Actually, no. I'm lying. It's a little boy, Alex. Feels like a girl, though, sometimes. His Auntie Jamie is spoiling him."

He scoffed all the cookies, dipping them in his tea, making a horrendous orange sludge at the bottom of his cup. Things were almost pleasant between them when he said his goodbyes.

"Oh, I've been meaning to say," he said at the door, as if in an afterthought, "I'm sorry about what happened at the theatre."

"I beg your pardon?"

"The Scottish Play, remember?"

"Oh." Her mouth was round as an egg. The terror returned to her eyes.

He gave her a cheery smile in return. He tried to imagine her back in the darkness of the oubliette, but failed. That had been a completely different woman on a completely different continent in a different age. Now he almost felt sorry for her.

"Well, think about the theatre. Georgia would love to see you."

"We'll see. No promises."

He strolled back down the garden path, his hands in his pockets, some ghastly tune whistling through his lips. From where he'd parked the car, he winged a snowball towards her house. It fell short of its target, but he didn't care. He'd just climbed the beanstalk and paid the Giant's Wife a little visit.

A week after young Alexander's third birthday, the balloons still clung to the corners of the room, cards still ran along the window ledge, and G.I. Joe still had all his accessories. That Sunday afternoon, Wally was playing the tickling game with Alexander again. James was in the kitchen, fixing a late lunch. Georgia was expected back from her matinée performance by four-thirty. Weekend papers littered the carpet, the crossword abandoned in favour of games with Alexander.

"I wish you wouldn't do that, Wally," said Georgia, coming in through the door. "He hates being tickled."

"He loves it," Wally countered. "Look, he's laughing."

"He's gasping for breath, you big bully."

Wally stopped. Georgia calling him a bully was risible, after all, she was the one who loved to throw her weight around. He sulked back to his seat, sweeping up the newspapers in his great paw as he went, and buried himself back in the crossword. He was hungry. Waiting the extra hours for Georgia to finish her show always put him on edge. It didn't seem fair, but she always insisted that they put off lunch until she got home.

Alexander, recovering from the latest tickle attack, toddled up to his father and gripped the central fold of the paper from behind, tugged down, ripped it a few inches.

"Lunch!" called James from the kitchen. "Come and get it!"

Wally stood up and pushed Alexander rudely away, perhaps a bit angrily, perhaps a bit roughly, enough to knock the boy down to the carpet. It wasn't violent, nor was it focussed, but it was sudden.

"Wally!"

"What?" Wally turned at the door. "It's lunch. I'm hungry."

"Oh, my God. Look."

Wally followed her gaze. Alexander lay on the floor, shaking, locked in an unmistakable seizure. The body was rigid, the legs floppy, the eyes were rolled back to the whites in a head that jerked spasmodically. Georgia was kneeling beside him in a trice, her hands fluttering undecided in the air, panicky, not knowing what she could touch.

"Wally!"

The paramedics arrived long after the episode was over. Georgia had Alexander cradled in her arms, the two of them wrapped up in a Navaho blanket, laid out on the couch. She had finished her ten minutes of near-hysterical weeping and was now haggard and shiny. Exhausted. Wally showed the paramedics in, but hung back. He felt as if he was intruding.

The men knelt at the couch, like the shepherds at the Nativity, and whispered reverently, getting all the information they needed on what had happened. Then they extracted the child from Georgia's reluctant arms.

"No-o-o," she moaned. "He's all right, now."

"If he lost consciousness he may have a concussion, Ma'am," said one. "You can come with us, but we really ought to get him to a doctor."

"He just landed on the carpet," offered Wally from the transom. "Soft as a meadow. He's done it a thousand times before."

Georgia glared at him as she stood and gathered the blanket around her like a Native elder. "You hit him. You were torturing him."

"What?"

"You heard."

She was bitterly triumphant. It was as if she'd proven something unfathomable and that completely unnerved him. Some battle he wasn't aware of having been declared, let alone fought, had been won, he was sure of that. She was the victor and he the vanquished. Within moments, she had left the house with the paramedics. She left the front door ajar, as if she wanted the whole world to traipse in with the afternoon air. All the neighbours. Anyone who happened to be passing.

Wally wandered into the kitchen, where James was covering the lunch dishes with tinfoil. There was silence between them, but Wally felt an arrow of accusation fly his way. It was just a glimmer, but it was all he needed.

Anger consumed him in a flash. He slammed his fist on the table with such force that a fork fell to the floor. He remembers the pine of the tabletop, the fruit in the bowl, the stupid Niagara Falls salt-and-pepper set. He remembers gripping the edge of the table so hard in his fury that he thought his entire universe was twisting sideways and he had to haul with all his strength to get it back to rights.

The table tipped. Or, according to James, Wally upended it.

As the table cantilevered sideways, a corner caught James on the hip, sending him spinning spectacularly in the opposite direction. Plates flew. Apples bounced and bruised. James' casserole dish shattered against the wall and tiny white slivers of Pyrex spattered across the floor. The table landed askew, the legs and struts sticking in the air.

It had all happened in a beat; a vortex of one thing simply following another. Wally was mortified. In his mind, all he could see was Alexander in the other room, twitching his legs, flicking his eye-whites. Georgia's accusation: *You hit him.*

James started to pick himself up, to dust himself off, as Wally fell

to his knees with a groan. What had he done? A rocking sensation
pulsed up his spine, developing into spasmodic jerks as the smell of
burning filled his sinuses. He recognized the territory he was stepping into, but there was nothing he could do. He saw the edge of
the table rush towards his face as he keened forwards. He became
Da, stripped to the waist in the yard, and he wondered where the
sunshine had gone. Then his mouth struck pine.

"Wally! Stop!"

But he couldn't. Again and again he punished himself for a
crime he couldn't recall committing, pummelling his face into the
the table struts. It didn't stop until James dragged him bodily out of
the kitchen and into the hallway. Blood streamed down his chin,
from where he'd smashed four of his teeth clean out of his gums.

"I can't take any more of this," said James, leaving.

Wally lay, bloody, on the floor. The pain never seemed to arrive.
It was just one long extension of the same wound. The taste of warm
salt in his mouth.

Act V

22

A cold shudder awakes Wally in his bed. He's been sweating for hours and the duvet is clammy, his pillow tamped. He slept in his socks and underwear; his legs have been restless all night, kicking and running. Now, awake, he can't recall any of it, except that something tells him the madness isn't going to stop. The nightmare continues, as they say.

He'd worked late at the shop. The theatre is in the middle of technical rehearsals, the infamous "ten-out-of-twelve" hour days, of which today is the second out of a series of three, gearing up to the first preview the day after tomorrow. A technical run-through is expected tonight, and there's still so much to be done. Birnam Wood. Body parts. Swords. A bit of everything and no one to help.

Ned has been gone for weeks. No tattooed hide nor dog of him. His absence niggles at Wally, who keeps expecting him to return as if nothing had happened and get back to work with some flimsy tale of debauchery sufficing as his excuse. It doesn't happen.

Wally groans. His skull is still reverberating from all the banging, forging, mixing, honing, hammering of last night. *Two parts hot water, one part concentrated hot gelatin glue, with one part glue size to three parts dry whiting for heavy dope, thick texturing.* There's a cacophony playing inside his head. He would have stayed at the workshop overnight had he not stepped outside for a breath of fresh air at four-thirty in the morning and found his feet walking home. I'll have a bath, he thought.

A soak in two parts Epsom salts, followed by a good sleep on a firm mattress. He told himself he merely needed to renew his energy.

He lies on his back, adjusting to his waking state. Beside him, Georgia's steady breathing could mean that she's either dead to the world or really awake and waiting for him to bring her a damned coffee in bed. He can't tell which.

"Nnggh." Noisily, he pretends to wake up again. "Nnggh, mmph."

She joins in the groaning, turning over and nestling into the covers. He blows in her ear and she swats him away. Aha. So she *is* awake and faking it, too. He swings his legs off the bed. The room is stuffy, he craves air—some breeze on his face.

"Tell you what," he says, glancing at the bedside clock. "I'll go get you a coffee from the corner if you put the kettle on. The alarm'll go off in three minutes."

When he empties his bladder, he notices his reflection in the bathroom mirror: there's another hand print on his chest. Worse, his right eye is completely bloodshot. He wonders if he isn't running a fever, his skin is rubbery, his urine is dark orange. The whiff of burning is constant; it's as if a pot has been left on the stove for three days. He would check for an electrical problem in the house, except that he knows that the smell is inside his head. He splashes some cold water on his face. Within moments, his skin is dry without benefit of towel. For a second, he wavers, wondering if he should measure his temperature. He decides against it.

As Georgia dons her bathrobe, he pulls himself into some clothes. Trousers, shirt. Downstairs, he puts on his jacket and shoves his feet into his shoes, squishing the backs down with his heels. Then, he staggers out of the house, slamming the door behind him.

The day is grey, damp, and closed with cloud. The concrete of the road, the pavement, the corner store, the trees—even the mountains—everything presses in on him. It's mid November, it ought to be cold. He unbuttons his jacket as he walks. Too many layers. He gulps the air, enjoying a crisp vibration in his lungs, a pain.

At the corner store, he picks up the daily paper and pours a large cup of coffee from the Serve Yourself to take back for Georgia. Adding a couple of plastic-wrapped muffins to his load, he returns to the house, feeling an inch better for having taken his little walk.

Georgia is in the kitchen, leaning against the sideboard, grey light from the window bisecting her face. Wally tosses her the bran muffin and keeps the chocolate-chip one for himself. He sits at the table and tears messily at the cellophane shroud—he seems to have lost sensation in his fingers. The operation gets frantic. He flips to the entertainment section in the paper. His wife's smiling image jumps out at him—there is a preview article on the show. Suddenly repulsed, he spins the paper over to her.

"How's the tea coming?" he asks. "Almost brewed?"

"Oh, look, the piece came out." She holds the page at arm's length. "It's not a bad picture, is it?"

"Not bad. You look like a drag queen."

Muffin crumbles over his fingers and spills onto the table. He shoves chunks of it into his maw but it has no taste nor texture, it's like eating cotton. The chocolate chips are dry and gritty on his tongue.

The phone startles them both. Georgia takes it on the third ring, after rolling her eyes and sighing. The day has begun.

"Yes?" she says, with a tired resignation. "What is it? . . . No, I'm sorry, you must have the wrong . . . yes, this is she speaking . . . Ned McLean, you mean? Yes, but he doesn't live here, why don't you try . . . Oh, hello Parker, I didn't recognize your voice."

Her eyes shiver at news. She betrays herself with a sudden glance at Wally, then just as quickly looks away. Wally doesn't need to hear her say "Oh, I'm so sorry," to know what's happened. He pours himself a cup of tea to wash down the sludge in his mouth and pretends not to eavesdrop. There's nothing much to overhear, though. Georgia gives occasional monosyllables of assent or sympathy, along with the repeated line of not knowing where Ned is.

"Yes, well, I'll tell him to call you if I see him . . . Yes, I will . . .

Yes, I'm so sorry . . . Goodbye."

Eventually she hangs up with a little exclamation of bemusement meant for nobody but herself. To help compose her thoughts,
she tucks her hair behind her ear and breaks off the cap to her
muffin.

"Well," she says, examining her breakfast. "That was Parker."

"She's dead, isn't she?" Wally says, making certain. "Peggy?"

Georgia nods. "I think so. Well, he used the euphemism 'no longer
in pain' so yes, I think that means 'yes'. Dead, I mean." She pops a
muffin morsel into her mouth and turns into the grey light. A smile,
incongruous. Click. Wally's stomach lurches. Just for a moment, he
fancies he can see Peggy's face there, cream-cake smeared on her lip,
seagulls circling overhead, the scent of Welsh sea air in his throat, the
taste of powdered sugar. *I'm never growing old!*

"Too bad," he says with a grim smile, the first relief he's felt all
morning. "I'm sure she would have made a really lovely old woman."

Her death, he realizes, means nothing to him, not as he supposes
that it ought. As with the others, those close travellers who have made
their exits from his life, he feels detached at the news, knowing his
reaction is always delayed. As with Ma, Da, James, Monty, and
Georgia's trips to Brighton, he never saw the corpses, he just imagined them through the words of the messengers. They become
indistinguishable from other news-of-the-day trivia, such as the
price of gasoline, a distant war, celebrity gossip, AIDS. Third-hand
grief, at best.

These ghosts, of which Peggy is now one, taunt Wally from afar.
They sing of his missing their demise, his abandonment of them in
their hour of need. He wasn't there. And with this accusation, they
burn scars across his psyche—atrocities that itch, tease, and push him
to the brink. Not being there at the deathbed leaves the event up

to his imagination to absorb. Not being there, in some twisted way, makes it his fault.

He's angry that Parker didn't have the decency to call and tell him straight out. Oh, no. He had to make a song-and-dance about getting in touch with Ned, so that he, Wally, almost found out by accident. Through Georgia, at that. He wonders whether Parker tried to get one of the twins to make the call. *No longer in pain.* That was so typical; all spineless euphemism, all ancient protocol followed as if writing an address, line by line, staggering to the right as he goes down the envelope.

> *Mrs. Margaret McLean, née Chingford,*
> *1936–1987, No longer in pain,*
> *Kingdom Come,*
> *AMEN, B.C.*

In the end, they are just so many words; a collection of scratches in the dust; or sounds, fleeing from the constraint of lips and tongue, mere echoes of the real events. So how could they hurt him?

"Are you all right?" Georgia lays a hand on his shoulder. Then she tests his forehead. "You're burning up."

"I'll be fine." He shakes her off.

"You don't look fine. What's with your eye?"

He wants to tell her that it's nicotine withdrawal, or the massive amount of work he's had to do lately, that it's a wayward blob of scenic dope, or any one of a myriad of superficialities, but he knows the cause is deeper than excuse can bear. It's life. His heckling life, pelting stones and rocks at him as he rushes down a blind gully to his cliff. One of those missiles glanced him in the eye; a war wound. Nothing to get excited at.

"I got it dreaming," he says. "Some stupid nightmare."

"Use it," urges Georgia. "Use her death to change something in your life. Like I did with James."

"Oh, don't be so wet!"

He sneers at her Age of Aquarius banter. It was easy for her; she has no shame. Self-improvement doesn't carry a stigma for her as it does for Wally. When they returned James' dog tags to her, she'd used it as an excuse to quit smoking, managing to turn her culpability into a personal triumph. Such was her blindness, it was impossible for her to see the hypocrisy.

"Besides," chides Wally. "What have I got left to improve? I gave up smoking three weeks ago."

She gives a forced laugh. "You're such a liar, Wally Greene." Her hand brushes his beard. "I can smell it from here. You stink like a bonfire."

Wally's chest feels as if a hand is pushing right into him. He clenches his fists. He *has* stopped smoking. He swears he hasn't had a cigarette for days. Surely he isn't so crazy he wouldn't have noticed?

"Didn't Parker want to talk to me?"

"I got the distinct impression, not."

"Bloody scaredy-cat. I'll cream the bastard."

He takes a taxi, he can't really afford the time. Traffic snarls all the way across to the North Shore. Above, a helicopter burrs. There's a jumper on the Lion's Gate Bridge, the full details of which are on the radio, courtesy of the eye-in-the-sky. They creep along, Wally dreading the meter's click, hoping he has enough cash to cover the fare. After a wrong turning on the residential slopes that requires some back-tracking and angry words flung around the cab, he feels justified in lopping ten bucks off. Twenty dollars, that's all the idiot gets. No tip. He should count himself lucky he gets anything at all.

The McLean homestead. Wally's been here a few times before, usually with Georgia acting as chaperone. The place is one of those faux Alpine ski-lodge constructions with lots of acute angles and glass panels that must have had an expensive architect behind them. Set into the hill, the house was designed to fit perfectly into its environment and has been photographed doing just that in more than one international magazine. There is a fantastic view from the deck.

"I can't believe this is February," Georgia announced on their first surprise visit, flinging her arms into the sunshine. "What a beautiful home. Isn't it beautiful, Wally?"

Wally grunted in reluctant agreement. He was still angry that Georgia had made him sit and wait five minutes in the car while she went inside to test the waters with Peggy. "She'd love to see you," Georgia whispered, letting Wally out of the car. "If you ask me, she must have the memory of a fish. Just no sudden movements, compliment her house, remember to call her Margaret, and you'll be fine."

"You've done well for yourself, Margaret," Wally announced, staring at the misted pine trees, at the Lincoln Log gabled overhang against the blue sky, at the slick plate glass. "You got yourselves a good architect."

"Cornelius Ffadden." Georgia tapped Wally's nose with her finger. "He's more than good, Wally. He's the poor man's Arthur Erikson, and he's our man."

"Our man?"

"I didn't tell you?" Georgia knew she hadn't, she played it like a memory lapse. "I'm putting together a proposal for the theatre to expand. You know, better dressing rooms, nicer lobby. With a good plan the place could really go somewhere."

"Oh." Wally took in the information. "Does Dickie know about this?"

"Dickie's getting tired of running the place all by himself. I'm thinking of investing. Time, talent, money." She grinned mischievously, first at Wally, then Peggy. "Besides, I'm sick of the winters in Ontario. I can't believe how warm it is—in February!"

"Oh. You're not thinking of moving out here?" Peggy's voice went watery thin through her smile, trying not to meet Wally's eye. "Is . . . is that a good idea? I mean, in your business, theatre, that is,

I wouldn't have thought . . . is there much employment? I thought
you were just here on tour."

"Spitting at Petruchio for my living, yes I know. But I've always
wanted my own little theatre. And that building is so sweet. It would
be like having my own little chocolate box."

Peggy's hackles were bristling with panic, probably wishing for
Parker to come home and deal with her unexpected guests. Her
chin wobbled with the effort of maintaining control.

"Oh, *Margaret*," chided Georgia. "Don't tell me you're frightened of this big idiot. He's harmless, didn't anyone ever tell you?"

They laughed, the two women, together, at Wally's ineptitude.
Peggy smoothed her hair and allowed herself to be flattered by
Georgia's attention. Soon she found herself telling the story of
Parker's West Coast success. It wasn't long before her breath bloated
with pride; a confidence entered her voice.

"We're having a cocktail party next month," she gushed, the oxygen dripping from her high-altitude social calendar. "Do come. You
too, Wally, if you like." She became serious for a second, adopting a
patronizing tone, as if publicly forgiving herself for saying such a
thing even as she said it: "But you have to promise to behave yourself."

The party was Wally's second visit to the place. Not a success.
He was livid that Peggy still pitied him like a dangerous child and
he would almost certainly have made a scene if Georgia hadn't doped
him into a chemical straightjacket, and then abandoned him by the
buffet table while she swanned the crowd. Wally sunk to a leather
Ottoman, where he stayed, favouring the wall, and sipped his way
through the evening at crotch level. He played the eccentric, tucked
away in a corner, enjoying everyone else's discomfort. And there
were a lot of gangly rich people to laugh at—more than a hundred
well-heeled guests congregated as proof of the McLean's western
success. Wally held court with the gullible and ignorant, teaching
them how to swear in Welsh and toss grapes into their mouths. Every
so often, Parker appeared, suspicious, but there were too many guests

around for him to be anything other than civil.

"Peggy tells me you're thinking of staying in B.C.," he said, politely, bowing at the waist.

"Oh, yeah," drawled Wally, back up at him. "The Wild West. The last frontier of civilization, isn't it? It's like Wales, only bigger."

"I never went to Wales," Parker laughed, straightening back up and hoping to continue with his host's duties. "I hear it's very pretty."

"Noh. It's just Scotland for wankers, *boyce bach*," spat Wally, amazed at his self-control, and delighted at the effect his self-deprecation had on Parker, who bolted.

Georgia joined him on the floor later with a plate of canapés.

"Well, I've got us half a board of directors," she beamed, as she pried her shoes off. "Two lawyers, a dentist, a real-estate agent, a professor, and our architect. God, my feet are killing me."

"You're enjoying yourself, aren't you?"

She nodded. "Mmm. Parker really hates you, did you know that? Did you really just call him a wanker?"

"Not in English."

"Hmm." She chewed her lip. "I'm going to have to soften him up if I want to get myself invited back."

"Just leave me at home next time. They both think that you're pureblood and that I'm just the unfortunate boil on the royal bum."

"I know. Sad, isn't it?"

"It's not sad. It's the truth."

And the last time he'd been to the McLean homestead wasn't an official visit at all, but to drop off the car after the ill-fated camping trip in Squamish. Peggy and Parker had, of course, flown in the emergency helicopter to the burns unit with Ned, Parker nursing a bloody nose. Georgia drove her old Mercedes with Alex and the twins, while Wally got the McLean's Volvo, with all the camping gear. He got stuck in the mud, had to be pushed out with sticks and sheets of cardboard shoved under the tires. He drove back along the coastal road so full of vim that he had to keep notching the volume on the car radio to sing along with the Pointer Sisters and the Village People.

The house then had seemed huge and empty. Dark and hollow. A light had been left on to deter burglars. He got out of the car, then waited twenty minutes on the stoop for Georgia to turn up. When she arrived, he wasn't invited inside. Somehow, it was generally understood that Wally was *verboten* in those hallowed halls. He's forgotten what the inside of the place looks like; probably wouldn't recognize it without a buffet table.

The front porch, however, is known territory. The oak door beneath the angled overhang. The cast-iron knocker that looked like a Picasso. The long, vertical strip of glass. A scraper for the mud from your shoes. It hasn't changed in eight years, except for today, in honour of Peggy, a black ribbon is tied to the knocker.

"Wally Greene? What are you doing here?"

"Hello, Parker, old chap." Wally tries to rub the itch off his nose. "Two teas wiv' a sticky bun, then?"

"I beg your pardon?" Parker has grown into an oblong slab over the last decade. His eyebrows are now bushy, his jowls soft. The Scots accent, however, hasn't changed a bit. And he wears well-appointed leisure wear like a man who has become acclimatized to comfort but doesn't quite understand why. His socks are white. "I beg your pardon?"

"I heard about Peggy," nods Wally, his head thick. "I've come to pay my respects, haven't I?"

"But the funeral won't be for a couple of days, she's only just ..."

"Oh damn. And we've got a show opening day after tomorrow." Wally's right eye twitches; he can feel the little bloodshot veins throb. "Would you like tickets? We can get you some tickets if you'd like. Complimentary. Absolutely. I'm sorry. I'm an idiot."

Parker blinks, his mouth turns thin against his teeth. Wally tries again, the breath coming in spurts.

"Is Ned here? I could do with his help down at the shop."

"No-oo. We thought maybe you knew where he was."

"Why would I know where he was?" Wally's stomach clenches in time to his heartbeat. "What, am I related to him or something?"

"Easy there, Greene."

"She lied to me!"

He can contain it no longer. His fury hurls out of him, spittle and curse. Anything to smash that old, immovable cliff face of Parker, the boy from Tufnel's Bakehouse.

"She fucking lied to me!"

Wally's arms flail, madly. Parker steps forward, trying to contain them, to calm them, catch them, thwart them.

"Hey-hey-hey! Easy, easy, easy."

But it isn't easy. It's as difficult as it could possibly be, thinks Wally. All the ancient animosities, the Chingfords' sneer, the sick across the table, Peggy's ridiculous hairdo, smart shoes. Her yellow rubber gloves as he sat in her kitchen dunking biscuits in his tea and she'd lied to him. Lies!

"I'm sure there's been some mistake."

"What?"

"Mistake." Parker glances back into the house, where shadows of men gather in the hallway. "I think you've made a mistake. God knows, Greene, you've . . ."

Not letting his quarry finish, Wally pulls back with his right fist, feigns a swing. Parker ducks, swerves, spooked. Which is exactly what Wally had hoped for. His left hook screams victory on a brutal, short arc. He can feel the dull crunch of knuckles hitting jawbone. Sparks burst in his vision at the contact. Blood. Ha! Twice in the same lifetime!

Men are shouting from the house, now. The twins, burly and fit descend on Wally, running like rugby players, catching him in their arms and taking him down. They smell of clean wool against their biceps.

"I saw the fucking birth date!" Wally yells from the ground.

"You think I'm a fucking moron? Right there on the Family Court papers. 1963, Parker. She lied to me!"

He sees himself, then, as if from a distance, from high up. An eagle, perching in the treetops, perhaps, watching the scuffle down below. He is a distant, spitting ball of some frenzied animal being sent packing down the driveway, all arms and legs and crackling fur. Then swoop. The eagle's viewpoint plummets earthward, whistling wind towards its prey and—so it seems—directly into Wally's skull. He feels the talons grip his ribcage as he runs away, down the hill, towards the bus stop, running, lopsided Quasimodo on the tarmac, heart pounding into a stitch, thighs pumping, relentless, imagination squeezing the air right out of him.

23

Birnam Wood. The Forest of Arden. A wood outside of Athens. Stanley Park. Formidable trunks grow straight out of the earth and reach to the clouds like beanstalks, ready to be climbed. That's it, old man, climb up through the tree canopy, up to the Giant's Castle, Valhalla, and steal the singing harp, the golden fleece, the dragon's tooth, the Holy Grail.

The bus through Stanley Park is near empty; a couple of chatting women with shopping bags and a kid with a radio. Wally sits on the back seat with his head against the window, letting himself get bounced around. The rhythmic knocking against his cranium is comforting; the shaking vision of the old rain forest through the mud-splattered glass actually calms him down. Loneliness overpowers him and for a brief moment he catches sight of Peace, quixotic and silver, dancing in the trees outside.

Wally licks the blood from his left fist. It tastes good. Parker, he reflects, had always been an obstacle. Well, now he was dealt with. During those later years in Ontario, it was Parker who had protected Peggy, as if he was some annoying trained dog. There was such an air of self-righteousness about him that Wally could never take him seriously. The man was nothing more than a working lad from Inverness made good. He deserved the punch in the jaw.

The bloody hypocrite. He must have known that Ned was Wally's child from the get-go. How it must have twisted in his gut like a coring knife. They'd raised the boy as one of their own, not because they wanted to, but because, Wally is convinced they thought it was the right thing to do. No trips to the Brighton tea shop for Peggy; Parker wouldn't have stood for it. So together they'd built a false world for themselves and their family in Canada, never dreaming that Wally would one day turn up on their doorstep and bring it all crashing down.

Of course Peggy had lied. He'd known it at the time on some level; he was too familiar with her ways. But because she'd placed Ned's birth at two years after it really was—Year of the Snake, she'd said, instead of Year of the Rabbit—Wally could lean on her lie as heavily as she did herself. But it didn't jive. Deep down, he knew. And all those years of telling himself he wasn't the father, knowing instinctively that something about the whole arrangement was suspect. No wonder he'd picked at the scab.

Now, rumbling through Stanley Park, the truth of the matter finally out in the open and forced into Parker's cakehole with a fist, Wally begins to breathe easier than he has for years. Finally, his emotions ebb. He feels the endgame approach.

By the time he reaches the theatre, his humours have subsided enough to allow him to focus on work. He slips backstage, intending to have a look at the Birnam Wood rigging attachments. The stage, however, is inaccessible: the cast is doing a cue-to-cue and won't be done for at least another six hours. So he checks in with the Production Manager on the status of the day's schedule and what priorities he can expect.

"Dickie wants Birnam Wood to fill the stage," he's told.

"Well," he offers, "I've got another dozen branches ready to come over. And I was planning on doing six or seven more."

"He says he'll tell you when to stop."

"Oh, he will, will he?"

Swallowing his anger, Wally drives the theatre truck over to the workshop. He loads up with the props that are ready—most of the weaponry and the finished branches of greenery. The workshop is in turmoil, much as he'd left it last night. Body parts litter the floor, drying on sheets of newspaper, the dull varnish still tacky to the touch, the sharp scent of polymers in the air. Give them an hour, thinks Wally, and they'll be ready, too. In the meantime, he can whip up a few more leafy boughs for Dickie.

"I'll give him when to stop," Wally mutters to the staple gun as he loads it up. "He doesn't know who he's talking to. I'll give him a fucking Forest of Arden, so help me God."

He sets to with wood, staples, three shades of green vinyl sheeting, craft knife and binding tape. He mixes up a small pot of scenic dope with a flexible base. Anger transforms into craft: he loves the work. He finds it easy for his fingers to act as conduits for his energy. Making props is, after all, his *métier*—this is where his body and mind are best attuned, and he knows it. Just as Georgia is exalted when she's treading the boards, so Wally is at his zenith when he's working the gaff. Thespians, Wally laughingly realizes, may use their roles as a kind of therapy to work through their psychoses, and he is no different in what he does. Nobody, however, is paying twenty dollars a ticket to watch him imagine that he's staple-gunning leaf-shaped bits of vinyl to Parker's head. Dickie's head. Georgia's, Ned's. His own.

The time chunks by. Wally becomes absorbed.

Wally's tangle with the kitchen table that Sunday afternoon in Stratford smashed a hole in the affairs of the household. Unable to deal with the madness, James finally abdicated his avuncular position, ran back to Long Island and, soon after, enlisted for K.P. in Vietnam, where he vanished for good if not for better. Alexander was grabbed by a scrum of pediatricians, neurologists, dieticians, and the like, and put through a steeplechase of tests, observations, and programs, with no real diagnosis beyond medication to control his seizures.

300mg/day Dilantin, as produced by Brandt Pharmaceuticals. The irony wasn't lost on Georgia.

It was Georgia who was affected the worst. The events were too incomprehensible, too dramatic, as if a page or two of melodrama had blown off her résumé and into her life, where they made no sense. She grew distracted, unsure of herself; her lines escaped her, her smoking increased. Her work suffered. She started casting her eye around other companies, in Toronto and further afield, guessing that she might not be invited back to Stratford for the next season if her clomping performances continued. On more than one occasion, she took Wally out for dinner, with some ulterior motive that stayed occult beyond the final brandies. He suspected she wanted to ask him for his help, but that she didn't have the faintest clue how to go about it. It must have been awful for her. She was stuck in a chain-smoking nightmare for months—until she got the dog tags in the mail.

Wally, on the other hand, suddenly had four tooth gaps of fresh Canadian air blowing into his head. Once the bleeding stopped, he was full of pep, strutting around looking like a hockey player, the gape in the front of his mouth giving him what Georgia called a "cocksucking grin." He practically revelled in his ugliness, smirking at girls at the bus stop, frightening them silly, or blowing kisses to the fairies in the park. The repair job, from a master prosthetist, was almost anticlimactic. Almost, but not quite.

Magic. His new dentures were exceedingly well-made, as well they ought, given their cost. Wally admired them for their craft, from one artisan to another. But most miraculously, when he slipped this brand new set of chompers into his mouth, something of the Old World vanished. He gained a North American sheen. His vowels flattened and his Welsh lilt became less conspicuous, almost non-existent. It was uncanny. He'd stare at himself in the bathroom mirror, mesmerized by the charm of his pearly whites and the new confidence they gave him.

"Hi, there," he'd say with an affected accent. "How's it goin'?"
He'd snap his jaw, pleased as a con man and virile as a pop star. At
thirty-seven, he started running around as if he was ten years younger.
But the occasional young filly he found would only be interested in
him because of who he was married to. The town was too small,
too full of thespians.

Then Georgia got better. She got work in Ottawa, Calgary,
Vancouver, all over. Acting and directing. Sometimes she took Wally
and Alexander with her on the shorter gigs; sometimes she went
alone. She started talking about her dream theatre again. A toned-
down version now: Canadian, modest, and dedicated to the classics.

"It's what I want to do, Wally."

It didn't take Wally long to realize that what *he* really wanted to
do was to go back to North York and have another go at Peggy. He
wanted to show off his new teeth to her, rub her nose in how well
he'd assimilated to driving on the wrong side of the road in this
classless society. Show her how he'd succeeded where she'd failed.
How he'd turned himself inside-out over the Atlantic, revealing the
brashness he always knew he had. How Canada had ironed out their
social differences. He craved the taste of her sweat again. He didn't
want her sex—he wanted her fear. He was only mildly shocked at
this realization, more titillated than anything; it was like watching a
horror film through the cracks of his fingers.

Georgia would take Alex to Toronto for regular visits to a top
neurologist. One Saturday morning, Wally went with them, dropped
them off at the hospital, and sneaked up to North York and laid in
wait. He sat in the Mercedes, smoking roll-ups and winking at himself in the rear-view mirror. After three quarters of an hour, his
quarry appeared at the end of the street, laden down with groceries.

"Hello there, Peggy," he beamed, rolling down the window.
"Those bags look heavy. Let me help you."

"Wally? What . . . ?"

"I just happened to be in the area again. Thought I might look you up."

"Well, I . . ." she searched his face, trying to discern what it was that was different about him. "No, really, I can manage."

But he insisted, getting out of the car to take her shopping from her, and she relented. It wasn't far, he reasoned. Just up the garden path, and in any case, it was so good to see her looking so happy. She believed him just long enough for him to get inside the house again.

"Parker," she bleated, "we're in the kitchen!"

The sound of someone practising clarinet could be heard, honking through the house. Wally followed his ear, led by a pied piper, to the front room, where a small mousy boy of about ten or eleven was standing at a music stand, a clarinet stoppered in his mouth.

"Hello, there," said Wally. "I'm your Uncle Wally. Was that you making that awful wailing noise?"

"That's Ned," said Peggy, catching up, breathless. "This is Wally. Say hello, Ned, where're your manners?"

"Are you really my uncle?"

"Parker!?"

Parker appeared: a salivating bull-pup at her side, obedient and ready to defend her honour and correct avuncular misconceptions about the family tree. Crag-faced and fearful, with hair already turning grey at the temples, he escorted Wally to the front door, polite but firm, aware that he was being watched and observed by a young, impressionable child.

"Margaret told me you'd turned up in Canada," he said with his tenor burr. "Your wife is here doing a drama play or something, isn't she?"

The way he said *your wife* laid claim to his own. Wally shrivelled at the simplicity of Parker's world.

"You want to introduce that Ned of yours to some real sports, Parker," he said in a low voice, "instead of wasting your money on music lessons. Did I catch you at a bad time?"

"No, but . . ."

"How about a cup of tea, then?"

"We were just on our way out."

The conversation got terse. Yes, they ran a successful baked-goods business now. No, Wally couldn't sample a sticky bun, it wasn't that sort of bakery. No. In short shrift, Wally found himself back at the garden gate, saying his goodbyes.

"Sorry you've wasted a trip, Greene," said Parker, "but as I say, we're in a bit of a hurry. We have to go pick up the twins from school."

"I've got my car." Wally flashed the irresistible grin. "Let me go get them. It's a Mercedes."

"No," they said, rushed, in unison.

"No," repeated Parker, firmly. "But thank you. Goodbye, Wally. All the best."

Undaunted, Wally sent her letters, usually a promotional post-card from one of Georgia's upcoming productions with *Free tickets if you want them!* scrawled under a little note. *It's so good to see you slumming it in Canada, ha ha!* He imagined his Hollywood teeth nipping her fingers as she read.

It was Parker who finally came to see Wally down in Stratford. He tried to imitate Wally's style by turning up at the house unannounced, but he failed miserably, simply because he was too square. Formality was in his blood. Besides, Wally had been expecting them in some form. *Drop by if you're in the neighbourhood.*

He answered the door and ushered Parker into the living room, where he'd been reading the paper. Wally was cordial to a fault. He greeted his guest breezily and apologized for Georgia's absence: it was a Sunday matinée, why didn't Parker run over to the theatre and catch the second act? But the small talk fizzled. Parker stood in the middle of the room like a pastor in the snake pit.

"Please, Greene. You have to stop this nonsense," he said, dropping a packet of Wally's letters onto the coffee table. "For your own good."

"What nonsense?"

"Writing to Margaret."

"Peggy and I go way back," said Wally, avoiding the threat. "You don't understand our relationship. We were childhood sweethearts."

"Well it has to stop." A twinge of sudden suspicion cramped Parker's face as the implication of *childhood sweethearts* hit him. "Margaret never . . . she wouldn't . . . she's not . . . she's worried for your mental health, Greene."

"You mean you're worried for yours." Wally picked up the stack of envelopes and riffled through them. "Does Peggy know you've been reading her personal mail?"

Parker left at that, exasperated. At the moment of his departure there had been such a tangible knot of raw comedy in the room that for days afterwards, Wally giggled out loud at the memory. Of course, he continued to write. He would decorate his letters with little red-and-green flying penises around the edges.

The Ontario Court, Family Law Division, saw fit to give Wally a social worker. After all the nastiness of lawyers' threats and mandatory mediation with a disapproving Judge-of-the-Peace, it was a surprise to find, that at the end of it all, there was a harmless middle-aged man in a beige office. Spider plants hung from the ceiling and filing cabinets ran the length of a wall. The desk was clean. Mr. Cook liked things uncluttered.

"Your sentence has been commuted to community service," he said, playing with his pen, his one prop. "Do you know what that means?"

"Shovelling snow from pensioners' driveways?"

Mr. Cook smiled, revealing a genuinely sharp wit. From a drawer in his desk, he handed Wally a two-sheet list of registered charities and non-profit organizations in the area and told him to sort himself out for ten hours a week for a period of eight weeks. He didn't care where, as long as there was a signature from one of the names on the list at the end of two months.

"Oh look," said Wally. "The theatre's on the list. It's a non-profit society, what do you know? How about I just put in some overtime?"

"As long as you don't sign your own time sheet."

"That's it?"

"That's it, Mr. Greene." He was about to put his pen back into his breast pocket. "Oh, and don't forget to write your letter of reparation. You know, something along the lines of 'Dear Mrs McLean, I apologize for all the pain I have caused,' and so on, I'm sure you get the picture."

Wally liked Mr. Cook. He was so straightforward, a man after his own heart. They had similar smiles: predatory occlusions, both crafted by clever dentists.

At the end of his two months, there was another meeting. Mr. Cook took Wally's four-page letter of reparation and read it twice. He seemed confused.

"What's this about hockey tickets?" he asked, pointing out the paragraph in question.

"Oh, it's nothing, really," said Wally, glibly. "It's just that we can arrange for tickets at Maple Leaf Gardens. My wife was given a time-share on a box. I just thought the . . . the McLeans might like to make use of a little cultural edification."

"Hmph." Mr. Cook was suspicious. "You do know, don't you, that they've moved to B.C.? I don't think they'd be interested in your time-share at Maple Leaf Gardens, somehow."

Wally winced at the information. British Columbia? Had he frightened them that much? Was he that powerful to fling them so far west?

"It was just an idea," he shrugged. "They're good seats."

Mr. Cook didn't care about the quality of the seats. He did, however, reluctantly agree to send the letter on to the McLeans' lawyers. The file was closed and Wally had paid his debt. He'd learnt his lesson, or so he said: no more letters, no more penis doodles. That final four-pager was his swan song.

He was lucky that the sentence was commuted, so it didn't affect his citizenship papers, which arrived, along with Alexander's, in 1975. His photograph showed his hair slicked back and his teeth bared and plastic. He liked to think he looked like Jack Nicholson. Movie Star.

When Georgia took Co-Artistic Directorship of the West Coast Sunshine Theatre in 1975, the first thing she did was to persuade Dickie Flemming to fire most of the board and get in new blood. A wise move. With all the changes she proposed, the old board would have dug in their heels and resisted. The new board members, however, were dazzled by her résumé and eager to prove themselves up to the task of helping to realize her vision. Within a year, she had the Capital Development Plan moving into a second phase, and the theatre was now called The Phoenix—more in keeping, she maintained, with the mythic scale of live drama.

She continued to plunder the McLeans' cocktail parties, more for season subscribers now than board members, although she really had no need. She attended for a perverse kind of satisfaction, Wally was convinced. Somehow, she managed to create the widespread belief that the McLeans were dear, close friends from her days in London, and that the two families were as beloved of each other as siblings.

"Margaret lived with Wally in Wales during the war," she took pleasure in telling people. "She was a refugee."

For Wally's part, he was too busy keeping her gaff in order to pay much attention to her social forays with the McLeans; however, he delighted in her tales of adventures up at the chalet, the "goat-herder's hut" as she called it. So Wally got his vicarious thrills of Peggy- and Parker-taunting through Georgia.

"Oh, I backed him into a corner tonight," she crowed, one night in '79. "How do you fancy a camping trip to Alice Lake this summer?"

"Alice Lake? Where the hell's that?"

"It's near Squamish. Up the coast a bit, I think. Who cares?" She twirled Wally's hair around her finger as if he were there simply to please her. "The important thing is that Parker invited us. Us. You, me, Alex: us. In front of witnesses. I should get James' old camping equipment sent out. What do you say?"

She clapped her hands excitedly like a little girl, as if proposing a fun trip to Wales. She was mad. She scared him.

Alice Lake was all about bugs. Flies during the day, mosquitoes at dusk and moths by night. Wally's soft, white flesh was a magnet for the biting, chewing, stinging, malicious creatures. The discovery of a hotel bar, two miles from the campsite, changed what could have been a nightmare into something tolerable. It had been over five years since Wally had last seen either Peggy or Parker. Georgia had done an excellent PR job in his absence.

"Wally, how lovely."

"Peggy. Margaret."

She hugged him. She actually hugged him. In that foolish, North American liberal greeting that must have taken years to break through the English briar. Wally couldn't resist giving her waist a little squeeze and watching her eyes pop, as if they were connected to her stomach. Deep lines around her eyes now.

"And this must be little Alex," she cooed.

"Hi."

"You'll be excellent company for Ned." She tousled Alex's hair. He tried to wriggle away from her. "He could do with someone younger to boss around. Do him the world of good."

"Got him playing hockey, yet?" asked Wally.

In the silence that followed, Parker stepped forward and shook Wally's hand and commented on how fit he looked. Wally was almost beside himself, laughing silently, running his tongue along his plastic teeth.

"Well, you're looking not half posh yourself there, Parker, my lad. How's about a cup of—"

"Now look here—"

"Parker!" Peggy's voice was sharp and commanding. Wally had never heard her use that tone before. "I told you: none of that. Wally's here as my old friend."

"Getting older by the minute," agreed Wally. "With a bit of luck, they'll have my pension sitting at the post office when I get back to town."

They all laughed. Together and separately. Not because anything particularly humorous had been said, nor because of nervousness to cover insecurities or apprehension. It was simply laughter at having aged, at the whims of time, at the surreal reality of finding themselves pitching tents together up the bung-end of Howe Sound in British Columbia, twenty years, thirty years, forty years on.

"I'm being eaten alive," shrieked Wally, slapping at the dusk. "Anyone bring any gnat cream?"

No one had. No one had even been camping before. They had to be shown the ropes by the kids.

"I thought you had four. Didn't you have four of them?" asked Georgia. "Or are the twins confusing my counting?"

"Bill's off tree planting again this year," explained Peggy. "Besides, he's at that age where the last thing he'd want is to go camping with the old 'uns."

"Speak for yourself, paleskin," muttered Georgia, glancing at Wally, "but I'm not calling myself old until I start wearing double-knit and white shoes."

"Georgia . . ."

"Yes?"

Peggy tried to say something, but her mouth got stuck in a little wooden *o*; an empty stage with no actors, no script. Panic snapped across her eyes as she looked for the security of Parker, who was off, helping with the tent-raising.

"It's so good to see Wally again," she said, eventually. "Isn't this fun?"

"Oh yes," agreed Georgia, and clicked her tongue.

Later, they went to pick up provisions at the store in Squamish. It was one of those low-ceilinged buildings, filled to the brim with everything anyone might need: can openers, ground sheets, baked beans, fireworks, insect repellent, packets of seeds . . . the task became enormous. Peggy and Parker became frantic and giddy, surrounded by the kids, unable to control them. Wally grabbed Georgia and took her to the Squamish Arms Hotel next door. He convinced management to crack a bottle of single malt that had been gathering dust above the bar. They drank two shots each in silence.

"There's something seriously wrong here," Georgia said. "It's like they've taken up membership in a brainwashing cult. EST or something. If I didn't think them incapable, I'd say they were being nice on purpose just to freak us out."

"If I hear Parker tell me how good it is to be alive one more time," warned Wally, "I'm going to smash his nose flat into his face."

"Shh! Here they come. Act natural. Watch."

"There you are. What are you drinking?"

"Single malt. Care to join us?"

"Well, maybe just a small one. The boys have gone on ahead to the campsite with the supplies. We said we'd only be five minutes or so. Parkie?"

"I don't . . . Oh, all right. You only live once, eh?"

Cheers all round. Glass clinked to stilted, lip-service professions of friendship and bygones being bygones. They drank, they laughed about not bringing any insect repellent or toilet roll, and they marvelled at how, here they were, in their forties, canvas virgins. Worse, their children knew more about roughing it than they did. It no longer sounded fun; it began to feel foolhardy.

Parker leaned over when Peggy went to the washroom. He gripped Wally's biceps and stared earnestly into his eyes.

"You can keep a secret, can't you, Greene?"

"Oh, sometimes, I think I can."

"She's too good for me. You know that, don't you. She's an angel."

"Well, I wouldn't go—"

"She's dying, Greene." Parker's fingers dug further into Wally's arm. "She's dying."

"Oh." Wally threw a glance at Georgia. Explanation blossomed between them: so this was why they were treating Wally so nicely; why they were forcing themselves to be so positive; why the whole camping trip in the first place. "Oh. That's so sad."

"It started when we were back in Ontario. When you were . . . you know," Parker continued, suddenly caressing Wally's shirt, trying to smooth away his tracks. "It wasn't your fault, of course, it wasn't. I don't blame you . . ."

"Thanks."

"But the doctors did say she needed a change of location. Sometimes it helps ease the stress, you see. And the climate, of course . . ."

"Forgive me," Georgia said, expertly defusing Wally's spark of affront, "but what exactly is she dying of, Parker . . . other than old age, like the rest of us? She looks fine to me."

"Well, she has a lump . . ."

"Cancer?"

". . . in her breast . . ."

"And it's metastasizing?"

"Well. Yes. I suppose so."

"And she's going to have a mastectomy?"

"I don't know . . ."

"Or just a biopsy?"

"Um . . . I couldn't say . . . the doctors . . ."

Wally got up and left the table. Went out for a cigarette in the open air. He couldn't believe Parker had the audacity to blame him for Peggy's cancer—not out-and-out blame, in so many words, but worse. He'd forgiven Wally. In one magnanimous bourgeois sweep of his hand, he'd pardoned Wally for the crime of having given his wife a disease—a disease about which he hadn't even bothered to find out the first thing. The ignorant prick.

Wally tasted bile. He couldn't imagine spending the next two weeks with these creatures. Sharing a vacation. It was a nightmare. Sooner or later, someone was going to get hurt. He licked the knuckles on his left hand. He could already taste the blood.

There isn't time for a cup of tea. Wally's fingers are red and swollen from the work, splotched with scenic dope, but he pushes on with Birnam Wood. He'd spent four years, once, on a production of *As You Like It* that never, ever arrived. Those four years had slipped by like four weeks. What was this by comparison?

There is a knock on the workshop door. Wally looks up from his work, startled. He isn't expecting anyone.

"Wally?" It's Georgia. "Can I come in?"

"Just a minute!" He wipes his hands on a rag, wincing at the pain. "Come in!"

He's pleased that she asked his permission before entering; she could have easily just barged in. But she understands the nature of territory, does Georgia. The workshop is Wally's turf.

"I thought you were in rehearsal."

"We've finished for the day, it's gone midnight." She looks at the mount of branches. "I think that's enough Birnam Wood, Wally. Let me give you a hand loading up the truck."

"If you like." Wally shrugs, bewildered at her offer, but inwardly thankful. "Here."

As they transfer Birnam Wood out of the workshop, Georgia leaks the reason for her visit. The McLean twins had turned up at the theatre again. They were getting to be such a regular fixture, she said, that she was thinking of giving them a plaque on the wall.

"It's your theatre," Wally reminds her. "You can put up whatever you want."

"They told me what happened, Wally, up at the goat-herder's hut." She gives him her old hairy eyeball look. "I had to give them the Quality of Mercy speech. Wally, what's going on? Should I be worried?"

"Don't be silly. It's out of my system now."

"Are you sure?" She waves a branch in the air. "It doesn't look like it's over to me. Show me your hands."

Wally balks. Damn Georgia and her clarity of vision. He tries to wriggle away from her, but she wrests his arms from behind his back and jerks them forward. With the experience of a police matron, she twists his hands palm up, exposing raw fingers to the world. Blood. A couple of staples are embedded deep in his flesh.

"Oh, Wally!"

"It's the staple gun … it's got quite the kick to it, that's all … It doesn't hurt … I … I'm working under a deadline here, Georgie …"

Her gaze is too solid for him to avoid. He makes the mistake of looking into her eyes. Sadness pours through her. She's exhausted with him, he can tell, but since she's made the effort to come all the way out to the workshop, it must mean that she still thinks there's something worthwhile about him. The kindness is intolerable. Hope against hope. Wally so wishes he could weep, but it's impossible: he's wrung dry.

"So what am I going to do?" he asks, simply.

"You tell me."

He blinks at her, unable to see through a third of his right eye. A film of red now covers the edge of his vision. He feels the throb, the pain running up the side of his face, and he wonders how long he's been ignoring it.

"I don't know," he says, without an ounce of self-pity. "Everything hurts. I just want it all to stop."

"Come here," she says, opening. "Come. Come."

Unable to resist, Wally falls into the centre of her bloom, obedient. Her little dog.

24

The piano, thinks Xander, is a ridiculous invention. Look at it: a percussion instrument, technically, but more a hybrid of strings, cabinetmaking and mechanics. Who could have thought it up, this unwieldy piece of musical furniture? Take the basic idea—a hammer hitting a stretched wire across a sounding box —and how many constructions could be built before a machine recognizable as a piano emerges? And yet, the keyboard rules as king of the orchestra. In sound, it is unlike anything found in nature. Not air vibrating across a reed, as in the human voice; not the friction of one surface rubbing against another, such as the cricket's stridulation; nor skin vibrating on a drum as in the ear. The trumpet, the ram's horn, has a more legitimate claim to the crown than does the piano. Did the walls of Jericho fall to a Chopin nocturne?

And how did the keyboard itself evolve? Those eighty-eight keys of mathematical division, from the lowest A to the highest C, giving regular widths to each sound, the width of a human digit. Like a sheet of musical notation, it forces its tyrannical black-and-white view upon an entire art form. To be a pianist, you need the soul of a juggler. To be a pianist furthermore, thinks Xander, you need nimble fingers—and that, as of the present moment, turns the piano into a useless lump of twiddly furniture.

Three of Xander's metacarpal bones on his right hand are broken. The X-rays revealed a fracture pattern consistent with a boot.

Now bound and taped, swollen and blue, his fingers are as immobile as a package of sausages. No *Well-Tempered Clavier* is in their immediate future. Rachmaninoff is as distant as the Hermitage in St. Petersburg: an exclusive collection of gilt and sparkling treasures, the very best that civilization has to offer. And it's inaccessible.

Juan sits by the bed. He reads a music magazine with a picture of David Bowie on the cover. At Xander's stirrings, he looks up. Blue mascara.

"Hey, baby. You crying or is that pain? Would you like me to call the nurse?"

"Pain," says Xander, screwing up his nose. "It stinks in here. Can you smell it?"

"It's your dinner coming down the hallway. Tomato-fish-spam cakes. Here." He rummages in his pocket and produces a little tin of flat yellow pills. He places one on Xander's tongue, like a sacrament, then washes it down with unconsecrated water from a plastic mug. "Mexican Percs from the private collection. Don't ever say I don't love you."

"And I love you too, Juanita," whispers Xander, once the bitter tablet is down. "Shouldn't you be at work?"

Laughing, Juan tells him not to worry about it; he's taken the evening off to play nursemaid. Despite some polite protestations, Xander is thankful for the company. Lying here, brooding about his misfortunes both past and future, would be frightful if he were alone. Not that he's so naïve as to believe himself surrounded by concerned friends; he knows that Juan's presence is as much a combination of guilt and jealousy, of outrage and ownership, as it is of altruism. The effect of Ned's chaos is not confined to Xander's broken ribs, fingers, collarbone, cartilage and damaged kidney; it extends to Juan, to Roxie, to all those kids up there in 612. And the dog.

"Is the dog . . . ?"

"Dead. You're in heap trouble, oh chubby white boy, for killing dog belonging to crazy fucker." He drops the Wild West shtick.

"Actually, Ned's disappeared off the face of the planet and taken his wacky drugs and bitch with him. Not that I give a shit."

"And Roxie?"

"Oh, she's a bit upset. She's too embarrassed to come and see you right now, but she'll be okay. Feels like an idiot."

"She's not the only one." Xander raises his bandaged hand. "Looks like I've screwed my chances at Juilliard. I'll never be able to get back in shape in time. If ever."

His eyes well up again at the thought of his loss. He can hear the music playing within him, looking for a way out. It seems so unfair to him that something as intangible and as deliciously emotional as a *dolce cantabile* passage should rely on ligament, bone, and muscle for its execution.

"Hey, your left hand's fine," suggests Juan, playing the optimist. "You could take up the violin. We'll get you outfitted with a socket for the other hand to attach the bow. How's that?"

"What, like the six-billion-dollar musician?"

"Sure, why not? Androids are cool."

Xander sighs, frustrated. He doesn't understand how things got to this stage. He'd indulged a fantasy. He'd had a little dance with the devil. It had all felt so exciting, so fashionable, so well within control. But then, without warning, it had all exploded in his face like a pipe of freebase cocaine in the *Hollywood Reporter*, and all that remains is a sordid movie of the week. He hadn't counted on Ned being anything other than an extension of the rough, tough, sexy image. Image. It wasn't supposed to be real. God forbid that there was a violent, irresponsible, insensitive, selfish, and confused bastard under all those tattoos.

"Want to know a secret?" he asks Juan, the bitterness creeping into his voice. "He's my brother. Ned. My half-brother. Can you believe it?"

Juan bites his lip and nods. "I know, baby," he says, uncomfortably. "He told us last week. He made us promise not to tell you."

Xander feels trapped on the bed, caught in a calumnious web of half-revealed truths, the perversity of Ned's game revealed. He'd known all along. There had been a vein of deep sickness running through Ned's every smile, every fuck, every proffered delight of ecstasy. Buried behind each orgasm, there was an untold connection to his mother's cancer, to his own father's wild oats, to the Squamish incident. A revenge scenario? Xander feels such a pawn, as if he'd been singled out to be the fall guy months ago. Patsy. Idiot. Moron. Faggot.

"If it makes you feel any better," says Juan, returning to his magazine. "My brother's an asshole, too. Can't stand him."

He is woken from a drugged snooze by a touch on his hand. He raises his head and opens his eyes. It feels late; the lights are dimmed in the corridor, a nighttime hush permeates the hospital. His mother is perched on the edge of the bed to his left, holding his healthy hand. She still wears her stage makeup, her eyes are unnaturally enlarged and outlined, her face contoured and powdered, fraught with concern.

"Alex?" she whispers, gently, trying to keep the emotion from spoiling her voice. "Alex, honey?"

"Mom." He coughs. "How long have you . . . ?"

"I came as soon as I could." She corrects herself. "As soon as I found out. We had a dress rehearsal, I almost cancelled it."

"What day is it?"

"Wednesday."

"I've been here five days." He readjusts himself on his pillows. "We need your signature on some consent forms."

"Oh." She stares at him as if through glass. "I didn't know."

"How could you?"

He realizes that not only did she not know, but also that she hadn't thought to ask. Her arrogance assumed that she would have been one of the first to be told her son was in hospital, if not the

first. Watching her process the truth of the matter is painful. Her
hospital scene is no longer a flight to her one and only son's bedside
after a horrible accident. It's now all about her betrayal. She looks
as if she's chewing rotten meat.

"Mom?" Xander knows that if he doesn't rise to the bait, it'll
be forced down his throat. "Mom, what's up?"

"I don't understand," she says, sucking her teeth, "I don't understand why I'm always the last to know."

And so it goes, *à la* Mary Tyler Moore from *Ordinary People*. The
things she's done for him, the sacrifices she's made for him, and the
thanks she gets. The role, Xander notes, doesn't fit her, she's much
too corrupt. He wants to tell her to stop it, to just be honest, but he
doesn't have the strength.

"Have you told Dad?"

"What? No, of course not. Your father's not—"

"Then you're not the last to know, are you?"

She switches tactics faster than a crimp in a three-card-monte,
asking him how it had happened, the where and why and all the
whats of it. Had he seen who it was? No. Would he recognize them
again? No. The white Camaro, maybe. Faces? Not a chance. Then,
unaware of his lies up until then, she hits him with what she thinks
is the clincher.

"What were you doing round the back of the Aquatic Centre
at that time of night?"

"What do you think I was doing?"

Anger buzzes behind the bandage over his nose at her attempt
to make him say it aloud, forcing him to wound her, so that she can
pretend her pain is equal to his. How dare she. He wants to scream
at her, tell her how he'd heard her argue with Dad, that he knows
full well that Ned McLean is his bastard brother, that knowing this,
they'd fucked their brains out together, high on designer drugs, until
he'd gotten so high the sun melted the wax holding them together
and he'd fallen, crashing to the earth.

"Your fingers!" She is riveted by the sight of the swollen sausages. "Oh, Alex, no."

The Juilliard school of fantasy, so lovingly painted and worshipped, dissolves. The great cathedral of her desire crumbles into golden mud. Other scenarios follow quickly in its wake: the proud, famous mother; the grateful celebrity son; the legends printed in magazine articles, the documentary biographies. All mud. Through the gaping holes of what is left, they look at each other, perhaps for the first time without the patina of future promise getting in the way. He sees a middle-aged tart with expensive clothes and paint on her face. She probably sees a puffy-faced young gay boy with a shaved strip down the side of his head and a ring through his nipple. They are, in essence, similar creatures. Their scars are immaterial; it is the Great Desire that unites them now. Their mutual lust for the jangle of the tambourine.

"You look like an old whore," he says. "And I mean that in the nicest possible way."

"And you look like a freak."

"Thanks. Who is it you're supposed to be, again?"

"What?" She's caught off guard. "Oh, Lady Macbeth. I thought you knew."

"Figures."

He watches drips of saline solution and imagines he can feel the cold impact in his bloodstream. Time passes to the fall of salty water. His mother picks at the cuff of her coat.

"Well," she sighs, making the best of it. "Now that you've got me down here, I might as well make myself useful. Where do I sign?"

The following morning, Xander is taken downstairs to a treatment room. After a wait of three pages in *Time* magazine, a friendly woman with a mass of orange curls takes charge, leads him into a curtained-off cubicle.

"Alexander Greene is it?" she says, consulting her notes. "Do I call you Alex?"

"Xander. Alexander."

"Well then, Alexander. This is going to take about six hours. I hope you have some reading material, because it can get quite boring. But if we're lucky, you won't have to go through it again." She looks at him properly for the first time. "Oh dear, what have you done to your collarbone?"

"It's broken."

"Oh." She makes a face as if she were going through pain herself. "Well, this might hurt a bit. I have to get a catheter into your subclavian vein."

"A what in my what?"

Not bothering to explain beyond showing him the scary apparatus she intends to ram into his neck, she gets on with it, fussing with his dressing and attaching tubes to his collarbone. She was right: it hurts like hell. Her scatterbrained state doesn't help matters. At one point she gets confused as to which tube goes where, but in the end, she seems satisfied that she has it under control.

Once everything is hooked up and running to her satisfaction, she draws the curtains, revealing a square window that gives a partial view of the sidewalk and a glimpse of Nelson Park beyond. They are a few feet below street level, so Xander-Alexander is left to endure his treatment watching people's ankles go by, whilst his guardian-nurse putters around the other end of the room at her station. His companion for the day is the dialysis machine by his side.

It's about half the size of an upright piano, but twice as complex. Green and menacing, exuding a 1950s solidity, it swooshes and gurgles to a tune of its own devising. On every visible surface, it sports dials and gauges as if they were medals. Warning lights and beeps occasionally punctuate the proceedings. He wonders where he might find Middle C.

After an hour or so, he bites into the tedium of the experience, allowing his mind to wander. Disappointment is the first and recurring theme, followed by the slightly cheering thought that he's not alone. The entire city is experiencing a post honeymoon depression, it seems. After the big party, and the threat of actually fulfilling its own wild dreams of popularity, the city is in a slump of compromise. It seems that the rest of the world doesn't care. Worse, it appears that the opinion of the rest of the world doesn't really amount to much. It's strange, thinks Alex-Xander, how we need someone else to tell us how great we are, or what a fantastic time we're having.

He can't deny he had a good time. The memory of Ned is still juicy, but only in isolation. Beginning, middle and end unto itself it was such a wild fantasy that Alexander wants to cut it out, stick it in the pages of a thick encyclopedia, press it like a flower and treasure its fading colours for the next century. Frame it somewhere between hemlock and belladonna, mark it with an *x* for Xander, or Xtasy, or *XXX*, and pass it down from generation to generation, let the apocrypha run rampant. He never needs travel that route again. The beast is sated. He sees it for what it was: a craving for attention.

Now, he has all the attention he needs. His decidedly unfashionable sidekick is giving it to him. With its gentle swish and gurgle, hum and buzz, it filters out the poison from his blood. It echoes the music within, the melody striving to get out.

A thought strikes Alexander, as he stares out of the window at the grey Vancouver winter's day, the scuffle of shoes passing at eye-level. Perhaps he doesn't need to play the piano after all. Perhaps he can find another way.

Quietly, underneath his breath, he begins to sing. Soon it transforms into a laugh.

25

The Phoenix Theatre was originally built as a Presbyterian church. From the outside, despite its renovations, it looks much like a giant, ornate cake—both stodgy and superficial. It squats just off the main Granville strip, south of Davie, where the hotels turn into pool halls and the restaurants into night clubs. This part of town is a mixed bag. The Orpheum with its Mighty Wurlitzer is within walking distance, as is the Empire Ballroom, as are some of the seediest strip bars in town. Hookers mingle with symphony matrons, business suits with punks. Given the cross-section of humanity running past its front door, the Phoenix is in a prime location for a theatre. The age has gone when it would have been prime location for a church.

It's strange, thinks Wally, as he walks in through the Stage Door, how theatres in this new country are so often converted from existing buildings and so rarely built from scratch. The tradition isn't there, he realizes, it has to be adapted. One-time churches, fire halls, railway stations, stock exchanges—these are the successful theatres in this bold and open country. The ones that are built new, the clean and modern art centres, the acoustically pristine concert halls, don't have any human dirt in their walls. They don't necessarily fail; they simply don't have the centuries-old traditions of greasepaint and gaff with which Wally is so familiar. But there's no going back now, he tells himself, he's stuck in Canada for good. And although he feels the loss, he has wit enough to question his nostalgia. If he went back to London, would it not be just as alien to him now? Nothing stands still.

Inside, the Phoenix Theatre has kept the original gilt-and-plush balcony that curves around the second floor, but of course the clever architect has added some of his own touches: bold chandeliers, Deco sconces, sleek railings, and blood-red chairs. Georgia got her chocolate box, but she also got a functioning five-hundred seat theatre with a full lighting grid and wing space. Part of the genius of Cornelius Ffadden is in what is unseen, like the acoustics, which are such that there are practically no dead spots on stage.

The black obsidian replica of The Globe Theatre stage is impressive at full scale, Wally has to admit, and it complements the circular auditorium with a hostile authority. He settles himself into his favourite seat: house right, front-row balcony, on the aisle. He sighs.

Thankfully, his day has been calm. As was yesterday, the day of the dress rehearsal, which Wally didn't watch because Georgia had made him stay home, sedated. He heard her call Dickie on the phone, arrange for Wally's slack to be taken up by students from the Art College. He winced at the thought of his workshop being spoiled by strange hands, but Georgia was right. He was in no state to continue the work. Damn her, she is always right.

He feels as if he's been weeping for a month. Exhaustion manifests itself in a narcotic trickle down the back of his throat. When Georgia had handed him a couple of diamorphine tablets, he'd been grateful. He bowed to her wisdom and acquiesced like a six-year-old when she'd tucked him into a makeshift bed on the couch. She bound up his damaged fingers with gauze and unguent, one step away from singing "This Little Piggy" as she did so. Throughout the day, intermittently, Wally's eyes have been welling up whenever he thinks of how much she must truly care for him, this strange and wonderful wife of his. He's never known anyone else to come close to her peculiar breed of benign dictatorship. She is his Queen.

And now she's letting him attend the first public preview, almost as a consolation prize for having had to back away from the show at the last minute. He isn't there in any official capacity, for in truth, he couldn't change anything now should he want to. The art students have the gig. But it gives him a sense of security just to be there. He still has a place.

The auditorium fills up with the preview audience and their excited chatter of being present at, if not the official opening, then the first public performance. Georgia calls these shows Special Sneak Previews, and consequently, the audiences who attend are known as "Special Sneaks." Wally spots Dickie down in the stalls, fussing around and causing importance all around him. Assistants go running, the houselights dim, the warmer lights on the set glow in anticipation. A drum. Smoke.

The play begins.

The actor playing Macbeth is a lightweight, as Wally well knows. Right from his entrance on his fair and foul a day, he struts and over-enunciates in all the wrong places. All the shiny black obsidian sets and hydraulic lifts through smoking pits, pretty though they may be, are for naught when the centre isn't strong enough to hold. Again, thinks Wally, it's a lack of tradition. In London, this bantam wouldn't have reached the prompt box, everyone would have laughed him off. Here, there's always someone willing to praise mediocrity.

"It doesn't matter how bad we are," Georgia often says with disciplined irony, "there's always someone, somewhere, who says they like it."

"I know," is Wally's response. "And I've met her."

The play limps along, compromised.

But when Georgia makes her upstage entrance in scene five, the story comes alive. In two pages of text, both prose and iamb, the enormity of Shakespeare's proposition becomes palpable. There will be blood spilled tonight because this woman demands it. And that's just the way it is. Cruel and unstoppable. As with any good theatre, Wally feels that what he's witnessing ought to be somehow illegal. It thrills him. Suddenly he is aware of what he's watching. The Scottish Play. Up until that moment, he'd managed to fool himself that he was watching something completely different.

Damn his wife for being so good tonight! Even when this Dullard Mackers enters into the picture, Georgia—or, rather *not* Georgia, for she has retreated behind her thespic mask—makes it work, by keying into some mythic energy that stretches back through time, through audience after audience, to the core of storytelling.

"My dearest love," says Macbeth, flatly. "Duncan comes here tonight."

"And when goes hence?" She's plotting aloud so that her dumb husband can figure it out, thinks Wally. She's using his stupidity to make the drama.

"Tomorrow, as he purposes."

Wally's brain shudders at the words. Tomorrow.

"O, never," says Georgia, the vowels coasting from her lips, "Shall sun that morrow see!"

Wally's hand flies to his mouth. He chews at the bandages taped on his fingers. His calm is dissipating as the play hurtles forward, unstoppable. Come what may, he thinks, he must do everything in his power not to betray himself.

"The Queen, my lord is dead."

Act Five has arrived, the tragedy is almost over. Macbeth's mouth drops open, startled at the news from his messenger; his expression is a crude rendition of someone going mad, a studied stereotype. Now the poor sod is on his own.

"She should have died hereafter," he intones, his lip wobbling. "There would have been a time for such a word . . ."

Wally's breath catches involuntarily in his windpipe. Here comes the speech; he can't stop it now. Without realizing, his lips move, synchronized with those of the orator down below.

"Tomorrow, and tomorrow, and tomorrow
Creeps in this petty pace from day to day . . ."

Wally's heart pounds at a hairbreadth's pace faster than the remainder of the passage. His fingers twist and worry at his bandages. Those lines, those words, reverberate. He warns himself to be careful.

And all our yesterdays have lighted fools
The way to dusty death.

"Out, brief candle . . ."

A hook catches in the fabric of time. A word is missing, ripping across Wally's memory, making his stomach lurch. "Out, *out,* brief candle" is the line; he's missed an "out." Wally is mortified. And he's not the only one. The actor realizes that he's made a mistake. Fudging, he backs up, tries the line again and, like a junky stabbing at a vein, makes the same error. This time, however, a shadow crosses his face, and he stops mid-line, unable to continue. It is as if some god has descended to the stage and stuck in the cork. There is the hideous embarrassment of irreparable silence.

Whatever peace has blessed Wally with its presence up until this point today, now abandons him utterly. The last drop of calm evaporates like pools of water on a desert rock. His heart picks up the pace as he smells his own fear.

Into his seat he sinks, struggling for breath, wishing he could merge with the plush. The mad king's coronet settles on his brow, a circlet of sweat. A throbbing pain bulges up his temples. The chair could swallow him. The seat could tip up and he'd vanish in a trice, with nothing but a little plaque to commemorate where he'd been.

An age passes and the silence, unbearable, continues onstage. There are sporadic coughs from the audience. Soon, it reaches the point where hissing prompts can be heard coming from the wings. Wally recognizes Georgia's mellow tones.

"Life's but a walking shadow . . ."

Too late. There's the smell of burning in his sinuses. It won't be remedied with a patched-up monologue. Somewhere in the distance, Wally hears the lost actor taking up the cue and continuing the speech, but it is muffled as if heard from the wrong side of a trapdoor, distorted.

For Wally, time is hemorrhaging. Part of him is back in the Whitehall Theatre, confronting Peggy, reciting the forbidden words himself. She is watching him, her head tilted in that curious way of hers. The Professor winks. He can smell the mazarine. The excitement of ritualized sex in the oubliette and the taste of blood.

He daren't move. He sits transfixed and stares at the stage. Fear blocks out his vision as his head jerks, loosely, to this side then that. Who's that laughing? Someone's laughing, or is it the blood rushing through his ears? He clenches his jaw and tries to discern where the noise is coming from.

For a moment, his vision clears, as if a curtain has been lifted. Contrary to every impulse rushing through his body, he dares look to the stage.

Ned is standing there.

Wally blinks. Yes, Ned—a grin of tattooed insolence—then he's gone, replaced by the actor playing Macbeth, who is lost in a whirlpool of embarrassment. But that moment is all Wally needs to trip headlong into the void.

". . . that struts and frets his hour upon the stage . . ."

Steam rises, the periphery warps, the Phoenix Theatre bubbles, shakes, and Wally, tasting the grit of medication, erupts. The blasphemy is too much.

He bursts from his chair, jerked up like a marionette. Suddenly, he is dancing a red-faced jig in the aisle. His bandages are in shreds, the trailing ribbons twisting through the air, where they catch the light like the debris of an erupting volcano.

"It is a tale told by an idiot!" he yells, no longer caring. "Full of sound and fury signifying nothing!"

He dances a Ned dance in honour of the moment. A crazed, leering, giggling, screaming monkey fandango. A bloodthirsty rabble, that's all he is. The dregs of the dregs. An evil, crusted scum washed up in a stinking tide, flushed from his dark fuck-hole underneath the stage. His nose wrinkles; he smells like soup that's been left on the stove a week too long. He shakes away black fragments of burnt gauze that stick to his fingers. He feels in terrifying proximity to the truth.

He laughs, bellowing now. The truth? The truth is always somewhere else—offstage, beyond the footlights, past the stage door —carrying on, parallel to him, but always out of reach and inside-out, back-to-front. Outside the theatre, that's where the truth is. Sometimes it was closer, sometimes further away, but always it was playing against him in a ruthless, incomprehensible competition. It's all a game. And Peggy has lost, hasn't she? Peggy's dead. He's won.

Silence.

He concentrates on the sound of his breathing, trying to push away the other sound of the audience's mutter of disapproval. He feels them turn in their seats, rows of chairs creaking and tongues rustling. He smells their perfumes and aftershaves, tastes their venom dripping down the back of his throat. He swears he can hear snippets of laughter.

He has to get away. Everything's closing in upon him, it's all so unbearably hot and wretched. People are staring, but he won't subject them to his tantrum for much longer, for, with the force of a tropical storm, he is unaccountably propelled towards the door. He can't stop himself, he is obeying a power greater than his comprehension. The demons have control.

And the next thing he knows, he is outside. Outside, and running through the Welsh fields, with the wind in his hair and a knife in his hand.

The sky is on fire. Flashing neon billiard balls and dancing girls careen through the kaleidoscopic mist. Cars swish their tires in the wet, honk their horns as Wally dances, twists, and runs through the traffic. He doesn't care where, as long as he doesn't have to stop. It feels good to run: oxygen rushing in and out of his lungs, legs chugging forwards, forwards, shoes slapping the concrete. He tilts his face to catch every last drop of refreshing night drizzle.

He bumps into Ned. Damn that insolent grin, that tattooed machismo, leather jacket, barring his way.

"Hey, look out, buddy! Watch it!"

Wally swats him away, his knife slicing, glistening in the street-light. Blood flecks his hand, he licks it off, crows with delight and runs on into the fog. Past the hookers in their legwarmers and their rabbit-fur jackets. Past the seedy hotel doorways. That showed the bastard!

But at the next corner, he runs headlong into Alexander. The collision knocks the wind right out of him, and Wally has to pause to regain his breath.

"You!" he gasps. Purple mohawk, black trenchcoat, but it's his son, despite the disguise. "I thought I just told you to keep away."

"Hey, dad, chill."

Half a dozen more encounters and Wally reaches the water. No more Neds or Alexanders to get in his way. He runs across Pacific Avenue, the dark night wrapped around him. Concrete, steel, the giant rooks of the Burrard Street Bridge up ahead. God, how he wants a cigarette! He sucks his knuckles, tasting damp, salty gauze, and craving that hit of nicotine. What would it matter now? Everything was buggered to blazes, wasn't it? The world is crashing down around his ears and why? So that from the wreckage, once the smoke clears, he could emerge to face the cameras and the reporters to say, "But I never had a cigarette the whole time"? One small victory in the face of Armageddon. Bollocks to all that.

He's just killed his boys. He must have. He heard the owl scream and the crickets cry. Over and over, he sees the dagger going in and the blood running out. Murther. Now they're going to come after him like a pack of bees. He can hear the sirens already, the crackle of the walkie-talkies. Birnam Wood do come to Dunsinane.

Ka-boom!

He ricochets to the centre of the bridge—Doppler effect—a taxi honks and screeches, warps into the distance. Facing the old Expo site Wally sees the source of the noise.

The sky really is ablaze. Fireworks. Great chrysanthemums of green and blue. Golden boughs of sparkling gunpowder rain down from the heavens. *Ka-boom! Ka-boom!*

He hikes a leg over the edge and climbs up the strutwork a couple of yards. He jumps up to a small platform; more of a ledge, really, than anything else and continues on his way up the girders sure-footed. The fireworks above him are indistinguishable from the ones inside his head. As he pauses, he is assaulted by reflections in the water of the city, of fire, of conflict, wars both old and new, of mystery, ambition, secrets, loves, and hatreds, all exposed, laid bare. Enough! The world is gauche sufferance, too melodramatic to be believable. He laughs, flinging out an arm to bask in the wonder of his private fireworks show.

"*Mae 'na Duw!*"

An ugly, gurgling sensation draws his attention to his stomach. Just below his solar plexus, across the saddle of his belly there is an acidic burning. Indigestion? He fumbles in his pockets for some more of Georgia's pills and struggles with the childproof lid, but the pain takes over. Pills scatter like a shower of sparks, acid rain for the fish of False Creek.

"Sir! Sir!"

Wally laughs them off. If it wasn't for this infernal buzzing in his ears, the world would be quiet. Bugger it. Why can't it all just shut up?

"Sir!" The voice is insistent. A young, uniformed policeman is stretching out a hand towards him from below. "Please. Sir!"

Oh, how his skin hurts! Itchy and raw, it chafes with every brush of his clothing. He divests himself of his jacket in one easy move; it falls away from him to the water far below.

Someone's telling him to breathe. Yes, that's it. Breathe. Yes. Long, slow breaths flowing right down to the diaphragm, the seat of breath. Pretend it's a speech class and swing that ribcage open to a calmer, more serene, controlled plateau. Push those North American vowel sounds into your sinuses, you Welsh moron! *New Yorrrrk's Unique.* He spits the dental plate out of his mouth; it spins into the darkness.

Air rushes in through the gap in his front teeth. For a moment, everything is clear. He's standing at the topmost point of the green bridge girders. The dark road with police cars, ambulances, and flashing lights is below him, a little to his right. He crouches, feeling the cool metal beneath his hands. Soothing. He runs his palms along it, gathering a sluice of water. Wind bites into his face.

"Wally?" They know his name, now, it appears. "Wally, can you reach my hand?"

He glances down. Old Man Greene is leering up at him from the safety of a few girders away. Old Man Greene in a policeman's uniform, holding out his hand. His right hand. What does he want? A shot of Welsh in his tea?

"Fee, fie, fo, fum! I smell the blood of an Englishman!"

Wally starts to reach out, naturally, with his left, then stops. Right hand to left hand—it won't work. Jack can't make it back down the beanstalk because everything's the wrong way round. He is unsaveable, he realizes, and so reality and memory merge. The old saw about not being mad if you suspect you're going mad, he discovers, is rubbish.

"Give me the knife, Wally!" yells Old Man Greene in his face, followed by that awful, dredging laughter. "Gelding!"

Is it Old Man Greene, thinks Wally, or is it just some stupid sheep, bleating, bleating, like a broken siren? He covers his ears to keep the sound out. He doesn't have the knife! He threw it away and no longer knows where it is. He looks down. There it is, at his feet, like a silver sardine. Red flashes in his peripheral vision swarm across his sight, taking over, usurping, scorching. A hum, not unlike those damned wasps, whines in his ears.

"I'm sorry!" he shouts. "I didn't mean to steal . . ."

He bites his lip and tastes blood.

Fervently, he wishes himself back. He screws his eyes tight shut and tries to push his very soul backwards into the press of time, as if by sheer willpower he could traverse the years and put the knife back on the little shelf in Old Man Greene's bathroom. Maybe then he could rid himself of this intolerable heat.

But it won't happen, he knows it. Life is too smart to allow such an easy exit. He's trapped, encased in his fomented arrogance, clinging to the struts of a bridge, forcing the emergency services to talk him back down to safety. He can hear the helicopter. Will he jump? He doesn't know. Instead, he decides to pick up the knife. Bends down, reaches out, touches the metal—Ai—he drops it immediately, the heat too much to bear.

In anguish, he stares at his fingers. The gauze bandages are curling at the edges, wisps of smoke arise, tiny flames lick and consume. He brushes them, fearfully, away.

"Ai-ai-ai!"

It's coming from him. Inside.

Gasping for breath, Wally rips his shirt from his searing skin. A bubbling rash crawls over the pinking flesh of his belly; a crystalline brown crust forms, then smoulders, finally giving birth to a small, intense carpet of flame, like coals in the fireplace.

A mastoid chrysanthemum swells, explodes, followed by two more giant blooms of red, purple, green, blue. Its reflection in the water beneath shimmers with transient beauty, opening continually from the centre. The image ripples, then holds—waiting for him. And at this, he knows, at last, the decision to jump can no longer be postponed.

Ignition.

A brilliant force writhes and bucks, shimmers and hews its way through Wally's body, bringing with it a perverse satisfaction, slaking his bile. Yes. This is the way to get rid of it all, to expunge the foul constipation. If he can't burn up, he'll burn down. Not burning out, but burning in. Upside-down and back-to-front. Jump across the twisting Atlantic Ocean. Live your life from right to left. The way of the Gaff.

He feels so peaceful. At last! It's all so easy when you're at the centre of everything.

His arms are writhing with flames; he holds them out before his face, marvelling at the svelte blue shoots emerging at his fingers. There are tendrils of fire at his wrists, so close to the skin, so snug to their source of fuel. Him. He's their source. Their God. Their nova.

They rage around his torso now, entwining him like bindweeds. What with all his fat, he could burn like a candle forever! Ha-ha! A tightness grips him as he laughs. A great roar escapes from his lips. The horizon sears open, a fearful strip of light, like that terrifying moment before the curtain goes up and the audience bites its tongue. But not he! No! He is no longer afraid.

Howling, he reaches up, stretching, bouncing on his toes. His fingers scrape the memories of vomit from the cobbled stars. This is his moment. His delicious cliff dive at the final curtain of flame. He blinks through singeing eyelashes, through polyps of fire.

"Ai . . ."

And what visions in the heart of the fire. The world is but a molten echo. Consciousness is a girdle round the earth, it fires synapses simultaneously from the pineal sparkplugs of four and a half billion souls. The current is too much for any single one to bear; it must be shared. Blindly. So with no regard for truth, he jumps.

His body arcs into the air. Blazing through the night, framed against the blue-black-shadowed struts of the bridge. A perfect dive, suspended in time. Arms above his head, his entire body stretches taut in space.

Up, up, like Apollo to the moon. What a glorious moment, thinks Wally, what a glorious view.

The descent, now, head first, dynamic and fast. Breathing is irrelevant. Air speeds past, singing a glimpse of peace in his ears. Beauty.

Like a flaming arrow rushing to the bull, Wally Greene cuts the surface of the water at the very centre of the flower, the core of the spark, the wink of the Cyclops' eye. The lotus blooms. A seed, a burning acorn, falling down, down, down into the well.

CURTAIN

Praise for Greg Kramer's work:

Couchwarmer: A Laundromat Adventure
"[An] acid tongue, gleefully sick sense of fun and warped imagination."   — *NOW magazine*

"Forget Thomas Pynchon. Forget *Last Exit to Brooklyn*. Kramer mythologizes a new nation of anti-heroes and, if nothing else, he deserves a (dis)Order of Canada for proving we can harbour disaffection as well as anyone else. . . . This tale of intersexuality and narcotic conspiracies draws the reader archly, gleefully, into events we might reassess as repulsive only in hindsight. This is Kramer's gift: the logic of each character appears weirdly unassailable and whole, only to be smashed apart by the next one who takes up the narrative. . . . *Couchwarmer's* rewards remind us that humanity comes bearing all kinds of labels."   — *Quill & Quire*

"Combining bizarre coincidence, gender-bending mystery, bingo, and a cast of colourful denizens of Toronto's nocturnal underground, author-actor-director Greg Kramer has concocted a witty, fast-paced adventure with more tangents than a Tom Robbins novel, as much camp as a John Waters movie, and enough plot twists for an Elmore Leonard story."   — *The Georgia Straight*

"A vein-popping, high-octane look at fast-paced life in the underground."   — *The Globe and Mail*

"Kramer's almost impossibly letter-perfect turns of phrase are eclipsed only by his inexhaustible supply of them. *Couchwarmer* is a carnival of spiritual advancement, an Alice's Adventure Through the Glitterball, with Lady Luck either squashing you flat or handing you a flashlight."   — *Motion*

"It is astounding that Kramer, with deceptively easy strokes, succeeds in painting this story in day-glo colours, without sacrificing subtlety. The fact that the book holds together, never threatening to crumble, is nothing short of fantastic."   —*Xtra!*, Toronto

Hogtown Bonbons

"A master of hallucinatory humour and effervescent insights."
— *The Globe and Mail*

"A great collection of vignettes . . . a book populated by colourful characters on the fringes of big-city life—with sprinkles of Thomas De Quincey and William Burroughs." — *The Globe and Mail*

"If such stories are bonbons, then they're a fizz candy that erupts in your mouth. As their chemicals balloon and writhe, you find yourself surpressing a pleasant, embarrassed laugh." — *Hour*, Montreal

The Pursemonger of Fugu: A Bathroom Mystery

"Hilarious, cruel, witty, and licentious." — *Eye* magazine

"An entertaining marriage of classic whodunit and a spoof of world-class urban pretentiousness." — *Books in Canada*

"*Ten Little Indians* meets *Valley of the Dolls.*" — *Venue*

"There hasn't been a murder this gruesome since P.D. James pumped caustic down the lavage tube in *Shroud for a Nightingale* . . . A writer to watch." — *The Globe and Mail*